"SUSPENSE IS BAYER'S FORTE . . .
THE READER IS CONSTANTLY SURPRISED BY THE TWISTS AND TURNS,
THE DEAD ENDS AND OPTICAL ILLUSIONS."
—*Mostly Murder*

MIRROR MAZE

"Gripping . . . thought-provoking."
—Donald E. Westlake

"A plot more cunning than any maze."
—Ross Thomas

"Brilliant and riveting . . .
Bayer again proves himself one of the true masters of the American psychological thriller."
—Roger Simon

"It's great to see Janek back on the street in this fascinating, top-notch thriller."
—Gerald Petievich

"Janek proves himself to be good company:
a likable and believable hero,
more than a match for the monsters he eventually finds."
—*The Wall Street Journal*

"Refreshingly offbeat."
—*Los Angeles Times Book Review*

And don't miss William Bayer's previous novel, featuring Detective Frank Janek . . .

WALLFLOWER

"*Wallflower* is a knockout!"
—Robert B. Parker

"Enthralling . . . inventive . . . brilliant.
This is Bayer at his most suspenseful and resonant."
—*Kirkus Reviews*

Also by William Bayer

WALLFLOWER
BLIND SIDE
PATTERN CRIMES
SWITCH
PEREGRINE
PUNISH ME WITH KISSES
TANGIER
VISIONS OF ISABELLE

Mirror Maze

William Bayer

JOVE BOOKS, NEW YORK

The first chapter of this novel originally appeared, in somewhat different form, in *The New Mystery*, published by Dutton, an imprint of Penguin Books USA, Inc., in 1993.

This Jove Book contains the complete text of the original hardcover edition. It has been completely reset in a typeface designed for easy reading and was printed from new film.

MIRROR MAZE

A Jove Book / published by arrangement with
Villard, a division of Random House, Inc.

PRINTING HISTORY
Villard edition published February 1994
Jove edition / July 1995

ISBN: 0-515-11523-1

A JOVE BOOK®
Jove Books are published by The Berkley Publishing Group,
200 Madison Avenue, New York, New York 10016.
JOVE and the "J" design are trademarks
belonging to Jove Publications, Inc.

PRINTED IN THE UNITED STATES OF AMERICA

10 9 8 7 6 5 4 3 2 1

For Paula,
who walked with me through the maze

"I never understood the pattern of my life so that I have blundered through it in a maze. I did not know until now that in places the walls of this maze were cunningly polished so that the perils I have endured, my fears and hopes . . . those I have loved and hated have been mirrored images of one another. In all my life I never learned from one experience how to encounter its reflected twin."

—MICHAEL AYRTON

Mirror Maze

Mirror Girl

Always on those rainy nights when she decided to drive into the city to play the game, she would first revisit the mirror maze. . . .

All that afternoon, warm rain danced against the tin roof of the loft, and the faint howling of a dog, somewhere on the fringes of the park, made her think of pain.

With darkness, light from the sulfurous street lamp across the road, cut by the blinds, cast soft stripes across the walls and floor. She sat on her hard wooden stool listening to the patter on the roof and the squeak of the ceiling fan as it thrashed the humid air.

When, finally, she made her decision, she moved with swift resolve. She rolled up the little blue rug beside her bed, opened the trapdoor beneath, then made her way by memory and touch down the wooden ladder to the catwalks.

These she crossed with the grace of an aerialist. When she reached the switchboard, she turned on the lights below. Then she lowered herself deftly to the floor down a soft, thick white gym rope. Finally she stripped off all her clothes and walked out to face the mirrors.

The ones in the sharply angled Corridor met her like angry sentinels—fattening, elongating, disproportioning her body. She strode rapidly past them, wound her way through the labyrinthine Chamber, exited via the sinuous Fragmentation Serpent, then entered the Great Hall of Infinite Deceptions. Here, in the middle of the vast room, she stopped, then slowly turned like a skater cutting a figure on a patch of virgin ice.

Her glossy tresses of dark brown hair, so dark they looked almost black in the mirrors, cascaded down her neck, broke upon her shoulders and edged her pale back. Pausing to regard her high cheekbones and sculpted lips, she smiled gently at her likeness. Fair skin, brown irises, dark brows, modeled chin—she was a beauty and she knew it.

She basked before the multiple images. The reflections ravished her eyes. Then she began to look beyond herself, searching out corners and crevices in the silvered glass. There was secrecy in mirrorspace, places to hide and to conceal, corridors of sparkling light, endless shimmering passages and tunnels.

She positioned her image into one of these, stared hard at her eyes, willed herself entry. Then, in an instant that no matter how often she experienced it would always seem magical, she passed through to become her dream-sister—the one she'd known since girlhood, the one who lived in mirrorworld.

She felt safe then, in a place where so many things were possible, where the rules and laws that governed the world outside were null and void. Here, in the land of mirror-reverse, normally forbidden acts could be performed without fear or guilt and to degrees of intensity undreamed of even in deepest sleep.

Later, wigged blond, dressed smart, artfully made up, she drove into Manhattan through the tunnel beneath the river, then onto the city's rain-slick streets. She kept all her car windows shut. Only music from the tape deck, dizzying arias sung by great divas, reached her ears.

Cruising the avenues of the upper East Side, she raised

her eyes from the herd of taxis to gaze into her rearview mirror. Glimpsing the reflection of her dream-sister, she shivered at the sight. What if she were trapped? What if the mirrors turned cruel and refused to let her out? *Then I will be lost forever,* she thought, dread dissolving in the vision of street lamps reflected in the gleaming wet black avenue ahead.

She was searching for a bar, one she'd never been in before. She would know it when she saw it. There would be an aura: a rich warm glow, laughter and conversation spilling out, perhaps a handsome, well-dressed man entering alone.

Marks were always to be found in such places. Diana had taught her that. For the first months after she had left, she had continued to follow her old mentor's rules. She had always been better at the game than the other girls—subtler, slicker, far more credible. Diana had told her that she had a gift for it, was a "natural," that with concentration she could outgross the others ten-to-one. Now, a year and a half after striking out on her own, she had begun to rely on her instincts. Now, too, she played only on rainy nights.

She chose a place called Aspen, a preppy jock hangout with an "*après* ski" look: glowing yellow lamps, a glistening U-shaped bar, the whole place carefully defined by its adornments—tarnished athletic trophies, crossed ski poles and lacrosse sticks, framed amateur team photos crowding the walls—all calculated to create instant nostalgia for some nameless generic school distinguished by its love of sports.

She was standing just inside the doorway, taking in the buzz, inhaling the aroma of smoke, perfume and beer, when she noticed a man glance up at her from the bar. Late thirties, expensive striped Italian shirt, thinning light brown hair. He appraised her briefly, met her gaze, grinned in welcome, then turned back to his drink.

In the instant when their eyes met and locked she recognized him as her mark. Not the flashy type of salesman or conventioneer Diana had taught her to seek out, but someone better and less gullible. A superior man with cultural interests, perhaps moderately successful with women. A well-educated man, possibly divorced, who most likely owned an apartment in the neighborhood.

Striped Shirt looked up, smiled at her again. Already she felt regret; this conquest, it seemed, would not be difficult. She turned slowly, a signal that she noticed him but chose not to recognize his interest. Spotting an empty table, she moved toward it, knowing he was watching to see if she sat alone.

The waiter was a puppy: bright eyes, cute polka-dot bow tie, tail of frizzy hair tied back with a rubber band. He flirted with her ("How're *you* tonight?"), then asked what she'd like to drink.

She squinted at him. "Have I seen you in something?"

He smiled. "You a casting agent?" She shook her head. "Well," he admitted shyly, "I was in an ad in *Details*. You might've seen me there."

They chatted briefly about his career. He was looking to break through with a TV commercial. "Just in case you know someone in the biz . . ." he added, wandering off.

When he returned with her vodka, he told her she had an admirer.

"Striped shirt. Over there." He gestured. "He picked up your tab."

"Nice," she said, "but I like to pay for myself."

"Sorry, too late, I rang it up. But if you wanna make things even, you can always, you know, reciprocate." He grinned. He'd put many a boy and girl together; it was what he liked best about his job. "Actually, Roger's a pretty nice guy. Comes in a couple times a week. Works for a magazine. Never heard any complaints."

She glanced at the bar. Striped Shirt was grinning again. She nodded her thanks. He raised his glass in acknowledgment.

"Well?" asked the waiter. She shrugged. "A girl could do worse." He gave her his best kid-brother smirk.

"This girl usually does better," she said.

"Want me to tell him that?"

She laughed. "Sure. Why not?"

Striped Shirt appeared two minutes later, hovering at a respectful distance.

"Hi. I'm Roger."

She stared at him. "Hello, Roger."

He stared back. He looked a little unsure of himself. "Welcome to the pub."

"Thank you."

He gestured to the empty chair. "May I?" She shrugged. He sat down carefully.

"You're—?"

"My name's Gelsey, if that's what you want to know."

"Hello, Gelsey." He stuck out his hand. She looked at it, hesitated, then shook it casually.

"Thanks for the drink," she said. "But I wish you hadn't." She reached into her bag, pulled out her wallet.

His face fell. "Please, oh, no, don't! I know I should have asked."

She noted his wounded pride. "Well, just this once." She put her wallet away.

He sighed his gratitude. "That would have been really humiliating." She smiled to show she understood. "I haven't seen you in here before."

"I haven't been in here before."

"Well, figures." He was floundering. "What made you—?"

"I was out in the rain. I must have walked a long time. Then I felt thirsty and saw the glow and—" She shrugged. "Guess I was looking for some kind of refuge."

"Glad you chose Aspen. It's a friendly place. I know most of the regulars." He hesitated, then took the plunge. "Which is why I can honestly say you're the most attractive woman to drop in here in quite a while."

She pondered his compliment before accepting it. She wanted him to know she could not be so easily won. Finally she smiled, a signal that she would allow him to warm her up. Encouraged, he set eagerly to work.

He did his job well, careful always to offer a personal revelation before soliciting one from her. Still, he was thorough. After half an hour he had touched upon all the appropriate questions.

He was a staff writer at *Smart Money* magazine. She told him she worked in publicity at Simon & Schuster.

He was from St. Louis and had gone to Dartmouth. She told him she was from Oakland and had attended Cal.

He was thirty-six, divorced, an excellent skier, an earnest tennis player, also interested in art. She told him she was twenty-six, had broken up two months before with a live-in boyfriend, belonged to a health club, and, as for tennis—if they ever played he'd better watch out!

They discussed some of the concerns of people in their cohort: how difficult it was to live in the city with so much crime, homelessness and AIDS; how hard it was to meet nice people outside of work; the relative virtues and drawbacks of the alternate coast.

They oriented themselves by social-economic class (he was a child of the suburbs; she was brought up near a university where her father taught history); by personality type (he was gregarious; she thought of herself as more of a loner). Then they talked about their jobs.

He told her he'd been thinking about recycling as a TV correspondent. But the truth was he believed in print.

She did, too, she said, which was the only reason she stayed in publishing, where the workload was heavy and the pay disgracefully low. Still, she was thinking of moving on. There'd been some sexual harassment at her office. Subtle but unnerving, and, in its own way, insidious. In fact, the reason she'd gone out to walk in the rain that evening was to try to think through her options.

He turned compassionate. He knew exactly what she meant because he, too, had suffered something similar a couple of years back from a female superior.

"And it *was* insidious, because I knew if I complained I'd look like a total jerk. What could I say? That she made comments about my clothes, my build, told me I played 'a major role' in her fantasies? I should have been flattered, right? Physically speaking, she was a fairly desirable woman. Under other circumstances I might have been interested. But not in the workplace. Not for me, anyway. There's a time and place for everything, don't you think? A place to work and a time to play. . . ."

Gelsey picked up a half dozen signals from that little monologue. She made her eyes gleam so he would know she had caught them all.

He stared at her. There was a silence. They listened to a little burst of laughter from a table in the rear.

"Are you comfortable here?" he asked.

"Tell you the truth, there's too much smoke."

"Well," he said, "I hope this doesn't sound pushy. But I was wondering—see, I practically live around the corner."

This was it: the bar pickup endgame. She stared at him, noncommittal. She wanted to make him work for it.

He swallowed. "Like I said, I don't want to sound pushy. But I've got an interesting idea."

She leaned forward slightly. "Tell me."

He grinned to dispel any intimation of aggression. "I was thinking we might mosey out of here, go over to my place and, you know, have a nightcap . . . or something."

She reached across the table, took hold of both his hands, lightly played her fingers along his wrists. "Is that all you had in mind?"

He tried not to show too much excitement. "Well, that would be up to you," he said carefully.

She met his gaze, then lowered her eyes demurely. "What if we went up to your place and then I told you I'd like us to take off our pants?" She gazed at him again. "What would you think about that?"

He shook his head. He was enormously aroused.

"I'd think you were about the most intriguing person I'd met in a very long time."

His building was a fifteen-story white-brick-with-doorman, constructed as a rental in the sixties, converted to a co-op in the eighties. There were several mirrors in the lobby, one nice one between the elevators. They entered, Roger pushed the button for the penthouse, they leaned against opposite sides of the cab and smiled at one another as they rode up.

"Let's get these wet raincoats off," he said, fumbling with his keys.

Once inside, he switched on a set of track lights, then dimmed them down. There was a classic Manhattan penthouse view: squared-off apartment buildings against soaring midtown towers, a hundred thousand lit-up windows, golden cages hanging in the sky.

She looked around. The sparse furnishings were expensive: Matching soft black leather couches faced one another across a spare glass-topped cocktail table. Smooth white walls served as background for a small collection of average-quality contemporary prints. She knew the look: downtown gallery. She peered about more carefully, hoping to be surprised. But she could find nothing personal; the decor spoke to her of risklessness. Yet Roger had taken a major risk—he had invited her into his lair.

"I've been saving a bottle of very good wine. Think I should open it up?"

She thought a moment, then shook her head. "Actually, I'd rather have a drink."

"Great. What would you like?"

"Let me make it?"

He grinned at her. "I bet you can mix up something pretty good."

"Gelsey's Special."

"Sounds interesting."

"It is. I promise," she said.

He led her by the hand into his kitchen, showed her where he kept his booze, glasses, bar tools and blender, then excused himself to dry his hair.

"Just call me if you need anything." His voice trailed off.

She set up a pair of highball glasses, quickly marked one with a slight smudge of lipstick against the rim, then set to work creating her potion. As she was finishing she heard music. He had put a Mabel Mercer CD on the stereo.

She carried their drinks into the living room. He was slouched on one of the couches, jacket off, hair engagingly tousled.

She handed him his glass, sat down on the opposite couch, took a little sip from hers.

He grinned at her. "Starting to mellow out?"

"Very much so." She leaned back, flicked her hair, then casually stuck out her legs. She looked around. "I imagined you'd have a place like this."

"Really? Like what?"

"Cool. Hard-edged."

He looked perplexed. "Am I really that predictable?"

"We'll soon find out," she replied in a throaty whisper. Then she lightly touched her breasts.

It was a fine moment, the kind she tried to create every time she played, full of the promise of lust—tastes, aromas, moves and caresses that could not be predicted and would therefore surprise and delight. It was a moment that a worthy opponent would want to savor and prolong, knowing that anticipation is almost always sweeter than closure.

They drank in silence, matching one another sip for sip. When, finally, he had drained his glass, she excused herself.

"Don't get up," she said. "I'll find it on my own."

As she passed him she studied his eyes. They were beginning to glaze. Unaware of just how tired he was, he broke his yawn with another grin. She paused behind him, turned, placed her hands on his shoulders, then bent her head down to his ear:

"I think it's getting time to take off those pants," she whispered. Then she patted his head and retired to the bathroom.

She spent three minutes staring into her dream-sister's eyes in the cabinet mirror, then flushed the toilet and wandered back to the living room. She found him dozing, pants down, caught around his ankles. She knelt, placed a hand beneath his chin, carefully raised his head.

"Roger?"

He opened his eyes. "Sorry." He stared at her. "Maybe too much to drink." He gestured toward his glass on the cocktail table. "What did you—?"

She gazed at him. Her voice turned stern. "What did I *what*?"

"I dunno. . . ." He slurred his words.

"You lied to me at the bar."

"Huh?" He blinked.

"That little story about sexual harassment at the office—that never happened. Did it?"

He blinked again. "Whassa problem? I don get—"

"Get what, Roger?" she asked kindly.

He glanced at his glass again. "You put something—?"

"In your drink? Yes, as a matter of fact, I did." She nodded sweetly, then watched as the realization struck and the terror filled his eyes.

"*Why?* What're—?"

"Don't panic. Just go to sleep." She cooed at him like a pigeon from the park: "Sleep, sleep, sleep. Let yourself go. It'll make it so much easier. . . ."

He tried to strike out at her. She pulled back, but even if he had connected, his thrust was too feeble to have hurt. After that he drooped; the effort had wasted the last of his energy. She watched as he tried to fight off his exhaustion the way they always did, shaking his head, fluttering his eyes. She peered at him closely. He was terrified. He knew he was defenseless. He was probably wondering whether she had poisoned him, whether he would ever wake up.

"Please . . ." he begged.

She waited until he closed his eyes and his heavy rhythmic breathing told her he was out. "Good night, sweet prince," she whispered as she rose, then hurried to the kitchen where she had left her purse.

The first thing, always, was to put on a fresh pair of surgical gloves, thoroughly wash the highball glasses, then clean every spot she had touched with her fingertips. There weren't many such places: a few in the kitchen—the refrigerator and freezer doors—the bathroom doorknob, the edge of the medicine cabinet. When she finished with her chores she checked again on Roger. He was snoring deeply, lost in sleep. She nodded and began her search.

She removed his wallet from his fallen pants and emptied out all his pockets. She took the cash (more than four hundred dollars. *Surprise!*), but left the credit cards and IDs arranged neatly on the cocktail table. The point, as Diana had always taught, was to rob the mark, not enrage him. She also removed his watch. It wasn't anything special, but it was part of the game that he be deprived of his way of marking time. Then, when she had finished searching his person, she began a methodical search of the apartment.

It took her five minutes to discover that everything of interest was concentrated in the bedroom. The front closets and drawers were virtually empty. The bedroom, however, offered all sorts of treasures: a pair of gold Cartier cuff links, a Krugerrand, a gold pocket watch (probably his grandfather's) and, in the bottom of a drawer filled with hand-ironed shirts, a worn airmail envelope containing various denominations of foreign currency and five one-hundred-dollar bills.

All of this she took. She discovered and rapidly rearranged a good deal more. There was a trove of personal letters which she laid out, like cards dealt for solitaire, neatly on the living-room floor. And a collection of photographs which she separated and then propped up in various places around the apartment—on top of the bureau, on the bedside tables and along the windowsills.

She uncovered a small cache of ho-hum sex toys—a pack of condoms, a vibrator with attachments and a pair of domino masks. She partially superimposed the masks in the middle of the bed, to suggest classic symbols of comedy and tragedy, then unraveled the condoms and arranged them symmetrically so that they radiated from the masks like rays of the sun. Finally, she completed the work by circling the masks and condoms with the vibrator cord. Then she stepped back and squinted at her design.

It was fine as far as it went, she thought, but not, she decided, sufficiently bizarre. Feeling it could use a little more embellishment, she looked around the room and then, recalling a tangle of jockstraps she'd seen in one of the drawers, thought of a way to have some fun. She withdrew a pair of surgical scissors from her purse, retrieved the jocks, snipped off the fronts of the pouches, then added them to the bed display.

Pausing, she thought of inflicting similar damage on all his trousers and undershorts. But that, she decided, would take too much time and demonstrate too much hostility. She felt that in Roger's case she would make a deeper impression if she showed a certain elegant restraint.

But there was one final assault upon his dignity that she would not resist. The "inscribing," Diana called it. All of Diana's girls were instructed to do it and were tutored in its importance. Yet Gelsey's particular manner of inscription was unique. She employed it always. It sent a message to the mark, and, at the same time, doubled as her signature.

She hurried back to the living room. Roger was still snoring. She knew from her experience with various dosages that he would remain unconscious for at least ten hours. Now it was necessary to place him on his back. She lifted his legs, still bound by his dropped pants, pulled them around ninety degrees, then laid him out full-length on the couch. Then she bent down, unbuttoned his shirt and pulled it open so that his upper chest was exposed.

Indelible black marker in hand, she straddled him like an equestrienne and began to write in script upon his flesh. When she was finished she smiled at her handiwork. To an ordinary viewer it would appear an incoherent scrawl. But she could read it easily. And so would Roger, when, awakening, he stumbled into his bathroom and examined his groggy features in the mirror. Then the message she had written on his chest would leap out at him with diabolic force. And the fact that she had inscribed it as one long word in mirror-reverse would haunt him far longer than her robbery:

Down in the apartment-house lobby, she paused before the mirror between the elevators. Pretending to smooth her hair, she willed herself egress from the glass. Her dream-sister stared back at her, and then, in an instant, disappeared. Now she was once again herself.

Smiling sweetly at the doorman, she strode out into the open air. It was two A.M. The rain had stopped. The sidewalk was still wet. The air smelled faintly of iron.

She walked the four blocks to her car, got in, then drove leisurely along the empty avenue. At an intersection, when she stopped for a red light, a homeless man approached with a squeegee. She nodded encouragement when he began to wash her windshield; before the light changed, she handed him a twenty-dollar bill.

As she entered the tunnel she did not think about what she had done. Rather, she reveled in feelings of purification and release. The events of the evening seemed like a dream, not surprising since it was her dream-sister who had engaged in them. Still, the gratification engendered by the acts of violation now belonged to her.

Forty minutes later, approaching Richmond Park, she pulled off her blond wig and glanced at herself in her rear-view mirror. This time it was her true image that stared back.

A Small House in Queens

Not much of a place, Janek thought as he pulled in front of the house and parked. It was just an ordinary little house on a modest residential street that ran parallel to the Van Wyck Expressway, one of a thousand "starter houses" he'd passed countless times on his way out to Kennedy Airport from Manhattan.

It was two A.M., a humid August night, with a scorching wind blowing in from the south. Street lamps burned sulfurous in the gray-black haze. Janek, sweating, sat in his car in front of the house, listening for the sound of shots. He didn't hear any, but wouldn't have been surprised if he had. It was summer, the season of random gunfire, bullets discharged in rancor, piercing windows, killing babies in their cribs and grandmothers waiting to cross dusty, savage streets. All that summer, it seemed to Janek, the city had teetered on the edge of a breakdown.

He glanced at himself in his rearview mirror. There were bags under his eyes, but his features, he was pleased to see, were still intact. *Forty-four years old and I can maybe pass for forty-eight. But what about ten years from now? Will I end up with a turkey gobbler neck and one of those old-cop faces that remind me of a shattered piece of safety glass?*

He wiped his forehead with a handkerchief, stuffed it back into his pocket, then stepped out of his car. The house, he saw, was covered with some sort of synthetic siding made to look like roughly finished stone. The tiny front yard was enclosed by a chain-link fence, high enough to imprison a dog.

Janek unlatched the gate, entered and carefully closed it behind him. Three narrow brick steps led to a front stoop defined by a surprisingly delicate iron railing. From there he looked back at the street. There was a small wooden structure set out by the curb to hold garbage cans. Except, Janek knew, there'd never be any garbage in front of this house; if someone were in residence, the garbage would be hauled off in a van with blacked-out windows.

He wiped his forehead again and pressed the buzzer. A moment later the door opened and he was staring into Baldwin's chilly little eyes. The balding borough commander, wearing baggy shorts and a gray police T-shirt, looked different than in uniform—smaller and much more ordinary.

"Frank—"

"Harry," Janek said.

"Kit's here. She's waiting for you."

Baldwin, who was standing too close, stared at him for a moment, then stepped aside. As Janek crossed into the narrow front hall, he smelled deli food on Baldwin's breath.

"That you, Frank?"

Janek followed Kit's voice into a small living room where a bare bulb illuminated functional secondhand furniture. There he found her, reclining in a maroon lounge chair, sipping coffee from a Styrofoam cup. A short, dark, intense woman with sharp Greek features and burning eyes, Kit Kopta was chief of detectives of the city of New York.

Janek crossed to her, bent and kissed her cheek.

"Just you, me and Baldwin?" he asked.

"The others are with the prisoner." Kit raised her eyes to the ceiling.

A prisoner upstairs. Made sense. This was a police safe house. But the presence of the C of D and the borough commander suggested a prisoner of more than ordinary stature.

"Get yourself some coffee, Frank." She gestured toward the kitchenette.

When Janek walked in he found Baldwin hunched over the counter, making himself a corned beef sandwich. There was a sweat line on the back of his T-shirt. Janek noticed the flab on his biceps.

"Been a while, Frank," Baldwin said.

"Yeah, about a year, I guess." Janek filled his cup. Beside the pot on the stove, there was a spread of deli meats, sliced bread and Danish laid out on the counter, an open jar of mustard and a neat pile of napkins and paper plates.

"Big one, huh?"

Janek nodded knowledgeably and returned to the living room. Kit was dozing. When she heard him, she opened her eyes.

"Baldwin says this is a big one," Janek said.

"Could be."

"Am I supposed to guess?"

Kit smiled, a warm, dazzling smile that took him back nearly twenty years—to the time when they'd been young detectives, heady on each other and the job. Their affair had lasted three months. They'd been close friends ever since.

"We got a guy upstairs says his sister was Mendoza's maid."

Mendoza. Of course. The case had haunted him for the better part of a decade. Mendoza's maid had been the missing witness. Janek had been assigned to find her. He never had.

"Jesus," he said. "Does this thing never stop?"

"Maybe now it will. You see why we called you, Frank?"

Sure, I see. Who the hell else would she call?

There wasn't much of a story, at least not so far. The prisoner, one Angel Figueras, had been apprehended by an alert patrolman the previous evening, emerging through the back door of a mom-and-pop jewelry store on Queens

Boulevard, pockets stuffed with watches and engagement rings. Figueras was arrested, booked and awaiting arraignment when he asked to see a criminal defense attorney named Netti Rampersad. "She's upstairs with him now," Kit said.

"Rampersad. Never heard of her. Is the name for real?"

Kit smiled. "It's real and she's a powerhouse. Anyway, they had a little conference, Rampersad went to see the D.A., and now here we are, about to make a deal."

"He locates his sister—we let him off."

"That's about it," Kit confirmed. "He especially requested you, Frank. You're the one he wants to tell it to."

"He knows me?" Janek was surprised.

"Seems that way. Meantime his story checks out. He's Tania's brother and he swears he can give you her address. All we gotta do is give up a small-time safecracker for a shot at a woman we've been wanting to talk to for nine years. Not a bad deal, seems to me."

"No guarantee she'll talk to us."

"No. But we know you'll give it your best shot." Kit smiled at him again, her gorgeous smile. "Don't we, Frank?"

They went upstairs. Baldwin didn't join them, just grinned at them, jaws masticating meat.

"What's he doing here?" Janek whispered when they reached the upstairs hall.

"Harry? Well, it's his safe house." Kit lowered her voice. "Also . . . he's Dakin's friend."

"Looking out for Dakin's interests?"

Kit shrugged. "A case like Mendoza—who knows?"

Four of them were sitting on plastic chairs around a card table in what Janek took to be the master bedroom. There was a stained rust-colored shag rug on the floor. Figueras, a short, lean, hard-bodied, mustachioed Hispanic in a soiled tanktop, looked fairly relaxed considering he was handcuffed. There was a slicked-down young A.D.A. named Gabelli, who wore his sleeves rolled up Manhattan district attorney–style; Detective Sergeant Tommy Shandy, who guarded the portals to Kit's office; and Netti Rampersad, clearly the dominant personality in the room.

Janek studied her. She looked to be in her early thirties, a tall attractive woman in tight jeans, with a lush mane of red-blond hair and a galaxy of freckles on her upper chest, exposed by a scoop-neck blouse that looked like it had cost a lot of money. There was a glow on the lady, too, a glow Janek had observed on certain female attorneys when they thought they had a group of men by the balls. Evidently Ms. Rampersad thought she had the assembled males exactly that way tonight.

"Tony and I've worked it out," Rampersad said to Kit. "No typewriter, so we wrote it up by hand."

She handed Kit a handwritten document. Gabelli turned to Kit at the same time.

"Sure you want to do this, Chief?"

"Why shouldn't I?"

"I'd prefer to see him plead, do a deal on the sentencing."

"We've gone over that, Tony." Rampersad stared at Gabelli, not bothering to conceal her annoyance. "No plea, no felony on the books. That's the only way he's going to talk." She turned to Kit. "Take it or leave it, Chief."

"We'll take it," Kit said.

"I thought so. Now all you've gotta do is sign. . . ."

Later, alone with Figueras in the smaller bedroom, Janek asked him if they'd ever met.

"No, sir. But I know your name. My sister said, 'Someday, Angel, the cops pick you up, I'm your ticket out of trouble. Ask for *Teniente* Janek. Tell him where I am.' That was her good-bye present, see."

"She went away?"

Figueras nodded. "She went back to Cuba, Lieutenant. Now I give you her address."

When Gabelli heard, he turned on Rampersad. "Cuba! Fuck! You're trying to screw us, Netti!"

"What?"

"The deal's invalid."

"Fuck you, Tony!"

Janek glanced at Kit. She didn't look angry at all.

"I didn't know where his sister was," Netti Rampersad said. "But it doesn't matter if she's in Timbuktu. The information's good, the deal's good." She turned to Kit. "Are you satisfied, Chief?"

"Sure I am, Counselor."

"Good. Now can we all go home?"

Kit nodded to Tommy Shandy, who unlocked Angel's cuffs. The little Cuban shook his wrists and grinned.

"I'll drive you," Netti Rampersad told him.

"Drop me at the subway's okay," Angel said.

While Angel retired to the bathroom to clean up, Janek followed Rampersad downstairs. She went into the kitchen, poured herself a cup of coffee. Janek joined her. She was still glowing.

"Feeling victorious?"

She raised her eyebrows. "Interesting situation, you have to admit."

"I'd like to ask you something."

"Sure."

"Angel asked for you. Does he know you? You don't exactly strike me as a legal-aid type."

"Oh?" She arched her eyebrows higher. "Fill me in, will you, Lieutenant? Exactly what type's that?"

Janek shrugged. "Hollow eyes. Bitter mouth. Lots of yak about prosecutorial misconduct and infringed constitutional rights."

She smiled. "Go on."

"Well, let's see." Janek scratched his head. "Polyester

blouse. Ten-buck hairdo. Hmmm . . . way too many cigarettes.''

She laughed. ''Tell you the truth, Angel and I didn't meet until this morning.''

''Then, why—?''

''His sister told him to request me. Just like she told him to ask for you.'' She paused. ''I'm thinking I should go to work now on Mendoza's appeal.'' She met his eyes carefully, as if she wanted him to understand how strong and confident she felt. ''How many lawyers do you think he's had?''

Janek shrugged. ''Three or four. They keep getting grungier.'' He looked at her. ''Think the tide's turned?''

''You never know, do you? But Angel's not lying. Everything he told you's true.''

''I have your word on that, Ms. Rampersad?''

''Oh, sure,'' she said. ''You have my word.''

Suddenly she was bored. She glanced at her watch. ''Gotta go.'' She yelled roughly out to the hall: ''Angel! Let's haul ass!'' She turned back to Janek, stuck out her hand and then, to his amazement, addressed him in a mock Chinese accent: ''Velly nice to meet yoo, I'm shoo.''

It was three-thirty by the time he left with Kit. She'd dismissed Tommy Shandy, who'd driven her in from Manhattan. Baldwin stayed behind to straighten up the safe house.

Janek and Kit sat together in Janek's car, trying to decide where to go. It was the deadest hour of the morning, the favored time for shootouts between drugged-out thieves and trigger-happy clerks and therefore the most dangerous time to enter a twenty-four-hour convenience store. It was also the hour when desperate battered wives put bullets into their sleeping husbands' heads. Most of the bars had closed and most of the coffee shops hadn't yet opened. Kit suggested they drive to Hunts Point Market. She knew a place where they could get themselves a good breakfast there, she said.

On the way to the Bronx they passed Shea Stadium, silent, looming, and for a moment Janek saw grandeur in it. Then, for no particular reason, he recalled a vacation he'd taken two years before, a late-summer camping trip to the MacNeil River in Alaska.

He and the woman he'd been in love with, a German psychiatrist named Monika whom he'd met on vacation in Venice, had gone there to hike, fish and observe the wild brown bears. It was a glorious time. The wildflowers were in bloom, the sun had blazed, and at night the northern lights had glowed like jewels in the sky. In the mornings he'd gathered birch twigs to make a fire, mixed batter, flipped flapjacks, then served them to Monika from an old black skillet.

She had told him she loved him. He had told her the same. But when they got back to civilization, the romance started going sour. Her life was in Europe; his was in New York. Her friends were academics; his were cops. She had patients; he had snitches. She wanted to relieve people of torment; he strove for an ideal that he laughingly called justice. In the end, being adults, they acknowledged their incompatibility and agreed to part. They vowed to stay friends, and genuinely tried, but it had been nine months since either had written or called the other.

"It's like the Dreyfus case," Kit said.

Janek, reverie broken, turned to her. "What?"

"Mendoza. It's haunted us the way the Dreyfus Affair haunted the French army. It's made us question our honor. That's why we've got to get to the bottom of it, Frank."

She seemed to sigh then, a sound he couldn't remember hearing her make before. He looked at her. She was huddled, eyes closed, against the passenger door, head crooked between the window and the seat. Turning back to the parkway, his brain flashing with memories of the labyrinth everyone now called, simply, "Mendoza," Janek was inclined to give out a sigh himself.

The crime-scene photos had been horrific, even to cops who thought they'd seen it all: shots taken from various angles of the body of Edith Mendoza, naked, gagged, wrists cuffed, feet tied together with rope, then suspended upside down from a hook implanted in the ceiling of the double-height mirror-lined studio apartment in Chelsea that she and her husband had kept for fun and games.

There was one shot in particular that Janek remembered. The photographer would have had to have taken it on his belly. Janek could still recall the way Edith's finely sculpted features filled the frame, the way her thick dark hair hung loosely, barely scraping the polished floor. What was memorable was the tranquillity of her features, the lack of any expression of anguish, the repose. Her face had been the only part of her that had not been bruised. Her torso, beaten mercilessly by her killer, had borne terrifying marks.

The moment they reached Hunts Point, Kit came awake. They passed men tossing food crates off the backs of trucks, Korean shopkeepers bargaining with Italian wholesalers, piles of eggplants and tomatoes, carrots and onions, multiplying wildly in the huge main selling hall.

Kit guided Janek to a diner just behind. Teamsters, who'd driven produce in from Long Island and New Jersey, crowded the counter demanding coffee.

"My cousin's place," Kit explained as she nudged him toward a booth. Janek smiled. He knew that Kit, who always seemed to enjoy telling him how lonely she was and how she spent most holidays at home watching sports events and sipping ouzo, was actually a member of a vast extended Greek-American family that owned coffee shops all over the city.

"I didn't like Baldwin's coffee," she said when they were seated. "And I didn't think much of his spread."

"He'll take it home and feed it to his kids for breakfast," Janek said. "It'll give them bad breath. Later at school they won't understand when the other kids turn away."

Kit laughed. "You've got everyone figured out, don't you, Frank?"

"Not everyone," he said. "Not you."

She stared at him, blinked.

"Hi, Chief!" A handsome young waiter with a Greek accent took their breakfast orders, then moved away.

"My nephew," Kit explained.

"I know what you're thinking," Janek said. Kit looked at him curiously. "You want me to interview Tania. I'm wondering how you think I'm going to do it."

"Only one way I can think of," Kit said. "Fly down to Cuba and knock on her door."

"You're kidding!"

"Uh-uh, not kidding, Frank. There's no extradition, no cooperation, but there's nothing to stop you going down there as a tourist."

"Sure. Without my badge, without my gun."

"What do you need them for? You're just going to talk to the woman. It's perfectly legal to go. There're charters out of Miami—though I wouldn't advise taking one. Your best bet's Mexico. You don't want to attract attention by going as a cop, so you work up a cover identity under your own name, something they'd appreciate, something slightly socialist, like . . . labor organizer? Yeah, that sounds right. Then go to a tour operator and arrange a week's vacation. The Cubans are hungry for dollars. They'll show you a good time."

"Then one afternoon I just slip out to the address." Janek pulled out his notebook, laid it on the table. "Ring the buzzer. Ask for Tania Figueras. Ask her if she'd like to fill me in on a few little matters that happened one night nine years ago."

"Sounds good to me."

"I don't believe this!"

"Why not?" She eyed him sternly. "You know you're going to go. You knew it, same as me, soon as you heard where she was."

Kit was right. But somehow he hadn't been able to picture himself playing detective in a country where he would have no authority, where, at best, he would be tolerated only because he carried hard currency.

"We thought Tania was dead. Now it turns out she's been living this close for years. She has to know what's been going on. But she never came forward, never even wrote a letter. Why should she talk to me now? What's to stop her, soon as I identify myself, from slamming her door in my face?"

"She may do that. She may even call the cops and have them heave you out. But can you think of any other way to handle it? Be honest, Frank. Can you really imagine yourself, now that you know where she is, shrugging the information off?"

The waiter brought their food. Kit dug into her scrambled eggs. Janek sipped his coffee and watched her eat. *How can she feel so ravenous?*

"No."

"No—what?" she asked, not looking up.

"No, I can't imagine that."

"So—?"

"So, I'll go." He paused. "Want to know why?" She nodded. "I'll go there for you—because you want me to."

She looked up at him then, her tired face breaking into a grin.

"You'll not only go, Frank. You'll bring back the goods." Her smiled turned truly beauteous. "I know you will."

He spent the next several days in a small bare room off Central Files reviewing the Mendoza folders, scanning the documents, rereading the notes, trying to fill in the well-remembered outlines of the case with its texture, smell—

what he thought of as its "buzz." Halfway through the material he was moved to pity. Mendoza was a cop's nightmare, and, for New York City cops, it was a great nightmare shared.

The photographs told the initial story well. There was one, clipped out of an issue of *New York* magazine, that had appeared a year before the killings. It showed the Mendozas in happier days: short, chubby, balding Jake, the corporate-takeover genius, standing proudly beside Edith, his younger, taller, slimmer wife. Both Mendozas gazed at the camera. Jake wore his shy, dimpled, baby-face grin; Edith's smile was more restrained. What came through strongest was their confidence—"Look at us, we've made it big. Now we're reaping the harvest."

The setting for this shot, the vast living room of their Central Park West apartment, was as interesting to Janek as the portraits. Polished floors, priceless antiques, radiant old-master paintings mounted on glazed and glowing walls—the artifacts spoke of wealth and striving, props in a room conceived of as a theater in which the elites of Manhattan mingled, and by so doing imbued their hosts with glamour.

Jake and Edith had been involved with the great cultural institutions of the city—Metropolitan Museum of Art, Metropolitan Opera, New York Public Library, New York City Ballet. But there was a dark side unseen by their attractive society friends, bizarre scripted encounters enacted in another, smaller, less-glittering theater: the covertly rented, mirror-lined studio in Chelsea in which Edith Mendoza had been found hanging from a hook.

There were photographs in the file of *that* apartment, too, showing the Mendozas at play with partners recruited from the lower depths. The pictures had been discovered in the suburban home of an undercover narcotics detective named Howard Clury a week after Clury, while starting up his Cadillac, had been blown to bits by a plastic explosive expertly wired to his accelerator. It was the discovery of Clury's cache, and the coincidental timing of his execution (one day after Edith's), that pushed the case out of the category of "brutal society sex murder" into another, more esoteric realm of criminal phenomena.

Janek inspected the Clury pictures closely. They had been taken with an extreme wide-angle lens so that everything in the Chelsea studio could be seen. The mirrors that lined the walls tripled the impact of the images. They showed Edith, bound naked to the bed with rope, being ravaged by a muscular black man (later identified as an aspirant boxer named Carl Washington), while Jake, bound tightly to a chair, looked on with anguished eyes.

But was Edith truly being violated? Or could her expression be characterized as ecstatic? Was Jake helpless and humiliated? Or was he simply fascinated? Janek compared one of the pictures from this series with the portrait in *New York* magazine. Except for their nakedness, the Mendozas looked the same. Jake's grin was just as broad. Edith's smile was similarly enigmatic. Their expressions projected the same smug sense of entitlement, perhaps tinged in the sex photos by an additional blush of almost otherworldly delight.

After three days of studying the file, Janek arranged to meet his former partner, Timmy Sheehan, at a pub called O'Malley's on Second Avenue near Ninety-third. O'Malley's was a typical neighborhood Paddy bar, catering to a mix of blue-collar people, brassy local women and apartment-house doormen of Irish descent. It was not a cop hangout, which, Timmy said, was why he found it tolerable.

When Janek arrived a little after six P.M., Timmy was waiting at the bar. Janek didn't spot him at first; the afternoon sunlight was so bright he was temporarily blinded when he walked in. But then, as his eyes adjusted, he made out Timmy's face—pink cheeks, squared-off chin, thick gray hair rising straight back from the forehead. Timmy was staring at him, waiting to be recognized. A TV, set above the bar, was carrying the local news.

"Have I gotten that fat, Frank?" he asked as Janek approached.

"Yeah, I think so. In the jowls," Janek said.

They cuffed at one another, ordered beers, then moved to a booth in the dark back half of the room. There they chatted briefly about a former supervisor named McGavin who had shot himself the week before, after seven years' retirement, in Arizona.

"Way I heard it," Timmy said, "he ate his Popsicle in a service-station rest room."

"Leave a note?"

Timmy shook his head. "He just sat down on the toilet. Then . . . *ping!*" Timmy formed his right hand into a pistol, pulled an imaginary trigger. "His wife, Jo—remember her, Frank?—she was out by the pump filling up the tank. When she heard the shot she knew what had happened. People at the station started going crazy, but Jo just stood there pumping gas till it ran down the side of the car."

"Jesus!" No matter how many such stories Janek heard, he never became inured to them.

"McGavin was always an inconsiderate bastard." Timmy squinted. "Anyway, Frank, what's on your mind?"

Janek met Timmy's eyes. They were smart and quick. There had always been something cool about him, swift and cold behind the banter.

"Heard the latest on Mendoza?"

Timmy laughed. "Like what? He still hates my guts?"

"We located the maid."

Timmy nodded slowly. "That *is* news. What does she have to say?"

"Haven't talked to her yet."

"Then, I guess there is no 'latest,' is there?"

Janek had noticed Timmy tighten up at his mention of the maid. The tightening was barely perceptible and quickly covered by a smile. Mendoza was like that. It made everyone connected to it tense. The waves keep coming, he thought, the way they do when you throw a stone into a lake—concentric waves that keep widening until they disturb lives far removed from the original crime.

"Tell me your version."

"Oh, shit, Frank. Just read the file, why don't you?"

"Been reading it. It's thick. And my part, looking for Tania, was a sideshow. What I remember, I guess like everyone, are the things that happened later on—the stuff with Dakin, the forged-evidence charges, the aftermath."

"The important stuff."

"Yeah, but I'm not going to talk to Tania Figueras about that. I'm going to talk to her about the Mendozas. I want to get a feel of what the case was like at the beginning, before you connected it to Clury, before anything."

Timmy sat silent. He gazed at Janek, then suddenly stood up, walked into the men's room, emerged a couple of minutes later, walked over to the bar, brought back a second set of beers, sat down, groaned, looked at Janek with great forbearance and began to talk.

"There was a call to nine-one-one. It came a little after seven P.M. A woman in Chelsea reported shrill screaming in a neighboring apartment. Couple of hours later a pair of patrolmen showed up. The dispatcher had billed it as a possible domestic disturbance. You know what they found—Edith Mendoza, hanging upside down. I caught the squeal. You were down in Dallas, working on . . . I can't remember now."

"Drug case. I was testifying."

"Right. So anyway, I went over there with Jim Rankin, the only other guy in the squad room at the time. Neither of us ever saw a crime scene like it. It was a good-sized studio, about twenty-by-twenty, with lots of mirrors around and a double-story ceiling. There was this beautiful lady hanging from there, bruises all over her, track lights aimed down, floor lights aimed up, spotlighting her like she's in some kind of show. And she's even twirling a little, too, like the rope had been wound up, you know, like when they'll twirl someone in a circus. But there was one big difference. The lady was dead."

"Wouldn't the rope have unwound by then—after so many hours?"

"I guess. So maybe it just seemed that way. Maybe it was the air that moved her when we opened the door. I remember she was moving in a kind of circle. Counterclockwise, I think."

"That's interesting," Janek said. "That's not in the file."

"It wasn't really relevant."

Janek nodded. "So then—?"

Timmy shrugged. "I did what I was supposed to do."

He described how he had contacted the med examiner, called in a Crime Scene squad, IDed the victim—standard procedure, everything by the book. A little before eleven, he and Rankin drove uptown to Mendoza's building, a block-wide Art Deco tower on Central Park West. Timmy called Jake Mendoza from the lobby. Mendoza, sounding groggy, complained that Timmy had woken him up. When Timmy asked if he could come upstairs, Jake demanded an explanation. When Timmy told him he couldn't go into it on the phone, Mendoza said fine, in that case it could wait till morning. Then he hung up.

"Think about it, Frank—two cops call you middle of the night, tell you they got something important . . . and you hang up on them?" Timmy rolled his eyes. "We had to see him, so we went to work on the elevator man. We finally persuaded him to take us to the penthouse. We rang the buzzer and waited a long time. Finally Mendoza opened the door. He was wearing pajamas.

"I didn't like him, not from the first. I thought he was a phony. His hair was mussed like he'd been sleeping, but the pajamas looked fresh to me. Anyway, when we told him about his wife, he gaped at us. Then, I swear, he grinned. Like we were putting him on, like it was, you know—hardy-har-har. But when Rankin showed him one of the Polaroids, he got serious real quick. He went into another room and called his lawyer. When he came out he said he'd been advised not to talk to us. Then he said he wanted to see the body.

"We waited while he dressed, then took him downtown. And we were very careful, Frank. We didn't say a word to him in the car. I watched him. There was something about him. He sat very still and there was this smell coming off him, like bad fumes, you know, something like that. Actually, it was some fancy men's fragrance he'd splashed on himself, but it was going bad . . . like something was eating him up inside and turning that fragrance to shit. That's when I knew he was behind it.

"His lawyer was waiting for us at the morgue, a tweedy, WASPy type named Andrews. They huddled, then Andrews motioned us aside. Mendoza had been at his office until nine o'clock, he told us, working on a deal since noon with lunch and dinner delivered in. Andrews gave us names of people on Mendoza's staff who would verify Mendoza hadn't left the entire time. When he came home and Mrs. Mendoza wasn't there, he'd assumed she was out seeing friends. He didn't know anything about the Chelsea studio. He had no idea what his wife was doing there. Finally Andrews said Mendoza was too upset to talk, but in a couple of days, after the shock wore off, he'd probably be willing to sit down. Now, did we have any problems with that?" Timmy laughed. "Oh, sure we did. But we didn't say anything. That was it. End of discussion."

"What about the maid?" Janek looked at Timmy. No sign of tightening this time. Two men, who'd been arguing about baseball at the bar, inexplicably burst into song. Timmy glanced at them, then back at Janek.

"We found out about her the following day. The night doorman filled us in. Around nine o'clock, about the time the patrolmen got to the studio, Tania Figueras came down to the lobby of the Central Park West building with a suitcase, told the doorman she was leaving the Mendozas' employ, got into a taxi and drove off. The doorman said she looked terrified. We were too busy to look for her, but when you came back from Dallas I put you on her."

"And I never came up with anything. She disappeared."

"Right. But by that time she didn't matter all that much." Timmy sat back in the booth and smiled. "By that time the case was getting complicated. Because once we got Clury factored in, we knew we had a double. . . ."

Two nights before Janek was due to fly to Mexico City, he met his ex-wife, Sarah, for dinner. Their meeting, arranged at Sarah's request, took place in a small family-run Czech restaurant called Praha on West Thirteenth in Greenwich Village.

Praha had been a favorite dining place during the years when they'd been married. Personal attention by the staff and the friendly gemütlichkeit atmosphere made it an ideal spot to celebrate promotions and anniversaries. Janek still went there; the owner, Josef Jellef, had been a friend of his father's. At first he was surprised when Sarah had suggested it, but as the evening approached, he became concerned. *Suppose she wants to meet there to stir up nostalgia for years I'd just as soon forget?*

She was seated when he arrived. Josef had put her at his best table, visible through the front window. Pausing out on the sidewalk to observe her through the glass, Janek tried to imagine how she would appear to a stranger glancing in: a svelte, well-groomed woman in her forties with intelligent eyes and a well-modeled face. But would it occur to this stranger that the handsome woman he was looking at had once been the wife of a cop? Janek didn't think so. Sarah looked more like an attorney's wife, privileged, perhaps even spoiled. There could be, he knew, something attractive, even sexy, about such a woman—a woman, like Sarah, who knew exactly what she wanted.

"Frank . . ." Her smile was warm, her voice throaty and

full of feeling. ‘‘It’s been so long. I hope you don’t mind meeting here.’’

‘‘Not at all,’’ Janek said. ‘‘It’s good to see you, Sarah.’’ Suddenly he felt gallant toward her. The bitterness he had harbored for so long faded rapidly in her presence, leaving him with a mellow, protective concern he had not felt toward her in years.

When Josef came over to greet them, he kissed Sarah’s hand. After he took their order and moved away, she giggled slightly. ‘‘I’m still a sucker for old-world manners,’’ she said.

She asked a lot of questions about people in the Department, detectives with whom they’d once socialized. Most of them were people Janek didn’t see anymore and a few of them were dead. But Sarah chattered on about them as if the years had never passed.

When she asked about his current cases, he responded cautiously. When she asked if he still attended pro-hockey games, he sensed she had something on her mind and was trying to warm him up before exposing it.

He knew how to deal with that: keep shifting the topic to throw her timing off. So he sparred with her until halfway through the main course, when he suddenly realized he was treating her like an interrogee. Then he was annoyed with himself. He hadn’t wanted the dinner to turn out this way. *Lighten up,* he told himself. *Try and make it pleasant.* But then it was too late; Sarah looked uncomfortable.

‘‘All right,’’ she said, breaking in on him in the middle of a story, ‘‘there’s something I want to discuss.’’

He lowered his silverware. ‘‘Sure, there is. That’s why you asked to meet.’’

‘‘I thought it would be nice to see you, Frank.’’

‘‘But it hasn’t been all that nice, has it?’’

‘‘I didn’t say that. You make me a little nervous, that’s all.’’

‘‘Sorry. I wanted this to go well. Anyway’’—he looked

at her—"what's on your mind?"

She lowered her eyes. "I need more money."

He stared at her blandly. "So do I."

"I mean it, Frank. I can't keep up, not on what you send me."

"I don't follow that." He spoke carefully. "You have a full-time job. Plus I send you a monthly check. The amount was agreed to long ago. You can't come around now, years later, and expect to renegotiate."

"Times change. Things are more expensive these days."

"For everyone. Not just you."

"Look, Frank—"

"No, *you* look," he said. "You still going out with what's-his-name?"

"That has nothing to do with—"

"It has everything to do with it. You're going out with a professional man who earns a hell of a lot more than me. And he sleeps with you in a house I spent twenty years paying off so you'd always have a roof over your head."

She bristled. "Guess what, Frank? The damn roof on that damn house leaks."

"So, get it fixed."

"They say it has to be replaced."

"I'm sorry," he said. "It's your house now. Fix it up or sell it and move someplace else."

She gazed at him. She made no attempt to conceal her disgust. "I had a feeling you'd say something like that. I was hoping you wouldn't."

He laughed, fighting off the old bitterness. "Shameless as ever. You haven't changed."

She stared at him, outraged. "What've I got to be ashamed about?"

The transparency of your manipulations, he thought, but he didn't say it. Instead he shook his head. Then, in a tone as kind as he could manage: "Why don't you ask your rich boyfriend to help you out?"

"I can't, that's all." Tears filled her eyes. "Oh, Frank—don't you understand?"

"Sure, I understand. You're in a relationship with another guy. I don't know why you two haven't gotten married—that's none of my business. But my responsibility to you ended long ago. The fact that I'm still paying alimony galls me no end."

She lowered her voice, then mumbled as if to herself, "I suppose I could go to court, ask for a bigger allotment."

"I wouldn't do that if I were you. Believe me, that would be a mistake."

"I'm not threatening. It was just an idea."

"When you talk about court I take it as a threat."

"I'm only asking, Frank. If you can't do it, you can't." She smiled. "I don't want to be like one of those wives we used to talk about. Remember? The ones who took their exes 'to the cleaners'?"

"You'll only be counted among them when you act like one of them." He signaled to the waiter. "How about some dessert?"

"Please do one thing?" He stared at her, waiting to hear. "Think about it, that's all. Just think about it. Will you do that, Frank?"

He swallowed. He could feel his resistance melting, but he couldn't help himself—he'd always been a sucker for a well-turned plea. "Tell you what. I'll consider helping with the roof. Get an estimate and let me know."

She brightened. "That would be wonderful!"

"I'm not promising anything."

"I understand."

"First let's see what kind of money we're talking about."

"I'll call the contractor tomorrow."

The waiter came over. They ordered pastries. Then their conversation mellowed. Again, he felt the similarity to an interrogation—how, after manipulating a source into giving him what he wanted, he always felt the need to smooth things over, descend from a summit of intensity and conflict to a plateau of amiable banter. But this time he hadn't gotten anything. Sarah had. So, what about himself, what role had he played in their little joust? Sucker? Dupe? He knew he'd been the one to lose control.

After dinner they strolled through the Village, down quiet residential streets. It was a warm summer night, people were out, sitting on portable lawn chairs or lingering before their doors. On the stoop of one building a girl was playing a guitar; her friends, assembled on the steps, sat around her, listening.

''How's Kit?'' Sarah asked in a tone intended to sound nonchalant. Sarah had never been able to bring up Kit's name without pretending she was doing so casually.

''Kit's fine,'' he said.

''I hear she's sending you on a little trip.''

Janek stopped walking. ''Who told you that?''

''A little bird,'' Sarah said gaily.

He was angered that word on his Cuba venture had gotten out. ''Whoever told you broke security.''

''It was a cop's wife, someone you don't know. You don't know her husband, either.''

So, despite Kit's precautions, the Department was still a sieve. Janek wondered if Baldwin had leaked the story. He would certainly have passed the news to Dakin, then Dakin's crowd would have spread it fast.

''It's that damn Mendoza thing, isn't it?'' she asked. ''I *hate* that case. I always did.''

He started walking. ''I'm not all that crazy about it myself.''

''It ruined our marriage. I never told you that before, but that's really what I think.''

He looked at her. Was she serious? Didn't she understand that her selfishness had ruined it—her refusal to have children, her insistence on having abortions the two times she'd gotten pregnant, as if the presence of a child in the house would somehow diminish her, cause him to pamper her

less, make her feel less like a prin
of his life, he knew, was that he had sp
with a woman who had insisted on a barren ma
all the time he had yearned for a son or daughter wh
could lavish with his love.

"Mendoza is an unpleasant fact of life," he said. "My only interest in it is to put it to rest."

"And Kit—is that her only interest?"

He stopped again. "What are you getting at?"

She turned to him. "Just raising a point. Everyone in the cops has his own agenda. I learned that from you long ago. I was just wondering if maybe Kit had one. Like why, now that everyone's forgotten about Mendoza, does she want you to go back and beat on it again?"

"Our honor's at stake."

Sarah laughed. "Is that what *she* says?"

God, you're impossible! "Why do you care, Sarah? What's it to you?"

"Oh, I care, Frank," Sarah said softly. "I care because I hate to see you waste your time on something that can only bring you grief." She paused. "Mendoza is a tar pit. Everybody knows it. Everyone, that is . . . except maybe you."

Lies & Consequences

Early on a Sunday morning in September, the day before Labor Day, Janek flew "naked"—without shield or gun—to Mexico City. Besides his toilet articles and a week's worth of clothing, he carried a microcassette recorder, a half dozen cassettes, a photocopy of his police ID, an ink pad, a blank fingerprint form, and a small 35-mm camera, loaded with color film, which a detective in the Forensics Division had assured him could be operated by an idiot.

On takeoff, Manhattan looked spectacular, silver towers reflecting golden light. It also looked clean and still. Staring down at the city as the plane rose in a graceful arc, Janek felt grateful to be off its torrid, squalid streets.

He had never met Howard Clury, but he believed he knew the type: a detective who could have chosen to become a criminal. In fact, in performance of his duty, a criminal was, essentially, what Clury had been.

In photographs, he even looked a little like a hood, at least a movie version of one. He had a hulking, bullish body, his neck was thick and his cheeks were heavily scarred. Most troubling to Janek were Clury's eyes. He searched them for signs of vulnerability, but could find nothing but slits in a mask.

Clury had had an exemplary record. He was a loner, specializing in undercover work, with lots of acquaintances but no real friends in the Department. He had been married to a younger and, by all accounts, pretty woman named Janet, who, he told people, had deserted him for another man. He lived alone in the one-story tract house they had shared, in a middle-class suburb on Long Island. His only extravagance was the baby-blue Cadillac he parked conspicuously in his driveway near his door.

For the first few days after he was killed, no one made a connection between the blown-up undercover cop on Long Island and the beaten-to-death society woman in Chelsea. NYPD investigators, working with Nassau County police, were convinced that Clury, engaged in a dangerous narcotics investigation, had been found out and executed by the ring he had penetrated as an agent.

There were reasons to believe this: His car was wired professionally; the people he'd been dealing with were ruthless; by blowing him up so spectacularly, they made him an example. But when these same investigators, searching Clury's house, uncovered his cache of photos of the Mendozas, a new police theory was instantly born: Clury was blackmailing the Mendozas; Jake Mendoza had paid to have him killed and at the same time arranged the murder of his wife.

On the plus side of this theory were two linking facts: Clury, who moonlit as a private investigator, had been hired by Jake Mendoza the year before to collect compromising information about an opponent in a business deal; second, an examination of the victims' financial records showed recent cash withdrawals from an account controlled by Edith that matched perfectly with recent cash deposits by Clury.

But there were many unanswered questions: How did Clury come into possession of the compromising photographs? Why did Mendoza want his wife dead? Why, if Clury was engaged in blackmail, did he bank the money and thus provide a paper trail for the police and the IRS? Finally, if the killings were linked, why were they so dissimilar—in Clury's case, quick and clean; in Edith's, slow and painful?

It was Timmy Sheehan's focus on these questions that caused him to regard Tania Figueras's disappearance as a relatively inconsequential tangent to the investigation.

The air over Mexico City was neither clean nor clear. On the descent, Janek craned to view the sprawl but caught only quick glimpses through a canopy of haze. On the ground, he collected his bags, passed customs, then made his way through the mob that thronged the terminal. After a chaotic scene at the Cuban Airlines counter, he boarded his plane for Havana.

After being boarded, the aircraft taxied to one side of the field and sat there, sputtering, for an hour and a half. Every once in a while the engines would rev, and then, failing to catch, would subside. There was a loud electrical hum, the air grew stifling. Passengers began to sweat and curse. A pair of stout stewardesses passed out pieces of hard brown candy. Janek noted that the bins above the seats, stuffed with baggage, were not secured by doors or even rope.

Finally, with an ear-splitting roar, the plane attacked the runway. Shaking violently, it surged up through the smog. Janek looked down, saw nothing, closed his eyes. He wanted to rest. He wanted to be fresh when he reached Cuba. He conjured the familiar features of Tania Figueras, and then the stories about her that Timmy Sheehan's task-force detectives had uncovered—the pretty Hispanic girl who lived in the Mendozas' apartment, cooked, cleaned, attended Edith Mendoza as a personal maid, and also brokered the couple's trysts.

It was the boxers who identified her. Timmy's people traced the muscular black participant in Clury's photos to Pinelli's Gymnasium, which was three blocks from Jake and Edith's Chelsea studio. Pinelli's was not a Yuppie health club; it was a serious liniment-and-leather gym catering to boxers, pro and amateur.

The black man's name was Carl Washington. He was quick to spill his story. Yes, he told the detectives, he had been hired on a number of occasions to play games with the Mendozas. Specifically, he was instructed to arrive, sweaty and bleeding from a workout, tie up the gentleman and make rough love to the lady, for which labor he was paid excellent money. He also received the expressed gratitude of both Mendozas, who, he assured his interrogators, always enjoyed their mutual encounters.

But there was more. According to Washington, he was not the only one who had performed such services. Several other regulars at Pinelli's had also played: Cash Royalton, a cruiserweight contender; Rudolfo Peña; Gus "the Animal" Metaxas; and a tough, young, promising white welterweight named Tate. The meetings, Washington said, were always set up by the pretty Cuban girl named Tania. Tania would arrive at the gym, call the chosen fighter aside, outline the desired scenario, then hand him the key to the studio and the cash fee. Sometimes, when one of the guys performed particularly well, Tania would return to pay a bonus.

Why did Tania disappear only hours after Edith Mendoza was killed? What did she know? Had she been involved? Since the med examiner concluded that Edith had been severely beaten by human fists, and since Washington, Royalton, Peña, Metaxas and Tate all named Tania as the broker of their deals, it was logical to assume that Tania had also played a role in setting up her employer's final assignation.

That had been the premise behind Janek's search nine years before—a search that had taken him, photo of Tania in hand, into bodegas and santería parlors throughout the city. He had checked airline manifests, immigration lists, Social Security computer printouts; had spoken to priests, taxi drivers, building superintendents, Cuban-American leaders in New Jersey, Miami and Los Angeles. *Did anyone know the girl? Had anyone seen her?* And the longer and more thoroughly he searched, the more worried and suspicious he became. Tania Figueras, as far as he could tell, had disappeared off the face of the earth.

Cuban airport formalities were lenient. A female immigration inspector in a tight, unironed khaki uniform asked Janek the purpose of his visit. Tourism, he said. And what was Senõr Janek's profession. Labor organizer, he replied.

The wait for baggage was interminable. The sky was dark by the time Janek wandered out of the terminal. In the line for transportation into the city, he and a Mexican businessman agreed to share a dollars-only tourist taxi. They didn't talk much on the way. Janek peered out the window at the dimly lit streets. He saw palms, lots of bicyclists, very few cars. In the distance he could see stark high rises, but the buildings along the road struck him as bedraggled. There was a muted smell of rot, night-blooming plants and decaying vegetation—the rich, soothing aroma of the tropics. At intersections he observed small congregations of teenage males. At several points along the route people waited with weary expressions in roadside shelters.

"Thirty years of socialism," his Mexican companion commented, "and they still have nothing here. *Nada.*"

After Janek checked into the Habana Libre, where the ragged towels still bore the old Hilton crest, he went out to walk on La Rampa. There were crowds on the wide avenue, not moving in any direction, just milling about. A light breeze was blowing off the bay. The odor of malfunctioning sewers scented the air. A grandiose movie palace with an unpainted façade was playing the Spanish-language version of *Gone With the Wind.* Janek was able to read the title on the marquee even though half the letters were missing.

Following the flow of people, he found himself drawn into a small park. Here he discovered an impromptu rumba band entertaining people waiting for service at the understaffed counters of an enormous ice cream parlor named Coppelia.

Occasionally people stared at him. His clothes, he realized, gave him away. He was a Yankee, a gringo, citizen of the country that had blockaded Cuba for three decades. But the people who stared did not regard him with anger. They seemed more curious than hostile, he thought.

He was approached several times by men offering to exchange pesos for dollars and twice by sultry young women, wearing tight tanktops and sporting flashy watches, who asked if he needed an escort. After he shook his head, a male youth approached, offering discounted Monte Cristo cigars. Janek shook his head again, then walked back to his hotel. The lobby was swarming with young people, expressions blank, milling or sitting, waiting for something to happen. The dollars-only shops were deserted. He thought: *This is not a happy place.*

He had bought a package tour through a Mexican travel agency. For six hundred dollars he got round-trip air transportation from Mexico City, five nights at the Habana Libre, breakfast and a second meal of his choice for four days, a bus tour of old Havana, an optional visit to the Hemingway Museum, and one admission to the floor show plus a prepaid champagne cocktail at the ''world famous'' Tropicana Nightclub.

He decided to spend his first full day getting a feel for the city, then make his initial approach to Tania early the following morning. There was risk in this plan—if things didn't go well, he would be trapped in Cuba and vulnerable for two additional days. But there was more risk in waiting until the end of his visit because there was a good possibility that Tania would refuse to speak with him, would not be at home or would be unknown at the address given by her brother. In any of these events, he would need time to convince and/or find her.

And so, on the first morning, he set out on foot for the

Malecon, the wide avenue that rimmed the elegant curve of Havana Bay, with the intention of following it along the seawall to the center of the old city. From there he planned to return in such a way that he would inconspicuously pass Tania Figueras's address.

Even at ten A.M. the heat was punishing. But he enjoyed the notion that he was walking freely in a foreign capital visited by few Americans. Again he was struck by the small number of private cars on the street, the shabby condition of the buildings, the clusters of people waiting stolidly for buses that perhaps would never come.

Near the end of his walk, within a mile of La Punta Fortress, he noticed he was the only pedestrian on the Malecon. Cubans, he decided, were too smart to take long walks under the broiling Caribbean sun. Perhaps he would do better to move from the hot, sunstruck bay side of the avenue to the shady sheltering arcade that linked the buildings across the way.

He crossed, entered the arcade. Each of its sections was supported by a unique set of columns matched to the architecture of the building above. Some columns had Greek-style capitals, others were plain. Most were flaking, but one was freshly painted a bright, vivid blue and another a soft Pompeian red. What was most spooky, he thought, was that all the stores that had once fronted on this arcade were now abandoned and gated shut.

He was in the center of the red section when he noticed two men, in leisure suits and perforated shoes, bearing down on him fast. Sensing danger, he turned to find two more men, similarly dressed, coming up quickly on his rear. Clearly these were not street thieves. They moved with precision and were closing in.

There was, he could see, only one route of escape—he must run out of the arcade into the street. He was about to do this when a small black car pulled up, blocking his attempt. Its arrival, he noted with a certain admiration, could not have been more perfectly timed.

A middle-aged man with handsome features, gray hair, a soft gray mustache and a steady gaze leaned out of the right front window. Janek immediately recognized him as a cop.

"Señor Janek?"

"Yeah, I'm Janek. What's going on?"

The man, who wore a white shirt open at the neck, flashed an ID bearing a red diagonal stripe. Janek saw the name Fonseca and the words *"Seguridad de Estado"* stamped across the top. Fonseca's voice was disinterested, a well-practiced monotone. "You are under arrest, señor. Please get in the car."

Janek turned. The four men who had trapped him stood in a close semicircle behind.

He looked back at Fonseca. Fonseca nodded gravely.

"Yeah, right," Janek said.

He sat in the back squeezed between two of the young men from the street. The other two got into a second vehicle which had pulled up and now followed behind. His car, a small Russian model, moved rapidly down the spacious avenue, then abruptly entered a labyrinth of narrow streets. Unfamiliar with the city, Janek soon lost all sense of direction. Meantime, the bodies of the men on either side confined his arms, and his knees were crushed against the seat ahead.

Several times he tried to speak, to ask his captors what they wanted. Each time Fonseca turned around and made a zippering motion across his mouth. When he did this the young men on either side of Janek looked out the windows and grinned.

So, all right, they would take him to their headquarters and there he would get an explanation. But why had they arrested him? He had done nothing and they couldn't possibly know why he had come.

Yet they knew his name and had trapped him flawlessly on a deserted stretch of sidewalk. Which meant, he realized, that they'd been following him from the moment he'd left his hotel.

He knew better than to blame himself. He was a detective, not an espionage agent. It was in the nature of his work that he follow others, not look out for others who might be following him. At that realization he was struck by the thought that this was the first time in his life he had been the subject of a police arrest.

Suddenly the car swerved off the road, entered a dirt track, stopped in the middle of a weed-choked field. The sun outside was blinding. For a moment Janek felt like throwing up.

"Close your eyes." Fonseca issued his order without any emphasis. "We are going to take a security precaution. Do not be unduly upset."

Janek looked into the man's eyes and saw a hardness he often affected himself. It was a no-nonsense way of looking at a person in custody, a signal that the person is without any power and must do as he is told.

The moment Janek closed his eyes, the men beside him grasped his wrists, pulled them together behind his back, snapped on steel cuffs. Then he felt them pull something pliant, smelling of oiled leather, over the top of his head. He struggled as they pulled it down over his face but relented as soon as he realized he could breathe. He felt a strap being buckled around his neck. He opened his eyes and then, for the first time, felt fear. They had blindfolded him, he understood, because now they were going to take him to a place *they did not want him to see.*

He had no idea how long he'd been sitting there, perhaps twenty-four hours, perhaps longer. The room was dank and smelled of disinfectant. There was a plastic bowl of water on the floor and a plastic bucket that served as a toilet. In area the room was not much larger than a closet. Its ceiling, however, was very high. There was no window. A dim red bulb, the kind used in darkrooms, burned from a socket far out of reach. Also on the ceiling was a small ventilation grill. *So at least,* he thought, *I'm not going to suffocate.* Sitting on the floor, arms wrapped about his knees, he tried to take some comfort in that.

There was little else to take comfort in. When the car had stopped, the young men on either side had helped him out, then taken hold of his arms. When he had tried to speak, one of them had slapped him across the mouth. It had not been a hard blow, but it had stung, a message that he was not to speak again without permission.

They pulled him along between them into some sort of building, down a long corridor, down a steep flight of stairs, then marched him along another corridor until they reached a room. After they shut the door, one of them removed his handcuffs.

"Take off your clothes." Fonseca's voice was colorless. Janek could feel the presence of others, perhaps all four of the young men who had cornered him on the street.

"I demand to see the American consul."

For that he received another blow across the mouth, harder than the first. It made him reel.

"Shut up and take off your clothes. This is a standard precaution. Do not be afraid. We will give you something to wear."

The time had come to take a stand. He would not assist in his own degradation. He stood facing them with as much dignity as he could summon, considering that his head and upper face were encased in a hood buckled to his neck.

"You refuse. Very well. We will assist you."

There was nothing sadistic or even exasperated in Fonseca's voice, just the flat intonation of a cop doing his job. He gave his orders in Spanish and then Janek felt strange hands grasping at his body. Someone roughly opened his shirt, popping off the buttons. Someone else pulled off his watch. A third man unclasped his belt, then harshly extracted it. After they stripped off his shirt, they handcuffed him again, pushed him down to the floor, grabbed hold of his legs, then tugged off his shoes, socks and pants. He did not fight them but resisted by going limp. That didn't slow them down. They yanked off his underpants with the dispatch of men who stripped prisoners every day.

Lying on his back on the cold tile floor, his cuffed wrists crushed beneath him, he sensed them standing in a tight circle around him and assumed that they were staring down. Yes, he was certain, they were studying him, a middle-aged captive lying helpless, hooded, naked, at their feet. And their faces, he guessed, reflected a certain repugnance, too, a certain distaste, for, he knew, he could not be a pretty sight. He could smell himself, an aroma of sweat and fear coming off his body, which was probably inducing expressions of mockery and derision on the faces of the men above. He had seen far better men than them wear the victor's smirk. He had even worn it himself occasionally and so knew its purpose—to mask a bully's shame.

Now he sat on the floor of the tall locked closet lit only by the red bulb. His wrists were no longer cuffed, his head was no longer bagged, but he wore a particularly humbling garment, a kind of hospital gown secured by a single clasp behind his neck. It left a good part of his back and buttocks exposed and its skirt barely covered his thighs.

He heard footsteps approaching, then a key turning in the lock. Crouching back against the wall, he felt like an animal cornered in a cage.

"Stand!"

The order came from a muscular black man wearing an unmarked khaki uniform. He had a thick, bushy mustache and poorly shaved, heavily pitted cheeks. The timbre of his voice, cold and abrupt, was different than Fonseca's. He thought: *This one's a guard, not a cop.*

"I demand to see the American consul."

"Stand!"

Janek took his time getting to his feet.

"Turn!"

Janek turned slowly. The man snapped cuffs over his wrists, then yanked him backward out of the closet.

"Move!"

"Where?"

"Move!"

The guard placed his hands on Janek's back and shoved him hard. Janek stumbled.

"Fast!"

The man pushed him again. Understanding he had no choice, Janek obeyed. The man continued to shove him down a long corridor lined with doors. *More closet cells,* Janek thought. At the end of the corridor he faced a steel door enclosing a small thick window of wired glass. His guard reached over his shoulder and banged on the door. The face of a second guard, older, lighter-skinned, appeared in the window. He stared at Janek, nodded and unlocked the door. As soon as it was open, Janek felt the hard hands of his escort on his back.

"In!"

Another shove as Janek staggered through the doorway into a room with a stained terra-cotta tile floor. He thought: *This was probably where they pulled off my clothes.*

His escort grasped his arms while the older guard approached him with the head bag. This was the first time Janek had seen it. Although he knew they were going to put it on him again and despised the thought, he couldn't help himself—he peered closely to see how it was made. Constructed of dark brown leather, it was shaped to fit over his entire head except for the nostrils and mouth. It looked much like an old aviator's helmet, except that the flap, which would normally extend only to the top of the forehead, had been cut lower to cover the prisoner's eyes.

As the older guard approached, he grinned sheepishly as if to say "Sorry, these are the rules." Janek smelled the oil again, then realized with disgust that he had unconsciously bowed his head to make it easier for the guard to put it on.

He thought: *Prisoner for only a day and already I'm trying to help.*

Her eyes! That was his first reaction when his guard pulled the hood off his head and he found himself face-to-face with his interrogator.

The woman possessed a kind of bizarre beauty, he thought. Her eyes, a pair of smoldering emeralds, glowed out of her gaunt, dark face. Her chocolate-colored skin looked smooth as satin and her cheekbones were exceedingly high. Thin, sinewy, she held herself straight in her chair behind a little wooden desk. Her hands were clasped in front of her on top of a closed folder. As she switched on a portable tape recorder, he noticed that her nails were painted camouflage-green.

Janek looked around. His guard, expressionless, stood just behind his stool. Janek turned back to face his interrogator. She wore the same khaki uniform he'd seen on the guards, but with red dashes on the epaulets. She was inspecting him, her eyes moving slowly down his body. His smock was bunched up beneath him, partially exposing his genitals to view. He wanted to squirm, but fought the impulse. The whole situation, the way he was dressed and seated, had been contrived to make him feel devalued and insecure.

"I am Captain Valdez," she said, raising her eyes. "An officer of the Agency for State Security." Her English was formal and barely accented. "You will address me as Captain."

Janek stared back. He did not want to reveal his fascination with what was happening and the strange way this woman was forcing him to view himself. It was odd to be on the other end of an interrogation. He thought: *So this is what it's like.* But he knew that if Captain Valdez was experienced, she would pick up on his interest and use it against him. His best policy, he felt, was to ignore all attempts at intimidation. He resolved to maintain his dignity no matter how scornfully she might behave.

"There are two ways an interrogation such as this can go," Valdez said. "Friendly or hostile. We can work as partners or become antagonists. It depends on you." She stared at him. "Have you been mistreated?"

"I was hit and pushed around. Your people took my clothes and watch."

"That's standard. Anything else?" Her voice was impatient, her tone clipped.

"I asked to see the American consul. They hit me in the mouth for that."

"They did not understand."

"They understood. Now I'm asking you. I want to see my consul. I have that right."

She ran her tongue slowly over her lips. "Perhaps."

So, it's going to be like that. He wasn't surprised. The important thing now was to find out why he was there. He wriggled on the stool, trying to ease himself into a few more inches of smock. She watched his struggle with a smile.

He looked into her eyes. "Why am I here?"

"You know why."

He shook his head. "I have no idea."

"You lied to an immigration officer. Just as in your country—lying to an official here is a crime."

"I did not lie to her."

"You told her you had come to Cuba for tourism."

"That's true."

"You told her your profession was labor organizer. But in your suitcase we found this." She laid the photocopy of his police ID on the table. When she spoke again, her tone was contemptuous. "This is your true profession, isn't it, *Lieutenant*?"

So . . . they'd been to his room, searched his luggage, which meant they'd also found the ink pad and the blank fingerprint form he'd brought to ID Tania.

"Yes," he said, "I'm a police detective. I work for the city of New York."

"So, you are not a labor organizer?"

"No," he admitted, "I'm not."

She stared hard at him and in that moment he understood how good she was. Her timing, expressions, control over the interview were extremely well managed. He was also aware that he had begun to sweat. He knew what that meant: She had gotten to him—he was guilty, he had lied. *This is why the pressure always works,* he thought. *You show them how you know they lied about one thing to force them into conceding they lied about another.* He had used the same technique a thousand times. Now it was being used against him. And, to his great discomfort, he was discovering he could not resist. He wanted to confess to Captain Valdez. He wanted to regain her trust.

"You are now, by your admission, in considerable trouble," she said. "The penalty for lying to an official of the government can be severe."

Her amazing emerald eyes were glittering. He thought: *She's the lepidopterist, I'm the insect. Now she's going to pin me to the board.*

"If you insist, I will telephone your consul. In that case this interrogation will be terminated. You will be tried, perhaps as early as tonight. The immigration inspector and I will serve as witnesses. This photocopy of your police identity card and the tape recording of your confession will be placed in evidence. The judge will find you guilty. The sentence will be"—she shrugged—"three years, perhaps four." She stared at him, licked her lips, then smiled. "Our prisons are well known for their conditions. Perhaps you've read or heard." She paused. "That is one way we can proceed."

She wasn't bluffing; that was her message. She was using all the leverage she had gained to force him to assist in his own destruction.

Janek looked at her. "There is another?" She nodded. "What do I have to do?"

"Simple," she said. "Tell me truthfully why you have come to Cuba. Think about it." She rose, picked up her file and tape recorder, then nodded to the guard. "It would be best to decide before we speak again."

She started toward the door. When she reached it she paused. For a moment Janek thought she was going to say something, but she left without looking back.

Head bagged, roughly shoved into a room, he felt the presence of other men. He heard them shuffling, and then, without a word, one tore off his smock and others began to rough him up.

They were methodical. One would hit him then shove him at another, who in turn would pummel him then shove him on to a third. This went on for approximately five minutes. Because he was blindfolded and was turned around many times, he lost his balance and fell.

When he was on the floor, they stood around him and kicked his body with their boots. But they were careful, he noted, not to strike him in the face or groin. In fact, he realized, after his initial terror, their kicks, like their blows, were light and not injurious. It was a symbolic beating. They were not trying to hurt him; they were working to increase his sense of helplessness and fear.

How arrogant of me to think I could just come into this country and do as I liked. I came for you, Kit. Where are you now?

Locked back in his closet, he thought over his situation. A number of things were clear. First, he had no rights. He had lied to them, and because of that they felt entitled to treat him brutally.

Second, they had had only two opportunities to find his police ID: at the airport during his long wait for his luggage, and during the short period when he was out walking on La Rampa. The airport was the more likely possibility—they had searched through his things *before* he went through immigration. Which meant that the moment he had lied to the inspector he had become a suspect. *But of what?* he wondered. *Why are they so concerned? Why do they think I'm here?*

Finally, he was disgusted by his reactions to what was happening to him—his detachment, curiosity, admiration of their technique. *It's like I'm on a damn busman's holiday.* But then, considering the gravity of his situation (*My God! I'm in a stinking Cuban jail!*), he decided that his professional interest might be the one thing that was keeping him from panic.

"Hey! Gringo!" *Tap-tap-tap.* "Gringo? You there?" *Tap-tap-tap.*

The whisper and the tapping cut to him through the wall. The voice had a rasp. The speaker was in the adjoining closet, head down near the floor.

"I'm here."

"Shhh! Not loud, gringo! Be careful. If they hear us they will beat us. I have been beaten enough today."

Janek pressed his ear against the wall. "What's your name?"

"Ernesto. Yours?"

"Frank."

"You are all right, Franco?"

"Yes. You?"

"Not so good." Pause. "Who is your interrogator?"

"Valdez."

"The woman? Dark skin? Green eyes?" Ernesto sounded excited.

"Yes."

"Ah, my friend, you have bad luck. Her name is Violetta. She has no lover—this is what they say. Be careful. She is dangerous. She will never touch you herself but will order others to hurt you. They say she likes to give such orders. Everyone fears her here."

"What did you do?"

"They will not tell me. They wait for me to tell them. This is their method. They break you and then you tell them everything."

"I don't—"

"Shhhh!"

Janek heard steps approaching down the corridor. They stopped in front of Ernesto's closet. The guard yelled something in Spanish, kicked the door, then strutted back. After a while, Janek heard a cautious *tap-tap-tap.* He pressed his ear against the wall again. This time Ernesto's whisper was faint.

"Safer not to talk. Good luck, gringo. God keep you!"

Janek settled back against the wall. Of course it was a scam—well executed, too. Plant a fellow convict in the next closet, then have him *tap-tap-tap* you a message after you've been left to simmer after a beating for—how long had it been? Another twelve or fourteen hours? With the right prisoner it could be effective. The question now was what was the message—what had Ernesto really meant to convey? It had to do with Violetta, he was sure—that she was not to be trifled with, and that, since he was certain to be broken sooner or later, he would do well to come clean with her at once.

Many hours later the muscular black guard opened his closet, threw a hunk of bread at him, then slammed the door shut.

Janek sniffed the bread. It smelled all right so he ate half of it. He wondered what time it was. He guessed it was night. He figured he'd been confined for at least two days. He curled up as best he could on the tiny floor.

I came here for you, Kit, he whispered to himself. Then he closed his eyes and tried to sleep.

• • •

"Stand!"

The black guard stood in the doorway. Janek raised his head and blinked. The harsh light that broke around him hurt his eyes.

The guard kicked him. *"Fast!"*

Even before Janek had fully risen to his feet, the guard grabbed the back of his smock and yanked him out.

"Move!"

The ignominious shoving and bagging routine began again.

Violetta didn't bother to look up when the hood was removed from his head. She was reading her dossier and continued to read even as he sat facing her, waiting for the interrogation to begin.

Since she refused to acknowledge him, there was nothing to do but try to read her document upside down. It was in Spanish, so he gave up. But then she turned a page and he felt heat rising to his cheeks. There was a color Polaroid stapled to the page—a photo of himself, head bagged, lying naked on the stained tile floor. They must have taken it just after they beat him.

He glanced at the image, then, burning with anger, turned away. He looked terrible, like some kind of thing lying there, naked and exposed, red splotches over his body. To be photographed like that, in such a state of vulnerability, and then to have the picture examined by this woman while he sat before her in this ridiculous revealing smock . . . it was too much. He thought of what Ernesto had said: *They break you and then you tell them everything.*

He told her everything. There was no need to withhold a single detail. His only need was to convince her that he had not come to Cuba for any political purpose and was no threat to its regime.

As the Mendoza story poured out of him, he gazed steadily into her cold green eyes. They revealed nothing, which only spurred him to be more truthful, more precise, more sincere.

Occasionally she interrupted to ask a question, but most of the time she simply listened. When her tape ran out she held up her hand, flipped the cassette, then motioned him to continue. He guessed that he had spoken for nearly an hour before she signaled that she had heard enough. Again, just before she left the room, she paused as if she had something to add. He watched her back as she stood still in the doorway. Then, as before, she left without a word.

Perhaps he spent another full day in his closet. There was no way to know. He ate the bread they threw at him and drank the water, and sat on the floor trying to imagine how, if he were a Cuban investigator, he would go about checking out his story. The only way that he could think of was to go straight to Tania Figueras.

Later, he thought about Sarah, the way she'd looked through the window of the Praha—so calm, svelte—and then the glow of greed in her eyes when she'd told him she needed more money. He thought of the way she'd snickered when she boasted that "a little bird" had told her he was being sent to Cuba, and the sadness in her eyes when she'd warned him about Mendoza: "It will only bring you pain. . . ."

He was dozing when he felt a prod. He opened his eyes to find Fonseca bending over him.

"Your story is true, Lieutenant Janek." Fonseca spoke without expression, without severity. "We confused you with someone else, someone who might have come here with a less innocent purpose. You must understand, the moment you lied to our immigration officer we had no choice—we had to find out why you had come."

Janek nodded.

"Your clothes will be brought to you and then you will

be taken to your hotel. Even now they are sewing back your buttons. Tomorrow you will meet with a detective from the Urban Police. I have spoken to him and he is ready to assist you.'' Fonseca offered his hand. Janek took it. ''Enjoy your stay in Cuba, *Teniente*.'' For the first time Fonseca smiled. ''I doubt we will meet again.''

Janek felt cleansed as he rode back to the Habana Libre in an unmarked Seguridad car driven by a silent driver. The deserted night streets were dimly lit and the bay of Havana, smooth as glass, reflected the light of a three-quarter moon.

Yes, he felt cleansed, although he was not physically clean at all; his body was sore, he had not shaved or washed and the stink of imprisonment was still upon him. Rather, it was the sensation of having come clean that suffused him. For years he had employed the purgative effect of confession in his work, holding it out, in interrogations, like a cool glass of water, telling suspects how good they would feel and how clean, once they owned up to what they had done. Now he was experiencing that sensation. How else could he explain his feelings of calm and innocence? He *had* lied, *had* come into their country under false pretenses. But now his lies were purged. He had been punished. Now he could go on about his work unsullied.

The King Is Dead

There were days when, no matter in which direction she turned, she would find herself facing her own reflection. . . .

The rows of mirrors along the wall doubled the space in the room in which thirty women, bodies honed, exercised in unison. The instructor, a rail-thin redhead dressed in no-nonsense workout clothes, led the drill.

"High-er! High-er! High-er!" she ordered, ponytail bouncing. *"Im-pact! Im-pact! Im-pact!"*

Gelsey, in the back row, center, pranced to the commands. Panting, sweating into her leotard, exhilarated by her own incipient exhaustion, she couldn't take her eyes off the images dancing across the mirrors ahead. Faces, torsos, arms, legs—limbs scissored and eyes flashed. Tails of hair swung like whips. Thirty pairs of twins performed synchronous jumping jacks. *"Up-down! Up-down! High-er! High-er! High-er!"*

Gelsey was not the only one to regard the reflections. The entire class watched itself, for the silvered glass seduced. The wall of mirrors became a huge screen inspiring effort and discipline. It was like being in a theater, performing and watching at the same time—thirty female narcissi, each regarding and loving her own reflection, each asking: "Mirror, mirror on the wall/Who is the fairest one of all?"

On the edge of fatigue, Gelsey wanted only to merge with her mirror image, meet her dream-sister on the glass. But, understanding mirrors, she knew that although one can stand outside looking in, or inside looking out, to linger on the surface plane is impossible.

"High-er! High-er! High-er!" the instructor cried.

After aerobics she met up with Tracy. They grabbed towels, mopped off, strolled together past men and women working out with weights. There were mirrors in the locker room, too, big ones over the sinks.

"Some class!" said Tracy when they reached their lockers. "That Ms. Ponytail's a real bitch!"

Gelsey pulled off her damp leotard. "Don't be a wimp. She gives us our money's worth."

"Wimp! Give me a break, Gelsey." Tracy stared at her, pretending to be angry. Then suddenly she beamed. She was a small true blonde with a pretty face, features good but not quite good enough to allow her to earn her living as a model.

She was also the only one of Diana's girls whom Gelsey saw—not that they had all that much in common besides a devotion to high-impact aerobics. Still, their time together under Diana had forged a bond. Gelsey knew that Tracy respected her—for her expertise at the game and for daring to leave Diana and strike out on her own. She had her suspicions as to why Tracy kept up the friendship. It had occurred to her that Diana had put Tracy up to it, to spy, to make sure that she didn't horn in on the easy marks and that she kept her distance from the hotels. Still, Gelsey preferred to think Tracy was genuinely fond of her.

"So, what's going on with you lately?" Tracy asked. Towels wrapped about their bodies, they walked toward the shower room, passing a lightly steamed mirror. "Good scores? Bad scenes?" Tracy giggled. "Actually, we had a lulu the other night."

They stood beneath adjoining showerheads, a tiled shoulder-high partition between them. Gelsey closed her eyes, reveling in the sharp sting of the water against her back.

"What happened?"

"Remember the new black girl I told you about?"

"Sooky?"

Tracy nodded. "She was over at the St. Moritz hitting up on a Jap. He had all the signs—diamond ring, Rolex, solid-gold lighter, the whole bit. So, comes time to go upstairs, Sooky's slobbering. Guy looks like Mr. Bucks. In the elevator she's already tasting the score, maybe thinking how she can screw Diana out of most of it." Tracy laughed.

"I know what's coming." Gelsey stepped out of the stream of hot water, started to soap up.

"Do you, now?"

"He was a plant. He worked for the hotel."

Tracy gazed at her through the spray. "How comc you're so smart?"

"You said it was a lulu. Anyway, the guy sounded too good to be true."

"Sometimes you'll meet a Mr. Bucks like that."

Gelsey gazed back. "Sure. Like Kirstin did, remember? Remember what that cost her?"

Tracy turned away. "I'll never forget."

"Diana *wants* you never to forget. That was the point of the exercise. After that night I knew I had to quit. It was either fight or flight, so I flew." Gelsey stepped back under the showerhead and stood still, allowing the spray to rinse away the soap. "What happened with Sooky? The house dick bust her?" She looked down at the foam swirling around her feet.

Tracy nodded. "He found her KO kit, took her in, but first Sooky called Diana from the hotel. Diana called Thatcher. Thatcher met Sooky at Central Booking. He got her out that night, which was too bad for Sooky because Diana was totally pissed. Thatcher gets a grand and a half for a night call like that, so soon as Sooky shows up at the apartment, Diana starts slapping her around. 'Stupid slut!

Cunt!' You know how crazy she gets. Then she fined her Thatcher's fee. Which means Sooky'll be working free the next two weeks.''

After they dried off, dressed and groomed themselves, they went downstairs to the snack bar for lunch. The place, low-ceilinged with a sleek, sterile look, was crowded, filled with healthy-looking young people, most dressed in work-out clothes or sweats.

There were mirrors down there, too, behind the service counter and along the wall opposite the windows. Mirrors to pose before. Mirrors to admire oneself in. Mirrors to check out a stranger's butt. Mirrors everywhere—mirrors and reflections. Sometimes Gelsey thought she would scream if she saw one more cheap, stupid mirror.

''How long're you going to stay with her, Tracy?''

Tracy picked a piece of watercress out of her salad. ''I wish I could quit,'' she said without looking up.

''Do it! Walk out. *Adiós.*''

''Sure. Then what?'' Tracy gestured toward a girl in an apron taking an order at another table. ''Waitress? Bank teller? Squirt toilet water at old ladies in Lord & Taylor? There're all sorts of shitty jobs.'' Tracy shook her head. ''Sorry, Gelsey, I don't have anywhere else to go.''

''Ever think about going back to school?''

''You mean college?'' Tracy bugged her eyes. ''First I'd have to get my equivalency. Meantime, who'd pay the rent?''

Gelsey stared at her avocado. She had no answer for Tracy. ''Listen to what you're saying. You're saying you're trapped.''

''Damn right!'' Tracy's eyes turned fierce. ''You just don't get it, do you?''

''Oh, I get it.''

''Uh-uh, no, you don't. Because you've got another career. You go after marks just for fun. And you own your own place, too.'' Tracy arched her eyebrows. ''Wherever it happens to be.'' She stared into Gelsey's eyes. ''I'll know when you've accepted me, Gelsey—when you ask me over for a drink.''

Gelsey acknowledged Tracy's hurt. ''I'm sorry about that. I told you, I've got problems.''

''Who doesn't? But you gotta admit it's a barrier. We're supposed to be friends. But I don't rate enough to know your phone number or even your address.''

''It's not a question of how you rate.''

''What is it, then? Personal privacy? Screw that! 'Cause I got none. Diana's on my back about everything, controlling everything. Like we all belong to her. Like we're all her . . . you know, slaves.''

''Well—?''

Tracy finished off her fruit juice. ''Think I don't know it? You were one, too, before you ran away. So, how's it feel to be free, girl? Lucky you!''

''Try it sometime. You'll like it,'' Gelsey said gently.

They parted on the street. Traffic was heavy on upper Broadway. Gelsey saw bits of herself reflected in chrome parts on rapidly passing cars.

''Same time next Friday?'' Tracy asked.

Gelsey nodded. ''It's fun to work out with you.''

''Except for the gripe session afterwards, right?'' Tracy beamed, then glanced at her watch. ''Shit! I'm late. Diana'll kill me.''

The two young women embraced.

''Take care,'' Gelsey said, and then, after Tracy flagged a cab: ''Score big! Good luck!''

Mirrors: There were so many on Broadway, Gelsey couldn't have avoided them if she'd tried. They surrounded shop windows, or, narrow and vertical, were set in the panels between stores. Stainless surfaces, hubcaps, buildings with skins made of metal or glass—sometimes the whole man-made world seemed to consist of reflections and reflecting surfaces. Nature, too, provided mirrors—puddles, lakes, pools of still water. Gelsey knew there was hardly a place on earth where one could not turn and find a double of oneself.

Mirrors: at times they seemed to swallow her being, suck her deep into their world of reverse. She knew she should regard them as her friends, for they offered her a place to hide. She recognized that they could be her enemies, too. The things she saw in them were frightening, terrifying sometimes.

Dr. Zimmerman's office was in a Victorian brownstone on a shady, quiet street between Columbus and Central Park West. Gelsey walked there from the health club, ever watchful, wary of running into someone she might have hit on in a bar.

That was the risk she ran whenever she ventured into Manhattan—not robbery or rape, but recognition by a mark. Her wigs provided some disguise, but there were men, she knew, who would never forget her eyes. A confrontation with one could be disastrous. Whenever she walked the streets she was on her guard.

There were two buttons marked "Zimmerman" on the panel. The upper one rang in the doctor's residence; the lower one alerted him in his ground-floor consulting room. She pressed the lower one then waited, nervous, hand poised on the doorknob, because Dr. Zimmerman had a singular response to entreaties to enter his domain. He would first ring back fast, so quickly a visitor would barely have time to push open the door. Then, after several seconds (maddeningly, the interval varied), he would send forth a second, longer peal, which would echo in the visitor's ears long after entry.

Gelsey always tried to make it in on the first buzz, but she rarely succeeded. This bell game, as she thought of it, was a strange little quirk on the doctor's part that either irritated her or warmed her heart, depending on her mood.

• • •

"Hello, Gelsey!" Dr. Zimmerman spoke her name even before he craned his head into the little waiting room. Today he was feeling affable; sometimes his greeting was more restrained.

Gelsey rose and followed him into his office. She detested the waiting room, with its bland wallpaper and disheveled magazines, some of which she'd seen grow ragged over the year she'd been in treatment. But she hated the room most for the tawdry dime-store mirror on its wall, provided, she supposed, for patients who needed to compose themselves after particularly intense sessions of psychotherapy.

Dr. Zimmerman's office, however, was something else, an extraordinary world. Gelsey loved it on account of his collection of artifacts of primitive cultures mounted on the walls. African ritual objects made of wood and copper; Oceanian fetish items; Native American headdresses; an array of African and South Sea island masks. "Totem and taboo, mirrors of the unconscious self—that's what they're all about," Dr. Z would say, sweeping his arm expansively, his gray goatee wiggling.

Mirrors: There it was again, that damn word, the concept of reflection and reverse that consumed her, ruled her life. She had come to Dr. Zimmerman to seek escape from her obsession only to find that the words *mirrors* and *mirroring* were essential to his discourse.

"How're things going?" Dr. Z's standard opening; he usually glanced away from her when he said it. He was a medium-sized man, stout, bald on top, with well-groomed gray hair on either side. He had a confidence and composure that made her doubt she could take him in a bar. Just the thought of such a battle made her shake.

"Well, I keep looking into mirrors," she said.

"Nothing new about that." Dr. Zimmerman smiled. "It's what you *see* in them that should concern us."

"I see my dream-sister."

"Sure. Your twin. Your opposite. Forever separate yet forever bound. That's your fantasy, Gelsey. The mirror fantasy equals the double delusion. It's a beautiful equation. So symmetrical. And so . . . convenient for you, too."

Dr. Z smiled again—a little smugly, Gelsey thought. Oh, he was sly, the good doctor, with his perceptions and equations, devised to penetrate her defenses, disrupt her neurotic ways of coping with the world and set her on the high straight road to mental health. *Of course* her dream-sister was a "double delusion." *Of course* it had been engendered by having spent her childhood above a mirror maze. She craved more, much more—a deeper, more liberating analysis.

She looked at Dr. Z. She wondered sometimes if his glib responses were devised to force her to peer more deeply into herself, or if they were nothing more than the mutterings of a lazy, aging analyst.

"This twin of yours who writes in mirror-reverse—she's not just your mirror-sister, Gelsey—she's your inner sister, your shadow."

That was sort of new. He had talked a lot about her "shadow," but had not offered that equation before. Perhaps Dr. Z, sensing her frustration, was going to give her her money's worth today.

"Shakespeare wrote: 'This thing of darkness I acknowledge mine.' Do you see how it might apply?"

"You're saying if I own up to my dream-sister, accept her as my shadow, then—I—what?"

"You can eat her. Eat your shadow. Swallow her up. Ultimately that's the goal of therapy." Dr. Zimmerman paused. "Tell me something—when you come back from one of your expeditions and look at yourself in the mirror, what do you feel? Please note before you answer that I didn't ask you what you see."

She thought about it. "I think I feel a little surprised."

"Why?"

"I think it's because I look the same. As if the experience hasn't changed me a bit. As if the mirror—'' She stopped. There was an important idea floating in her head, but she couldn't quite catch hold of it.

''Does the mirror reject you?''

Gelsey stared at an Indonesian mask. She shook her head.

''Defy you?''

''No.''

''Try to describe it?''

She shook her head again.

''Perhaps it just stares at you. A blank, unforgiving face.''

''Yes, it stares. But I don't want forgiveness, Doc. No, it's something else.''

''Tell me?''

''I can't.''

''Try, Gelsey. You must work hard on this. Shadow work is always difficult.''

''It—''

''Yes?''

''It almost seems to—mock me.''

''Mock you?''

She nodded. ''Like, 'See, you did all that, seduced that guy, dumped on him, and now you're just the same as always. You wanted it to change you and it didn't.' '' She turned to him. ''Does that make any sense?''

''I think it does.'' Dr. Z spoke slowly. ''It's a reference to your mask. Like those.''

He pointed at a grouping of African masks made of ebony and embellished with savanna grass. One in particular had always fascinated Gelsey. Although a single mask, it offered two nearly identical carved faces. The cheeks of each were puffed, the eyes were slits, the mouths were open as if for whistling.

''You want to be like Dorian Gray—looking at his portrait, seeing the evil in himself. But your mirror refuses to show your bad side to you. Which means, of course, that you refuse to see it.''

Well, she had to admit, she rather liked that view of things. It explained the mockery she felt when she gazed into her own eyes after taking down a mark. The problem was that Dr. Zimmerman had no idea of what she actually did. She had told him she went to bars, picked up strange men, went home with them, had sex with them, then slipped out without a word while they slept. She had never told him what she really did to them, that she *never* had sex with them although she always made them think she would—how, instead, she fed them KO drops, then stripped them, searched them, robbed them, uncovered their secrets, left behind a display of power, even wrote them messages in mirror-reverse on their chests.

''You haven't talked about the maze in a while,'' Dr. Z said, changing tone, indicating he wanted to start along a different tack. ''You told me your father built it. But I've never been quite sure why or for whom.''

''He built it for himself.'' She paused. ''For us.''

''Your family?''

''Maybe for just the two of us,'' she said.

''Do you think of it as his legacy?''

''It was all he left me.''

''I didn't mean that way.''

''Well, sure, it kind of sums him up. I mean, it's got all his traits.''

''Please explain.''

''It's slick and complicated. You can get lost in it. It draws you in. He was a charmer that way.'' Dr. Zimmerman nodded. ''It's cruel, too,'' she added.

''How is it cruel?''

''The way it confuses you, drives you nuts. A maze is a fiendish thing.''

''I'm sure it is. Sounds like he used it to express his aggression.''

''I think so,'' Gelsey agreed. ''It also makes you look

funny. Actually, it makes you look like shit. The Corridor of Distortion—that really takes you apart. Someone with a body-image problem wouldn't be able to take it. And the Fragmentation Serpent—that breaks you into little pieces.''

Dr. Zimmerman was silent. She glanced at him. He was staring intently at a Melanesian mask, one with huge eyes and a grotesque looped nose. She had touched it once when he had gone out of the room. A film of oily soot had stained her hand.

''Why have you stopped, Gelsey?'' he asked softly.

''You want more?''

''Have you more to give?''

She shook her head. She knew what he was waiting for, and she knew that if she started talking about it she would end up sobbing like a little girl. *Dammit! Why doesn't he have a mirror in here?* If she could only look at herself, she could—what? Escape?

''Escape,'' she said.

''Escape—yes. Go on. . . .''

''My mother would lock me down there when I was bad. As a punishment. 'You can just be with yourself awhile,' she'd say. You know what happens?''

''Tell me?''

''Locked up with weird images of yourself—after a while you forget what you look like.''

''Yes, I can imagine.'' Dr. Z changed position in his chair. ''And then, perhaps, you would need to keep looking into mirrors to reassure yourself that you still were you.'' He shook his head. ''But I think there was more to your parents' cruelty. Locking you up down there wasn't the worst they could inflict. Your father, for instance—''

She felt sweat on her forehead. Suddenly she wanted to run away—jump out of her chair, bolt out of Dr. Z's consulting room, rush out of the building into the open air.

''I know what you want. You want me to talk about playtime.'' Dr. Z was silent. ''I don't feel like it today.''

''That's all right,'' he said kindly.

"I wonder—"

"Yes?"

"—if I want to come back anymore." The words leaped out of her mouth as if of their own accord. When she heard them she was shocked. She turned to Dr. Zimmerman to see if he was surprised.

"Quit therapy?" he asked. He didn't look upset.

"Yeah—I guess that's what I meant."

"That's one way to handle it, isn't it?"

"You think I want to run away from the truth?" He shook his head. "What *do* you think?"

"I'm not sure I want to say."

"Hey! Come on, Doc! I'm paying you fancy money. Don't hold out on me. You got something—hand it over." She liked the way she sounded—a tough young woman who didn't take any shit.

"Leaving therapy means leaving me."

"Of course."

"That means killing me."

"I don't see that."

"If you don't come here to see me anymore, Gelsey—then I'll be as good as dead for you, won't I?"

"I suppose . . . in a way."

"Kill me and you kill your father."

She looked him square in the eyes. "What are you talking about?"

He smiled at her, his sly, therapeutic smile. Then, very quickly, he stuck out the forefinger of his right hand and drew it swiftly across his throat.

"Kill therapist! Kill father!" He leered at her suddenly, in a way she'd never seen before. "Aha!" He nodded vigorously. "The equation's simple. *The king is dead!*"

Out on the street, she felt that, indeed, Dr. Z had given her something special. She felt unburdened, although she wasn't certain of exactly what. Perhaps, she thought, she was free for a time of the weight of carrying around her dream-sister on her back.

Looking about her, she took in the tranquillity of the street. Two children were playing jump rope. A repairman, tool box in hand, was stepping out of his panel truck, double-parked a few houses up. A mother was wheeling a baby carriage toward the corner of Columbus Avenue. The sun glinted off the well-washed windows of the row houses. From one of the apartments she could hear someone playing a piano, awkwardly practicing scales.

West Seventy-first was quiet, residential, a street of urban professionals like Dr. Z, who had bought up the old town houses, renovated them and by so doing created an island of serenity.

How I wish I could live on a street like this, Gelsey thought, *where everything is so subdued and sweet. Instead of in a loft on top of a mirror maze beside a deserted old amusement park that doesn't amuse anyone anymore, least of all myself.*

Tania

Janek, awakened by loud knocking, opened his eyes. For a moment he was surprised to find himself in his hotel room. His body still ached from the beating, but the bed was soft and he didn't feel much like leaving it.

"Yeah? Who's there?" he called.

"Police." The response was delivered in a surprisingly gentle voice.

Janek shook his head. *Maybe they think they made a mistake. They've come to take me back.*

He wrapped a sheet around his body, went to the door and opened it. The corridor was dark. A short, slender mid-thirties Cuban, dressed in a neat white shirt and a well-pressed pair of slacks, peered at him through wire-rimmed spectacles.

"Lieutenant Janek?"

Janek nodded. The young man smartly saluted.

Well . . . this is a change. Janek examined the visitor's ID. His name was Luis Ortiz. He was a lieutenant in the Homicide Bureau of the Havana Urban Police.

"I have been assigned to assist you."

"With what?"

"Your investigation of the Mendoza case. You are an esteemed visitor, sir. All the facilities of my bureau are at your disposal."

Janek gazed at the man, then gestured him into the room. Ortiz entered, looked around, warmly shook Janek's hand.

"Aren't you laying it on a little thick?" Janek asked.

"Excuse me?" The young officer stared at him, confused.

"You're the first person around here to call me 'esteemed.' "

Ortiz shook his head. "A mistake was made, sir. I am here to set it right. I have located Señora Figueras and have discussed the matter with her. She is waiting for us now." Ortiz peered around the room, then continued, more relaxed. His English, Janek noted, was excellent, although his accent was unmistakably Cuban. "At first she did not wish to speak with you. But when I explained that you had come a long way and that your presence here had become a matter of"—he smiled shyly—"state security—well, she will be very pleased to answer your questions. Whether she will be truthful, I cannot guarantee."

Ortiz paused, squinted at Janek, smiled again, cupped his hand to his ear and pointed at the ceiling. Then he gestured toward the windows. The message was clear: They could not speak freely in the room; it would be better to talk outside.

"All right. Give me fifteen minutes," Janek said. "I'll meet you in the lobby."

After Ortiz left, he went into his bathroom, dropped the sheet and inspected his body in the mirror. There were some bluish marks on his flanks and thighs from the kicks, but the tenderness was dissipating fast. He looked at his face, saw the eyes of a man who had been humiliated and abused. Recalling his feelings of the night before—of gratitude and purgation—he was angry at his captors but even more furious with himself. *Am I so weak it only took them a couple of days to bend my mind?*

"*The segurosos* are shits," Ortiz said as soon as they were out on the street. Now, suddenly informal, the Cuban policeman turned to him, large, brown, bespectacled eyes flashing outrage. "They had no business arresting you.

Some heads will roll, I believe. But perhaps not. They protect one another, cover each other's—how do you say it—ass?''

''Yeah, that's how we say it,'' Janek said. He thought: *This guy's pretty funny.*

''Is it not precisely the same in New York?'' Ortiz asked.

Yes, that, too, was true, Janek agreed.

Ortiz guided him to a small black Russian car parked around the corner. It was identical to the car in which Fonseca had picked him up under the arcades three mornings before. Ortiz unlocked the passenger door, held it open for him, closed it, then came around to the driver's side and got in.

''Are you all right, sir?''

Janek stared at him. Ortiz's concern seemed genuine. His manner conveyed a younger cop's respect. He thought: *Isn't it amazing how quickly my situation's changed?*

''I'm okay,'' Janek said. ''They didn't hurt me. They just wanted to get into my head.''

''But you saw through them.'' Ortiz smiled, then lightly bit his lower lip. ''Torture does not exist in Cuba. It is the law. It is forbidden.'' His irony, which verged on bitterness, was unmistakable, but Ortiz did not continue to project it. Rather, he shook his head to dismiss the subject, started the car and pulled into the street.

''We have many problems here, Lieutenant. The *segurosos* are only one of them. Colonel Fonseca told me they thought you were someone else. They often make such mistakes.''

Janek studied Ortiz as he drove. He liked the efficient way he handled the little car, wheeling elegantly around a traffic circle, then merging smartly behind a convoy of military trucks. *But can I trust him?* he asked himself. *Couldn't all this affability be part of some complicated scam?*

They passed a food store with a long line in front. Ortiz gestured toward it. ''They have bread today. Not much else.''

"So, we're going to be partners," Janek said.

"It will be an honor to be your partner, sir."

"Partners should get to know one another."

"I agree."

"Call me Frank, Luis—I'd appreciate that. You have a family?"

"A wife and two daughters." Ortiz grinned.

Janek turned back to the street. A billboard loomed ahead. The words were in Spanish, but he had no difficulty understanding them: SOCIALISMO O MUERTE—"Socialism or Death."

"Are you a Communist, Luis?"

"I am not a counterrevolutionary." He glanced at Janek. "And you, are you a capitalist, Frank?"

Janek smiled. "Where I come from cops don't accumulate much capital."

"Nor here . . . if they are honest."

"And you're honest, is that what you're telling me, Luis?"

The answer, when it came, was a good deal more serious than Janek expected. "In these difficult times that is the only thing I can hold on to," the young man said gravely.

They drove a while in silence. A bus ahead of them spewed thick black smoke. A truck barreled past them, radio blaring. Havana seemed more lively than three mornings before, perhaps because it was early and people were on their way to work.

"Let's get some coffee."

Luis shook his head. "Coffee is rationed. There are no more cafés."

"There must be a place—"

Yes, Luis told him, there were several hard-currency restaurants that catered exclusively to foreign visitors.

"I've got hard currency," Janek said.

"But Señora Figueras—"

"She can wait."

For a moment Luis hesitated, then he nodded. "Yes, of course," he said.

He turned the car around and drove west toward the suburbs. In an area called Miramar, Janek noticed mansions with spacious gardens and sentry posts. Luis told him these were foreign embassies or the homes of high officials. He turned down a side street, passed through a wooded area, pulled into a parking lot and stopped before a vast open structure with a thatched roof.

As they walked toward it, Janek could see that it enclosed numerous tables set with plates and utensils. But except for a lone waitress, the huge place was empty.

"The tourists will come later, perhaps a group tour in the evening," Luis explained. He selected a table, ordered coffee. After the waitress drifted off, Janek leaned forward.

"What do you know about the Mendoza case?"

"Only what Señora Figueras told me."

Luis outlined Mendoza as if it were nothing more than a case of a man who had arranged the brutal murder of his wife.

"She told me she knew you had been looking for her after the homicide. She was surprised to learn you still wanted to speak with her. She said these events took place many years ago and that Mr. Mendoza has been in prison for a long time."

"That's true."

"Then, why are you still investigating, Frank?"

"There are still many unanswered questions."

"You will tell me about them?"

"Maybe. First there's something else."

The waitress returned with two cups of Cuban coffee. Janek waited until she slipped away.

"There was a woman who interrogated me. Do you know the one I mean?" Luis nodded. "Who is she?"

Luis exhaled. When he spoke it was in the manner of an efficient, well-informed cop.

"Her name is Violetta Bonilla. She is well known in Havana. Actually, she is a member of our National Theater troupe.''

Janek stared at him. ''An actress?''

Luis nodded. ''The Seguridad uses her because of her English. She was brought up in Miami, where her father lived in the exile community, one of our best penetration agents until they pulled him back. Violetta went to school in the States and claims to understand Americans. There is a rumor that her lover is a Minister of State. I cannot confirm that for you.''

''She said she was a captain.''

Luis shrugged. ''The ranks of nonservice personnel are simulated, a method of flattery the *segurosos* learned from the KGB. But be assured that when Violetta examined you she was but a marionette dancing to Fonseca's tune. He is a colonel. What we call 'a serious man.' '' He paused. ''Perhaps you would like to see Violetta in another context?''

''What context?''

''She is performing now in a play. I can get us tickets. Tonight we can go together, make ourselves known.'' Luis smiled. ''Your presence in the audience might unnerve her a little bit.''

Janek smiled. It was a tempting idea. He actually liked Luis for proposing it. But there was a side of him that wanted never to see Violetta Bonilla again.

''No, thanks,'' he said. ''I only want to know why they arrested me.''

''You drew their attention.''

''How?''

Luis shrugged again. ''The *segurosos* do what they like and explain nothing. That is one reason they are dangerous.''

Janek stared at him. ''I don't get it. I've thought back over everything. I can't figure out where I gave myself away. I know they can't search everybody's bags. So, why'd they choose mine?''

"This bothers you?"

"Of course."

"Because you are a professional."

"Because I must have made a mistake."

Luis stroked his chin. "I am not certain, but I believe they thought you were a bounty hunter."

"What?"

Luis nodded. "Fonseca mentioned it. There is a rich American living here. I am sure you have heard of him—an extremely crooked financier wanted by your government. Several attempts have already been made to capture this man and abduct him back to the States. I believe they thought you were another abductor, perhaps the advance man for a group."

"That's ridiculous!"

"Of course. But, you see, they have nothing else to do but think up plots and then find suspects to fit their fantasies. Which is why, in the end, it is impossible to penetrate their thinking. Better to forget about them, Frank. You are finished with them now. You are with me. We understand each other because we are real cops who deal with the reality of the streets." Luis smiled. "It is my pleasure to work with you, if only for a day. I know you will teach me many things and perhaps you will learn a thing or two from me as well."

Tania Figueras's apartment was one of twelve carved out of a huge old house that had once belonged to a wealthy family. Although the building had been crudely subdivided, there were still traces of grandeur—high ceilings, delicate moldings, fine if scarred tile work in the entrance hall. As they entered, Janek noticed a faint smell of sewage, a sign that the plumbing was overworked.

He and Luis climbed the rear stairs. Tania's apartment had been created railroad-style out of three small servant's rooms on the top floor.

When she opened the door, she and Janek gazed at each

other. *Yes, it's her,* Janek thought. The smooth features he knew so well from the photos he had carried around with him nine years before had grown more prominent, and the seamless skin was beginning to crinkle a little around the eyes. Her body was thicker, but her black hair was still glossy and her lips still slightly petulant. She was a good-looking woman, and evidently an amused one, for she smiled as she searched Janek's eyes.

"What took you so long? I've been waiting nine years."

She laughed, turned, led them through her kitchen, a bedroom where clothing hung exposed, then into a pleasant sitting room with a view upon what had once been a lush tropical garden, but was now a desiccated patch of weeds dominated by the stump of a giant palm and an overgrown, browned-out banana tree.

"You've met my little brother?" she asked casually, seating herself beside the window.

Janek nodded.

"How is Angel?"

"He's in trouble," Janek said.

Tania shrugged. "If he had come here with me he might be a doctor today." She turned to Luis.

"Sometimes we think we have too many doctors," Luis explained.

Tania snickered. "Most of them do the work of nurses, but since they have diplomas we must call them *'médico.'* Isn't that right, Ortiz?"

Luis, embarrassed, did not respond.

Janek glanced around the room. It was nicely furnished. There was an old stereo, a small battered TV and shelves crammed with books and long-playing records. It did not look like the room of a woman who worked as a maid.

"What do you do, Miss Figueras?"

"I work for the revolution."

"Can you be a little more specific?"

"I am a bureaucrat at the Ministry of Finance. But not today." She smiled. "Today I assist the cops."

"You're married?"

She nodded. "My husband manages a citrus farm twenty miles outside the capital. I also have a son. He hopes one day to be a baseball player. He is at school now, no doubt studying revolutionary principles." She glanced at Luis again, to see whether she'd overstepped. Evidently satisfied, she turned back to Janek. "Well, shall we begin?"

He photographed her, fingerprinted her, then set up his tape recorder. There then followed a brief discussion about whether she could be deposed under oath.

Since they were outside the United States, they agreed that after the interview Janek would prepare a statement in English based on what she told him, Luis would translate the statement into Spanish, then Tania would sign both versions and swear to their truthfulness before a Cuban judge. When all that was settled and Tania assured him she was ready, Janek turned on his tape recorder. Then he hit her with his first question, designed to set a no-nonsense tone and catch her off guard.

"Did you have anything to do with the murder of Edith Mendoza?"

Tania laughed. "Are you serious?"

"Please answer the question."

"Of course not! I know what they said. I read all about it. I can tell you that what they said about me was lies." Her black eyes flashed.

"You ran away the night of the murder. Why?"

"I was scared! As you would have been if you'd been in my position. Mrs. Mendoza told me she was meeting a friend that afternoon at the studio. She asked me to come by afterwards and clean up. Nothing special about that. That was a normal part of my duties. I remember exactly what happened, almost as if it were yesterday. I got there just after seven. I saw her as soon as I walked in, hanging there in front of me, body battered, deep purple most of it. I screamed. I believe I screamed a lot. I had never seen anything like that before. Then I ran out, flagged down a cab, rushed back to Central Park West, packed my stuff and left. I hid out that night with a friend in Harlem, then, next morning, caught a bus to Montreal. I spent my second night at the YWCA, bought a plane ticket in the morning and flew down here. I've been living here ever since."

"The Metaxas letter—"

"I know all about it," she snapped. "What he wrote about me was a lie."

"Peña backed him up."

"Peña lied!"

"Everyone lied—is that what you're claiming?"

"Sure, and why not? I wasn't there to refute them, so they said whatever came into their heads." She smiled bitterly. "You police lied, too, because I never met Metaxas, I never arranged anything with him, I never even knew what he looked like. Why are we talking about this anyway?" Her tone showed impatience. "I read that that letter was a forgery. Wasn't it? Isn't that what they said?"

Uh-oh, here we go. Janek shook his head. Tania sat beside him, glaring, breathing in short, tight, angry gasps. She was smoldering and his only thought was that it was always this way with Mendoza—it made people crazy, everyone who touched it, every single person, including himself.

"If what you say is true—"

"It's true," she added scornfully.

"Then, why didn't you come forward?"

"Why should I? What did it have to do with me?"

"You say you knew about the Metaxas letter. Then, you must have known it was that letter, along with Rudolfo Peña's testimony, that got Mendoza convicted."

"So what?"

Oh, the lady's tough! "You didn't care if an innocent man was convicted of murder?"

"Who said he was innocent?"

"You think he—?"

"Who *cares* what I think? You don't understand."

Janek shook his head. "I guess not."

"It didn't matter to me that Metaxas never wrote that letter. Or, if he did, that he lied in it. Your great American judicial system! You're so puffed up about it, you don't see how most of the time it doesn't work. Poor, innocent dark-skinned people are sent to prison while rich, white, guilty old men walk free." She made a vulgar gesture. "I shit on your judicial system! Do you understand, Lieutenant Janek? I puke upon it! And anyway"—she worked to control her breathing—"I am sure Mendoza killed her." Tania shrugged. "Not that it mattered. They were both pieces of crap. What did I care? And who would have believed me anyway? When I came down here I went to see a friend of my father's, a lawyer. He told me I did the right thing, that the way things work up in gringoland, I could have been convicted with Mendoza as an accessory." She laughed. "You make people's beds, pick up their dirty underwear, scrub shit crust off their toilet seats, and you're supposed to care! They were rich, foul, vulgar people. Far as I'm concerned, they got what they deserved!"

Tirade finished, Tania sat back, then stiffly crossed her arms. The message was clear: *That's how I feel and to hell with what you or anybody thinks.*

Janek called a break. Tania—passionate, educated and articulate—was not what he had expected. He turned off the tape recorder, Luis cracked a little joke, the three of them laughed, then Tania went into the kitchen to prepare tea. While they waited, Luis asked Janek about the Metaxas letter.

"What is it, Frank? Why is it so important?"

Janek explained that Gus Metaxas was a failed Greek-American boxer, nicknamed "the Animal," who had allegedly been one of several boxers from Pinelli's Gym who engaged in paid sexual encounters with the Mendozas.

Three weeks into the investigation, Metaxas, who lived in a cheap hotel room near Penn Station, was found dead in his bloody bath water of self-inflicted cuts across his wrists. On his bedroom dresser was a suicide note, written in what police experts testified was his hand. In his note Metaxas wrote that he had been hired by Tania Figueras to have a sexual assignation with Edith Mendoza the day of her murder, and that the night before, at a private meeting, Jake Mendoza had paid him twenty-five hundred dollars to beat his wife to death. Twenty-five hundred more was to be paid after the deed was done. Metaxas had killed himself, he wrote, out of remorse for his awful crime.

''Was there supporting evidence?''

''Plenty,'' Janek said. ''Metaxas's mother, who lived in Chicago, received a money order for five thousand dollars mailed the day of Gus's suicide. Since everyone knew Gus was broke, his possession of that much cash supported his story. Then there was the testimony of his best friend and sparring partner, a Cuban-American fighter named Rudolfo Peña. Peña testified Gus had confessed the whole thing several days before he took his final bath.''

''Sounds convincing,'' Luis said.

''It was, although the defense tried to laugh it off. They had their own theory—that we, the cops, forced Metaxas to write the note and kill himself, that we provided the five thousand dollars for the money order and pressured Peña to give false testimony. The jury didn't believe that, so Mendoza got convicted.''

''And then—?''

''Then what, Luis?''

''Tania said something about a forgery.''

Janek exhaled. ''That came up a couple years later. A high-ranking officer named Dakin, chief of our Department of Internal Affairs, brought in some evidence he claimed showed that the defense theory of a police conspiracy might have been correct after all. There was a departmental hearing. In effect, my old partner, who'd headed the Mendoza investigation, went on trial. I acted as his defense counsel under a special provision whereby one officer may call upon another, rather than an attorney, to manage his defense. We successfully rebutted Dakin's so-called evidence.

After that Dakin resigned. But from then on the case was tainted. Worse, it split our department. There're still people, including many cops, who think we fabricated the evidence against Mendoza because we couldn't make a legitimate case."

"You don't believe that?"

"I try to keep an open mind."

"That's why you came to Cuba?"

Janek nodded. "Trouble is, if Tania's telling the truth, then something was very wrong."

After they drank their tea and the examination resumed, Tania dropped her second bombshell of the morning: Edith Mendoza, she said, had not been blackmailed by the murdered cop, Clury; rather, Edith had hired Clury to gather evidence against Jake.

"She hated her husband. She told me many times. She found him disgusting and wanted a divorce. But she wanted a big financial settlement, too. So she hired this detective, Clury, who had done investigative work for Mr. Mendoza. She paid him to collect embarrassing material about Mendoza, so she could force Mendoza into a good settlement."

"How did Clury get hold of the sex photos?"

"Mrs. Mendoza gave them to him."

"You're certain?"

"She told me so."

"You didn't note any of this down?"

Tania smiled. "I didn't keep a diary, if that's what you're asking."

"Did you know Carl Washington?"

Her mouth tightened. "Yes."

"Did you arrange meetings between the Mendozas and the boxers?"

Tania looked extremely uncomfortable, but she answered. "Three of them. Washington, Royalton and Peña. But not Metaxas, or that other man—what was his name?"

"Tate."

Tania nodded. "I never met him and never paid him.

Not him or Metaxas. The others—well, I did what Mrs. Mendoza told me. She explained that the games were to Mr. Mendoza's taste, not hers, and that he forced her to join in. She told me Clury had placed a hidden camera in the studio, and that she went along with Mendoza's pleasures in order to get pictures to embarrass him."

"So, there wasn't any blackmail?"

Tania laughed. She looked relieved that they were done talking about her complicity.

"That was so stupid! I kept reading that people thought Clury was blackmailing the Mendozas, when actually it was Mrs. Mendoza who was going to blackmail her husband. The money she paid Clury was for his investigation." She turned solemn, met Janek's eyes. She wanted to convince him. "I think Mendoza found out what she was up to. I think he had his wife killed and Clury, too. I can't prove it. But I can tell you I didn't have anything to do with Metaxas. Never! So, if he's the one killed Mrs. Mendoza, it wasn't the way it said in that note. . . ."

Janek spent the rest of the morning trying to tear apart her story. He asked long, complicated, sympathetically phrased questions, then short, jabbing queries designed to confuse and/or unnerve her. He pressed her on specific details, and, when she claimed she couldn't remember them, demanded to know why her memory was so selective. He forced her to separate what she knew from what she thought. He helped her to finesse her worst inconsistencies and attacked those portions of her account about which she seemed most certain. He complimented her on her composure and needled her for her disloyalty to her mistress. He was kind and cruel, subjecting her to glances of skepticism, snarls of ridicule and, when, suddenly, she dropped her head and began to weep, nods of humane compassion. In the end he thought that she had stood up well, that her story, as he forced her to refine it, was credible and that the lapses in it were justified by the passage of time. In short—he believed her.

"I have never witnessed such an examination," Luis said as they descended the stairs of the house. "You are a master of interrogation, Frank."

Janek shrugged. "Shucks . . ."

Luis looked at him, admiration clouded by confusion. "What is this 'shucks'?"

"It means I can't handle compliments." He looked at Luis. "What do you say I buy you lunch?"

They drove to an oceanfront restaurant a few miles east of Havana, where, at Janek's insistence, they ordered lobsters. They were the only customers. While they waited, Janek asked Luis what Tania did at the Ministry of Finance.

"She's an economist."

"Does she have a degree?" Luis nodded. "And she calls herself a bureaucrat."

"She is a modest woman."

Janek smiled. "A hard woman. A modest woman. A maid who arranged sex parties, now turned government economist. You know what I'd call her, Luis? I'd call her a very interesting woman."

When the lobsters arrived, Janek was amazed. Their tails were so large they literally fanned out of their shells. They were delicious, too.

"This is the sweetest, most tender lobster I ever ate," Janek said.

Luis, who had been eating very slowly, looked up. His eyes were sad. "Do you know how long it's been since I ate one?"

Janek shook his head.

"Twelve years. I remember the occasion very well." Luis set down his fork. "I had just gotten out of the army. My father arranged a celebration at Las Americas at Veradero Beach. It was a wonderful evening. Near the end, when we were almost finished, a convoy of vehicles pulled up and a very special person walked in. It was Fidel. The only time I had seen him that close. Of course I was thrilled. My father got up and approached his bodyguards. They let him through. Then I saw him whisper into Fidel's ear. A few moments later he brought the president to our table. I stood and Fidel looked me in the eye. Then, very emotionally, he embraced me. 'It is for young people like you that we made the revolution,' he said. As his arms grasped me and his beard grazed my cheek, I felt as if some of his strength, his incredible power, was flowing directly from him to me. It was a fine moment—standing there before my family, on the brink of manhood, embraced by our leader, this man who had single-handedly re-created Cuba, delivering us from oppression and corruption. Even now, twelve years later, if I close my eyes I can feel the pressure of his hands."

Luis paused. He removed his glasses. His large, brown liquid eyes seemed even sadder than before.

"But you see, and I must say this very carefully, Frank—when I open my eyes I can no longer feel that strength. When I open my eyes now I see the truth, which is that that man, who has done so many remarkable things for our country and whose every word so moved me when I was young, has held on to power far too long. The regimes in Eastern Europe have fallen like matchsticks, but he tells us we must die before we allow the slightest change in ours. If there is no fuel for our tractors, so be it, he tells us—we shall plow our fields with oxen. And if there is no food for us to eat, so be it, he tells us—we shall suffer hunger for the glory of our revolution."

Luis shook his head.

"The world has passed him by, but he does not know it because he believes he is like a god. I think he is mentally disturbed, Frank, and that he is turning this poor, tired country into an asylum to harbor his madness . . . and the madness of his failed dreams."

It was an eloquent, anguished, heartfelt speech. Janek

was moved by it, and, he could see, Luis felt better for having made it. Janek also knew that by sharing his perception of Fidel, Luis had given him a gift. *He has given me his trust.*

After lunch they drove quietly to a large, drab, gray building—headquarters of the Havana Police. It was an ominous, labyrinthine place of echoing footsteps—long corridors lined by bureaus with frosted-glass doors. Yet the faces of the people who roamed its halls reminded Janek of the faces in the halls of any precinct house in New York—anguished victims, frightened witnesses, worried relatives, bantering cops. The buzz was the same and the smell was similar: stale coffee, stale cigarette smoke, the bad air that is generated wherever there is a gathering of people concerned with crime and punishment. It was, he recognized, the universal smell of law enforcement, no different in Havana than in New York.

They passed through an archway beneath the word HOMICIDIO inscribed in ornate letters—as if homicide were an elegant thing. Past this point the noise dropped off. Luis explained that in Cuba murder was not a common event. Most homicides were committed within families and required little investigation. But still the word had a certain mystique. ''People always feel a chill when they walk in here,'' he said.

He led Janek to an empty, dusty room with a high ceiling, unwashed windows and mold-stained walls. Here an ancient black Royal typewriter sat upon a bare wooden table. He brought Janek a chair, then left him alone. Janek sat down, pondered for a while, then began to pound out a summary of his interview.

As he typed, the room echoed with shifts and returns, an old squad-room sound he hadn't heard since the introduction of computers. But no matter how hard he hammered the keys, his words were barely imprinted on the paper. When he examined the ribbon he understood why—it was so old, so used, that in many places it was torn all the way through.

When the affidavit and translation were done, Luis dropped Janek in front of his hotel. He would take the documents to Tania for approval, take her before a Cuban judge for the swearing-to ceremony, then return.

Back in his room, Janek took off his clothes and again inspected his body in the mirror. Although there were still a few sore spots, the blue marks had nearly faded.

He lay down on the bed. He didn't want to think about his experience with the Seguridad. He needed to think about Mendoza.

Is it possible, he asked himself, *that Timmy faked the Metaxas letter and pressured Peña to commit perjury?* The thought was so chilling, he put it out of his mind. Then he fell asleep.

At nine that night Luis was back, treasures in hand. The executed documents, sworn to by Tania in the presence of official witnesses, bore a variety of flamboyant signatures, indented seals and one big red wax seal securing a piece of multicolored ribbon to the paper.

"These are beauties!" Janek said. He embraced Luis. "Thank you. You've really saved my ass!"

Since neither one was hungry, they decided to take a walk. Luis led the way from the boisterous atmosphere of La Rampa to a well-kept area of suburban blocks nearby. Here old-fashioned lamps lit silent shady streets and the air was perfumed with the aroma of night-blooming shrubs.

They talked about police work—what they liked about it and what they didn't, the boredom and the pleasures of it, the exhilaration that always came when an investigation began to break open a case. They talked about detectives who solved crimes by the numbers, and others, like themselves, who worked more by hunch and touch.

"I usually go in the way you go into a labyrinth," Janek said, "trying to feel my way around. Sometimes I'm clumsy. I run into the walls. Other times I get completely lost. In the end, if I manage to get to the center of the thing, it's because on some level or other I felt it. Know what I mean?''

Luis nodded. ''A sixth sense about people, what they are like, what they are likely to do.''

''Right,'' Janek said. ''So, let's talk about that. What did you feel about Tania?''

''My professional opinion?''

Janek shook his head. ''Your gut reaction.''

Luis paused. ''I felt she was a very strong woman.''

''But maybe not so strong as she wanted you to believe.''

''Perhaps not.''

''So, what do your instincts tell you about her, Luis? Did she lie to me? Did she tell me everything?''

Luis thought again before he answered. A parrot, his cage secured to the railing of a porch, screeched shrilly as they passed.

''She is safe here, the case is old, so she has nothing to gain by lying. Still, she is human. She could be holding something back or leaving something out.''

''Why?''

''Perhaps to make herself look better in our eyes.''

''Or in her own. That's something I've learned about stories, Luis. People have to live with themselves, so they interpret what they've done in ways that make them feel good.''

Luis nodded.

''Thing is,'' Janek continued, ''if Tania set up the final date with Metaxas, she'd have to bear some responsibility for what he did. She doesn't want to bear any responsibility for it. That may be why she ran—''

''Do you think she lied about that?'' A dog howled in the distance.

''I'm not sure it makes much difference. She says she screamed a lot when she saw Mrs. Mendoza hanging in the studio. That's something we didn't know. We didn't know she'd gone over there that night. But I'm certain she's telling the truth.''

''How can you be?''

''A neighbor called our emergency number, nine-one-one, to report screams just after seven o'clock. That's when Tania says she arrived to clean the place up. All these years we've assumed that the neighbor heard Edith's screams, something we couldn't reconcile with the fact that our people found her gagged.''

Luis spread his arms. ''Well, there you are—Tania was truthful.''

''About that, yeah. But I still have a problem with Metaxas. He was slow-witted, known for being sweet and well mannered, except of course when in the ring. Suppose Tania *did* set up the date with Metaxas, like he wrote in his note. Does that mean the note couldn't have been faked or forged?'' Janek shook his head. ''There're too many other things that don't fit—like why would Mendoza risk a face-to-face meeting with a hired killer and why would sweet Gus use a woman's body as a punching bag? If he was capable of that, why would he feel remorse about it afterwards? There are four things that tie Metaxas to the murder: his suicide; his note; the five-thousand-dollar money order to his mother; Peña's testimony. All four could have been manipulated. It would have been difficult, but it could have been done. What Tania has to say has little bearing on that . . . if she lied a little or left a few things out. But suppose Tania told us a very big lie.'' He glanced at Luis. ''Suppose she brokered the whole deal for Mendoza, not just the date but the killing instructions and the murder fee, too. Suppose she hired Peña, the only other likely hit man, then ran away with enough money so she could buy a plane ticket here and set herself up when she arrived. Did Jake Mendoza pay her off? Was part of the deal that she run down here to divert attention? That script might work.'' He paused. ''It certainly isn't impossible.''

''But only if she told a very big lie,'' Luis added.

"Right . . ." Janek paused. "For me the issue isn't whether Mendoza arranged the killing of his wife. I'm pretty sure he did. The issue is whether my old friend, Timmy Sheehan, decided that if he couldn't legally nail Mendoza, he'd fake up a chain of evidence using sweet, dumb Gus Metaxas as his fall guy. That, Luis, is such a horrifying possibility, it makes me sick to think about it."

"I understand. But what's the answer? Do you think Tania was telling a big lie or not?"

"I don't think she was, but I can't be sure."

As they approached La Rampa and the hotel, Janek explained how he was going to proceed.

"Even with my tapes and documents, they'll ask me about Tania's demeanor. That'll put me in a position where I can skew what she said."

"Skew?"

"Slant it. Put a spin on it."

Luis looked worried. "How will you skew it, Frank?"

"I'll act like I believe everything she told me. I'll put her statement out, then sit back and watch what people do."

"You believe someone will do something and give himself away?"

"I hope so. If someone gets provoked, it might answer a lot of old questions."

At the Habana Libre they stood in silence by the door. Janek turned to Luis. "You've helped me so much. Is there some way I can repay you? Anything I can send you from the States?"

Luis shook his head. "Perhaps one day I will come see you in New York."

Janek nodded. The pride of the man continued to impress him. "Have you been to America?"

Luis said that he had not, but that he had relatives there among the exiles, as did his wife.

"Most Cuban families do. In that way the revolution was expensive for us—it split us up. Now we wonder what will happen if things change here and our exiles come home.

Will they try to dismantle our medical and educational systems, demand their old property back? It is better for us not to think about such things, better to simply go on as we have for thirty years. And if we have no paper or fuel and barely enough to eat—well, then, at least we know we are defending our revolution. That, Frank, is the beauty in our pain, the luxury of it. Do you understand?''

Janek understood. He also understood what Luis was really telling him—that because he did not share this total belief, the suffering he and his family endured on account of the shortages was neither beautiful nor luxurious, it was simply pain.

They embraced a final time, then Luis got into his car. Janek came around to the driver's window.

''Good luck,'' he said.

He slept well. In the morning, he took a dollars-only taxi to the airport. There were few cars, lots of bicycles, the usual throngs waiting glumly before the bus shelters. He passed a group of joggers and then a convoy of military trucks. On the outskirts he was struck by the way the early-morning light cut through the sugarcane that lined the road and painted the worn asphalt splendidly with bars.

At the airport, when he passed through immigration, a supervisor stepped in to examine his documents.

''Ah, the labor organizer!'' the supervisor said. Then he laughed. ''Good news, señor. Due to unforeseen circumstances this morning's flight for Mexico City will depart on time.''

Half an hour later, as his plane soared upward, Janek stared down at Cuba glittering below. It seemed to him that the country looked quite beautiful from the sky—a long, thin, verdant island set in an emerald sea. In his five days there he had experienced some of the worst moments of his life, had been blindfolded, stripped, beaten and humiliated. He knew he would never return.

Gelsey's Special

He always called it "playtime" when he coaxed her to join him alone down in the maze. He was always tender with her there. She adored their games, and, when his caresses became too ardent, she would simply turn away, face the mirrors, then watch her dream-sister and the Leering Man perform inside the glass. . . .

Gelsey was evoking him again, the Leering Man in the mirrors, the man she had drawn, painted and sculpted so many times. She thought she knew who he was and what he meant to her and why she felt compelled to re-create him. What she did not understand was why she could never seem to get him right.

But this morning was different. She had awakened with a new idea, had been working on it since dawn. Now, standing back from her easel, seeing the way the fragmented mirror portrait was taking shape, she felt exhilarated by the process. *Perhaps this time I'm really on to something,* she thought.

She used the skylit end of the loft as her studio. The space had been her father's workshop; it was here that he had constructed the many parts which, when joined, had become the fabulous mirror maze below. Here, amid his old benches and tools, she kept her easels, paints, brushes and canvas, her supplies of pastels, charcoal, paper, plywood, mirrored glass and clay. She loved the fresh, clean smell of unused art materials and the feel of them in her hands. She remembered something an old art teacher had once said in class: "Every bucket of clay has the potential to become a work of art. In every fresh tube of paint there is a masterpiece waiting to be released."

She had started that morning to paint the outline of Leering Man onto an irregular slab of mirror. Then she had covered this mirror with a towel and smashed it carefully with a mallet. Now she was reassembling the shards onto a plywood board coated with glue. But rather than fitting the pieces back together the way they'd been, she was rearranging them into a more expressive order.

She knew what she was doing: She was putting Leering Man through her own personal "Fragmentation Serpent," then packing her image of him with her rage. When she was finished, a viewer would look at the portrait and, confronted by bits of himself reflected in the shards, be caught in the web of her art.

At noon she paused briefly to eat an apple, then went back to work, gluing the shards on faster, with greater concentration, thinking that if she applied herself, she might complete the portrait by night.

Just before five, she heard a roll of thunder. She paused, looked outside, saw storm clouds forming in the east. She shrugged and began to put away her tools. A few minutes later sheets of rain began to sweep across Richmond Park. She stopped all work, sat by the window, watched the water spray the glass then run down in rivulets. As she listened to the rain pounding the metal roof, a new compelling need took hold. Tonight, she knew, she would drive into the city, seek out a mark and take him down.

She did not linger too long in the maze. A few steady gazes at herself standing nude in the endless mirrored galleries, then she returned to the loft to disguise herself and to dress.

At eight-thirty, wearing a conservative navy business

suit, a classic pearl strand with matching earrings and a well-cut red-haired wig, she was on the rain-streaked highway heading for New York.

Because she had barely eaten that day, she felt gripped by pangs of hunger. But she didn't stop. *It makes me feel powerful to feel hungry,* she thought. She rarely ate before a foray, preferring to work with an edge, then treat herself afterward to ice cream. Self-discipline followed by satiation, taking down a mark then receiving a reward—the sequence made her feel like a warrior.

She was just emerging from the Holland Tunnel when the notion of infringement struck. The rain was still coming down, though not so forcefully as before. She smiled when she thought of driving to a hotel, working a hotel bar and thus encroaching on Diana's territory. If doing that meant going to war against Diana, then so be it, she would be prepared to fight.

Instinctively she wheeled her car toward lower Manhattan. She would make a hit against the Savoy, the new hotel across from the World Financial Center. She found a parking space near Battery Park City in sight of the twin towers. She checked her makeup in the rearview mirror, wished her mirror-sister luck, then locked her car, opened her umbrella and strolled to the hotel entrance.

There was a convention in progress. Men and women, well lubricated with alcohol, were pressed together conversing loudly in the lobby. They all had red "Hello! I'm ________" badges stuck to their lapels. Gelsey eased her way through the throng, checked her raincoat and umbrella, found the lobby lounge and entered.

No ebullient conventioneers in here; the mood was dour. The customers, nearly all male, sat by themselves in gloomy booths. She sat down, looked around: dim lighting, dark carpeting, chairs and tables finished in black lacquer. A long, curving modernistic bar, with a dark, mottled mirror behind, carried out the Deco-style motif.

Gelsey had forgotten how mournful a hotel bar could be,

so different from the stoked-up gaiety of the neighborhood joints she was used to working. But sitting there brought back memories of her days with Diana, when she was still learning the game. It was the particular lonely qualities of hotel lounges, Diana had taught her, that favored their special work: all those out-of-town businessmen sitting alone after dinner waiting for their fantasy strangers to appear. Someone young, attractive and mysterious who would hold out the promise of an erotic adventure. "That's you," Diana had told her. "You're their fantasy. And then, of course, their nightmare afterwards," she had added, smiling.

Gelsey summoned the waiter, ordered a Bloody Mary, then stared off into space. Sooner or later her mark would find her. The more aloof she held herself, the more attracted he would be.

His name was Philip A. Dietz, according to his card, and he was everything Diana always told her girls to look for. He was from out of town ("San Jose—you know, Silicon Valley, computer chips"), he wore a wedding band ("Very important," Diana always said), an expensive Rolex ("A sure sign of flash," Diana always said) and when he picked up their first round of drinks he glanced at his room key, then wrote his room number on the check. ("Be careful if he shows too much cash, girls—he just might be a plant.")

Perhaps the most important thing about him, from Gelsey's point of view, was his blatant conceit. She spotted him for a womanizer the moment he sat down. *He could be Leering Man,* she thought, *reeking of gloss and self-assurance. Leering Man before he leers.*

She played with her swizzle stick as she looked him over. "I don't usually do this sort of thing."

Dietz leaned forward. His thick black hair looked dyed. "What's that, dear? What don't you do?"

"Let strange men buy me drinks in hotel bars."

"Am I 'the bad stranger'?" He grimaced. "Anyway, I thought you looked like a—" He smiled. "You know . . . adventuress?"

She shook her head. "You definitely had me wrong."

"Okay," he said, turning serious. "You're a lawyer from Chicago. What brings you to New York?"

"I'm taking a deposition in the morning. I'll fly back in the afternoon."

"First class, too, I bet. And you'll take your time with the dep at two hundred thirty per. Right?"

She gazed at him with faint disgust. "I don't talk about my fees."

"Sorry."

No, you're not. She leaned forward, engaging his eyes. "What about you, Phil? You look like a player. So tell me—what's your game?"

He laughed. " 'Player,' 'game'—I like that!" He took a long sip from his Scotch. "I'm here to make a deal. If it goes down—well, old Phil here is going to be rich. *Very* rich."

She stared at him. She detested braggarts. *You won't be boasting like that in the morning.* Then she noticed that he was looking her over like a shrewd gambler inspecting a filly before a race.

"You're a very attractive woman. But you know that already, don't you?"

She winced. "Is that your idea of a clever remark?"

"Take it any way you like."

The hook was in, she knew, although he was trying not to show it. "Well," she said, stifling a yawn, "time for me to be getting back upstairs."

"Whatsamatter?" He pretended to be surprised. "It's early!" He showed her his watch. "Just eleven-fifteen." He paused. *Now he'll go for it.* "What do you say we move someplace . . . you know . . . a little more comfortable?" He grinned.

She studied him coldly. "My room—is that what you're thinking?"

He shook his head, opened his palm, showed her his key. "I was thinking of old sixteen-sixty-four."

"Sorry. It's been fun."

Her rejection caught him short. "What's the matter, Gelsey?" There was an edge to his voice. "Have I offended you? Did I do something wrong?"

She reached for his hand, rubbed her finger across his wedding band. "This, my friend, is where I draw the line."

"Oh, that old thing."

"Yeah, that old thing."

She let his hand drop. He stared at her, deflated.

"All I meant was, you know . . ."

Now he's sputtering! "Yeah? What *did* you mean?"

"Just a drink, from the minibar. No obligation, no expectation. You can leave whenever you want." He showed her a sincere expression, then raised his hand as if taking an oath. "Honest Injun!" His smile did not disarm her. *It wouldn't even fool his mother.*

"Well . . ." She pretended she was considering his offer. He peered at her eagerly. "Well," she said again. "All right. Just one drink."

In "old 1664" she moved to take control.

"Lie back," she told him. "Loosen your tie. Take off your shoes. Get comfortable." She took his key from his hand, unlocked the minibar, set to work. Dietz, amused, reclined on his bed and watched.

"You make a very attractive bartender," he observed.

Hey! Wow! The Great Seducer!

"I worked my way through law school tending bar." She turned slightly, slipped the KO drops into his drink, then turned back and handed him his glass.

He looked at it like it was poison. "What's this?"

"Gelsey's Special. Drink it. It'll make you feel good."

He sniffed at it, made a face. "I'm more of a straight Scotch guy myself."

"What's the matter? Afraid of something new?"

"Not really . . ."

She studied him. "I didn't figure you for a stick in the mud, Phil."

The taunt upset him. "I'm not a stick in the mud."

"A little stodgy, then?"

"Not stodgy at all."

"Good." She grinned. "I like an adverturesome man."

"I just prefer—"

"Come on, Phil. Drink up," she said kindly. "You might like it. Wouldn't that be a surprise?"

He hesitated for a moment, then clicked his glass against hers and quickly drank off half the potion.

Gotcha! All she had to do now was string him along a couple of minutes more.

"What do you think?"

"It's different, I'll say that for it."

"Of course it's different." She felt flushed with confidence. "And so am I," she added.

"You got a point there."

She laughed, started toward his bathroom.

"Where're you going?"

"To the powder room. I'll be right back. I just have to make a few"—she giggled—"preparations."

She shut the bathroom door, pressed her back against it. *Jesus!* She'd been worried when he sniffed the glass, as if he'd actually suspected something. But in the end he was an oaf like the rest of them, unaware of anything except that he was alone with an attractive woman and that he ought to get busy bedding her down, because, of course, that's what she wanted even if the sultry little bitch didn't know it yet.

When she felt enough time had passed, she opened the bathroom door and peered across the room. He must have heard her because he turned his head. His face was pale. He didn't look well at all.

"You okay?"

"A little wheezy." He tried to hold up his empty glass. He didn't have the strength. "What'd you give me?"

"Nothing."

"Something . . . know it. . . ."

"Love drops," she said. "I gave you love drops."

"Love drops?" He rubbed his eyes. His voice had lost its edge.

"Umm-hmmmm."

"You mean like a . . . aphrodisiac?" he asked.

"Uh-huh . . ."

She watched him silently, curiously, as he let go of the glass. It rolled across the bed and fell with a gentle thud onto the carpet. *You're dead meat,* she thought.

"My eyelids . . . heavy . . ."

"Let yourself go, Phil. Try and sleep."

A mild glare of anger in his eyes. "You spiked it, didn't you?"

"A nice girl like me?"

She waited for the flash of terror, but he was too far gone. He closed his eyes and began to snore. She smiled, shook her head, then slipped on a fresh pair of surgical gloves and set to work cleaning up the room.

In the end she decided not to freak him out. No scissors work tonight—just pick the guy clean and split. She put his cash (three hundred dollars plus change), Rolex and wedding band into her purse. *He'll* really *sputter when he tries to explain that missing ring!* She pulled off his already loosened tie, unbuttoned then spread open his shirt, sat astride him with her marker poised just above his skin. *Think of a good message, one that'll really get to him.* It didn't take her long to come up with an appropriate slogan. She wrote across his chest in mirror-reverse:

[illegible]

As she was dismounting his prostrate form, she noticed something—a little edge of khaki fabric peeking out of the top of his pants. *Aha! What have we here?* She unclasped his belt, unzipped his fly and pulled down his trousers to his knees. There it was, a money belt, and she'd almost missed it, too. *Okay, let's see what you're hiding. Let's see if you're Mr. Bucks.*

She pulled the belt off him. It had been strapped on so tight it left a pink imprint on his skin. She opened the flaps, explored the pockets, came up with a thousand dollars in hundred-dollar bills and a small object carefully wrapped in plastic foam.

Expecting a diamond, or at least a ruby, she was disappointed to find a piece of hard, transparent material covered with tiny lines. She held the object up to the light. What the hell was it? Some sort of computer chip? Dietz, she remembered, had spoken of a deal that would make him "very rich."

Well, good-bye deal! She popped the chip into her purse with the other loot, then went back into the bathroom, checked herself in the mirror, returned to the bedroom, looked around, saw everything was clean, moved over to the room door, looked back at Dietz and blew him a kiss.

"Sweet dreams, lover boy," she whispered.

She switched off the lights, cautiously opened the door, checked out the corridor. It was empty. She hung the DO NOT DISTURB sign on the handle of "old 1664," closed the door softly and strode swiftly to the elevators.

Descending to the lobby, she was nearly overcome by nausea. It was hunger, knotting up her stomach. She retrieved her things from the checkroom, walked inconspicuously through the lobby to the street, walked faster until she reached the corner, then broke into a run.

Rain was still falling and there were puddles everywhere. She splashed through several, drenching her shoes and feet. *Ice cream!* She drove to an all-night truckers' diner near the entrance to the tunnel. A few minutes later, sitting at the counter in the midst of pigging out on a huge chocolate sundae topped by a swirl of whipped cream mounted with a cherry, she paused to observe herself in a decorative strip of mirror on the opposing wall.

The sight offended her. She was filled with revulsion—for what she was, for what she had done, for what she feared she might one day do. She knew then that in her next session she would have to tell Dr. Z about the marks. And about a lot of other things, such as Leering Man and "playtime" and the compulsion that came upon her when it rained. Most of all, she thought, she'd tell him about the secrets of the maze.

Mirror-Reverse

When Janek emerged from customs at Kennedy Airport, he found Aaron Greenberg waiting at the gate. It was just after midnight, Janek was happy to see him, but he was startled. No one except Kit knew where he'd gone and when he was flying back.

"What is this—VIP treatment?"

"Kit's orders, Frank. She told me to pick you up."

Janek cuffed Aaron on the shoulder. They'd been partners since Timmy Sheehan retired. Aaron was a short, taut, wiry man with weather-beaten skin, sad eyes and a sweet, sometimes heartbreaking smile. He was wearing his usual short-sleeved Hawaiian shirt. Tonight the colors were green and black.

"Some guy's been assassinated downtown at the Savoy," Aaron explained. "Kit slotted it to us."

"I've been in planes and airports for fifteen hours. Don't suppose there's time to go home and change?"

"Probably be better if you didn't."

Janek wasn't surprised to be assigned a case. Kit had told him she was going to put him on something when he'd called her between planes from Mexico City: "I want you busy, Frank. I don't want everyone talking about how I've got you reopening Mendoza." But he'd expected she would want to debrief him on Cuba first.

"When did this come up?"

"Hour and a half ago." Aaron glanced at his watch.

"Crime Scene team's due now."

They walked through the International Arrivals building. There were fewer than fifty people in the lobby, a sharp contrast to the hordes that had thronged the terminal in Mexico. Actually, he thought, it was good to have something that would take his mind off Cuba—the scorn he'd seen in Violetta's eyes, the degradation of the beating, the stink and boredom of the closet cell.

Aaron led him to his car, a beaten-up green Chevrolet parked illegally in front. There was a ticket on the windshield.

"Port Authority cops!" Aaron snatched it off the glass, then laughed.

They sped along the Van Wyck, empty of traffic. Janek looked up when they passed the safe house in which he'd met Angel Figueras two and a half weeks before. They were going too fast for him to make out anything more than a blacked-out ordinary little house on an ordinary little street.

"She's not fooling anybody. You know that, Frank?"

"Kit?"

Aaron nodded. "Everyone knows where you've been and what you've been doing down there."

"They don't really know."

"Not officially. But there're rumors around."

Janek recalled Sarah's "a little bird told me." "If there're rumors, they probably track back to Baldwin," he said.

"Sure. Baldwin and Dakin were big buddies back then."

"Still are."

"So, if you're working on Mendoza, and everyone knows it—why bother with a cover?"

"Ask Kit."

"Yeah . . . but, see, that's what bothers me. Kit's supposed to be smart. But she's acting like she thinks putting you on this hotel homicide is going to make people think you're occupied full-time."

"Don't underestimate her."

Aaron laughed. "Impossible!" He paused. "Anyway, you're close to her. Maybe you can clue her in."

He cut onto Queens Boulevard, followed it to the Brooklyn-Queens Expressway, then crossed the Williamsburg to lower Manhattan. From the bridge the city looked truly majestic: clusters of buildings lit from within, stark forms of varying heights that seemed to float against the night sky. Moved by the sight, Janek felt seized by the naked power of New York, a place he alternately adored and loathed.

"You have to be strong to live here," he said.

Aaron nodded. "The slightest show of weakness and you're doomed."

Sue Burke met them in the hotel lobby. She was a short, intense young woman, a skilled martial artist, with dark, short hair cut butch. An upfront lesbian, she was impatient, brash, smart and fiercely loyal. Janek had always held to the view that it takes ten years to make a good detective. Sue was the exception—she'd only been in for three, but, he felt, she was nearly there.

"Victim's name is Philip Dietz," she told them as she guided them to the elevators. "Registered two days ago. Gave an address in San Jose. This morning there was a DO NOT DISTURB sign on his door. Around noon, with the sign still there, the maid knocked softly, then looked in. This is standard hotel procedure. People go out and forget to remove the sign."

Janek nodded.

"So the maid looks in and sees Dietz lying on his bed. The drapes are drawn. She shuts the door and goes about her business. Meantime, some calls come in. Operator rings the room but Dietz doesn't pick up. Operator asks the callers if they want to leave messages. Dietz's wife leaves three."

They stepped into the elevator. Sue pushed the button for

the sixteenth floor. Janek could tell she liked recounting the story.

"Around nine o'clock tonight, Dietz's wife phones the desk. Says she's worried, says her husband should have called her back. She asks the assistant manager to go upstairs and check. He goes up, enters the room, sees Dietz lying on the bed, a pillow on top of his head. Meantime he notices the room's a mess, like someone's turned it over. The assistant approaches Dietz and tries to wake him up. Dietz is dead. Looks like he's been shot in the head through the pillow to muffle the sound. Hotel management calls us. They don't call back Mrs. Dietz."

On the sixteenth floor a uniformed cop was standing by the elevators. Aaron clipped his shield to his lapel. Janek hadn't taken his shield to Cuba, but the cop recognized him and waved him through.

"Have we called her yet?"

Sue shook her head. "Waiting for you, Frank."

"Right . . ."

"Anyway, like I said, the room's been ransacked. Some stuff gone. Watch, cash, probably his wedding band—I noticed a ring mark on his finger. But not his credit cards or ID. Still, there're no papers, datebook, address book or other businessman's stuff. And his clothes have been sliced up, like someone's been looking inside the linings. The lining of his suitcase's been slit open, too."

"Doesn't go with taking a guy's watch and money," Aaron said.

Sue nodded. "There's more. Last night Dietz was observed picking up a young, well-dressed redhead in the hotel lounge. They talked a while, had a couple drinks. The waiter remembers them leaving together a little before midnight. That's the last time anyone saw him alive."

A small group was milling outside the door to room 1664. Sue introduced Janek to the hotel night manager. His name was Blinken, he spoke with a soft German accent and he was trying hard to act stoical, perhaps the way they'd taught him at hotel-management school in Lucerne.

The minute Janek walked in he felt a rush. Homicide investigations were his specialty. An assistant med examiner, Lois Rappaport, famous for her crooked mouth and wry attitude, was examining the body on the bed. A four-man Crime Scene team plus Sue Burke's partner, Ray Galindez, were conducting an evidence search in various parts of the room.

He greeted everybody then stood back, trying to focus on the scene. He felt at once that there was something wrong with it. He asked himself what it was. Then Lois Rappaport broke his concentration.

''Take a look,'' she said, pointing to Dietz's chest. Janek walked over to the bed and peered down. There were red ink markings on the flesh.

''What *is* this?'' Aaron asked.

Rappaport shrugged.

Sue craned forward. ''Think maybe one of those voodoo jobs, Frank?''

Ray Galindez joined them. He was in his late twenties, a tall, very lean good-looking man of Puerto Rican descent, with a serious demeanor, dusty skin and an elegant pencil-line mustache.

''Maybe Arabic?'' Ray suggested.

Janek shook his head. ''Shoot me a Polaroid, will you, Ray?''

Ray nodded. He and his wife, Grecia, were about to have their first child. Ever since Grecia had become pregnant, Ray had seemed to wear a special glow.

Janek turned back to the room. ''I better phone the wife.''

Aaron, perhaps out of sympathy for his exhaustion, offered to take on that unpleasant task. Janek thanked him. One of the Crime Scene detectives showed Janek a pair of empty miniature vodka bottles and a pair of fruit-juice cans in the waste basket. Janek shrugged. Mr. Blinken approached. He wanted to know whether Janek wanted him to close off the floor and move the guests to other rooms. Janek told him closing the whole floor wasn't necessary, but it would be a good idea to evacuate the nearest rooms. Ray handed him a Polaroid of the markings on Dietz's chest. Then Janek asked Sue to join him downstairs—he wanted to interview the lounge waiter.

On the way down he examined himself in the elevator mirror. His suit was wrinkled, his hair was mussed and his face did not show a proper sportsman's Caribbean tan. He recalled the Polaroid of himself in Violetta's folder. Again he felt a flash of anger at the memory.

The lounge was empty except for one man sitting by himself. The waiter and the bartender were the only staff. The waiter, who had slicked-back hair and a watery left eye, tried to be helpful, but he was anxious to go home. Janek asked him to describe the way Dietz and the redhead had acted. The waiter stifled a yawn.

"They were getting . . . you know, friendly. He seemed to be interested in her and she seemed the same. Sort of."

"What do you mean?" Sue asked.

The waiter shrugged. "I think she was making him work for it. Anyway, when I brought him the bill I overheard something made me think they were going up to his room to get a little . . . friendlier."

"Describe the girl," Janek said.

"Young, well built, pretty."

"That could be anybody."

"I know." The waiter paused. "There was definitely something about her. . . ."

"What?"

"Not sure. Just something. She had . . . moves, know what I mean?"

Moves: That could mean anything. Janek needed a face.

"I want you to work with a police artist. There's one on duty. Detective Burke'll escort you. Then she'll drive you home."

The waiter whistled. "Tonight?"

"A man's been killed. You saw him leave with a woman. She may know something or be involved."

"Sure," the waiter said.

Janek left him with Sue. On his way to the elevators he was intercepted by Aaron, who had just gotten off the phone with Mrs. Dietz.

"She took it pretty well, considering," Aaron reported. "At least she didn't go hysterical on me. I asked if there was anything I could do for her. She said someone in the family would be in touch." He paused. "The way she snapped up the phone I got the feeling she was expecting something. But, of course, not this."

"What do you think she was expecting?"

Aaron squinted. "Maybe some kind of news. She told me Dietz came East to meet with an executive recruiter. He hasn't been happy where he's been working. Maybe she expected to hear he'd landed a job. Thing is—on the phone I couldn't really tell what her reaction was."

On their way back up to the sixteenth floor, Janek pulled out the Polaroid of the chest markings and held it up to the elevator mirror. The markings spelled out a sentence.

Aaron read it aloud. " 'You couldn't get it up.' Jesus!" He looked at Janek."How'd you do that?"

"It's written in mirror-reverse."

"What does it mean?"

"I don't know. But it's interesting, isn't it?"

Back in Dietz's room, Janek asked Lois Rappaport what she thought. She showed him a plastic envelope. There was a spent bullet inside.

"Twenty-two. I found it under his head. He's probably been dead twenty-four hours. I may have something more for you tomorrow."

"Like what?" Janek asked.

"I'll let you know."

"You got a feeling about something?"

She showed him her crooked smile, then ordered her assistants to carry out the body.

Janek stayed in 1664 another twenty minutes, talking to the Crime Scene investigators. They had collected a vast number of assorted fingerprints, fibers and hairs—not surprising in a hotel bedroom. Janek asked Ray to get a list of women currently registered in the hotel, and a second list of women who had checked out within the past twenty four hours. Then he asked Aaron to drive him home.

There was a three-person TV news crew waiting in the lobby, led by a tired young female correspondent he recognized, a Chinese-American named Meg Chang. When she spotted Janek she sprang to life and crossed toward him, trailed by her cameraman.

"Hi, Lieutenant!" Janek nodded. "We hear a businessman was shot. Can you tell us anything?"

She tried to stick her microphone in his face. Janek gently pushed it away.

"Check with me tomorrow, Meg. I got nothing now."

He and Aaron walked out the door. The air was cool. A breeze was coming off the harbor. The stark towers of Battery Park City and the domes of the World Financial Center loomed like monoliths.

Following West Street on their way uptown, Janek asked Aaron if he'd taken a look at the Savoy lounge. Aaron shook his head.

"It's not the kind of place you'd drop in for the evening—unless you were staying at the hotel. Not many people live around here. It's not like your neighborhood watering hole."

"So, if the redhead wasn't staying there—?"

"Then, maybe it wasn't a pickup. Maybe the meeting was arranged."

"Or maybe the redhead was working the lounge. Twenty-two's a lady's gun."

"Or an assassin's." Janek glanced at the river. The water, lapping at the embankment, was black like oil. "I think we want to know a lot more about this guy."

"What do you want to do first, Frank?"

"Find the redhead. That's number one."

Aaron stopped in front of Janek's building. It was a bleak brick and graystone apartment house with an exterior fire escape on West Eighty-seventh. Someone had scrawled graffiti beside one of the pilasters. There was a pile of black polyurethane garbage bags stacked by the curb.

"Thanks for phoning the wife."

Aaron smiled ruefully. "Best part of the job."

Janek waited until Aaron drove off, then he entered. The lobby smelled of cabbage and cats. A crudely lettered sign was taped to the wall beside the elevator: NO HOT WATER TOMORROW DUE TO BOILER REPAIR. SUPT.

When he opened the door to his apartment, the only thing he could see was the tiny red light on his answering machine signaling there were messages. He set down his suitcase, made his way through the gloom, found a lamp and switched it on. The apartment was simply furnished, mostly with pieces inherited from his parents, including, most prominently, the old workbench from his father's accordion shop. A half-dozen instruments in various states of disrepair sat upon it. Janek knew it would be years before he got them all working.

His phone messages were routine, except the one from Sarah. She said she'd received three estimates from roofers and the lowest came in at ninety-eight hundred dollars. He found that information as irritating as the tone of her voice. He turned off the machine, stripped, looked at himself in the mirror. The marks were gone. He took a shower and lay down on his bed. Then he remembered—there would be no hot water in the morning. He went back to the bathroom and shaved. It was 4:15 A.M.

At two the following afternoon he sat in Kit Kopta's office on the twenty-third floor of the Police Headquarters building at One Police Plaza. Kit, dwarfed by her huge desk, came around to embrace him. Then she gestured him to the conference area by the windows.

He presented her with his treasures—exposed roll of film, fingerprint card, audiotapes and Tania's affidavits. He stared out the window while she read the English version. People crossing Police Plaza looked like ants.

"Beautiful, Frank." Kit's dark Greek eyes sparkled. "How'd you do it?"

"It wasn't easy."

She studied him. "Something happened down there." Janek nodded. "Want to tell me about it?"

"Not particularly."

"You had some trouble?"

"You could put it that way." She stared at him. He shrugged. "They put on a little show. I played the lead."

"That's kind of abstract."

"Yeah, I guess so."

"Hey—I'm your friend. Remember?"

"It's embarrassing, Kit. Let it go now. Please."

She nodded reluctantly. Eventually, he knew, she'd get the story out of him. It still pained him to think about his three days in detention; he felt no desire to describe them to her. And perhaps there was another reason, too. Since he had gone to Cuba to please her, whatever he had suffered there, he had suffered, he believed, on her behalf.

"Actually," he said, "the way it ended up, I got to work with a terrific Cuban cop. If it hadn't been for him, I wouldn't have brought back the goods."

Kit nodded slightly, sat back. "How do you like your new case?"

"Too soon to tell. You don't want me reporting to you?"

She shook her head. "To Deforest, as usual."

He looked at her. "Thing is, Kit, this little diversion isn't going to fool anyone. There're rumors all over the place about where I went and why. Even Sarah heard about it."

"Sarah . . ." Kit shrugged. "Doesn't matter, Frank. The case is legit. And the rumors are deniable." She cleared her throat. "Remember Netti Rampersad?"

Janek smiled. "To meet her is never to forget her."

"She does come on strong, doesn't she? Well, it seems now she's taken over Mendoza's appeal. Which means"—Kit stretched her arms over her head, then set her palms on the arms of her chair— "she'll want to see these affidavits right away. In fact, she called me twice to find out how you were doing. This morning she served me with an order to produce."

"Soon as she sees this stuff she'll move for a new trial. She'll claim that because Tania's statement contradicts Metaxas's note, the note should be thrown out."

Kit gazed out the window. "Yeah, that's probably what she'll do. It won't be easy for her to get a new trial. But she'll try. And maybe she'll succeed."

"Is that what you want, Kit? Are you using her as your cat's-paw in this?"

Kit shrugged again. "We're cops. Not lawyers or prosecutors. She's got her agenda. We've got ours."

"What *is* ours—if you don't mind my asking?"

"We want to know if someone around here did something corrupt." Kit pointed at the affidavits. "Give Rampersad the ball and let her run with it."

"Sure. And after?"

"You got a homicide case, Frank. Work it. It's what you do best."

"That's it?"

"That's it."

She stood to signal the meeting was over. He started toward the door, had just reached it when she called him back. "There is something else. I want you to see Dakin. You know, courtesy call. Fill him in on what you found."

He stared at her, outraged. "That's a pretty dirty task."

"It is," she agreed.

"So—am I your cat's-paw, too?"

"We're working together on this, Frank. That's the way I see it. Any problems?"

Janek nodded. "If I brief Dakin, I brief Timmy, too. Otherwise, get someone else."

"Sure, brief Timmy. Play it down the middle. I should have thought of that myself." She turned back to the papers on her desk.

Janek worked out of two interconnected rooms on the fourth floor of the Police Property building off University Place. The outer room of the suite, which bore the words SPECIAL SQUAD on its door, contained four beaten-up desks, as many chairs and a large blackboard at one end. The smaller inner room was his office. He kept it austere, without the usual departmental certificates, clippings about his exploits and personal photographs on the walls. He liked the notion that he worked in a plain city-owned space. He wasn't interested in personalizing it or in turning it into a nest.

When he arrived, Aaron and Sue were at their desks talking into phones. They waved as he passed through. In his office, he found the police artist's computer-generated sketch of the redhead and messages to call Lois Rappaport and Meg Chang at Channel 6. He dialed Rappaport, then examined the portrait. It showed a very attractive young woman with high cheekbones and a superbly modeled chin. *She looks good,* he thought.

"That you, Frank?" Lois's voice grated against his ear. He wondered if she had a husband, and, if so, how he felt about her when she smiled.

"Yeah, it's me. What's up?"

"I finished the workup on Dietz," she said. "Turns out I was right."

"About what?"

"Oh, thought I told you last night. Dietz was asleep when he was killed."

Asleep! "How do you know that?"

"From the drug screen. High level of triazolam in his blood. It's a classic, Frank. KO girls, dope-'em-and-rob-'em girls—call 'em what you like. They pick guys up, go up to their rooms, spike their drinks, take their cash. They used to use chloral hydrate, the old Mickey Finn. Now they carry triazolam. What they do is they grind up some pills, dilute the powder with vodka, then pour the mix into a vodka-based drink. No taste, no smell, puts you out in five minutes. When you wake up you can be disoriented, depending on the dosage.'' She paused. ''Only difference here is the girl doesn't usually shoot the boy in the head.''

After Janek hung up, he studied the portrait some more. Yes, he decided, there was something very attractive about the girl, something vulnerable in her eyes. He shook his head. *Why would you kill him? What were you after? How could you shoot a person who's asleep?*

Aaron came in. Janek told him what he'd learned. Aaron picked up the portrait.

''It's looking more and more like she's the one, isn't it?''

They discussed whether to hand out the police sketch or restrict its distribution. There were arguments to be made on both sides.

''Channel Six wants an interview. That would be a chance to show the sketches. But we need a lot more before we can name the redhead as a suspect. Meantime, she sees herself on TV, she could get spooked and run.''

Aaron agreed that for the time being they should keep the sketch to themselves. Then he said he was starting to wonder about Dietz. ''I've been talking to his brother. I think there's something wrong there. Like maybe the executive-recruiter story wasn't quite the truth and there was another reason Dietz came to New York.''

''You following up?''

''Sue's on it now. She's talking to his company. Ray's out showing the sketch around the hotel and the neighborhood.'' Aaron lowered his voice. ''How did it go with Kit?''

Janek shrugged. ''One minute we're pals: 'Only you can do this, Frank.' Next she's the boss and I'm the errand boy.'' He exhaled. ''By the way, we're reporting to Deforest.''

Sue came into the room.

"I just got off with Dietz's boss in San Jose—Eliot Cavanaugh, chairman of Sonoron Corp. I should say former boss. Seems Dietz was an executive there until six days ago, when there was a big blowup and he got fired. Cavanaugh says that on his way out Dietz may have stolen some kind of valuable prototype computer chip from a high-security area of their research lab. They think he brought it here to sell to a foreign competitor."

"Well, there you are, Frank. Whoever killed him tossed his room to find the chip."

"Did they report him for stealing?" Janek asked.

"They didn't have any proof it was Dietz, so they just reported it as a robbery. Cavanaugh said at first they were expecting Dietz to offer to return the chip in exchange for a heavy-duty severance package. When they didn't hear from him they figured he was out to screw them. Now Cavanaugh wants to send his security guy here. I got the impression he could care less about Dietz, that all he cares about is getting back his thingamajig."

Janek instructed Sue to run a check on all known KO girls and outstanding KO cases. He made a date to meet Aaron for dinner at Peloponnesus, then phoned Meg Chang. He tried to convince her that the Dietz story wasn't worth her time, but she wouldn't let go. Finally, he agreed to give her an interview in front of the Savoy at eight the following night. Then he called Netti Rampersad.

"Hi! I hear you got goodies," Netti said.

"Goodies for you could be baddies for somebody else."

She laughed. "You're funny, Janek. A witty fellow. Come on down. I could use a chuckle or two."

The address for her office was on Canal Street, within walking distance of the Criminal Courthouse, but the building, on the edge of Chinatown, was mostly occupied by Asian import-export firms and garment manufacturers inhabiting lofts designated by signs in Chinese characters.

Hmmm, this is curious, Janek thought as he mounted a steep stairway to the fourth floor. He was almost out of breath when he reached a bright red fire door. A neat little sign on it said RAMPERSAD & RUDNICK, CRIMINAL DEFENSE. Janek pressed the buzzer. He heard a click. Someone was examining him through a peephole. Then he heard several locks being unlatched. A moment later he was facing Netti, who was standing in the doorway wearing a black tanktop, red sweatpants and immaculate white sneakers. Her face, arms and chest were slick with sweat.

"Ah-so—you come velly fast," she said in the same imitation Chinese accent she'd used when she'd said good-bye to him at the safe house.

Her office was as surprising as her clothing: a vast open space broken up by columns and decorated with old framed posters for Tangier, Port Said and other exotic ports of call. A home Nautilus machine and a StairMaster were arranged like sculptures on a bright yellow platform. On one side of the loft a pretty young woman was working at a computer. On the other, a middle-aged gray-bearded man wearing a yarmulke was talking into a phone.

"That's my partner, Burt Rudnick," Netti said, gesturing. "This is our secretary, Doe Landestoy." Doe looked up and beamed.

"What's with the Chinese-waiter accent?"

"You don't like it?"

"I don't understand it."

Rampersad shrugged. "Just seems to come out of my mouth sometimes."

Maybe you should learn to restrain yourself, Janek thought. He peered around the room. "I've never seen a law office like this."

"It used to be a karate school. It folded and we picked up the lease. The clients like it, those who get to visit us. Mostly, of course, it's us who visit them . . . in jail, prison, wherever." Rampersad grinned. "I like it here. These old walls have seen lots of pain. Ever do karate?"

Janek shook his head. "Too much chop-chop."

She smiled. "Now that you've met everybody and checked out the joint, let's see what you got."

He handed her copies of Tania's affidavits, had her sign a receipt for them, then watched her as she read. She might, indeed, have strange mannerisms, but now, in defense-attorney mode, she was all business.

"My client's going to be pleased," she said when she finished. "You've just handed me his passport out of hell."

"Think you can get him bail?"

"If I get him a new trial, bet your ass he'll be on the street."

"I don't know." Janek shook his head. "He's a rich guy. He might make a run for it."

"He's served hard time. He's no threat to society. Anyway, what's it to you?"

"He killed a cop."

"Oh, sure," she said, turning sarcastic. "Howard Clury. How could I forget?"

At that she launched into a little tirade, working herself up as she went along like an actress delivering a curtain speech. Janek didn't much like her tone, but he was impressed by her passion. Toward the end she was spitting out her words:

"No one ever brought charges against Mendoza for that, did they? Maybe because there was no evidence. But still he had to be a cop-killer, didn't he? So, what did you guys do—excuse me, *some* of you guys? Cooked up as phony a chain-of-evidence story as this town has ever seen, probably even talked some lame-brained boxer into slicing his wrists while taking a bath. But that didn't matter because it brought the Great Cop-killer down. That was the only thing that mattered . . . except maybe to a few of us who happen to believe in the rule of law."

Janek stood back from her. Then he clapped. "Nice summation, Counselor."

"Never hurts to rehearse."

"I'm curious—do you see yourself becoming a legal heroine out of this?"

She shrugged. "Major victory in a high-visibility case—could do wonders for my practice."

"And if some good cops get hurt, Ms. Rampersad, that won't bother you a bit?"

She studied him. "Please call me Netti."

"That's short for—?"

"Henrietta. And don't worry about good cops. They won't get hurt. As for the bad ones—'You do the crime, you do the time.' Isn't that what they say these days?"

Aaron was seated when Janek arrived at Peloponnesus. He was nibbling olives and there was a chilled open bottle of Boutari Retsina on the table. The Greek fish restaurant on White Street catered at lunch to people in the criminal-justice field—court clerks, bondsmen, lawyers, judges. It was barely a quarter full that warm September night.

It was Janek's first chance to unwind since his return, but still he felt tense. He told Aaron about Kit ordering him to pay a courtesy call on Dakin, and then about Sarah and the ninety-eight-hundred-dollar estimate on the roof.

"There she is, two years into a relationship with her accountant friend, Gilette. Half the time he's sleeping over in my old house. I'm sure the only reason they haven't gotten married is she doesn't want to lose the income she gets from me."

"Ever confront her with that?" Aaron asked.

"No. Because I can't prove it. If I bring it up it'll just start an argument, and, for me, one of the great benefits of the divorce is I no longer have to fight with the woman." He shook his head. "Thing is, I feel like I'm being taken."

"I got news for you, Frank—you *are*."

"Yeah . . ."

"I used to like Sarah fine. But what she's doing to you isn't right. Why don't you get yourself a good lawyer, go in tough and cut off the alimony? At the least get it reduced.''

''I've thought of that. But the idea of fighting again after all these years . . .'' He shook his head. ''If we'd had children I think things would have been different. It was her decision, her fear. She was adamant. Whenever I'd bring it up she'd get irrational. After a while I stopped trying to convince her. Then it just seemed to hang between us, this unspoken thing that turned everything mean. We didn't talk about it but it was always there. Instead we talked about crap like the goddamn roof.''

They ordered a selection of *mezes* and two plates of broiled shrimp. Then they discussed the Dietz case.

''Try this, Frank,'' Aaron said. ''Dietz goes down to the bar, picks up the redhead, charms her into coming up to his room. But it's all a setup. She's after the chip. She works for the people he's contacted about buying it. She's sitting down there, available, ready to be picked up. Once upstairs she drugs Dietz, robs him, then shoots him so he can't identify her later.''

Janek smiled. It was a game they often played—Aaron tossing out theories which he then tore apart. They both enjoyed the exercise and it often helped them clarify their views. Also, on this particular evening, it made a good escape from bitter thoughts about Sarah and the prospect of having to face Dakin in the morning.

''Nice theory,'' Janek said, ''except for two little points. The first one bothered me soon as we walked in last night. I felt something was wrong. I couldn't put my finger on what it was. Now I think I know.''

''What?''

''The way the room was tossed tells us the person who searched it didn't find what he or she was looking for. Once you find the object of your search, you've got no motivation to keep ripping stuff up. But that room was torn from top to bottom. It would be an incredible coincidence if our redhead happened to find the chip at the very end.''

Aaron nodded. "Okay, that's pretty good. Now, what's the second thing?"

"The writing on Dietz's chest. Think about it. If the redhead wanted us to know Dietz couldn't get it up, why write on him in mirror-reverse? Only reason to do that would be if the insult were addressed to Dietz himself—which it was. She wrote it so Dietz would read it when he woke up and looked at himself in the mirror. But if she shot him, then she'd know he *wouldn't* be waking up. So why bother to write him a message?"

"Maybe she decided to kill him after she wrote it. Maybe she wanted to make it look like she was a psycho hooker instead of a paid assassin. Or maybe she just used the mirror writing to sidetrack us, the way it's doing now."

Janek laughed. "You're talking like a mystery-story detective."

"You gotta admit that message is bizarre."

"Not just bizarre. Very difficult to write. Here." Janek brought out his notebook, tore out a page and handed it to Aaron with a pen. "Try it. Try writing 'You couldn't get it up' in mirror-reverse."

Aaron stared at the pen and paper, laid down his silverware, took up the challenge. Janek watched, amused, as Aaron struggled to perform the feat.

"You're right," Aaron said after several attempts. "It would take a lot of practice."

"Some people write that way naturally. People with dyslexia, for instance."

"Well, there you are!" Aaron said. "Now we know something about her."

"*If* she wrote it."

"I think we can assume that. Bare skin. Getting it up. It adds up to some kind of sexual confrontation."

"I agree. But I still don't see why she'd kill him."

"She's crazy. A man-hater. Seduces, then kills. Or maybe they had one of those—what do they call 'em? Sexual misunderstandings."

"Like he tried to force himself on her, she said no, he wouldn't take no for an answer, so she shot him dead?"

"Could be." Aaron drained his glass. "What do you think?"

"No sign of a struggle."

"So, maybe she likes a steady target. Put him to sleep, then put a bullet in his brain. No movement, no back talk, no chance he'll cry out or try and take away her gun."

This, to Janek, was the best part of the game—the part where Aaron pressed him, forcing him to come up with a countertheory to fit his own objections.

"What if we're looking at . . . two separate layers of crime," he said.

"Two?"

Janek nodded. "Layer one: Redhead gets picked up in bar of businessman's hotel, goes up to guy's room, spikes his drink, waits till he falls asleep, then robs him of various valuables. Reducing it to schematic form: Two strangers meet, they don't know anything about each other, each has his/her agenda. The meeting ends badly for the man. The girl leaves. End of first crime."

"So then—"

"Second person enters room, someone who *does* know something about the victim. He knows Dietz has a valuable computer chip. Maybe he's the prospective purchaser, maybe someone else. All that matters is he's after that chip. Okay, he finds Dietz asleep, uses the opportunity to make a thorough search but doesn't come up with it . . . because the redhead, who was there first, already found it and took it away."

Aaron's eyes were glowing. "Go on. This is pretty interesting."

Janek sat back. "Unfortunately this brings me to the part that doesn't figure. The second intruder places a pillow on top of Dietz and shoots him in the head."

"I like the idea of two separate crimes. But you're right—killing Dietz doesn't add."

"It might, if we knew more. We've got a way to go on this. I keep asking myself what the intruder or intruders were trying to do—*really* trying to do. On this deal, everything makes sense up to the shooting. Then it falls apart. I can't think of any reason why either person, assuming there were two, would bother to kill a man already asleep."

Aaron thought about that awhile. "Gotta find the girl if only to eliminate her. Maybe in the end it'll turn out she's just a psycho."

"Maybe," Janek said without much conviction.

"Imagine," said Aaron, "a pure psycho killer. After all these brilliant ideas, wouldn't that be a gas?"

Dakin

There was an aura of darkness around Dakin, always had been, as far back as Janek could remember. Even from his first days as a police cadet, he had heard rumors about the chief of Internal Affairs, the man other cops called "The Dark One."

Shortly before graduation from the academy, Janek attended Dakin's famous lecture, affectionately called T&C by the students. Its long title was "Temptation & Corruption: The Dilemma of Police Work." Attendance was compulsory.

Every seat, Janek remembered, was filled that hot summer afternoon. The lecture hall, cooled only by fans, was stifling. Two hundred cadets, dressed in crisply ironed blue shirts, black ties, sharply creased dark blue trousers and gleaming black shoes, sat attentively as The Dark One alternately scolded and exhorted, admonished and implored, like a preacher conjuring up the eternal fires of hell.

Janek would never forget his first impressions—Dakin's fine red hair, fiery yellow eyes, angular body, reed-thin voice, tortured gestures and pale waxen skin. There was nothing dark about The Dark One's complexion, but there was something very dark about his soul. He never smiled. He discoursed about concepts (right and wrong, good and evil) as though they had no connection to living human beings. Dakin's passion burned like a pure blue flame exuding chilly, forbidding fumes. He was humorless, pitiless, steely, intimidating, respected and friendless. He was a "cop's cop" and a legend. Janek feared and disliked him.

Years later, he and Timmy Sheehan would confront Dakin at a special departmental hearing, and although Dakin held the rank of chief and Janek was only a lieutenant, Janek would manage to defeat and discredit him, driving him into a bitter, involuntary retirement.

Now, at 5:45 A.M., Janek sat in his car, parked in Cort City Plaza, across from the stark gray apartment tower where Dakin lived, waiting for the dawn to break.

Dakin's morning routine never varied. A lifetime bachelor, he would emerge from his building at six, stride briskly to the newsstand by the Baychester Avenue station a mile away, buy the *Daily News,* then walk briskly home. It was common knowledge that the best time to approach him was during this daybreak outing. But even then, depending upon the substance of one's mission and the quality of one's entreaties, one always risked dismissal.

Unfastening his eyes from Dakin's door, Janek glanced around. Perhaps, he thought, he might learn something about his quarry from a brief study of his neighborhood.

Cort City Plaza had been built on a forgotten strip of the Bronx separated by a narrow inlet from Pelham Bay Park. Until the day that someone envisioned it, it had been a swamp. Now it possessed the dismal aura of a hundred similar high-rise satellite communities constructed on the outskirts of major cities. In such places it didn't matter which part of the country one was in, because the satellite town always looked the same: bleak, gray, uniform, built on the edge of a great metropolis yet cut off from its rich offerings by high-speed roads on which cars hurtled day and night.

There was nothing in Cort City Plaza, it seemed to Janek, to become attached to; no corner of beauty to inspire a painter or a poet. The only texture was the lack of texture. The landscape was rubble and weeds, the spirit cheerless and forlorn. Yet such a place might well suit The Dark One,

Janek thought; here he could brood in anonymity over the loss of his terrifying power and the awful spectacle of his fall.

Promptly at six, Dakin emerged. Janek locked his car and hurried over.

"Morning, Chief."

Dakin's yellow eyes sliced him like razors. "It's *you,*" he snickered. "Been expecting *you.*"

"Can I—"

"Walk on my right. Hearing's better that side."

Janek positioned himself to Dakin's right, then glanced at his profile. The thin red hair had mostly bleached to white, but the skin was pale as ever, the body was still ramrod straight and the voice was as reedy as the day Janek had heard it deliver T&C at the Police Academy twenty-two years before.

"You got something for me. Spill it."

The imperial manner, too, was still intact. It was as if the heroic days of Dakin's reign had never passed, days when the only thing that mattered was the merciless rooting out of corrupt cops. As they walked together toward the subway station, and Janek began to summarize his interview with Tania, another part of his brain thought back upon the Dakin legend.

There were the stories, told and retold countless times, of how, arresting a cop for corruption or malfeasance, Dakin would call the man aside, place his arm fraternally across his shoulder, then gently recommend that the poor slob blow his brains out. "It's the only honorable way. Spare your family and colleagues the disgrace," Dakin would counsel in a whisper. More than a dozen men, according to the legend, had followed that withering advice.

At the height of his power he had been master of the sting, dangling enticing goodies in front of desperate cops to tempt them down crooked paths. The better the man, so the stories went, the more elaborately Dakin would contrive to sting him. It was as if he had to prove that there was no such thing as an incorruptible cop . . . except, of course, for himself. He, Dakin, was untouchable, inviolate, perfect in his virtue. Unable to face the darkness in himself, he hid behind a façade of rectitude, and from there searched out the weaknesses in others. Looking at him now, Janek understood the role he'd played: *He was our Robespierre.*

"So, that it?" Dakin said when Janek finished summarizing. They were less than a hundred yards from the subway station. The towers of Cort City Plaza, blocking the rising sun, cast lengthy shadows on the stony terrain.

"That's it."

"When're you going to arrest him?"

"Who?"

"Sheehan, of course."

"I'm not going to," Janek said.

Dakin gave him a sharp glance. His amber eyes flickered wildly. "I expect someone sure as hell is!"

Janek shook his head. "No one's going to arrest Timmy. Mendoza's got a new attorney, a brainy young woman with lots of brass. The information's been passed to her. It's up to her to decide what to do with it."

"You're kidding me!"

"I'm not."

"Who cares about Mendoza?"

"I would guess Mendoza does," Janek ventured.

"He's crap. It's us. We're what the case is about. NYPD. Who we are and what we stand for. Nothing less."

Janek exhaled. "I know you feel that way. But to me, that's just a part of it."

Dakin shook his head. Under his left eye a little muscle began to twitch; like an insect it jumped beneath the pale, sallow skin.

"I—" Dakin started to say something, then, unaccountably, he stopped. He stared at Janek, spat at the ground, then plunged forward toward the newsstand.

As Janek watched him buy his paper, he thought back seven years to the last time they'd met.

• • •

It was across an oval table in a nondescript conference room in the Headquarters building. A special departmental hearing was in progress. The judges, three high-ranking officers impaneled by the commissioner to hear Timmy Sheehan's charges, sat at one end, Timmy and Janek sat facing Dakin, and a female police stenographer sat at a little portable table by the door.

The events that led up to that hearing were recounted:

A year and a half after Jake Mendoza's conviction, Mendoza's first appeals lawyer went into court with a statement sworn out by a middle-aged, frizzy-haired Brooklynite, a graphologist named Phyllis Kornfeld. Kornfeld claimed that an NYPD detective, whose name she didn't know, had paid her a thousand dollars to forge Gus Metaxas's suicide note.

The judge convened the parties. Kornfeld gave her testimony and was then cross-examined by the prosecutors. She could produce no evidence to support her allegation, and under harsh questioning admitted she had spent several years in mental institutions. Police handwriting experts reaffirmed that the note had been written in Metaxas's hand. The judge ruled that there were no grounds for a retrial. Mendoza hired a new lawyer. The Mendoza case ground on.

But then a strange thing happened. Six months after the hearing, Phyllis Kornfeld was found tied to her bed, raped and strangled by an intruder. Her apartment had been ransacked. Some valuables, mainly family silver, were taken.

At first the case was treated as a routine robbery-homicide, unconnected to Mendoza, perhaps one of a hundred similar crimes committed in Brooklyn that particular year. But then Dakin's office asked to take it over. The case was reassigned to Internal Affairs. For a while nothing more was heard about it, until one night a panicked Timmy Sheehan knocked on Janek's door.

IA was after him, Timmy said. Dakin was trying to prove

that he, Timmy, had paid to have Kornfeld assassinated. They had a witness, a snitch named Ross Keniston, who would claim that Timmy had tried to hire him to do the job. According to Dakin's theory (leaked to Timmy by an old friend on Dakin's disaffected IA staff), Timmy found another killer, and the rape and robbery portions of the crime were added to divert attention from the motive: Timmy's need to prevent Kornfeld from speaking further about her role as hired forger of the Metaxas note.

"I'm not worried about Keniston," Timmy told Janek that night. "He's an addict and a liar. What worries me is Dakin. I hear he's around the bend, so crazy he's faking up evidence. He's claiming he interviewed Kornfeld before she was killed, and that she IDed me as the one paid her for the forgery."

Janek and Timmy spent the rest of that night frantically war-gaming the problem. There were, they decided, two ways to deal with an IA investigation: The first and most common was to let it take its course, dealing with it when and if charges were formally filed; the second method, rarely employed and filled with risk, was to preempt by lodging countercharges first. This was the route they decided to follow, with Janek acting as Timmy's counsel under a special provision in police regulations.

When the day of the departmental hearing arrived, they were prepared. They had cashed in on all the favors they were owed, and had used all their skills as street detectives to compile a list of Dakin's abuses. Rather than concentrating on his improprieties in the Kornfeld case, Janek launched a broadside attack. Believing Dakin was obsessed with duplicity and plots, he intended to goad him until he acted out.

Dakin, preening in his virtue, was flustered by Janek's litany. Attempting to take up each abuse in turn, he started out fairly well, then turned incoherent.

Janek let him ramble, keeping a close eye on the judges.

When he felt the moment was right, he gently interrupted.

"Everyone's against you. It's all a conspiracy. That's what you're saying, Chief—isn't it?"

Dakin, disarmed by the suggestion, which mimicked the very thoughts he was harboring, nodded fiercely and began to carve the air. He must have realized he was making a bad impression, because he suddenly sat rigid. Then, thrusting his trembling forefinger at Timmy, his reedy voice went shrill:

"That snake killed *my* witness! They're trying to get me now 'cause I'm on to them! Don't you see, it's a diversion, this fuckin' hearing! That snake's a fuckin' killer!"

After his outburst Dakin clamped his jaws. Everyone in the room could hear the crunch of teeth.

Janek turned to the judges, spread his hands and shrugged: "There you are," his gestures said, "the paranoid revealed."

The judges understood. Their voices turned solicitous. When one of them offered to fetch Dakin a glass of water, Janek knew he'd won. It was, he had felt at the time, a brilliant moment, perhaps his finest as a cop. He had successfully sandbagged The Dark One, and, at the same time, lifted suspicion from his friend.

But contrary to expectations, the cloud was not so easily raised. Because the IA case had been rendered incomplete, Timmy's role in regard to the Metaxas note was left unresolved.

The result of the hearing was that Dakin took immediate retirement and Timmy himself retired six months later. Although both men received full pensions, their reputations were besmirched. In the end the special hearing about Dakin's overreaching only added to the cluster of rumors and ambiguities that had come to surround the original Mendoza investigation, turning it into the phenomenon known around the Department simply as Mendoza.

• • •

"Whatsamatter? Dreamin'?" Dakin stood before Janek, clutching his paper, leering. "You took me. Didn't you, Frank?"

Janek glanced into Dakin's eyes. It was the first time the chief had ever called him by his first name. Dakin, however, quickly turned away. Then he started back toward his building, his stride awkward, urgent.

"It was right out of that damn *Caine Mutiny* movie. Get me up there, throw me cream puffs, then watch me destroy myself batting them down too hard. I was never a sophisticated man. I was always upfront direct. One-track mind. Eyes forward, with the blinders on. So you blindsided me and I never even knew it until I turned around and saw the looks on the faces of those judges. Lord, that was something! Then it hit me. I was cooked. I was going down and there was nothing I could do about it. Nothing . . ."

"Look, I don't think we should—"

"What?" Dakin snapped. "Rehash it? Want to pretend it never happened? We'd do better to act like a couple of old generals, crusty World War II types, shooting the bull at a reunion, finding out what the other had in mind the day of the big battle, maybe even fessing up to a few mistakes. Be interesting, I think."

Janek thought through his answer. "But we're not like two old generals. You were a chief—"

"Still am! Don't ever forget it!"

"—and I was and still am a lieutenant. Also, I don't think enough time's passed to heal the wounds."

Dakin nodded. "Fine, that's the way you want it. It was just my way of saying I respect you for what you did, even though I'm the one bore the brunt of it. Your job was to get me. You got me good. I don't hate you for that. The one I blame . . . well, never mind. . . ."

Who the hell does he blame? Janek wondered. *Some power behind me pulling my strings?*

In the end, he knew, it was impossible to probe the labyrinth of a paranoid's mind. There was always one step in the thinking you couldn't make yourself, one room full of conspirators you could never find because it was hidden too deep within the maze.

But Dakin was still rambling:

"Sheehan's your buddy," he sneered. "You don't have the balls to take him down. That's the trouble with having buddies, see. A man calls you 'friend'—he'll always expect a favor. Me, I never had any buddies and I never granted any favors. Not once! Ever! I'm proud of that. They can carve it on my gravestone if they dare. *'No buddies and no favors.'* I'd be pleased to rest under a stone like that. I could rest under it forever!"

Oh, Jesus!

But that wasn't the end of it—Dakin was on a heavy riff. The words continued to tumble out:

"Trouble today is everyone's forgotten the point. You got a department, you keep it clean, no matter who falls in sacrifice. A slime snake like Sheehan poisons the well, then everyone drinks from it gets sick. The Department's been drinking putrid water nine years. Soon the venom'll kill it. Then you'll see the ruin, my friend. The blood'll flow. The city'll drown in puke and gore. It won't be long now, unless someone's got the guts to reach deep down the well and pull the vile slime snake *out*!"

He must always have been this way, Janek thought, *and nobody noticed because they took his ravings as rhetoric.* But Janek knew that it wasn't rhetoric, that what he was hearing was deeply held belief. Dakin was too honest to obfuscate. With him, what you heard was what you got.

God help us! For years we treasured this man and all that time he was a lunatic. Then he thought: *Is it any wonder that so many of us end up putting our pistols in our mouths?*

The Threat

When Janek arrived at Special Squad, he found a fax on his desk. It was from an officer he didn't know named Tom Capiello, a member of the police artists unit. The message was simple and to the point: "Drop by. I've got something to show you."

While Janek was pondering what this might mean, he received a call from his zone commander, Joe Deforest. Deforest said a man named Stephen Kane, chief of security at Sonoron Corporation, had arrived in New York and wanted a briefing on the Dietz case.

"Fine, Joe," Janek said, "send him over. He can tell us more about that stolen chip."

There was a pause at the other end, then Deforest cleared his throat. "Seems Kane's boss, some big shot named Cavanaugh, called the mayor's office last night. Word came down from Kit. The briefing's to be held over there."

"Fine," said Janek. "I'm coming over anyway. I'll drop by early and fill you in."

When he put down the phone, he had no doubt about what had happened. Cavanaugh, the Sonoron chairman, had posed some difficult questions to the mayor—such as, how often are visiting businessmen assassinated in their rooms at top-of-the-line Manhattan hotels? By the time this needling query reached Kit, the order was clear: Kane, Cavanaugh's security chief, was to be shown special deference, which meant don't send him over to Janek's grubby Special

Squad, brief him in a plush suite in the Headquarters building.

Janek quickly gave instructions to Sue and Ray. They were to continue to show the police sketch until they got a lead on the redhead who had accompanied Dietz to his room. Leaving Aaron in charge of the office, Janek taxied downtown to Police Plaza. When he got there he went straight to the artists unit, where he asked the receptionist to point out Capiello.

She gestured across the busy room to a man sitting at a desk against the far wall. As Janek walked over he passed a row of artists working at computer terminals with witnesses.

"Now let's try some noses," he heard one say. "Was it short, long, fat or thin?"

"It was kind of squashed," said the witness, a black lady with steel-gray hair. "You know, like a boxer's."

Capiello looked up just as Janek approached. He was middle-aged with bags under his eyes and a sorrowful, earnest face. He was also one of the few artists in the room who was not sitting before a computer. From the array of art materials in front of him, Janek could see he was one of the last of the breed who sketched freehand with charcoal and pastels.

"Janek?" Janek nodded. Capiello gestured for him to take a chair. "Thanks for coming down, Lieutenant. I could have sent the material over, but I wanted to show it to you myself."

Capiello struck him as the sort of technical policeman who probably didn't get much satisfaction from his work. Now that he had come up with something, he wanted to squeeze a little pleasure out of it.

Capiello pulled out the sketch of the redheaded girl in the Dietz case.

"This isn't my work," he said. "I don't usually look at other artists' composites, but I was working late last night, and on my way out I noticed this one posted by the door.

Don't know why it caught my eye. It just did. I thought the girl looked familiar. But I was too tired to put it together. It didn't hit me till I got home."

Janek smiled. "Happens to me all the time."

"Anyway," Capiello continued, "I wasn't positive till I got in this morning. I came early to check and soon as I saw it I sent you the fax."

Capiello opened the center drawer of his desk, extracted a hand-drawn sketch. He laid it beside the computer-generated drawing of the redhead, then turned both portraits around so that Janek could compare them.

"I drew this three months ago, beginning of the summer, on another case. Hair color's different, cut's different, too, but otherwise the girls look the same."

Janek could see the similarity, especially in the eyes—the same vulnerable eyes that had held his interest the day before.

"What was the complaint?"

"Well, that's the thing," Capiello said. "There wasn't any homicide. Still, I think it's the same person."

Janek studied the two sketches as Capiello explained. *Something about this girl touches me. I wonder why.*

"It was an odd case," Capiello said. "The complaining witness was a magazine editor. I dug up the data." He passed a complaint sheet across the desk. "Anyway, this guy was pretty anguished about what happened to him and adamant about tracking the girl down. Seems he picked her up in a neighborhood bar, then took her home expecting to, you know. . . . But then she put something in his drink that put him to sleep. When he woke up she was gone and so was his money and his watch."

Janek looked up from the sketches. "Anguished?"

Capiello nodded. "That's why I remember him. He talked while I drew. He was very disturbed. Seems the girl did some fairly weird things while he was out, like going through his personal stuff and cutting up his underwear. She also wrote something nasty on his chest. It was strange the way she wrote it, he said. It looked like nonsense till he looked at it in a mirror.''

''So, how was Cuba?'' Deforest asked when Janek stepped into his office. ''You didn't get much of a tan.''

''It wore off,'' Janek said. Deforest laughed. ''I was supposed to be on a covert mission.''

''That's always the trouble when you get involved with Mendoza.'' Deforest shook his head. ''Sooner or later everyone finds out.''

Deforest was a big, blocky man in his early forties, with pale skin and arctic eyes. Although transparently ambitious for bigger and better commands, he was what Aaron called ''a stand-up guy.'' Janek respected him for his intelligence, his record as a working detective and his intense loyalty to subordinates. He also thought Deforest could end up one day sitting behind Kit's desk.

Janek briefed him on the Dietz case. Deforest agreed that finding the girl was the only way to go and that if the artist's sketch was shown on TV, it could scare her off. He also agreed that the mirror-writing connection to Capiello's complainant was a promising lead. ''But I'd hurry if I were you,'' Deforest said. ''A scent like this can go cold pretty quick.''

Promptly at eleven, Deforest's secretary announced the arrival of Stephen Kane. The moment Kane entered, Janek knew he didn't like him. The security man was in his mid-thirties, with a flashy, vain appearance. His loafers were fancy, crafted out of exotic reptile skins, with little tassels affixed to the tops that flopped back and forth as he walked. His watch was showy, a thick Rolex with a diamond-encrusted bezel. These accessories were consistent with the grooming of his hair—long on the sides, fastidiously combed back, meeting and crossing behind his head, then tapering down to a point. To keep up a cut like that, Janek thought, he'd have to see his barber every other day.

After introductions, they sat down in easy chairs at the

informal end of Deforest's office. Janek was amused to see Kane position himself so that he could give his primary attention to the zone commander.

''What've you got to tell me?'' he asked in a manner not contrived to endear him to Deforest.

Deforest looked over at Janek. ''It's Frank's investigation.''

''It's more like what can you tell us?'' Janek said. ''We understand Dietz was recently fired.''

''That's right.''

''What for?''

''Unsatisfactory performance.''

''What does that mean?''

''He wasn't up to the job. Also, he and Mr. Cavanaugh weren't getting along.'' Kane turned back to Deforest. ''You know, this is a very serious matter.''

''We always take homicide seriously, Mr. Kane.'' Deforest glanced at Janek. ''Is there some reason you think we don't?''

''Hey, please, no offense! And I'd appreciate it if you'd call me Steve.''

Deforest didn't respond. Janek was happy to discover he wasn't the only one who didn't like Kane.

''So,'' Janek said, ''why don't you tell us more about Dietz and this missing chip?''

''He took it.''

''Got proof?''

''We don't need proof. Dietz and Cavanaugh were negotiating the terms of Dietz's severance. Then Dietz stole the prototype.''

''Why?''

''Power play. He wanted to blackmail the company. He was going to sell it to one of our competitors unless we bought it back.''

''Dietz threatened that?''

''Not in so many words. But that's what he had in mind. The payoff would be his golden parachute.'' Kane paused, then he grinned. "I understand there was a redhead involved."

"Where'd you hear that?" Deforest asked.

"I'm staying at the Savoy. It's where our people always stay. This morning I had some time to kill so I asked a few questions. I got a look at the sketch your guy's been showing around."

Janek turned to Deforest, who was glaring at Kane. *You just blew it, buddy.* Kane, too, must have realized that he was not ingratiating himself.

"Hey, guys! What's the problem? All I did was talk to some people at the hotel. Nothing wrong with that."

"So long as you didn't leave the impression you were on my squad," Janek said.

Kane smiled. "Look, we're all pros. I used to work in the L.A. sheriff's office." When neither Janek nor Deforest acted impressed, Kane sputtered on. "Something valuable's been stolen from Sonoron. We feel we have the right to try and get it back."

"Tell us about this chip," Deforest said. "What does it look like?"

"It's small. Like this." Kane reached into his pocket and pulled out a mock-up. "You can keep this if you want." He handed the mock-up to Deforest, who inspected it carefully, then passed it to Janek.

"Find anything like this, Frank?" Janek shook his head. "If we find it we'll let you know," Deforest said.

At that point Kane had to understand he was in major trouble. But he seemed incapable of breaking his momentum.

"I hear Dietz's room was tossed," he said. "Look, guys—it would be great if we could share."

Again Deforest turned to Janek. "You want to respond, Frank?"

"It's like this, Mr. Kane," Janek said. "I'm investigating a homicide. You're looking for a chip. Maybe they're connected, maybe not. As for sharing, my suggestion is you tell me everything you know about Dietz and who he may have contacted here. Then go back to California. I'll keep you informed."

Kane's eyes turned mean. "Mr. Cavanaugh will hear about this. Your superiors, too."

"Hear about what?" Deforest asked. "That we won't co-investigate with a corporate security man? That's policy, Mr. Kane, so I don't see our superiors getting too upset about it. Anyway, they're not the investigator. Janek is, and he's one of the finest in the city. You're getting our best man. If Cavanaugh calls me, I'll be happy to explain that to him myself."

"Okay, all right." Kane looked resigned. "What do you want to know?"

"What's so important about this chip?"

"Proprietary information available to any knowledgeable person who examines it."

"They'd clone it, is that what you're worried about?"

"It's not that simple. There're other companies with a hundred twenty-eight megabit chips in development. It happens there're things about our Omega they'd all like to know."

"Such as?"

"What it's made of. It isn't silicon. Most important, if they got a good look at the prototype, they'd have a good idea how we plan to price it. For a competitor that would be an enormous advantage."

"You've got patents?"

"Of course. And if there's infringement we'll probably win our case—after twenty years. By then we'll probably be out of business, too. It's a rough game we're in. You have no idea."

"I still don't get it," Deforest said. "Once you manufacture the chip, anyone can look at it."

"Yeah, but then it's too late. We'd have two to three years' lead. We'd make a hell of a killing before the rest of the industry caught up."

"How much of a killing?"

Kane settled back. He turned smug. "If the Omega is as good as we think it is and Sonoron is first out with a one to twenty-eight—then figure . . . five billion dollars." Kane spoke slowly to make sure the magnitude of the sum sunk in. He turned to Janek. "I'd like to work with you, Lieutenant. I think there's a mutual interest here."

"How do you figure?"

"This redhead—she could have been a plant working for one of the Jap companies that would trade its left nut for a look at the Omega. They're all into industrial espionage. This is just the kind of operation they run."

"Tell me more."

"The way I figure it, Dietz came here and got in touch with one of them. He says he's got a prototype Omega. What would they pay to have a look? They're interested but they stall—they have to check with the home office in Tokyo. 'No problem,' Dietz says, 'I'm here at the Savoy.' So they sic their red-haired operative on him. She 'meets' him in the bar, gets seductive and things start getting cozy. Then, when they go up to his room for a little hanky-panky, she shoots him in the head and steals the chip."

"Interesting."

"It works for me."

"I'd like a list of competitors you think would do a thing like that."

Kane grinned. "I can make you a list. Then together we can run it down."

"Sorry," Deforest said, "we can't do that."

"That your final word?"

"It's policy."

Kane sat back. "I'm sorry, too." He reached into his pocket, pulled out a document and offered it to Deforest. When Deforest refused to take it, Kane laid it on the table. "This is a notarized consent from Dietz's widow authorizing me to inspect his effects."

Janek smiled. "You won't find your Omega there."

Kane smiled back. "I know you New York cops think you're hot shit, but you can screw up like everybody else."

Deforest shrugged. "You can go through his effects. There'll be a detective present."

"What about the hotel room?"

"You'll need a court order for that."

Deforest rose, started toward his desk, but Kane wouldn't let go.

"What about a picture of the girl?"

Deforest pivoted. "What about a list of your competitors?"

Kane grinned. "Talking a trade?"

"Slot your list to Janek and we'll see," Deforest said.

"I think that's him," Aaron said. They were sitting in the reception area at *Smart Money*.

Janek looked up. A tall, well-dressed man with thinning brown hair was conferring with the receptionist. The receptionist gestured toward them. The man approached.

"Lieutenant Janek?" Janek nodded. "I'm Roger Carlson. Please come this way."

He led them through an opaque door marked EDITORIAL, then down a corridor lined with cubicles. Janek heard the sounds of a typical Manhattan office: air-conditioning, faintly ringing phones, muted click of fingers striking computer keyboards, occasional human utterances too hushed to comprehend. Every so often a man or woman would emerge from one cubicle and slip into another. There was an aroma of coffee in the air, but not of cigarettes.

"Please, in here," Carlson said, opening the door to a small conference room. There was a round table, a set of pedestal chairs, a bookcase filled with back issues of *Smart Money* and, after Carlson shut the door, silence.

"My cubbyhole's a little small," he said. "Anyway, I want this to be private." He paused. "May I see the picture?"

Janek nodded to Aaron, who pulled the sketch out of his

briefcase and passed it to Carlson across the table.

"Yeah, this is definitely her," Carlson said, staring at the sketch. "The hair's different, but not the eyes. I'll never forget those eyes." He looked up at Janek. "I still find the whole episode pretty embarrassing."

"We're not here to embarrass you." He found himself liking Carlson and wanting to reassure him.

"I know that. But, see, I also find it painful. I was stupid and I paid the price." Carlson shook his head. "It's been months since it happened. I still think about it every day. It still pains me and it still makes me mad. I went to a shrink for a while but he couldn't help me. I realize it's something I'm going to have to work out for myself. I also think if you caught her—I told this to the other detective, Stiegel, but he didn't seem particularly interested."

"We're interested," Aaron said.

"Frankly, you guys seem a lot smarter. I hope you don't mind my saying that."

"There're all kinds of detectives, Mr. Carlson," Aaron said. "What did you tell Detective Stiegel?"

"I told him I thought that if you caught her, and I had the opportunity to face her in court and testify—I thought I might start to feel better about the incident. That is, if you can call it an incident. To me it felt more like a trauma."

Janek urged Carlson to tell his story from the beginning with as much detail as he could recall. Carlson nodded and began. As Janek listened he found himself drawn in. Carlson was articulate, not surprising for a professional writer, but there was a special quality to his narration that went beyond other recitals Janek had heard from other well-educated, well-spoken complaining witnesses. There was an intensity that etched out the scenes, making them extremely vivid. It was as if Carlson were describing an encounter that was, in some way, a defining moment in his life.

"She said she worked in publishing, that she was in the publicity department at Simon & Schuster. I've thought about that ever since—why she chose that particularly phony story out of all the other stories she could have used."

"Why do you think?" Aaron asked.

"Because, like a talented, intuitive actress, she spotted me as someone who would buy that particular line. She was totally convincing. She seemed just like a publishing type. I've even thought maybe she was, and that's how she was able to bring the impersonation off. Of course I checked with S&S. They never heard of her. Not that the name she gave me, 'Gelsey,' was any less phony than her quote occupation unquote, or her very comforting description of herself as a history professor's daughter. The way I see it, everything she said was contrived to make me believe we shared the same background and values."

"We'll check the publishing houses," Janek said to Aaron.

Carlson's response was touchingly grateful. "I was hoping you'd say that. The other guy, Stiegel—that didn't seem to occur to him."

"You're in good hands now, Mr. Carlson," Aaron assured him.

But Carlson seemed obsessed with the girl:

"She came out of the rain like a phantom. I remember thinking, as we walked back to my place: 'Well, say what you like about New York, life here sure can be sweet.' See, there I was, sitting in my pub, in my usual depressed state, staring at the door, hoping something interesting might happen and knowing in my heart that nothing would, when this blond creature suddenly waltzes in out of the sorrowful, soggy night. Slim, gorgeous, the girl I'd been waiting for . . . oh, probably the last five years. There she was at last, the prowling 'lone-wolf type' I keep reading about in magazines but never seem to meet. And if that wasn't enough, she lets me pick her up. And after an hour or so of gab she starts talking about taking off our pants. It was unbelievable, like something out of a movie, or a dream. . . ."

"You liked her?"

"I was crazy about her! She seemed like a really great girl. The kind you dream about, maybe even fall in love with." Carlson paused. "Notice I say 'the kind.' When I think back I keep coming up with the idea that she was a certain kind of girl, a certain *type.* And, of course, that was the core of her act—she was much too good to be true."

Carlson closed his eyes. "Something incredibly frightening about being put to sleep by a stranger. I'd picked her up a couple of hours before. Actually she picked me up; I understand that now. The stuff she told me—the lines were so good I could have written them myself. So, anyway, I lured her up to my apartment. At first she pretended she wasn't all that eager. I had to talk her into it. Then she made that remark about taking off our pants, so casually, so naturally, I couldn't believe my ears. It was so damn sexual. Soon as she said it I got incredibly turned on. Common sense—forget it! I just wanted to get her up to my place and make crazy love to her for hours. So there we were a few minutes later, sitting opposite one another in my living room. She starts touching herself, her hair, her breasts. Then she sticks out her legs. By this time I'm going nuts. Then, suddenly, I start to drift off. Then I notice she's staring at me, her eyes just the way they are in the sketch here, looking at me like I'm some kind of pinned-down bug. That's what struck me—the way she watched me, curious, very curious, like she was waiting to see how I'd react. That's when I knew she'd spiked my drink. But it was too late to fight it—I was going under fast. I knew in a few seconds I'd be in her power. I knew, too, there wasn't a damn thing I could do about it. I didn't know what her game was or what she was capable of doing. All I knew was that I was going to belong to her. I was utterly, totally terrified."

It was strange, Janek thought, the way Carlson described the girl's eyes in the sketch. He himself could see no evil in them. He could see only fragility and hurt.

Carlson shook his head. "I remember I tried to strike out at her. My arms felt like lead. I tried to stand but it was like I was wearing . . . cement boots. All I remember of those last few seconds is the way she was peering at me. So curious, so very curious . . ."

Carlson smiled to break the spell. "Well, I woke up. Thank God! Believe me, I was grateful. Even when I found myself in that strange position on my couch, pants down, shirt open, watch gone, credit cards and IDs spread out neatly on the coffee table. Then, on my way to the bathroom, I noticed the way she had my stuff arranged on the bed. She'd made a design out of my things, and she'd cut away the pouches on my jocks. There was a nasty message conveyed by that: 'I could have castrated you.' That's how I took it. Then I saw all my personal stuff—letters, family photos—spread around in this strange, orderly way. From that I got her second message: 'I know all about you, but you don't know shit about me.' So, okay, I stumbled on into my bathroom, and then, when I looked at myself in the mirror, I got her final message, the big one she wrote directly on my skin.

"At first I was scared. She'd used red ink. I thought: 'Shit! She carved me up. That's my blood!' Then I saw what she wrote, and, of course, every word of it was true. 'You are a total jerk.' Like, yeah! I was! She knew it and she wanted me to know she knew it, too. So, okay, that was her major message. A warning: 'You acted like an asshole, you got what an asshole gets. But, you better believe this, it could have been a lot worse!' I remember I smiled. I was very ashamed but also extremely grateful she'd spared my life. I figured I got off easy. I could chalk the incident up to experience. Why bother with the cops? You guys have enough to do. I could afford the loss. I'd learned my lesson. So why pursue it, right?"

"But you did pursue it, Mr. Carlson," Janek said.

Carlson nodded. "You bet I did! Over the next few days I thought a lot about what she'd done, how deep she'd gotten into me and how much worse it could have been. What if she'd given me an overdose? I could've died."

Janek studied Carlson. "There's more to it, isn't there?"

Carlson nodded again. "It was the writing. I couldn't get over the way she handled that, like she knew exactly what I was going to do—wake up, stumble into the bathroom, look at myself in the mirror. So, very thoughtfully she wrote the message in mirror-writing. Think about that. It's pretty amazing. It establishes total control. It also told me that it was important to her that I see myself through her eyes. I was a jerk, a sucker—so she put a dunce's cap on my head. It's like she knew exactly what to do, played her game to a fault. She was . . . I don't know, almost superhuman. That's why I think she's dangerous, Lieutenant. Why I think she's got to be stopped."

"We'll stop her," Aaron said.

"Stiegel told me there's a ring of these girls. 'Bad girls,' he called them. 'Happens to guys all the time.' " Carlson's smile turned ironic, but Janek saw a haunted bitterness in his eyes. "What're you going to do? The city's falling apart. It's the new Calcutta, the new Beirut. Who cares if some magazine writer got rolled and it freaked him out? I mean, shit! The bridges are crumbling, the tunnels are corroding, the subway's a nightmare, the infrastructure's shot. In the parks, gangs go on wildings. Kids shoot each other in the schools. So, what's the big deal? I wasn't wounded. No blood was spilled. I've just got a little anxiety, that's all. But, I'll tell you something"—Carlson lowered his voice—"I'm planning to leave this place soon as I can. I'll probably end up in the suburbs doing corporate writing, annual reports, boring stuff I wouldn't have touched before." He laughed. "Who'll care, right? I'm alive. A guy gets mugged and decides to leave—why should anyone care about that?"

Janek studied Carlson. The man had been deeply injured. "We care," he said softly.

"Yes, thank you. I can see you do. You're very kind."

Carlson paused. ''I don't sleep too well these days. I figure I was this close.'' He held his thumb and forefinger a fraction of an inch apart. ''Just this close to death . . .''

Descending in the elevator, Aaron glanced at Janek. ''To hear him tell it, we're looking for the most evil woman that ever lived.''

''That sure is the way he sees her,'' Janek agreed.

Out on the street he told Aaron he wanted to know everything there was to know about the ''bad girls.''

''How 'bout a briefing from Stiegel?''

''Do you know him?''

''I met him couple of times. Typical low-end detective.''

''Have Sue get in touch with him, line up a meeting for me around six.''

Aaron nodded.

''Meantime I want you to check out the Sonoron security guy, Stephen Kane. He says he used to work in the L.A. sheriff's office.''

''Something wrong with him?''

Janek shrugged. ''He didn't appeal to me. Maybe you can find me a reason.''

He found Timmy Sheehan at O'Malley's, waiting at the bar. This time he had no difficulty recognizing him. Timmy's cheeks looked pinker than usual, and his thick gray hair, rising straight from his forehead, was badly in need of a cut. On closer inspection, the pinkness proved to be a web of tiny broken blood vessels on the surface of Timmy's face.

When they moved to a table in the rear, Janek got the impression that Timmy had been sitting in O'Malley's for some time, perhaps most of the afternoon, guzzling beers, munching on a corned beef sandwich or two, watching the day's interminable Yankees game on TV.

''So, how's the world traveler?'' Timmy asked, arching his brows.

"You're looking at one tired cop," Janek said. "It wasn't the most enjoyable trip I ever took."

"Still, you made it back. Those Commies didn't eat you up?"

"They nearly did."

"Had some trouble, did you?"

"Nothing I couldn't handle. Anyway . . ."

"Yeah, anyway—you talked with the lady?" Janek nodded. "Always wondered what she'd be like."

"She's an educated woman. Works as an economist in the Cuban Finance Ministry. Married to a guy who manages a citrus farm. Has a kid, a boy. She's aged a little, just like the rest of us."

"Yeah, isn't it funny how you get a fix on a person, then five, ten years later you run into them, and they're older. Always takes a minute or two to reorient yourself."

Janek knew that Timmy was stalling, that he was eager to hear what he'd found out, but was deliberately prolonging the small talk to demonstrate how little he cared. Timmy, he knew, would rather die than show interest; his position, restated ever since Mendoza's conviction, was that Mendoza was closed.

Janek decided to drop a bomb. "I saw Dakin this morning."

Timmy's eyelids didn't waver. "That must have been fun. How's the old guy doing? Still live out in that crap hole—what the hell they call it? Cortland Park?"

"Cort City Plaza," Janek said. "As if you didn't know."

Timmy beamed. "Known me too many years, partner. You see through all my tricks."

"I'm sure seeing through the one you think you're pulling on me now."

"Are you?" Timmy grinned. "And which one might that be?"

Janek shrugged. "Every traveler's got a tale."

"That so? Come to think of it, my grandmother used to say something like that." Timmy scratched his head. "She had another saying, too. Want to hear it?''

''Why not?''

'' 'Never let them see you cry.' I never forgot that one. Kind of a good one to live by, don't you think?''

Janek put down his beer. ''Can it, Timmy. You're as keen to hear what Tania said as Dakin was. Maybe more.''

''I won't deny it, Frank—I'm a wee bit curious.'' He picked something out of his teeth. ''Not that I give a rusty fuck.''

''Of course not! So, now that's been established, let's get to the bottom line.''

Timmy's eyes went flinty. ''Yeah, let's get to it.''

''Tania says the letter lies. She never brokered any arrangement with Metaxas, not for that night, not ever. She also says Clury wasn't blackmailing anybody, he was employed by Edith to get the goods on Mendoza so Edith could get herself a ball-busting divorce.''

Suddenly Timmy's features started to contort, as if he were trying to keep control of his expression. ''If all that's true, why didn't she speak up? Pardon me for asking, partner, but why'd she fuckin' run down to Cuba and hide out?''

''She found the body. She's the one screamed so loud the neighbor called nine-one-one.''

''Oh, gracious me!'' Timmy's voice went mock falsetto. ''Such a ghastly sight it must have been!''

''She was scared,'' Janek said. ''She saw her employer hanging from a hook. She was sure Mendoza had done it. So she did the normal thing. She ran.''

Timmy bit into his lower lip. ''And now she wants to clear the air. What a good girl she must be, so straight and honest—the little bitch!''

''I cornered her, Timmy. That's why she talked.''

''Yeah.'' Timmy stared at him a moment, then got up from the table and walked over to the bar. Janek watched as he ordered an Irish whiskey, threw it back, ordered another, drank that one off, too, then lumbered back to the booth. Timmy stared at him again and this time Janek saw that his eyes were red and crazy.

"How can you be so fuckin' stupid, Frank?"

"Is that what I am?"

"About this. Forget Mendoza. It's a tar baby. The more you punch it, the more stuck you're gonna get. Let the others rant if they want. Dakin, Kit, the whole dumb crew downtown. Mendoza's in a cell where he belongs. It's over. End of story."

"If there's been a miscarriage, it's gotta be set right. You know that."

"Jesus! Listen to yourself! You sound like a scumbag attorney! The man's a piece of shit. He killed a cop. He deserves a living death."

"What're you saying?"

"What do you think?"

"I think you're saying there was something wrong with that note," Janek said, feeling a terrible ache beginning to rise out of his stomach.

"What the fuck difference does it make?"

"Oh, Timmy! Timmy!" The ache was curling around his chest. "I defended you, remember? I broke Dakin for you. Christ!"

Timmy sneered. "Oh, yeah, I forgot!" He coughed, then smacked the table with his fist. "Do I remember? What the hell do you think?" He glared at Janek, eyelashes flickering, his eyes watery and bloodshot. "We both know Mendoza had his wife beaten to death. We know he ordered Clury killed. How he did it, who he hired, how much he paid, the fuckin' details—who cares?"

"Christ!"

"You keep saying that! Don't 'Christ!' me, partner! You think law enforcement's a kid's game where winning's less important than playing by the rules? No cop worth his salt thinks like that."

Janek wanted to hit him then. Instead he just stared.

Timmy didn't look away. "You're telling me you faked the evidence."

Timmy laughed. "Am I? Would you believe me now whatever I said? Think it through. If you really believe I faked that note, you also have to think I had that old bat, what's-her-name, Kornfeld, knocked off, too. Like maybe I personally raped the cunt and stole her ratty silverware. Sound like me, Frank? Huh?"

Timmy took a draft of beer. The foam clung to his lips.

"You'd also have to believe Dakin isn't a psycho, Mendoza's pure as snow, and I'd risk everything, my pension, my whole fuckin' life, to close out a case because . . . *why?* I couldn't handle it? You have to believe the five grand I supposedly used to pay for the money order to Metaxas's mom came out of—what did Dakin say? Dough I took off of some coke dealer he couldn't name? I can't remember all the crap he tried to sling at me."

Timmy paused to wipe his mouth.

"Wanna know something, Frank? At this point I don't care. Hear what I'm sayin'? I'm sick of it! The whole fuckin' mess. You wanna try and get to the bottom of it, go ahead. Spend the next ten years on it if you want to. You won't get anywhere. Kit won't either. But be careful. Because if by some fluke you happen to stumble into the real heart of the thing, something bad might befall you. Personally speaking, I'd feel real sorrowful if such an event should come to pass."

"The real heart of the thing"—what the hell does he mean by that?

Janek stared into Timmy's eyes. "Is that a threat, Timmy?"

Timmy's hands were trembling. "Me threaten *you*? You gotta be kidding."

"Then, what're you saying?"

Timmy's eyes focused down to rivet points as he met Janek's stare. Suddenly he laughed. "Oh, hell! Do what you want. Nothing I say's going to stop you, is it, partner?"

With that, he set his palms on the table and slowly pushed himself to his feet. He towered over Janek for a moment, then turned his back and stumbled toward the door. Just as he reached it, he turned again, squinted and peered back at Janek through the gloom. Then he laughed a final time, a loud, high-pitched cackle Janek had never heard from him before. Then he stumbled out into the street.

Janek was still shaking when he met up with Sue in front of the Seventeenth Precinct on East Fifty-first. It was eight o'clock, the sky was dark, and he was exhausted from a day that had begun at dawn with one maniac and finished in the afternoon with another. *Dakin, Timmy—they're both crazy. Fuck 'em! Forget about 'em! Get on with your lovely, lonely life!*

However, the sight of Sue's glistening eyes and ardent, youthful face revived his faith in his fellow cops. He thought: *At least there're a few not tainted by that stinking case.*

"Stiegel's in a bar on First Avenue," Sue told him. "He was getting annoyed sticking around, so I told him to go get a drink." She paused. "I don't think you're going to like him much, Frank."

They walked three blocks to the bar. It wasn't what Janek expected. He knew some of the places in the neighborhood, overpriced Yuppie hangouts, but the one Stiegel had chosen was the crummiest of all—smoky, noisy, with a special aroma that told Janek it was a haunt for alcoholics.

Sue pointed out the detective from the door. Stiegel had the kind of sloping body that always reminded Janek of a big piece of fruit. His hair was crew cut and his eyes were tired. He sat alone at a small table nursing a bourbon, inhaling deeply from a cigarette and staring vacantly at the wall. As Janek approached he felt like an intruder, catching another man in an unguarded moment. While Sue introduced them, he studied Stiegel carefully. *There's no bottom to this guy,* he thought.

"I heard of you," Stiegel said. Janek nodded. He noted that Stiegel spoke in a hoarse whisper, a cigarettes-and-whiskey voice. "I heard you were down in Jamaica working on that Medina thing."

"Mendoza," Sue corrected him.

Stiegel nodded. "Yeah . . . right." Then he brightened. "Either you guys wanna drink?" Janek and Sue shook their heads. Stiegel shrugged. "I'm off-duty, so what the hell." He swallowed a mouthful from his glass, set it down carefully, pushed his cigarette into an ashtray, then sat back ready to talk. "Sue tells me you want a rundown on the bad girls. I don't know much—just they pick up guys in hotel bars, drug 'em, roll 'em and write on 'em." Stiegel grinned.

"Carlson wasn't picked up in a hotel. But his complaint got slotted to you."

Stiegel shook his head. A curl of smoke from the half-extinguished cigarette wrapped his face like a veil.

"You know how it is, Lieutenant—you luck into something couple of times, all of a sudden you're the Department expert."

"Sure, I know how that goes."

"Thing is, I got maybe seventy, eighty open cases, of which less than a dozen are bad-girl deals. A caseload like that, I can't worry too much about guys let themselves get rolled." Stiegel leaned forward. His eyes turned canny. "Still, I put it together. The victims give different descriptions but the MO's always the same. I figure there's a ring of 'em. 'Bad girls,' I call 'em." He laughed. "Not bad, huh?"

Janek glanced over at Sue; she rolled her eyes. Stiegel, Janek knew, was just the sort of third-rate detective she most despised.

"So, who are these bad girls?" Janek asked.

"Beats me, Lieutenant."

Sue tightened her lips to show disgust. "Just let the cases pile up, that it, Detective?"

Stiegel shrugged. "What else can I do? I send the victims over to the artists unit. Makes 'em feel better. Helps 'em get it off their chests. Not the writing, but the shame."

"You must have found out something," Janek said. "What about the body writing? What'd you make of it?"

"That's the best part, isn't it?" The canny eyes again. "See, most of the marks are married and from out of town. I think the girls're only interested in out-of-town married guys. Then, after they take them down, they write on 'em like you said. I've seen some weird stuff since I started taking these complaints. There's this one Oriental girl, she writes on the guys in Chinese. The others write in English, but they end up saying the same stuff."

"Which is?"

"Insults—'Asshole,' 'Shit face,' 'Stupid,' like that. There was this one mark, the girl wrote on him, 'Your cock's so small I couldn't find the worthless thing.' " Stiegel laughed. "Surprised the guy had the guts to file a complaint, but he was so mad he was willing to take the ridicule. Anyway, that's when I figured out why they write on them the way they do."

"Which is—?" Sue asked.

"To make the mark think twice about reporting it. Way I figure, he's got enough to do getting the writing off. The girls use indelible ink. You got to scrub yourself raw to get it out. And then I asked myself, how does a guy explain something like that? Does he say to the wife: 'Gee, honey, I was up in my hotel room having a little drinky-poo with this whore when she dosed me out and wrote this awful thing around my nipples'?" Stiegel shook his head. "I don't think so. Do you, Lieutenant?"

"Seems unlikely," Janek agreed.

"That's why they do it. Keeps the guys quiet. I figure they maybe do a hundred, two hundred jobs for every one gets reported."

Stiegel, Janek felt, had propounded a perfectly reasonable theory. It explained the skin writing, though not the use of mirror-reverse.

"Any other cases where the girl used mirror writing?"

"Just Carlson. Except for the blonde who took him, and the Oriental girl, the rest of them write their insults straight."

"And you never got close to anything?"

Stiegel shook his head.

"A dozen cases—there must have been something," Sue said.

Stiegel finished off his drink, signaled the waiter for another, then stared into Sue's eyes.

"There was this girl, a year ago . . . maybe two." His voice turned vague.

"What about her?"

"It was at Roosevelt Hospital. She stumbled into the ER, her face cut up real bad. What brought me into it was what she told the triage nurse. She said she'd been sliced up by some guy in a hotel room when she tried to dope his drink."

"You interviewed her?"

"Tried to. But she wouldn't talk. Maybe I could have pushed it, but the way her face was messed up, I just let it go. I got my own way of doing this job that you people probably wouldn't approve. If someone doesn't want to talk to me, I forget about 'em."

Sue gaped, as if she couldn't believe what Stiegel had just said. Janek brought out Capiello's sketch of the redhead. Stiegel squinted at it.

"No, that's not her." He looked up. "Looks a little like the one took down Carlson, doesn't she? But, I don't know, different somehow."

"This girl at Roosevelt—did you take notes?"

Stiegel shook his head. "I'm not too big on notes."

"Try and remember. What time of year was it?"

"Let's see." He scratched his head. "I remember it was cold."

"Last winter?"

"Maybe the winter before. February, March, something like that."

Janek nodded at Sue and she nodded back, their shared acknowledgment that they'd gotten about all Stiegel had to offer. As they stood to leave, Sue turned back. Stiegel was staring at the wall.

"Keep up the good work, Detective," she said. Her sarcasm was unmistakable, but Stiegel didn't notice.

Outside the bar, Sue vented her anger: "Couple more bozos like him and we can turn the city over to the felons."

"I've seen worse," Janek said. "His theory about the writing wasn't bad." They began to walk back toward the One-seven.

"Doesn't take a rocket scientist to figure that one out." She paused. "When I meet a guy like that, I'm ashamed to be in the same outfit."

"Worn-out detectives come and go. Don't hate him, pity him. Remember: 'There but for the grace of God . . . ' "

Sue looked at Janek curiously. "If I thought I was going to end up like Stiegel I think I'd eat my gun."

Janek winced.

They walked a block in silence. Then Janek turned to her: "What I want you to do is find that girl, the one who got sliced in the hotel."

"There ought to be something in the hospital records."

Janek nodded. "Find her, handle her right and she may put you on to the rest of them."

"And once we're on to the bad girls, maybe we can find the girl did Dietz."

"That's the idea."

When they reached the precinct, Janek started to look for

a cab. "I'm due at the Savoy for a stand-up with Channel Six."

"I'll drop you," Sue said, "then head over to Roosevelt. I want to get started on this right away."

Janek could have kissed her. "You like the work, don't you?" he asked as he slipped into her car.

"Want the truth?" Janek nodded. "I love it—every friggin' minute. I love it so much my lover's jealous. She says I'm more committed to it than her. And you know what, Frank? She's friggin' right!"

The interview went fairly well, he thought. There was the usual obligatory camaraderie with the reporter, or "wax job" as Aaron called it—which ended the moment the cameras began to roll. Then Meg Chang transformed herself into the shrewd, street-smart TV journalist she was, all canny questions and meaningful squints:

"We understand Mr. Dietz was shot in the head."

"That's correct."

"We also hear his room was ransacked. Was there a robbery, Lieutenant?"

"There are things missing. But we're not sure robbery was the only motive."

She examined him skeptically. "Does this mean that visitors aren't safe from crime even in a luxury hotel?"

"It doesn't mean that at all. We're still investigating. My preliminary opinion is that Mr. Dietz was targeted."

"There're rumors around the hotel that shortly before he was killed he was seen with a redheaded woman in the downstairs lounge."

"Sorry, Meg—you know I can't discuss an ongoing investigation."

She nodded curtly, then turned directly to the camera:

"There you have it. Lieutenant Janek will not confirm the presence of a *mystery redhead* seen with Philip Dietz just before he was killed. Meantime, the question hangs—are visitors to Manhattan safe, even inside two-hundred-fifty-dollar-a-night hotel rooms? This is Meg Chang, *Channel Six News,* in front of the Savoy."

Although he was exhausted, he couldn't get to sleep. The encounters of the day kept ricocheting inside his brain. Dakin, Capiello, Kane, Carlson, Timmy, Stiegel—as soon as he finished reviewing his meeting with one, memories of his meeting with another would intrude.

The confrontations had been too intense, the aroused emotions too inflamed, for him simply to push the skirmishes out of mind. These men haunted him—their sad, canny or glaring eyes; their ravished, hard or angry faces. There was a common element, he realized: Each, in his way, was a victim of the city and each had found his own way of coping with its violence. Even Kane, from out of town, seemed, with his threats and games, like a New Yorker.

Close the album, let their faces fade. Plenty of time to think about them tomorrow.

He shut his eyes tightly, then slowly relaxed until his eyelids gently met. The image of the redhead came into his mind, the two artists' sketches superimposed. *Yeah,* he thought, *something about her, something about her eyes . . .*

He took a half dozen deep breaths, rolled over onto his side, exhaled, then felt himself finally falling—falling into sleep.

A quarter hour later his telephone rang. Although it took him only a couple of seconds to come awake, the process seemed interminable, as if he were rising slowly from a deep, dark well. Grasping for the receiver, he knocked the phone to the floor.

"Frank? Are you there?" When he picked up the handset he heard Sarah's voice.

"Yeah, I'm here," he said. "I was asleep."

"Sorry. I didn't know. It's just eleven."

"I had a tough day. Maybe you could call back—"

"I want to talk about the roof. I left a couple of messages."

"I got them. Why don't we—?"

She interrupted. "That last estimate's pretty good. I told the contractor you wouldn't pay five figures."

He thought a moment, then made up his mind. "Yeah, well, I'm not going to pay anything."

Silence. Her voice went terse. "What do you mean, Frank?"

"Just what I said. Don't count on me. I'm out."

"This is pretty strange. I thought we had an understanding."

"I told you I'd consider it. I have. It's your problem now. So, please, let's not talk about it anymore."

A long silence. "May I ask why this change of heart?"

Sure, that's fair. "I don't feel like paying for it, okay?"

Another silence, then she hissed, *"You are a bastard!"*

"Don't start on me, Sarah."

"You broke your word!"

"I never gave you my word."

"Of course you did!"

"No," he said. "You heard it that way because you wanted to."

"Not true, Frank!"

"It's true."

"I can't believe you'd break your word *just like that.* Without telling me. Without even—"

Suddenly there was an explosion, so close it pained his ears. Then he heard pieces of metal cascading down upon the street. His first thought was that a gas main had exploded and ripped open the pavement.

"Hold on. Something happened."

He got out of bed. Carrying his phone, he went into the living room to look out the window. People in the building across the way were standing in nightclothes in lit windows staring down.

He moved closer to the glass to see what they were staring at. It was the wreckage of a car. There wasn't much left of it, just the frame, a hulk of smoldering steel. The hood, doors and other parts were strewn about.

Then it hit him. It was *his* car. The smoke was rising from the remains of his Saab, parked where he'd left it after returning from seeing Dakin.

"There, Frank?" Sarah's voice grated against his ear, still ringing from the explosion.

"I'm still here."

"What's going on?"

"You want to know what's going on?"

"Is it a secret?" She snickered.

"No, it's not a secret." He felt himself growing furious, at her and at the world.

"So, what is it?"

"They've just blown up my fucking car, that's what the fuck it is!"

After he hung up, he shouted the phrase again: *"They've blown up my fucking car!"*

It was only later, when he'd gotten over his anger and incredulity, that he asked himself just whom he'd meant by "they."

The Riddle

There were times when, staring into mirrors, she felt herself empowered. At other times, mirror-madness times, she felt as though mirrors were sucking out her strength, her very life itself. . . .

At first she didn't notice. She was lying in bed reading the latest issue of *ARTnews* with the TV set on across the room. As usual, she had the sound turned down so that the flickering television was little more than a barely audible presence. She probably would have missed the story entirely if she hadn't happened to look up just as a still photo of her latest mark filled the screen. She nearly choked when she saw it.

She sat up, grabbed her remote, thumbed down hard on the volume control, then clicked her VCR on to record. An attractive young Asian woman was talking to a tall, tired-looking man in front of the Savoy. They were talking about Phil Dietz. From the gist of their conversation, Gelsey understood that Dietz had been murdered in his room.

She watched spellbound. The tired man was a detective; the Asian woman was a journalist. The detective was middle-aged, and had searching eyes with bags beneath them and a well-sculpted chin. He also displayed a world-weary manner that she associated with certain French film stars of the 1940s. The reporter asked sharp, aggressive questions to which the detective responded with patient, noncommittal answers. *And then they started talking about her:*

". . . a *redheaded woman* in the downstairs lounge. . . ."

". . .a *mystery redhead* seen with Philip Dietz just before he was killed . . ."

After the segment was over, she rewound the tape and watched it again.

What was going on?

She got out of bed, pulled on her clothes, began to pace the loft. If Dietz had been stabbed with, say, a pair of scissors, she might have cause to worry that she'd done the deed, perhaps in the amnesic dream-sister trance-state into which she sometimes slipped after taking down a mark.

But she distinctly remembered hearing Dietz snore when she wished him sweet dreams from his door. So, whatever had happened to him had occurred after she'd left the room. She had left it neat, too—she remembered that. Yet the reporter had referred to it as "ransacked." That meant that someone had gone into it after she had left. Which meant, again, that whatever had happened to Dietz had had nothing whatever to do with her.

Except . . .

They were looking for her now. The detective's searching eyes told her he was a hunter. She knew the sort of man: quiet, sometimes gentle, but relentless in pursuit. He was a hunter and she was his quarry. Another thing she knew about him: He was serious—he was no Leering Man.

That night she didn't sleep. She had a painting to finish, her latest version of Leering Man—and this time she was determined to get him right.

At three in the morning, still haunted by Dietz, she thought of a way to put him out of her mind. She went to the drawer in which she stashed the loot she took off marks, pulled out the gizmo she'd found inside Dietz's money belt and brought it over to her workbench.

She centered it carefully, picked up a steel ball hammer,

raised it above the object, then brought it down with all her might.

The object jumped but didn't break.

She hammered at it several more times, but to no avail. Determined to destroy it, she set it lengthwise in her steel vise, then screwed the jaws closed. It buckled beneath the pressure. The transparent material, some sort of resin or plastic, split apart and fine metal tracing broke out. After that, by a combination of hammering and crushing, she was able to reduce it to irregular jagged pieces, which she added with glue to the other debris attached to the ground around Leering Man's face, and then covered with thick gushes of paint applied directly with a palette knife.

At dawn, exhausted but satisfied, she flung off her clothes, crawled into her bed, pulled the covers over her head and fell asleep.

Three days later she sat nervously in Dr. Zimmerman's office wondering what he was going to say. She had just delivered her confession. She was, she had just admitted, a species of poisoner, a thief and, worse, a destroyer of men's egos. Now she gazed at the empty eye holes in the masks on Dr. Z's wall and imagined eyes slowly appearing in them—twenty pairs of eyes that would glare at her in moral judgment until she bowed her head in shame.

"So . . ."

Dr. Zimmerman's soothing voice cut through her reverie. She tightened her elbows against her sides, fearful of his indignation.

"So . . . perhaps," he continued, "now you would like to tell me a little bit about 'playtime'?"

Is that what he wants now? God!

"Sure, Doc," she said in her best tough-girl voice, pleased at least that he had not condemned her. "What can I tell you?"

"Whatever you want, Gelsey," he answered kindly.

"And if you prefer not to talk about it—that will be all right, too."

What a gracious man. He deserves something nice, anything for sparing me a sermon. And his question relieved her of having to discuss her fear of being connected to the Dietz murder—a fear that had filled her life the past three days, ever since she'd seen the report on TV.

"Playtime," she said, "—it's not all that unusual from what I've heard. My father . . . well, you know . . . he'd make suggestions. And then we'd go down to the maze."

She stared at the masks again. The eyes were gone from the eye holes. She felt alone.

She continued: "We'd never enter through the outside door. We'd always descend to it from the loft—open the trapdoor, climb down the ladder to the catwalks, then shinny down the rope to the floor."

"Then?"

"Then . . . you know, we'd do it. Play."

"That was his word for it?"

" 'Play,' 'playtime.' That's what he always called it. Like: 'Hey, honey bunch—it's a rainy day. Let's go down the rope and play.' "

"He called you 'honey bunch'?"

More questions! Why can't he just leave it alone? "That and 'sweetheart.' Sometimes 'dolly.' Lots of different things." She smiled, a forced little smile. "Affectionate names."

"And then?"

"Then what?"

"What would he do?"

She glared at him sharply. "Christ, Doc! What the hell do you think?"

She was sweating, she realized. Her armpits were wet. But not her crotch. That part of her, she noted with grim satisfaction, was bone-dry.

She turned to Dr. Z. Was he titillated by all this? Was there an erection sprouting in his baggy trousers? She didn't look. Better, she decided, not to know. Her thoughts turned to the tired detective she'd seen interviewed on TV, the detective with the searching eyes. The hunter. Her enemy.

"You're angry with me now," Dr. Zimmerman said.

"Yes," she agreed, "a little."

"I think more than a little, Gelsey."

"What do you want me to do? Describe it to you blow-by-blow?"

"Were there blows?" he asked gently.

"No!" Now she *was* angry. "He was sweet about it. Really sweet. That's what's so maddening. He was tender. He didn't throw me on the floor and . . . force himself. He always tried to make it . . ."

"What?"

"Fun," she said.

She turned to face him. Dr. Z was stretched out in his chair, eyes half-closed, the point of his goatee aimed straight at his shoes. Perhaps he was trying to imagine what she was describing, not only to visualize it but so he could feel it as well. Perhaps he was being careful not to look at her, out of consideration, so she wouldn't feel ashamed.

"It was mostly with our hands anyway," she said. "We didn't do, you know . . . the whole thing. He wasn't a beast. He never did anything that hurt me."

"But he did hurt you."

"Yes," she agreed, "he did."

"Did he—?"

She interrupted. "He always wanted me to ask for it. Ask him to do this or that. Whatever. He wouldn't do it unless I asked."

"Did you?"

"I asked." It pained her terribly to say it. "I don't know why. I guess I felt I had to. That was part of the game, you see. I would ask and then he'd grant my wish." She paused. "I think I know why he did it that way."

"Why do you think?"

"If I asked for it, that would mean he wasn't doing anything wrong. Against my will, you know. It wasn't abuse. It wasn't forced. It was . . . by consent."

"How does that make you feel?"

"The same way it made me feel then." She knew that very soon she was going to cry.

"Which was?"

"That I really *did* ask for it. So I had it coming to me, didn't I?" The tears were welling. "I wish you could understand. It wasn't all that . . . bad. It really didn't hurt. It was really sweet. Afterwards I would feel as though I had dreamed it, you know. Like it hadn't really happened. The mirrors made it seem like that. I would watch what we were doing in the mirrors, and it would seem like I was watching other people. Maybe that's why he always wanted to play down there. So I could sort of . . . float away . . ."

The tears were streaming down her face now. It felt good to cry, so she didn't bother to wipe them even when Dr. Z offered her a box of tissues. Crying was better than feeling afraid.

". . . float away from it, into mirrorspace. It's another land, Doc. Everything's the opposite there. Right is left and vice versa. It wasn't me anymore. It was . . . the other girl."

"Your twin, your shadow."

"My dream-sister who lives inside the glass." Gelsey snatched up a tissue, wiped her face. "There wasn't just one of her either. There were hundreds. In that particular room—he called it the Great Hall of Infinite Deceptions—there were more images than you could count. Galleries of reflections extending in every direction, each one infinitely long. Of course not infinite. There isn't enough light for that and the mirrors can never be perfectly aligned, so the corridors tend to curve and eventually you lose the image. But you know they're there, continuing forever around the bend. That's the point, that they can go on forever." She turned to him. "It's hard to explain."

"I think you explain it very well." Dr. Zimmerman paused. "But I don't think it was all fun and games."

"I never said it was!"

"Did he?"

She nodded. "That was the idea, I guess." She paused. "There's something I never told you." She wiped away more tears, then tried to smile. *There're so many things I never told you until today. And other things I probably won't tell you ever.* "I sometimes thought I saw something else down there with us—amidst all the images, a creature's face. I'd catch just a flash of it and then it'd disappear. When I'd ask Dad about it, he'd laugh and say it was just the Minotaur."

"Minotaur—interesting. Was it real? Was someone really there?"

"I guess not. But it seemed so at the time. It scared me. Then this . . . creature would just disappear, and Dad would comfort me, and then I'd forget."

Dr. Z stroked his little pointed beard. It was getting toward the end of the hour. Gelsey stared at him, waiting to hear what he had to say. Perhaps he sensed that the time had come to venture an analysis, for he clasped his hands together, a sign that he was going to sum up.

She hoped he wouldn't talk about "shadow-work" and "eating your shadow" again. She needed more than that, something to make her feel less miserable about herself on account of the awful things she did to men.

"You believe you turned to the mirrors to escape the reality of what he was doing to you. But I wonder if there was another reason," Dr. Z said. "I wonder if you used the mirrors, mirrorspace as you call it, as a kind of stage to which you could turn and then watch the two of you perform."

"Perform?"

Dr. Z nodded. "Certainly turning to the mirrors was a way to disassociate yourself. It wasn't happening to you, it was happening to your dream-sister in the world of mirrors. With that fantasy you protected yourself from the pain of your father's betrayal and abuse. But I believe there was more. You were as much attracted to what he was doing as repelled. This is not unnatural. We often find it in incest cases. Your father was initiating you into a realm of arcane knowledge, the secret sexual knowledge of adults. You had to be fascinated. You were only twelve but already a sexual being. We know that children much younger than that can have extremely powerful sexual feelings. The point is—you watched. And not just one reflection either. A hundred reflections, a million . . . images reflected down those infinitely long mirrored corridors. You watched and you imagined and you dreamed that all this was happening to your twin. The mirrors were a theater and you were the audience. Oh, yes, you turned away from him. But you might have chosen to close your eyes. You did not close them. You chose to watch. That choice was yours."

Dr. Zimmerman paused.

"I don't condone your criminal acts, Gelsey. But perhaps I can help you understand them. With understanding, hopefully, you will stop. It would be easy to say they are simply acts of vengeance visited by you upon lecherous men, stand-ins for your perverted father, a man you both hated and adored. It would be easy to say that you always go down to the maze first in order to become your mirror-twin, thus making it possible to do these awful things without guilt or loss of self-respect. Your father made you 'ask for it'; you are so seductive that these men must 'ask for it,' too. Your father abused you on rainy days; you feel compelled to do these things on rainy nights. There are other parallels and they are all so clear that I am . . . just a little bit suspicious. The unconscious does not act with such precision. I believe there is another level of meaning hidden beneath this much-too-regular symmetry. Our task is to find it. I'm not certain yet, but I believe the key lies in the maze. I believe there is more down there than you're telling me, more than you may know yourself. This Minotaur, for instance. Who or what is it? Who or what does it represent? You look at yourself in mirrors all the time. Now I think you must ask yourself what exactly you are looking *for*. To put it another way, you must learn to look beyond your own reflection to something deeper, hidden, perhaps *behind* the mirrors. Then, I believe, you will see your real self."

He paused. He was looking at the little clock across the room, the clock that told him when a session was finished without his having to glance too obviously at his watch.

"Time is up. You know that as a therapist I don't pass judgment on my patients. But I'd be remiss if I didn't say something to you now—speaking as one most concerned about your welfare. I feel I know you well, Gelsey. I know you have good character. The terrible thing about compulsions is the way they force us to do things we know are wrong. You have a strong moral compass. So, please, my dear—I urge you with all my heart—please follow it."

He stood to signal the session was over. His parting words at the door were simple: "I believe we will look back on this session as having been very important for us both. Next time we will explore the Minotaur—who or what you think you saw in the maze. Perhaps that imaginary creature is the key to your locked-up memories."

When she left, the tears were back in her eyes. They clouded her vision even on the street. Dr. Zimmerman was a wonderful man. She was so fortunate to have found him. He had called her "my dear." He had urged her to be good "with all my heart." With such words he had given her a gift to carry through the week. He had given her, she felt, a big dose of love.

The Erica Hawkins Gallery occupied the sixth floor of a renovated loft building near Spring Street on lower Broadway. The building was not in the geographical center of the downtown gallery district, but close enough to justify its aura of self-importance—thick glass doors; austere all-white lobby; uniformed security guard; pair of shiny steel freight elevators.

As Gelsey rode up in one that Tuesday morning, the

names of the various establishments on the various floors were automatically lit in turn: Icarus Arts; Sofie Winter Gallery; Jeremiah Bones Art Books; Tannhauser Gallery; I. I. Sing; and, at the top, Erica Hawkins.

The elevator door opened directly onto the gallery floor, where Erica and her young assistants, Dakota Hutchins and Justin Barrett, were busy arranging sculptures for an exhibition. A willowy young woman, nearly six feet tall, wearing dark glasses and dressed in tight black leather pants and a black T-shirt overlaid with a black leather vest, stood to one side watching. Gelsey recognized her as Jodie Graves, the artist whose work was being mounted.

"Gelsey!"

Erica came toward her, arms wide to embrace. She was a large, rotund, gray-haired woman with a booming voice and a maternal smile. Impossible, Gelsey thought, to discern Erica's character from her looks. The gallery owner, for all her fostering of young artists, was a steel-hard businesswoman and a militant, occasionally raging radical feminist.

Erica wrapped her arms around Gelsey and squeezed her to her bosom.

"The new painting—I adore it!" She whispered in Gelsey's ear: "If I don't flatter Jodie a little more she'll go into a snit. Wait in my office. Be with you in a flash."

Dakota and Justin waved and there was a curt nod of acknowledgment from Jodie, the kind of nod an athlete might give a rival before a race. Gelsey glanced at Jodie's sculptures: commercial-store mannequins tortured into erotic positions, wrapped tightly in overlapping irregularly shaped pieces of black leather, the wrappings secured to the forms with chrome rivets.

"Nice," Gelsey said, smiling sweetly.

Jodie Graves turned away. *Nice* was the last word she wanted to hear; *disturbing* or even *trashy* would have been more happily received. But Gelsey would not give her that satisfaction. *I've been there,* she thought, *taken the risks, breathed the danger and the lust. The feelings Jodie goes for haven't been earned.*

In Erica's office she found her latest Leering Man hanging opposite the desk. She stood back from it, tried to see it fresh rather than as a work she had struggled with day and night through the preceding week.

She had delivered it the previous morning, leaving it wrapped with Dakota at the door. She hadn't wanted to be there when Erica first looked at it. She didn't need to hear Erica pontificate again on the subject of female artists defined by male abusers.

Now, examining the portrait for the first time outside her studio, Gelsey tried to imagine its impact on a viewer. The Leering Man figure, as she thought of him, was there as always, but in this version he was richly embellished with shards of mirrored glass. And there were also painted-over objects glued around his face: the innards of eviscerated watches, coins, keys, bits of smashed wedding bands, overlapping pieces of torn currency, and now the remains of Dietz's money-belt object—all artifacts collected on her forays to the bars. There was no chance that any of these objects would be recognized by a mark; if one happened to see the portrait, he would most likely find it strange. But perhaps he might also be attracted to the work by a mysterious magnetism he would not comprehend—the familiarity that exists between a person and his possessions even when those possessions have been broken, ripped, smashed and embedded in thick oil paint.

She was thinking about this when Erica breezed into the office, sighing the word *artist* and rolling her eyes to express the difficulty of dealing with such godlike beings—image-makers, creators, the blessed and cursed.

Then Erica gestured toward Leering Man.

"Now *that,*" she said, "that's special. It's by far your best, Gelsey. I mean it. Best!"

Gelsey felt a tremor. The Leering Man had been a recurring motif. He had appeared in numerous canvases over the years, usually in the background or hovering half-seen on the edge. But after she left Diana she began to isolate him as her principal subject. And within the past few weeks she had worked through a new approach, constructing and then deconstructing him out of the detritus of her expeditions. It was integral to the power of the portrait, she felt, that it be ornamented with these souvenirs and trophies. The Leering Man was composed of all men now, and would reflect all male viewers. He was singular yet generalized, specific yet abstract. He was also, she felt, beginning to enter the realm of art.

She explained to Erica that this new portrait was the first in a series by which she hoped to purge herself of her obsession with the leering face.

"I feel it strongly," Erica responded, eyes meeting Gelsey's. "You have the potential to become an important artist. We've done well with you these last couple of years, but I believe we're going to do far better now. Be bold. Keep doing what you're doing. Take as long as you like. Bring me a room full of paintings as good as that"—Erica gestured again at the portrait—"and I'll have the collectors begging on their knees."

She hugged Gelsey again. "We'll make them pay. Oh, how we'll make them pay!"

On her way out, Gelsey paused again to examine Jodie Graves's leather-wrapped mannequins. The sculptures, she thought, mirrored Jodie's sexual fantasies.

Then she was mad at herself. It was so much easier to see through the pretensions of others than to penetrate one's own. Just then Jodie sidled up.

"Erica showed me your painting." *And?* "I didn't like it much." *Well, fuck you!* "But then it grew on me." *La-di-da.* "That's usually a good sign. Means it's powerful. I really felt it. I guess it hit me hard."

"Gee, Jodie—thanks."

"Maybe we could have brunch one day and talk?"

"Brunch? Sure. That would be great." Gelsey smiled and turned away.

As she rode down in the elevator she felt the fear again—that she would run into someone who'd seen her around the Savoy with Dietz. She steeled herself. Fear could only crush her. She knew she had to stay out of bars. She was an artist, not a doper-girl; Erica Hawkins respected and admired her. She must hold on to that.

"Up-down! Up-down! High-er! High-er!" The cries of the red-haired, ponytailed aerobics instructor were relentless. *"Im-pact! Im-pact!"* she bellowed.

Gelsey strained to obey. Images of thirty exercising women pranced across the mirrored wall. "Mirror, mirror on the wall/Who's the fairest one of all?" Gelsey thought she might scream if she allowed that phrase to streak one more time across her brain.

"High-er! Im-pact!"

Mirrors! Would they never leave her alone? Why was she so drawn to them? Most people, brought up around such an obsessive thing, would spend their lives running away from it. Why hadn't she fled? Why did she feel she must live above the maze, the trap her father had built—that was now her prison?

"Im-pact! High-er!"

The images danced. "Mirror, mirror on the wall . . ."

Gelsey shut off the refrain. There were many snippets of mirror literature she could call to mind to blot out Snow White. Mirrors had been a literary subject since the first woman had examined her reflection in a pool of water. Her father liked to quote from Shakespeare and the older poets, but Gelsey preferred the moderns. Anne Sexton: "Take my looking-glass and my wounds/and undo them." Simone de Beauvoir: "Captured in the motionless, silvered trap." Sylvia Plath: "I am silver and exact, I have no preconceptions . . . I am not cruel, only truthful . . . most of the time, I meditate on the opposite wall."

"Up-down! Im-pact!"

Maybe Dr. Z was right. Maybe there was a secret down there in the maze, a secret she had been hovering above for years and still had not been able to see. Auden had urged: "O look, look in the mirror/O look in your distress." Dylan Thomas had raged: "Still a world of furies/Burns in many mirrors." Yeats had sung: "I rage at my own image in the glass." And Borges had written of hearing "from the depths of mirrors the clatter of weapons."

Leering Man, Mirror Man, dream-sister . . . mirrors, maze, mirror maze . . . mirror madness. *God, is there no end?*

The instructor signaled that the session was over. "That's fine, girls. Relax!"

Gelsey, panting, let her arms hang loose. *Finally,* she thought, *the torment is over, at least for a while.*

Tracy, in street clothes, was gesturing to her from the doorway. Gelsey approached through the mob of exhausted, sweaty women.

"Hi! You missed class."

"Gotta talk to you." Tracy's tone was urgent.

"Sure. Just let me take a shower."

Tracy shook her head. "Please! I've only got a couple minutes."

Gelsey shrugged. They descended to the snack bar. Gelsey ordered a bottle of mineral water, Tracy a Diet Coke.

"You look terrible," Gelsey said. "What's the matter?"

Tracy stared at her. "You did a number down at the Savoy."

Gelsey stared back, frightened. "You know about that?"

"Considering what happened there, a lot of people know."

There was a look of reproach on Tracy's face. "Why don't you stop beating around the bush," Gelsey said.

"The mark was killed."

"I know. I saw the story on TV. But it had nothing to

do with me, Tracy. He didn't OD. He was shot."

"The bar waiter saw him pick up a redhead. The cops say he was drugged, then shot while he slept. They say there was mirror writing on his body."

Gelsey cut her off. "How do you know all this?"

"Diana got it from Thatcher, who got it from his buddies in the cops. They're showing around a picture. Take a look."

She handed Gelsey a photocopy of a sketch. The words "Wanted for Questioning" were printed at the top. Gelsey stared at it. It was a crudely drawn frontal view. She didn't think it looked like her, or much like her dream-sister either.

"Who's this supposed to be?"

"Thatcher recognized you."

Gelsey didn't believe it. She was sure the mirror writing had tipped Thatcher. "Do you see me in this?"

"A little. The wig makes you look different, but the eyes are right." She stared at Gelsey again. "You really didn't do it?"

Gelsey met Tracy's stare head-on. "Here's what happened. I did a number and, yeah, I wrote on the mark. But I promise you I left him asleep. I don't own a gun. I'm extremely careful with dosages. Anyway, do you think I could shoot a person while he slept?"

Tracy shook her head. "Diana does. She's furious, Gelsey. She says you've ruined the business."

"She would say that."

"It's true. We're not going out here now. We've been working hotels in Philly the last few nights. Diana says we may have to move the operation to Baltimore until this thing blows over." Tracy looked away. "She wants us to find you. She wants to turn you in."

"I see." Gelsey nodded. "That's why you're here."

"No, dummy! You're my friend . . . even if you won't tell me where you live. Trouble is, Diana knows we're close. She asked me if I still saw you. I said no, but I don't think she believed me. I'm dreading the moment she decides I'm lying." Tracy paused. "You know how she gets."

"I know . . ."

Indeed, Gelsey thought, there was no resisting Diana; if she decided to put on the pressure, Tracy would be forced to talk. That meant they couldn't see each other anymore. The thought made Gelsey sad. She'd never had many friends; now Tracy was the only one. It would hurt to lose her. She'd be more isolated than ever. But if she really was a murder suspect and Diana wanted to turn her in, then, she knew, she would have to sacrifice the friendship. The important thing was not to panic.

"Okay," she said, "here's what we'll do. If Diana starts in on you, don't fight it. Tell her we used to meet here for workouts, then a couple of months ago we had a big fight and you haven't seen me since. Don't worry, I'll start going to another gym." She picked up a napkin. "Give me a pencil. I want to give you my number. I want us to stay in touch."

Tracy shook her head. "I think it would be better if I didn't have it."

"Sure, I understand. Thing is, I don't want to lose you." Gelsey thought a moment. "There's a supermarket across the street. They've got a community bulletin board near the salad bar. We can leave messages there. Put up a notice you have kittens for sale, then write what you want to tell me on the back. I'll do the same." She paused. "I want you to know I didn't shoot the guy and I don't know who did."

"I believe you," Tracy said, standing, "but someone did and the cops think it's you. Better stay out of the bars, Gelsey. And stay away from Diana. The way she sees it, you've fucked up her business. You know what that means?"

Gelsey knew: It meant Diana would just as soon see her dead.

° ° °

Driving back to Richmond Park, she thought about Diana, her coldness, cruelty, exploitation of her girls and total devotion to "the game." There was also a nurturing side that had attracted Gelsey at first, a kind of parallel to the nurturing she now received from Erica. Except that with Diana there could be no act of generosity that would not immediately rebound to her advantage, while with Erica, the quality of an artist's work was always more important than the profits gained from its sale.

Gelsey smiled as she remembered Diana's organized outings to the Museum of Modern Art, where she would point out important paintings and make sure each girl could properly pronounce the artists' names:

"The man who painted this was named Henri Matisse. Come on, girls! Let's hear you say it: 'Hen-ri Ma-tisse.' "

To that the group would respond in unison, imitating Diana's phony pronunciation, after which Diana would continue the cultural lesson:

"Now, remember, girls—Mr. Ma-tisse is famous for his bright colors, strong designs and love of flowers and the female form. Please repeat that for us, Tracy. . . ."

God! What a hoot!

But the sketch Tracy had given her wasn't funny. It was even more frightening than the TV report that Dietz had been killed. They had a good idea of what she looked like. Maybe she should turn herself in. But then what would happen? If she went to the detective with the searching eyes and told him her story, would he believe her? And even if he did, wouldn't he arrest her for robbing Dietz?

Down in the maze, Gelsey held the police sketch to the glass and compared it with the mirror image of her face. Tracy had said the eyes were right, but Gelsey could see no similarity. The sketch seemed to be of an entirely different person. She wondered: *Could this be how I really look?*

She thought back over Dr. Z's advice—that when looking into a mirror she should ask herself what she was really looking for. His suggestion puzzled her. It struck her like the Zen nonsense question: "What is the sound of one hand clapping?"

But come to think of it, Dr. Z had been sounding more and more like a Zen master lately. That morning he had also suggested that the key to her behavior lay not in the obvious parallel to her father's abuse, but in something hidden in the maze, some secret of which even she might not be aware. What was he talking about? A secret room? A chamber that might house a monster, a Minotaur? She had no idea, except that what he'd said had seemed right. It was as if there were something down in the maze and also vibrating deep within herself that resisted all her efforts to bring it to the surface.

Did Dr. Z have something specific in mind? She would have to wait until their next session to find out.

That night, lying in bed, staring up at her ceiling fan, she thought of something her father had told her when, after playtime, he had held her in his arms in the Great Hall and had spoken to her about his relation to the maze:

"This is my life's work. I've poured everything into it, all my money, all my sorrow. It's been my fortress and my prison, Gelsey. Someday it will belong to you. Remember: Somewhere in here lies the answer to a riddle. I'm not sure what the riddle is, except that it had to do with the way the mirrors catch the light and make something out of it, something you can't touch, but that's real—and that never existed before. Guard the maze carefully. Explore it. And maybe you'll be the one to understand. As for me, I'm only the maze-maker. Sure, I know how to find my way around. But sometimes I think I have no idea what's here. No idea at all . . ."

Kirstin

By the time Janek dressed and made his way down to the street, a patrol car and fire engine had arrived. Over the next ten minutes numerous special units poured in, the block was cut off, police barricades were erected, bystanders were herded away, traffic was rerouted and the night air was cut by the beeps and echoes of emergency communications gear.

As he approached the smoldering remains of his car, surrounded by vehicles flaunting revolving red lights, he breathed a thick, acrid aroma of cordite, scorched metal, burning rubber, burned-off gasoline. His front seat, blown out of the frame along with the sunroof, lay upside down in the middle of the street. Staring at the smoking vinyl, he imagined himself flying along with it through the air. He thought: *I'd be just a puddle on the asphalt.*

The bomb squad, grave young men with lean faces and haunted eyes, were busy gathering up pieces of wreckage. He watched them as they took measurements, shot photographs, talked quietly among themselves. They reminded him of Navy Seals: a small, efficient elite unit, polite but otherwise impenetrable.

''Hell of a mess.''

Janek turned. The chief bomb squad investigator, a short, stout, serious, mustachioed detective named Stone, had appeared noiselessly at his side. Janek recalled meeting him a couple of times. He remembered that everyone called him Stoney.

"Saabs are pretty solid. What year was yours?"

"'81," Janek said.

"Good shape?"

"It ran."

"Blue Book value—maybe eight, eight-fifty."

"My deductible's a grand."

"Too bad." Stoney shook his head.

"Any idea what happened?"

"You mean technically?" Stoney scratched his cheek. "Yeah, we got a few."

Janek waited for Stoney to continue, but the investigator went silent. *Maybe they call him Stoney because he stonewalls,* Janek thought.

"I want you to forget you're a cop," Stoney said. "Tonight you're a victim. That'll require adjustment."

"I'll manage."

"Good." Stoney smiled. "So, tell me, Frank—who do you know wants to blow you up?"

Janek shrugged. "Only person I can think of is my ex-wife."

Stoney wasn't amused. "Some kid could've been walking by. The blast could've taken a chunk out of his neck. This time you were lucky. Next time you probably won't be. So I want you to think carefully about who might've done this. Bombs are tools of terrorists and assassins. I'll want the names of anyone who'd want to terrorize and/or assassinate you."

By the time Janek turned to him again, Stoney had slipped away, leaving his questions hanging in the smoky air. Janek wondered what names he could give. The answer depended on the bomber's intentions. Had the explosion been a message or a serious attempt on his life? *If someone really wanted to kill me,* he thought, *there're so many easier ways.*

While he stared at the wreckage, thinking about what it

would feel like to be blown up, a patrolman approached. "Chief Kopta's here, Lieutenant."

Janek turned, saw Kit, dressed in a set of NYPD sweats, exchanging banter with several of the men. From their reactions he could tell how highly they esteemed her. Their regard went way beyond respect. It was eleven-thirty, one of her people was in jeopardy, so the tiny woman with the sharp Greek features and the gray frosted hair had pulled on her sweats and come out. Even Janek had to love her for that.

"Frank," she said, spotting him. "Let's take a walk."

She waited until they passed the barricades set up at Amsterdam Avenue, then asked him what he'd said to Stoney.

"Nothing yet," Janek said. "I didn't know how much to tell him." They were walking between a row of storefronts and a stack of black garbage bags piled by the curb.

"You saw Dakin and Timmy?" Janek nodded. "How did they react?"

"Like loony tunes," Janek said. "Dakin can't understand why Timmy hasn't been arrested. He went on about pulling the 'slime snake' out of the well."

Kit shook her head. "Timmy?"

"He said if I happened to get close to 'the real heart of the thing,' something bad might 'befall' me, and how 'sorrowful' that would make him feel."

"He threatened you?" Janek shrugged. She glanced at him and frowned. "Is Timmy capable of a move like this?"

Janek peered at her. "Is anyone?"

"That's not my question."

Across the avenue two slim young men walked slowly, arms tossed languidly across each other's shoulders. Janek figured they were returning from one of the fancy gay bars uptown.

He turned to Kit. "If you're asking do I see Timmy sneaking over and wiring my car, the answer's a cold-stone no. I partnered the guy six years. He was drunk this afternoon. If he's the same man I knew, he got even drunker after we split. Another thing, bombing's not his style. Timmy's a fist-in-your-face type. Finally, he knows me. He knows I don't get intimidated, that a stunt like this would only make me mad.''

''Unless it made you dead.''

They walked a hundred feet in silence, turned the corner and started east on Eighty-eighth. An elderly man, holding a pooper-scooper, waited patiently for his dachshund to defecate beside the tire of a Toyota.

''From what Stoney tells me, it looks more like a message,'' Kit said.

''How's he figure that?''

''He's speculating, but the charge was light and your ignition wasn't wired. They slipped a package underneath, then set it off by remote. Probably from up the block so they could be sure no one'd get hurt.''

''Who's this 'they' you're talking about?''

''Just a turn of phrase.''

''Funny, that was my first reaction— that there was some mysterious 'they' who did this to me.''

Kit grinned. ''Well, now we'll have to find 'them,' won't we?''

''Yeah, that's real funny, Kit. Meantime, what do I tell Stoney?''

''Tell him about the hotel homicide you're working on. Then take him through a list of your old enemies—who you sent away, who might have gotten out lately, the usual.''

''But not about Mendoza?''

''Up to you. I'm not going to tell you to withhold information.''

''I'm sure he knows I went to Cuba. Everyone else does.''

Kit turned to him. ''If this is connected to Mendoza, what can Stoney do about it?''

Suddenly she froze. A large brown rat, breaking for cover, scampered across the street, then disappeared into a drain. Janek took Kit's arm to steady her. After a few seconds, he felt her relax.

"Maybe it was someone from the old days," Janek said.

"If Clury hadn't been killed by a car bomb, I'd say, yeah, maybe so." Kit spoke as if nothing awkward had happened: There hadn't been any rat; she hadn't felt revulsion. "But the connection's too close. Anyway, think about it. Who stands to gain from a failed attempt to blow you away? Is the message 'Stay away' or is it more complex?"

"Like what?"

Kit shrugged. "Maybe one of the players muddying the waters a little bit."

Having circled the block, they arrived at the barricade on Columbus Avenue and Eighty-seventh. The officer posted there gave Kit a formal salute. As they approached the wreckage and the aroma of soot and gasoline and burned rubber, Janek saw Stoney, squat and short, staring at them from the center of the street.

"Better go talk to him," Kit urged.

Stoney was methodical. He wouldn't be hurried. His questioning took three full days. He was terse and, despite Janek's best efforts, rarely cracked a smile. He insisted on going over every case Janek had ever handled. Names that hadn't passed through Janek's mind in years conjured up images of old crime scenes and cornered suspects confessing in claustrophobic interrogation rooms.

There was the boy who had killed the two nuns; the "switch" case in which a man had killed two women on opposite sides of town, decapitated them, then boldly switched their heads; a set of voodoo murders; a roommate homicide; the famous actor who pushed the famous actress out the window; the case called "Wallflower" in which a female shrink had sent out one of her patients to exact homicidal revenge for past offenses.

But even as Janek related these stories, he got the impression that Stoney didn't think they were relevant. *He knows about Cuba,* Janek kept thinking. *He's waiting for me to bring it up.* He wouldn't lie if Stoney confronted him, but he'd be damned if he himself would introduce the subject of Mendoza.

In the end, Stoney didn't ask about it. He just stared at Janek as if waiting for him to talk. Janek found himself admiring the short bomb squad investigator, and also feeling uncomfortable in his presence.

As it happened, Stoney turned out to be right about the Saab. The high amount of the deductible, which Janek had chosen casually to save himself a few bucks, far exceeded the Saab's value, which meant he'd have to buy himself a new car. What especially rankled was his knowledge that it would be new only to him, since once again, he knew, he would be buying a used car.

By the time he broke free of Stoney, Sue Burke had located the "bad girl" Stiegel had met two winters before in Roosevelt Hospital. Her name was Kirstin Reese.

Janek met Sue in front of Kirstin's building, a walk-up tenement on Ninth Avenue in Hell's Kitchen. There was a busy fish market on the ground floor; its smell filled the hallway. The stairs were covered with some sort of green industrial carpeting that was badly stained and had been worn through in patches to the wood.

As they made their way up to the fifth floor, Sue filled him in:

"I found her name in the hospital records. She gave an old address. But with her Social Security number, I was able to track her through Welfare. I talked to her this morning for about half an hour. She's jumpy, Frank—fragile, too. It's like there's something wrong way deep inside. Reminds me of women I interviewed when I worked Sex Crimes. The broken-sparrow syndrome, we used to call it."

"Still—she talks?"

"About some stuff, at least to me. But there's other stuff

she won't talk about. The stuff we're interested in."

"Naturally," Janek said.

By the time they reached the fifth floor he was breathing hard. Also, the fish aroma wasn't fresh up there. It was as if the new smells downstairs were forcing the older ones upward, where they were heated to a condition of pungency by sunlight that poured in through the tent skylight above the stairwell.

"How much you think they get for a studio here?"

"Six-twenty a month, would you believe it?"

They looked at each other and shook their heads. Manhattan was crazy. There were people in rent-controlled buildings paying that much for six rooms with river views.

Sue rang the buzzer, there was silence, then the sound of rapid footsteps moving in the opposite direction, another silence, steps approaching, then the snap of a security lock.

The door opened a crack and Janek saw a sliver of a woman peering out over a taunt link chain.

"It's Sue Burke. I brought the lieutenant," Sue said. Silence. "What's the matter, Kirstin? You said I could bring him up."

"I changed my mind." The woman's voice was pitched with strain.

"Hey, come on," Sue coaxed. "You promised. Please."

For a moment Janek was sure the girl was going to shut them out. But then Kirstin unchained the door and stood aside. When Janek entered he saw a tall, young, blond woman with a slim figure and large ice-blue Nordic eyes. She wore jeans and a tanktop and there was a small blue tattoo of a crouching dragon on her right shoulder blade. She was attractive enough to be a model, he thought, except for the way she held herself and the zigzag scars on her cheeks. Her face had been slashed on both sides, and, he observed, not very carefully sewed up.

The studio was dark. The shades were pulled almost to the bottoms of the windows, allowing only narrow strips of light to break through. But the windows were wide open;

Janek could hear the roar of the avenue, cars and trucks inching their way toward the entrance to the Lincoln Tunnel.

Sue sat beside Kirstin on a brown corduroy couch, the kind that opens up and turns into a bed. Janek took a beaten-up leatherette easy chair. There was a small wooden table set between the couch and the chair, bearing rings and spots where spilled liquids had eaten through the varnish.

He sat quietly for the first few minutes while Sue drew Kirstin out. There was something grim about the girl, bitter and withdrawn, that made him think he'd do better to hold back. He needed her help; she was the only lead Stiegel had developed in two years of tracking the bad-girls ring. If she refused to cooperate, the odds of his finding the redhead would fall, he knew, to nearly zero.

"Things going okay?" Sue asked.

"So-so," Kirstin replied.

"I told you, I can get you some help. Think about it."

"Sure," Kirstin said.

"Kirstin's still got some savings, but Welfare doesn't know that," Sue explained. "I know someone might give her a waitress job, maybe even help her find a better place."

"It's okay here," Kirstin said, looking around. She was avoiding eye contact. Then she grinned, embarrassed. "The fish smell gets pretty bad sometimes."

"I've got an old air conditioner at home," Sue said. "Not too pretty but it works. If you want it I can probably get some of the guys to haul it up here."

"That would be nice," Kirstin said.

She was, Janek observed, deeply depressed. Although pale, she didn't look ill, but it was clear she wasn't functioning well.

As Sue and Kirstin continued to talk, Janek glanced around the room. There was a linoleum-topped table sporting a small TV, and two aluminum-framed porch chairs with green webbed plastic seats. On one wall was an old

Pan Am calendar showing a view of the Eiffel Tower. On another wall he spotted a pair of cheaply framed reproductions of large-eyed waifs with cats. Most of the furniture looked like it had been collected off the street. Janek wondered how much Kirstin had tipped the super to carry the corduroy couch-bed up the stairs.

When there was a break in the conversation, he decided to ease himself in. He turned to Sue. "Why don't you show her the sketch?"

Sue nodded, pulled out the sketch of the redhead and handed it to Kirstin. Janek watched her closely. He was certain she recognized the girl. There was a small glimmer of excitement, barely noticeable, followed by a denial that was a little too vehement. After that Kirstin set the sketch facedown. There was no reason for her to do that.

"Are you sure you don't know her?" Sue asked.

Kirstin shook her head, then stared at the floor. Her lie was so transparent, Janek wondered whether she even expected to be believed.

Sue exhaled. "Why don't you tell the lieutenant about what you used to do?"

Kirstin turned and engaged Janek's eyes. It was the first time she'd looked straight at him. Her eyes, he noted again, were a ghostly shade of blue and astonishingly beautiful.

"What do you want to know?"

"Whatever you want to tell me," he said. In the pause that followed he decided not to elicit information. *I need to open her somehow.* "Did you enjoy the work?" he asked.

She smiled slightly. "Why wouldn't I? I made a lot of money."

"Still living on some of it," Sue added.

Kirstin laughed, a short, cutting private laugh meant only for herself. Then she turned back to Janek. "Why'd you ask me that?"

"Whether you enjoyed it?" He shrugged. "I imagined there might be a certain amount of pleasure in the work."

"Yeah! Sure! It was really great!" The intensity of her bitterness told him he was getting through.

"You hated it, didn't you?"

"Sure"—she smiled—"that, too."

He could tell he'd awakened her. *How long has it been,* he wondered, *since someone's shown interest in her feelings?*

"What was the worst part of it?"

"The risk. I was scared the whole fucking time."

"Anything else?"

She shrugged. "Sometimes I felt sorry for the guys." She paused a moment, then undercut her small display of compassion with a tight, mean smile and a tough-girl remark: "But a girl's gotta make a living, right?"

They stared at her. There was nothing to say. A girl's certainly gotta make a living. But a girl didn't have to do it by drugging and robbing men. It took a special type to choose to make it that way, girls who didn't like men, who had it in for them, who wanted to humiliate them—perhaps to pay them back for violations suffered at their hands.

"Writing on their chests—whose idea was that?" he asked.

"Diana's."

"She was the boss?"

Kirstin nodded.

"How many were you?"

"Four or five. Girls'd come and go." Kirstin shrugged. "You know how it is."

More tough-girl talk, but Janek ignored it. He had roused Kirstin to the extent that she was no longer bothering to play a role. That was all he had wanted to do. It was time now to get some facts.

"Why did Diana want you to write on them?"

"To freak them out," Kirstin said. " 'Always mark him afterward.' She said marking made them embarrassed to go to the cops and kept them busy thinking how to hide the writing from their wives."

Janek glanced at Sue. She nodded back, her acknowledgment that Stiegel, mediocre as he was, seemed at least to have gotten that right.

"What's Diana like?" Sue asked.

The bitter laugh again. "Not a nice person."

"Why don't you tell us a little about her?"

Kirstin shrugged. "Sure, why not?"

Janek sat back.

"She started the business. She used to go after marks herself—in Texas, Houston, places like that. She was good at it, she told us. Really cleaned up. 'Picked 'em all clean down there.' She invested her money. 'I'm rich, girls. You will be, too, if you stick close.' She told us there were good livings to be made by girls who knew how to interest men, then put them to sleep. No one got hurt. No one got AIDS. No violence. Everything neat and clean. Oh, she could go on and on about what a neat, clean game it was." Kirstin paused. "Another thing she used to say: 'Don't give me any excuses. I've been there. I know every wrinkle.' Like anyone would dare give her an excuse! We were all afraid of her. Terrified."

Listening to her, not just to what she was saying but to the way she was saying it, Janek was struck by an idea. It was nothing he could justify, and he knew that if he brought it up and was wrong, he risked losing Kirstin's confidence. But he also knew that if he was right, he might be able to create a bond.

"Diana was the one who cut you, wasn't she?" he asked softly.

Kirstin's eyes glowed. "How did—!" She brought her fist up to her mouth. "I never said that. I—" Then she began to cry.

Janek nodded to Sue, who moved closer, offered her a handkerchief.

"Take it easy," Sue said. "We're not going to hurt you. No one's going to hurt you now."

Sue looked up at Janek. He stood and moved over to a

window. He wanted to release the shade, flood the dreary little room with light. But he knew that Kirstin wouldn't like that, that she'd pulled down the shades while they'd been waiting at the door. It was all right, he understood, if they saw her scars, just so long as they didn't see them very well.

After Kirstin recovered she was ready to open up. The information tumbled out.

She spoke with wistful nostalgia of her days as one of Diana's girls. Nothing, it seemed, was too good for her then. Great clothes. Shopping expeditions to designer boutiques. Haircuts at the top salons. The finest shoes and accessories.

"Catch a cold, Diana had this fancy doctor, Feldstein, to look after you. Get in trouble, she had this smart lawyer, Thatcher, to get you out of it."

There were cultural-improvement trips to museums and evenings at the ballet, parties, too, usually small corporate gatherings arranged by company publicists. After such affairs there was no requirement to, as she put it, put out. Sex was optional; if a girl was attracted to a man, she was free to date him, and if she wasn't, she could reject his advances. Diana demanded many things, but she never forced her girls to sleep with men for money. Their function at these parties was to glow and decorate. If there was payment for their presence, Kirstin didn't know about it.

When Janek asked how the girls put marks to sleep, Kirstin happily explained. Each one carried what she called a "KO kit" consisting of three small bottles containing triazolam diluted in white wine, vodka and Coke. This made it possible to dose a beverage no matter what the mark might choose to drink.

Janek was impressed by Diana's system of financial control. Kirstin explained how it worked. Each night, the girls would be collected at prearranged points by Diana's lover and chauffeur, a Korean girl named Kim. Kim would take the girls back to Diana's apartment, where they would pool the evening's take. Diana would take 50 percent off the top. The other 50 percent would be divided equally among the girls, regardless of how much or how little each one happened to bring in.

As for the watches, rings and other jewelry, each item was carefully logged in on a computer. After sale to Diana's fence, the girls would again be handed equal shares of 50 percent.

The purpose behind this equitable division of the spoils was to build camaraderie. It was also an acknowledgment that the gross take from any given hotel-bar encounter had much to do with luck. Some marks were loaded, some were not. Since each girl knew she would receive an equal share, an unsuccessful evening would not have a depressive effect. Diana insisted she was running a business. "In the end it evens out," she'd say.

But there were exceptions. If a girl's contributions were consistently low, Diana might decide she was a poor producer and cut her loose. Or, if she decided the girl was cheating by holding back on gross receipts, she might order collective punishment. The idea was that if you held back, you weren't cheating just Diana, you were cheating your co-workers, too. Punishment consisted of being slapped around by the group, confiscation of all clothes, jewelry and accessories, and permanent banishment. In her time with Diana, Kirstin saw two girls cashiered out that way.

"Is that why she cut you?" Janek asked, remembering how degraded he'd felt being shoved and kicked by the Seguridad guards.

Kirstin nodded.

"What happened?" Sue asked softly.

Kirstin took a deep breath. "I got lucky. It was at the Hyatt. The mark seemed fairly ordinary at first. I figured him for a businessman sporting a fancy watch. Diana always told us to go for the watch. If it was expensive, like a Rolex, it meant the mark probably liked to flash his cash.

We were supposed to stay clear of credit-card freaks, guys with fifteen different cards and just a pair of twenties in their pockets. We never stole plastic. 'We're not in the forgery business,' Diana said.''

Janek knew Kirstin was stalling, putting off telling what had happened. She seemed to realize she'd digressed, for she took another deep breath and went on:

"So anyway, I went upstairs with this guy, put out his lights, then started going through his stuff. Nothing too interesting till I got to the closet. There was a locked briefcase on the upper rack. Earlier I had found a key on a chain around his neck. The key fit the briefcase. Soon as I opened it up—ta-da! Lotsa cash.''

Kirstin's large blue eyes lit up. *She can still make herself high,* Janek thought, *recalling the memory of all that loot.*

"Maybe he was a dealer. There must've been thirty or forty grand. He was what Diana called Mr. Bucks. She always told us that's what the business was about—hitting up on a hundred marks, waiting for Mr. Bucks to show. 'You won't recognize him,' she'd tell us. 'When you find him, it'll be a surprise. But he's out there,' she assured us. 'Catching him's the high.' She was right. When I saw all that money, I felt . . . great. And the next thought through my head was: 'Hey! I'm not sharing this with anyone!' ''

Kirstin glanced quickly at Janek, perhaps embarrassed about admitting to her greed.

"I checked my watch, I was running late. I had less than twenty minutes before my pickup. I grabbed the briefcase, rode down to the lobby, then scooted through this tunnel that connects to Grand Central. I stashed the briefcase in the baggage claim, then ran back to my pickup point. I got there just as Kim drove up.''

"How did Diana find out?'' Sue asked.

"I was stupid. I had to tell someone. I picked the wrong person, that's all. I hinted I'd lucked into something big to a girl I thought was my friend. She was jealous, she told

Diana and when Diana heard she decided to make an example of me.''

Janek glanced at Sue; she was rapt. Even as he felt revulsion, he was fascinated, too.

''First thing, she forced me to turn over my money, not just the briefcase either. She made me tell her where I kept my savings from two years on the job. Lucky for me I kept some of it hidden in this couch. That's all I was left with. I've been living on it ever since. Basically she cleaned me out, kept half for herself and divided the rest among the others. Then she had them hold me down while she took a knife and . . .''

Kirstin brought her hands to her cheeks. Tears formed in her eyes.

''She cut me. She said it was to teach me a lesson. 'You won't be picking up too many guys now.' I think she liked doing it. She grinned when I screamed. Nobody said a word. Maybe I would have kept quiet, too, if I'd been one of them. Thanks to her, they all got rich, didn't they?'' Kirstin wiped away her tears. ''Maybe she was right. I knew the rules. I broke them. I deserved what I got.'' The tears began to flow again. ''I just didn't think she'd go that far, that's all. I would never have done it if I'd known she'd cut me up. . . .''

Janek was appalled, perhaps less by Kirstin's story than by her notion that somehow she had gotten what she deserved. It was a familiar paradox, the psychology of the masochist, the basis of most relationships between hookers and pimps. It never ceased to sicken him whenever he heard it expressed, especially by a victim to justify abuse by a tormentor on account of ''infractions'' of some phony ''code of honor'' devised by a psychopath to control underlings.

Sue seemed to have trouble imagining the scene. ''The others helped by holding you down?''

''Two of them did. The other three turned away.''

''What about the one who turned you in?''

"She held me the tightest," Kirstin said.

Sue's face was filled with indignation. "We're going to have to find Diana and put her away. What's her full name? Where does she live?"

As soon as Janek heard Sue speak, he knew she'd made a mistake. Her tone was wrong—abrupt, harsh, accusatory, when she should have been focusing on Kirstin's tragedy. Sue seemed to recognize her error; she reached out for one of Kirstin's hands. But she was too late. The dynamics had changed. Kirstin pulled her hand into her lap. It was as if she'd drawn a curtain.

"Okay," Janek said, "we don't want to tire you. You've helped us." No response. "There's just one thing." He picked up the sketch of the redhead, turned it right side up and placed it in front of Kirstin again. "I know you know her. It's okay." He studied Kirstin's eyes, detected a trace of liveliness. "We're not going to do anything to her. But we need to talk to her. A man's been killed. She may be able to tell us how or why."

Kirstin stared down at the sketch. "We were pretty good friends."

"Can you tell us her name?"

Kirstin nodded. "Gelsey. I never knew where she lived. None of us did. She was kind of . . . mysterious."

"She was one of the girls who turned away, wasn't she?"

Again Kirstin nodded. "She'd never hurt anyone."

"But she took down marks?"

"Like the rest of us."

"Anything more you can tell us?"

Kirstin looked up. "She had this thing about mirrors. It was spooky. She could do mirror writing, too. She told me she liked writing on marks that way. 'It's like signing my work,' she said."

Janek stood. He was surprised that Kirstin had been so forthcoming, and even more surprised that Gelsey had apparently used her real name with Carlson. But Kirstin had something to add:

"The night Diana cut me—that same night Gelsey quit. Way I heard it, she took off her clothes, threw them on the floor and walked. Diana was furious." Kirstin smiled. "Gelsey was her top producer."

On the way down the stairs, which were even more redolent now with the smell of fish, Sue apologized.

"I know I messed up, Frank. Sorry."

"Forget it," Janek said. "We learned a lot. Kirstin obviously knows where Diana lives. She'll tell you, too, if you handle her right. Let her think about it a couple days, then come back alone and talk about yourself, your work in the Sex Crimes Unit, how you feel about things—your job, your life."

"Girl talk."

Janek nodded. "Gain her confidence again and she'll probably tell all. Then you may get your chance to collar Diana."

In front of the fish market, he and Sue split up. She returned to Special Squad. He started walking east.

As he passed ethnic-food shops and mom-and-pop cigarette stores, he asked himself why he felt depressed instead of energized. His case was moving. Now he knew who he was looking for, had a name for his redheaded quarry. Her name was Gelsey and he even had a sense of what she might be like.

But for some reason that knowledge did not delight him. The hour spent with Kirstin had brought him down. He wanted not to think about the way she'd been deliberately scarred, the fear in which she lived, her belief that she deserved her fate, her rat-hole of an apartment, the smell of fish, the smell of a wasted life.

He didn't want to think about any of that, or that he could have been blown up inside his car, or about Mendoza, Dakin, Timmy and his demons, Sarah stirring up old regrets or his sadness that he had never fathered a child. But as much as he wanted to fasten onto something positive, he could not rid himself of the vision of Kirstin, hold down tight by the other girls, staring with terror at the gleaming knife descending in Diana's hand toward the sweet pink center of her cheek.

He thought of something Luis Ortiz had said within the first few minutes of their acquaintance—that, in such difficult times in Cuba, all he had to hold on to was his honesty.

So, what have I got to hold on to? Janek asked himself. *Pride in my skill? Pride in being a cop?*

Approaching Forty-second Street, that particular pair of virtues didn't seem half good enough. The city was mean. He knew the worst of it, had spent the better part of his life witnessing its cruelties. But, unlike so many of his colleagues, he had never grown inured to the malignancy. That was, he thought, his greatest strength, and also, perhaps, his weakness. He still could feel the pain of others, and each time he did he felt his own pain, too. Kirstin had brought him closer to the hurt within, a hurt deeper and more grievous than anything Fonseca and Violetta could inflict. They had only tried to break his pride. The real damage occurred when some of that hurt he shared with the injured of the world—the Kirstins, Stiegels, even his tormentors in Havana—spewed up from the secret lake inside. When that happened, as it had that morning, the melancholy nearly overwhelmed him.

That night he got a call from Kit. Netti Rampersad had, that very afternoon, filed papers on behalf of Jake Mendoza.

"Works fast, doesn't she?" Janek said. "I suppose she wants a new trial."

"You bet," Kit said. "And not only on the basis of your Figueras affidavit. She's got something else. A homicide down in Texas. Took place three years ago. Some society woman was strung up and beaten to death just like Mrs. Mendoza. Rampersad is pleading that the similarity shows the killer is still at large. Therefore Jake's conviction shouldn't stand."

Janek had never heard of the Texas case. "Did we know about this?"

"Sure. We figured it for a copycat job. We've been in touch with the El Paso police—who still haven't solved it, by the way."

"What if it wasn't a copycat?"

"That's Rampersad's problem. Let her convince a judge."

"How'd she find out about it?"

"Probably through her partner, Rudnick. He's a digger, smart and very good."

"I met him. Wears a skullcap. Seemed nice enough."

"I don't know if he's nice. He's the kind can find a legal precedent for anything."

"What's the story on Rampersad? I never heard of her until that night in Queens."

"No one heard of her till last year when she won a big case in Rockland County. Now she's the new hot defense attorney in town. We get a couple of those every year. Actually, she's better than most."

"Still, if the Metaxas note was fake, and there's someone going around killing women the same way—then the whole goddamn case falls apart."

"Makes your head spin, doesn't it?" Kit said.

After he put down the phone, he did feel his head begin to spin. With Mendoza the possibilities were mind-boggling, the permutations endless.

He tried to sleep, but couldn't. Ever since the bombing, insomnia had become a problem. Perhaps, he thought, he was afraid that if he let himself doze off, there'd be another explosion and he'd die. *I guess when they kill me I want to be awake.*

Still restless at one in the morning, he decided to call Timmy. He wasn't sure what he wanted from him: confrontation or friendship. What he got was banter.

Timmy, as it happened, was awake, too. He sounded as if he'd been drinking, but not so much that he was out of control.

"Heard about your car, partner." Timmy's voice was sweet and sad. "Too bad. She was a nice jalopy."

"I was wondering if you had something to do with her demise."

"Were you, now? And what might my motive have been?"

"Get me to stay away from Mendoza."

Timmy laughed. "If there's one thing I can think of that would keep you *on* Mendoza, it would probably be something like that."

"So maybe you wanted to take me out and the bomb went off early by mistake."

"Oh, that's grand, Frank. You always had a grand imagination. If you ask me, you should put it to better use."

"Is that your advice, Timmy?"

"Wanna know something? I can't believe we're having this conversation. I must be dreaming. That's the only thing can explain it. Maybe when I wake up this whole bad dream will go away."

"That'd be nice, wouldn't it? But I wouldn't count on it . . . partner."

Timmy hung up.

He and Aaron ate lunch at Aaron's favorite pizza place on East Ninth. Aaron, who was wearing a particularly gaudy yellow and red Hawaiian shirt, insisted that pizza was "a perfect food," high in carbohydrates, low in cholesterol and a treat for the palate, too.

While they waited for their pie, Janek talked about losing his car:

"I was having this awful conversation with Sarah when

I heard it blow. Soon as I saw the wreckage I started to shake. *Who the hell did this to me? Why?* Then, when Kit turned up, she was so cool, I managed to calm down. Now I'm mad again, but in a different way—like a deep, cold fury. Some jerk took away my wheels. I want to put him away for good."

"It's like you're a sheriff and an outlaw rides by and shoots your horse on the street."

Janek smiled. "Exactly!"

"So"—Aaron stretched—"when're you going to replace it?"

"I'm thinking of giving up the concept of car ownership. No more parking problems. No more insurance. Whenever I need wheels, I rent a set. The rest of the time . . . hell with it!"

"And don't forget, Frank—you've got loyal subordinates like me and Sue who'll chauffeur you around."

Janek twisted in his seat. "Tell me something."

"Anything."

He looked away. "What're the odds an adoption agency would let me adopt a child?"

"You're serious?" Janek nodded. "Okay, I'll give it to you straight. One, you're single. Two, you're middle-aged. Three, you're a cop. Three strikes like that and, basically, you're out."

"That's how I figure it, too. Anyway, it probably wouldn't be a good idea. Not that I don't think I'd make a pretty good dad. It just wouldn't work out, for me or the kid." He turned back to Aaron. "Tell me about Mr. Stephen Kane."

Aaron quickly filled him in. A personnel officer in the L.A. sheriff's office remembered Kane well. Kane had worked for the department for six years, first as an investigator and then as an intelligence operative in the Industrial Espionage Division. Near the end of his tenure there'd been some trouble. Kane was suspected of acting as a double agent, feeding sensitive information back to targeted people. There was no proof, but when two undercover informants were killed, Kane was transferred to a routine job.

"That double-agent stuff bothers me," Aaron said. "You'd think Cavanaugh over at Sonoron would have checked him out."

"Maybe Cavanaugh did," Janek said. "Maybe Kane's just the type he wanted."

In the middle of the meal, Aaron laid a brown eight-by-ten envelope on the table, then pushed it slowly toward Janek. Janek looked at it, but didn't pick it up.

"What's that?"

"Some stuff I dug up. On my own time."

"What kind of stuff?"

"It has to do with another matter."

Janek stared at him. Aaron was embarrassed. "What's it about?" Janek asked, casually.

"Look, we're friends, right?"

"You're probably the closest friend I've got."

"So, when you're friends with someone—real friends—you should feel free to be open about stuff even when you know it's going to hurt."

"Is the stuff in this envelope going to hurt?"

Aaron nodded. "Probably." He paused. "It's about Sarah and Roy Gilette, that accountant she's been living with."

Janek felt himself go tense. "They don't live together. They go out together. Occasionally he stays over. They're not kids. They're entitled to get it on like everybody else."

Aaron shook his head. "That's not how it is, Frank. He doesn't just stay over. He's moved in. His mail's delivered there. His driver's license lists him there. So do his tax returns. He doesn't live any other place."

Janek groaned. He'd suspected as much; now, he realized, he'd refused to face the fact because the thought of Gilette living with Sarah in his old house was too upsetting to deal with. Maybe that was why he'd decided not to help

Sarah with the roof—if she and Gilette were cohabiting, why should he pay the bill?

"I want you to know something, Frank." Aaron looked solemn. "It was not my pleasure to gather this information. But it wasn't hard to do and I felt you ought to have it. So now, if you'll allow me, I'll fill you in on what's been going down."

Janek nodded.

"This is going to be fairly painful, so I'm going to give it to you quick. First, Sarah no longer works at Saks. Gilette's got her on the payroll at his firm, where she pulls down forty K. Between the two of them, they're knocking down over a hundred seventy per and probably more with bonuses."

Janek winced.

"Two months ago they went to Hawaii for a two-week vacation. It wasn't one of those package deals. It was deluxe all the way. Credit-card records show they flew first-class. Then they stayed at the Kahala Hilton. That's minimum three-seventy-five per night. Hear what I'm saying, Frank?"

"Yeah, I hear—goddammit!" He felt like vomiting his lunch.

"I could go on. They left one hell of a trail. It's all there in the envelope. You can follow it yourself."

"Not necessary. I get the picture." Aaron, he knew, was one of the best paper-trail detectives in the Department. Whatever he'd found would be accurate.

"As I said—this was not a pleasant task."

"I appreciate that."

"Any thoughts about what you're going to do?"

"Yeah," said Janek, stretching, "I've got a few thoughts. They're flashing through my mind right now. There's this tough female attorney I met recently who seems like she likes to kick butt. Her name's Henrietta Rampersad. I'm thinking maybe I can induce her to take a swipe at Sarah's."

Aaron grinned. "I like the sound of that, Frank. Take no prisoners. Yeah, I like that a lot."

That afternoon when he passed through the outer room of Special Squad, Ray Galindez approached, asked if he could speak to him privately.

"Sure," Janek said, motioning him into his office.

Ray stood solemnly before the desk, then he touched a corner of his mustache.

"I feel a little awkward asking this. I want to make it easy for you to say no."

"Maybe the best move is just to ask, Ray. If it's about a transfer, you know that won't be a problem."

Ray grinned. "It's not about a transfer, Frank. It's about being godfather to my child. Grecia and I talked it over last night. We'd be honored if you'd agree to stand with us at the christening."

Janek was moved. He immediately stood up. "*I'm* the one who'll be honored."

"We had the test. It's going to be a girl."

"God, that's so great." He hugged Ray. "As if I'd even *dream* of saying no!"

At nine that night he was watching an old Bogart movie when his telephone rang loud. He must have moved the volume knob by accident. He nearly jumped as he fumbled for the receiver.

It was Sue. Even before she explained why she'd called, he knew something was wrong. She was over at Kirstin Reese's studio. She'd arrived to find the door unlocked and Kirstin's body on the floor.

"She doesn't look too good," Sue said. "I mean—" Sue paused. "She's dead."

When he arrived he found three police cars in front. Also, the med examiner's car, a meat wagon and a Crime Scene van. A small crowd had gathered on the street. People in adjoining tenements stood at their windows staring down. Ninth Avenue traffic, bound for Jersey via the Lincoln Tunnel, was snarled, with trucks and cars honking helplessly, trying to squeeze their way through the bottleneck.

Janek made his way up the narrow stairs, particularly ripe with the smell of fish. Near the top he heard Stiegel's rusty voice. As he drew closer, he found the old cop in a heated argument with Sue.

"I'm the one put you on to her. Next thing—"

"You didn't put us on to shit, Stiegel. You didn't even know her name!"

"So, how'd you find her?"

"I'm a detective, asshole!"

When they saw Janek, they broke it off.

"She was cut bad, Frank," Sue said. "Then shot in the head."

"It's gotta be the same guy cut her before," Stiegel said.

Sue turned on Stiegel. "You haven't been listening. It wasn't a guy who cut her. She told us who it was. It was the woman who runs the bad girls."

Stiegel turned to Janek, eyes pink. "You kept that to yourselves!"

"We didn't think you'd be interested," Sue said.

"Interested! Bad girls is my case!"

"That why you took such great notes?"

Janek studied Stiegel. He was drunk and about to get violent. "Take it easy," he said as soothingly as he could. Then to Sue: "Did you call him?"

Sue nodded. "Out of courtesy. Now I'm sorry I did."

Stiegel stared at her. "You don't like me, do you, Missy?"

"What do you think?" Sue asked.

It was time to separate them. Janek put his hand on Stiegel's shoulder. "Come on, Detective—I'll walk you downstairs."

Stiegel's eyes glassed over. Then, docile, he allowed Janek to escort him to the street.

"I'm overworked, Lieutenant. I told you the other night. I couldn't give priority to this . . . specially when the girl wouldn't talk. Then, out of the blue, your Missy Detective calls—I mean, Jesus! What the hell was I supposed to think?"

Janek wanted to show Stiegel sympathy, but he found it difficult. "Go home," he said. "Like you said—the girl wouldn't talk."

Stiegel nodded, stumbled onto the sidewalk. He mumbled: "Still think it was the same guy. . . ."

When Janek had trudged his way back up the five flights, he found Sue in the stairwell, head and hands pressed against the wall. She was shaking, crying softly to herself. Janek didn't say anything, just took her in his arms.

"You'll be okay."

"Oh, shit," she moaned. "I meant to come see her this morning. Then I got busy and couldn't get to it." She pointed at the floor. "See, I brought her my old air conditioner. Got two uniforms to carry it up. They set it down there, I rang the buzzer and the door popped open. There she was, lying by the couch."

He knew there wasn't anything he could say that would make her feel better, so he fell back upon a standard consolation: "It's not your fault. Don't think it is, even for a second."

When she was calmer, he entered the apartment to check in with Lois Rappaport. As usual, her face was sour, her smile crooked and her report toneless.

"Shot in the head at close range. Like Dietz down at the Savoy. Wounds indicate a twenty-two. Still looking for the bullet."

Rappaport beckoned Janek to join her beside the body. He complied although he didn't want to—to him Kirstin wasn't an ordinary victim. He'd spoken to her, seen her pain, had felt connected to her. Looking at her now—her pale broken face, her large, ghostly Nordic eyes—he thought he saw a less troubled person than he had interviewed three days before. Then, as Lois Rappaport traced the old scars on Kirstin's cheeks, he felt weighed down by grief.

"The way these cuts are drawn—you can see they were made carefully. Sue told me this girl was deliberately disfigured. But these new incisions . . ." Rappaport pointed. "These weren't done to mar her beauty. These are torture cuts, Frank. Looks to me like someone was trying to make her talk."

As Janek considered what Rappaport had said, he was struck by a thought: What if someone had tried to make Kirstin tell what she had refused to reveal to him and Sue—Diana's full name and address? *If that's what this is about,* he thought, *it's very likely she did talk.* How could she resist with a knife held to her face? And the fact that she'd been shot through the head suggested her torturer had gotten what he'd wanted.

He was angry. He had lost his only lead in the Dietz case. He was not waiting until the morning to go on. He phoned Aaron and Ray at home, told them to meet him at Special Squad. At eleven-thirty, when he and Sue arrived, the two men were waiting.

"Here's my theory," he said. "Someone was tracking us, hoping we'd lead him to the Omega. He followed us to Kirstin's, then came back later and finished up our interview. Now he's a step ahead."

"Who're we talking about?" Aaron asked.

Janek turned to Sue. "You were with Kane when he went through Deitz's effects?" Sue nodded. "What'd you think of him?"

"Cold. Arrogant. He tried to get me to talk about the case." Sue paused. "Do you think he killed Kirstin?"

"Maybe. Kane wanted to work with us. Deforest and I said no. Later that day, he met you. Suppose he started stalking you hoping you'd lead him to someone helpful. Suppose he saw you meet me and then the two of us go into Kirstin's building. It wouldn't have been hard to figure out who we were seeing."

Aaron shook his head. "But not Sonoron—?"

Janek agreed. "As much as they want their Omega, they probably wouldn't be party to a thing like this. But suppose Kane's gone into business for himself? In the L.A. sheriff's office he was suspected of being a double agent. The Omega's out there. If he finds it, it can make him rich."

Sue shook her head. "If that bastard—"

"It's just a theory," Janek said. "Now let's go to work and see if we can prove it."

He quickly gave orders. Ray was to search for Kane.

"Start at the Savoy. If I'm right, he's checked out, but the hotel will have a record of his calls. Maybe you'll get lucky—maybe he did something stupid like use his room phone to make a reservation at another hotel."

Aaron was assigned to dig deeper on Kane.

"If he killed Dietz and Kirstin, he's probably been violent before. Find out."

Sue was to keep looking for Diana.

"Kirstin gave us two important leads. She said Diana used a doctor named Feldstein and a lawyer named Thatcher. We gotta talk to them. To do that we need their full names. Check out all the Feldsteins who are MDs. If he's 'fancy' the way Kirstin said, he probably works out of the upper East Side. Then check out all the Thatchers who do criminal defense."

"What about you, Frank?" Aaron asked.

"I'm going to have a little talk with that Sonoron chairman, Cavanaugh."

It was midnight New York time, nine P.M. in San Jose. Sonoron was closed for the day, but a night operator at the company's answering service gave Janek an emergency number. When he called it, he was connected to a Ms.

Isabelle Brooks, who identified herself as Eliot Cavanaugh's executive assistant. Ms. Brooks said that she was speaking to him from her home and that she was hesitant to bother Mr. Cavanaugh after business hours.

"He's in San Francisco this evening. He and his wife went there for dinner and the opera," she explained.

"Has he got a beeper?" Ms. Brooks acknowledged that the chairman did. "Beep him," Janek told her. "Tell him to call me. This is an emergency." He gave her the Squad Room number, then settled back to wait.

Twenty minutes later, Cavanaugh called. "This better be good," he said.

"When did you send Kane to New York?"

"You paged me out of the opera to ask me *that*?"

Janek imagined him standing in his tuxedo at a pay phone outside the men's room at the San Francisco Opera House.

"Yeah, that's why I paged you," Janek said. "Answer the question, please."

"I don't remember exactly when we sent him. What difference does it make?"

"Here's the difference," Janek said. "A few days ago a detective named Sue Burke from my office called to tell you Dietz had been shot in the head. You told her you were sending your security man, Kane, to New York to try and retrieve your stolen chip. Wanna know what I think, Mr. Cavanaugh? I think that wasn't true. I think you sent Kane here to look for Dietz *before* we told you he was shot."

A pause on the other end. Janek imagined Cavanaugh's forehead popping sweat as he tried to dream up a decent response.

"And why would you think that, Lieutenant Janek?"

"Because I think Kane killed Dietz. Now I think he's killed someone else."

"That's wild!"

"Maybe. But if it turns out you lied about when you sent him, you could be implicated, too."

Janek heard a quick intake of breath. "This is really absurd."

"Then clear yourself by answering the question. Or would you rather consult counsel first?"

"You must be out of your mind!"

"It's a simple question—did you lie or didn't you?"

Cavanaugh went silent. When he spoke again his voice was calm. "As soon as Dietz's wife told us he'd gone to New York, we sent Kane there to look for him."

"That was before Detective Burke told you Dietz was dead?"

"I don't recall. Events were occurring fairly fast."

Slick bastard!

"Okay, Mr. Cavanaugh, we'll leave it like that for now. As for your Omega—wanna know what I think?"

"Tell me."

"Kane's gone rogue. If he finds it first, he's going to shop it around for his own account."

At noon the next day, with the squad reassembled, each of the detectives related his results.

Ray, stroking his mustache, reported that Kane had checked into the Savoy the evening Dietz was killed, and had checked out the day he'd met with Janek. Hotel records showed he hadn't made any calls from his room. Ray had begun a methodical check of all hotels and motels in the city, so far with no result.

Sue had found only one criminal defense attorney named Thatcher. His first name was Gilford and he was known as an efficient and very high-priced lawyer. As for Feldstein, there were numerous doctors with that name, so Sue, after consulting with Aaron, had called the Bureau of Controlled Substances in Albany. According to the bureau's computer records, a Dr. Isaac Feldstein, with offices at 780 Park Avenue, had written a large number of prescriptions for triazolam.

Aaron had found out more about Kane's last days in the

L.A. sheriff's office. After he was reassigned, there was noticeable deterioration—suspected drug use, then an assault on a fellow officer. The incident was ugly. The assaulted officer was female. Kane had picked up a pair of scissors, threatened to slash her up. Charges were filed. When it was clear that Kane was going to be dismissed, he resigned and moved to Northern California.

"I talked to the victim," Aaron said. "She says Kane took a swipe at her breasts."

Janek thought a moment. He had only Kane's and Cavanaugh's word that Sonoron's research department had developed the Omega. It seemed just as likely that Sonoron had stolen some of the ideas incorporated in the Omega, or had obtained them by bribing the employees of competitors.

"Right now it doesn't matter why Cavanaugh hired Kane," he said. "All that matters is that he's probably killed two people and he's out there now looking for a third."

Janek began to pace. "Think about it. For a double agent, this is a once-in-a-lifetime chance. First, Dietz steals the Omega. Then Sonoron sends Kane after him to get it back. Meantime, purely by coincidence, Dietz wanders down to his hotel bar, where he gets picked up by our redhead, Gelsey. Dietz invites her upstairs, she drugs him, cleans him out and, in the process, finds the Omega. She takes it and leaves."

"At this point Dietz is still alive?" Sue asked.

"Yes. But then Kane shows up. He's been tracking Dietz. Maybe he saw the bar pickup. Maybe he even saw Gelsey leave the room. So, okay, he finds Dietz drugged out asleep. He tosses the room, but . . . no Omega. What goes through his mind?"

"The redhead took it," Sue said.

Janek stopped pacing. He turned to his squad members. Their eyes were on him. "What's Kane going to do?"

The detectives looked at one another.

"The moral choice is to wait until Dietz wakes up, then

enlist his help in tracking down the girl. What would be his odds? Probably not too good, considering we haven't found her yet."

They nodded. Janek continued.

"There's also the criminal choice. Pump a bullet into Dietz, turn the robbery into a homicide, then stand back and let us do the legwork. Suppose we find the redhead, or at least turn up a lead. All Kane's gotta do is tag along, and then, at the right moment, jump ahead. If I'm right, that's just what he's done." Janek paused. "If Kane finds Gelsey and gets the Omega, he's got no motivation to return it to Sonoron. Instead, he'll do the very thing he says Dietz was going to do—sell it to the competition. If Kane does that, he'll never be suspected. After all, he didn't steal the Omega—Dietz did. Who'll know he found it? No one. So, if he's successful, he's home free."

Janek asked what they thought.

"Pretty theory," Aaron said, "but if you're right, and Kane forced Kirstin to tell him where to find Diana, then he really is ahead of us." Aaron paused. "What do we do now?"

"Play catch up," Janek said. "We're in a race. The winner gets to Gelsey first. We've got to get to her before Kane kills her for that lousy chip."

When he returned from lunch, Stoney was waiting for him. The short bomb squad investigator, looking solemn, asked to speak to him alone.

"Okay, what's up?" Janek said after he closed his office door. "We're busy. We're working a double homicide. So, if you don't mind . . ."

Stoney stared at him. "I'm working a homicide, too."

"Whose?"

"Howard Clury's."

Janek sat down. "Tell me more."

"A car bomb is handmade. You don't buy one at your local sporting-goods store. Every guy who makes one has his own way of doing it. That's what we call the bomb-maker's signature."

"Go on."

"The bomb set under your car and the bomb that blew away Clury nine years ago—without getting technical about it, they were similarly signed."

Janek picked up the police sketch of Gelsey. He remembered what Kirstin had said—that Gelsey referred to writing on her marks as "signing" her work.

"What does that mean?" he asked.

"It kind of eliminates the possibility that Clury was killed in a narcotics hit," Stoney said.

"There probably weren't all that many people who thought that's what happened even back then."

Stoney stared at him, then exhaled. "You and I have a problem, Frank."

"What's that?"

"You're working the Mendoza case and I'm working the Mendoza case. But we're not working as a team."

Shit! Here it comes! "You never asked me about Mendoza."

"I asked you to tell me anything relevant."

"You didn't—"

"Don't con me, Frank. You were a bomb target. So was Clury. Lately you've been investigating the Mendoza affair. Whoever bombed your nice little foreign car was trying to tell you to stay away from it."

"That occurred to me."

"Of course it did. It occurred to me, too, the night the bomb went off. But I didn't say anything. I waited for you to talk. When you didn't, I went out to Nassau County and spoke to the bomb people there. I wasn't with NYPD when Clury was blown. They filled me in. Now I'm asking why you didn't say anything."

"Look, Stoney, this thing's got a life of its own. It's bigger—"

Stoney stood up. He was a short, stocky man, but in his

anger he projected considerable size.

"I don't want to hear that. I don't want to hear any more bullshit about the Mendoza case—how it's bigger than all of us, how it's got a fucking life of its own! Hear me, Frank? I'm sick of that shit! Far as I'm concerned it's a bombing case. Only thing special about it is nine years ago a cop was killed and this week another cop was warned. I'm telling you this so you understand where I'm coming from. I'm going to find out who made those bombs—with your help or not."

He glared at Janek, then turned, walked out and slammed the door. Janek stared after him.

So now the bomb squad's working on the goddamn thing. Do I mind?

He decided that he didn't.

Mirror Madness

Once, to frighten her, her father told her there was a creature called a Minotaur hiding in the maze. From that day she believed the creature was real. Over the years, in her mind it took many forms. Always it was malevolent. . . .

She knew at once that something was wrong. When she rang the bell the response was not Dr. Z's. Instead of his eccentric much-too-quick buzz followed by one much too long, she received a normal, rationally timed response that told her someone else was ringing back.

With trepidation, she pushed open the door, crossed the small foyer and entered the little waiting room.

She had just sat down in her usual chair, was scanning the table for new magazines, when she heard someone emerging from the office. She looked up to find herself facing a woman she had never seen before. This stranger—middle-aged, slim, with handsome features and lovely glowing black-and-gray hair—showed her a warm smile.

"You're Gelsey, aren't you?" Gelsey nodded. "I'm Dr. Bernstein. I'm filling in for Dr. Zimmerman today."

The woman gestured for Gelsey to follow her into the office. Even as Gelsey complied she felt like fleeing. There was something about the woman's presence that filled her with dread.

Dr. Bernstein took Dr. Z's chair. "Please sit down, Gelsey," she said. "We would have called you, but there was no phone number for you in the files."

Gelsey stared at the masks on the opposite wall. The faces were taut, frozen, filled with foreboding.

"Something happened to him?"

Dr. Bernstein peered at her, as if measuring her ability to withstand a piece of devastating news.

"I'm very sorry to have to tell you this, Gelsey. Dr. Zimmerman had a heart attack over the weekend." The woman paused, then continued quietly. "Monday night he passed away."

No!

Even as Gelsey took in these terrible words, she choked on her denial.

NO!!

For a moment she wanted to grasp this strange woman's hands, tell her that what she'd said simply couldn't be true. But their chairs were too far apart, angled slightly from each other the way Dr. Zimmerman liked. And then Gelsey felt a rush of panic as she grasped the enormity of her loss.

Dr. Z, who had tried so hard to help her, was now gone forever from her life. She would never again hear his soothing voice. Staring at his masks, she felt as if she were standing on a tightrope, safety line suddenly gone, precariously balanced above a great, dark, terrifying abyss.

". . . we were close colleagues."

Dr. Bernstein was speaking. Gelsey, caught in a spiral of sorrow, tried hard to follow her words.

". . . he spoke often of you, Gelsey. He was fond of you, as I'm sure you know. Sy Zimmerman was not a man to hide his feelings. With that magnificent man, you always knew where you stood."

Dr. Bernstein shook her head. Her grief was evident.

"All the patients are in great distress. He was such a gifted analyst. I've been trying to meet as many of you as I can, to help you begin the important process of healing. If we mourn properly, we can mend ourselves and go on.

Sy would want that." She smiled. "I can just imagine him saying: 'Go on, Rebecca! Eat up that sorrow! Hurry, finish. Now . . . you're ready for your happiness, your dessert!' " Dr. Bernstein paused. "The funeral, of course, couldn't wait. But there will be a memorial service later in the month. If you give me your address, I'll make certain you're notified. All of Sy's patients are extremely welcome. . . ." She peered at Gelsey. "It's hitting you now, isn't it?"

Gelsey realized she was weeping; she hadn't noticed before.

"I don't know what I'm going to do," she blurted. "We were going to talk about something so important today."

"Well, Sy is gone, but he hasn't left you alone. There're several of us, close colleagues, ready to step in and help as best we can. I don't claim to be as gifted as Sy. He was my supervising analyst when I started out. The man gave to everyone—wife, children, students, patients. Now we must do what he would have wanted most—use what he gave us to grow stronger and continue our struggle with this marvelous, difficult process called life."

Gelsey liked Rebecca Bernstein. She was warm, perhaps even wise. But she could not imagine telling her the secrets she had shared with Dr. Z. Nor could she imagine Dr. Bernstein imparting the same quality of solace. Sy (how strange now to recall him by a first name she had never used) had been ready to explore with her the secrets of the maze. Looking closely now into Dr. Bernstein's friendly eyes, Gelsey asked herself: *How could I even begin to explain?*

But then she *did* begin. Suddenly the words began to tumble out. She wasn't aware at first of how fast she was speaking or how intimate was her torrent. It was all a jumble, the story of her life, fractured into pieces and then rearranged like the shards of broken mirrors she now applied to the surfaces of her paintings:

Her father, handsome, the charmer, the maze-maker, hitting the road with his tacky trailer, his funky fun-house mirror-maze-on-wheels. Traveling the carnival circuit, then returning to work on his great creation, his private labyrinth, secret work of art.

Her mother, depressed carnival worker, eyes wet, skin damp, sitting forlorn in the window, waiting, waiting . . . for her husband to return.

The world of mirrors. Mirror-madness times. Reflections that don't show you who you are. A dream-sister in mirrorspace. Mirrorworld. The mockery of mirrors. Their cruelty. Infinite corridors. Galleries of images. Slices of her face, body, soul.

Crooked crazy-house mirrors in the Corridor of Distortion. The sinuous, diabolical Fragmentation Serpent with its body-breaking mirrors and parabolic mouth that flips you upside down. The untouchable, unreachable attractions in the Chamber of Unobtainable Ecstasy. The Great Hall of Infinite Deceptions with its seductive multimirrored walls.

Disassociations. Shadow-work. Her double-delusion mirror-fantasy incest-secret. The forbidden mysteries hidden in the concealed chambers of angled silvered glass.

Mirrorsex. A Leering Man with a devil's grin. "You bitch! You slut!" Kisses that branded her pale, pale skin. How she knew all about men, their fantasies, their weaknesses, how she could turn them on at will. How she liked to tell them stories about her father's abuse, then watch how her stories titillated their desire. How she thought: *If I seduced him, I can seduce them all. If I was his love slave, I can make them mine.*

Mirror-art: The mirrors guard her. She gathers energy from them. They taunt her. Sometimes she believes she *is* a mirror!

Down in the maze. Down there. In the labyrinth. Among the mirrors. Nothing is real. We are only reflections, illusions, shadows on the glass.

Mirror-crime: Picking up marks, slipping them KO drops, putting them to sleep.

Looking beyond a mirror. What is she looking for?

Down there.

Deep within a mirror, behind its surface? Mirror-ache. Mirror-pain.

Down there.

Something hiding. A creature.

Down there.

Dark, malevolent, sexual.

Down there.

The secret of mirrorsex!

Down there.

The Minotaur.

''Hmmm, yes, I see . . .'' Gelsey looked up. Rebecca Bernstein was staring at her. ''While I was waiting for you, I read your file. Sy was concerned. He felt you were close to a breakthrough, a turning point in the analysis. I'd like to work with you, Gelsey. As I said before, I don't pretend to be as talented as Sy, but perhaps I can offer a few good insights. Perhaps, too, you could profit from working with a female analyst.'' She paused. ''You must think about it. I don't want to press you. You have been open with me today. Thank you for that.'' She spread her hands. ''We've all suffered a terrible loss. Perhaps together we can find a way to work through our suffering. Here's my card. Please call me . . . anytime.''

A minute later Gelsey found herself standing alone in the little waiting room, wondering what to do. Through the doorway she could hear Dr. Bernstein's muffled voice as she spoke to someone on the office phone. A kind woman, a good listener, but Gelsey knew she would not return. A good, kind, wise woman was not enough. She needed, and now had lost, a brilliant man.

She looked around the pathetic waiting room. Shabby chairs. Ragged magazines. The tawdry dime-store mirror on the wall. She had always despised that mirror. Now she found it touching.

She reached up, lifted it off its hook, held it tightly to her chest. She knew what she would do. She would steal the mirror to keep as a memento of Dr. Z. She would keep it and stare into it and perhaps one day she would see his face.

Back on Broadway, she hurried toward the health club. When she reached it, she paused outside. In the front window a muscular male mannequin, bare but for a pair of gym shorts, held hands with a muscular female mannequin dressed in shorts and a haltered sports bra. Smiles were painted on their faces. Mirrors revealed their attractive posteriors. The message was that if one joined this gym, one would find attractive objects of one's desire.

Oh, where are you, Dr. Z?

Thinking of Tracy, yet knowing it would be unwise to go in, she crossed the street to the supermarket, entered, pushed her way through the crowds to the community bulletin board posted beside the salad bar.

The board was crowded with slips of paper offering apartments for share, rides to the Hamptons, a male "maid" who promised to "bust your dust." There were numerous other notices offering items and services. Finally, in the upper right corner, Gelsey found an offering of newborn kittens. She untacked it, turned it over, found Tracy's message on the other side: "CALL DIANA! URGENT!"

She thought about whether she should call. By the time she reached her car, she had decided not to. But then, driving downtown, she changed her mind. When she reached the Village, she pulled into a metered parking space on Seventh, walked a block to an Italian coffee house on Greenwich Avenue, entered, ordered an espresso, then proceeded to the rest-room area, where she found a quiet pay phone.

Oh, Dr. Z . . .

Again she hesitated. She hadn't spoken to Diana since

the night she'd walked out. But when she lifted the receiver and inserted a quarter, the number flew back into her head. She was sorry she remembered it.

"Hel-lo. May I help you?" It was Kim, with her mechanical singsong, who painted Diana's toenails and slavishly handwashed her underwear.

"It's Gelsey. Is Diana there?"

"One moment, please." Not: "How are you, Gelsey?" or "How're you doing" or "Good to hear your voice again." Just that distant, mechanical response that brought back the strange alienated feeling that had filled her during her time as one of Diana's girls.

"Is it really *you*?" The oh-so-unctuous voice of Herself.

"None other!" Gelsey tried to sound cheerful.

"Tracy gave you my message?"

Beware! A trap! "No. But I ran into a mutual friend who'd seen her and passed it on."

A giggle. "Still mysterious. How long has it been?"

"About a year and a half."

"That long?"

This is boring. Time to get curt. "What can I do for you, Diana?"

"It's more like what I can do for you, my pet."

"I'm doing just fine, thanks."

"With the police looking for you?"

"I can take care of myself."

"I don't doubt that!" Diana giggled again. "Still," she said after a pause, "we may have a mutual interest."

"I can't imagine how."

"Let bygones be bygones, what do you say?" Then, in an unusual pleading tone: "I do wish you'd come back."

"I don't think so. Sorry."

"We made a lot of money together. We could make so very much more."

It was just what Erica Hawkins had told her. She thought: *Better to make money with art than marks.*

"Look, Diana—"

"What happened between you and the gentleman downtown was not good for business, not at all."

There it was, the reproach that always undercut the sweetness.

"It's your business, not mine."

"Oh, yes, I forgot! You do it for fun."

"What do you want?"

"To help you. You're a wanted woman. I can fix that. Have Thatcher get you out of this mess. Help you leave town, hide out, whatever. I'm still very fond of you, you know. I admit I was upset when you left. I'm well over that."

What could she say? That she didn't believe her, not for a minute, a second? That she never wanted to see her again, or sleazy Thatcher either? That Diana's proffered fondness was not reciprocated a single bit? That she didn't need any help hiding out because she always hid out—hiding out was what her life was about? *Isn't that right, Dr. Z?*

"Why don't we have tea, talk things over?" Diana crooned.

"Why not just leave things as they are?"

"You're not being very friendly, Gelsey. Considering the circumstances."

Gelsey felt her stomach tighten. "I don't know what circumstances you mean."

"The gentleman, the one you took down at the Savoy—I understand he was carrying something . . . unusual."

Her stomach went hard. "Where'd you hear that?"

"Around." Diana paused. Gelsey had a feeling that when she spoke again, her tone would be a good deal less ingratiating. "Listen to me. You killed a mark. That's not good for business."

"So you said. But I didn't kill him."

A haughty laugh. "I certainly don't expect you to admit it!"

"Get to the point."

"The point, my pet, is that I want what you took off

Dietz. Not his money or his watch. The other thing."

"Assuming I have it, why should I give it to you?"

"Because I know how to market it." Another pause. "You *do* have it, don't you?"

"Tell me what it is and I'll tell you if I do." Gelsey smiled the moment she said that, pleased by her shrewdness, for it occurred to her that although Diana seemed to know she had taken something, she had not yet said what she thought it was.

"All right"—Diana was now all business—"you have an item and I have a buyer for it. That's got the makings of a fifty-fifty deal."

"After you take fifty percent off the top?"

Silence. "Are you mocking me, dear?"

"I wouldn't dare."

Diana laughed. "You'd dare do anything you felt like doing. I know you better than you think." Gelsey kept silent. "You won't deal—is that it?"

Gelsey smiled. She had Diana on the mats. "You know I don't care about money." *And we both know you care about nothing else.*

"So you always said. I never believed you."

"Sorry, Diana. No sale. But if it'll make you feel better, I won't be playing the KO game for a while. It's suddenly gotten too dangerous—if you know what I mean?"

"Stupid, insolent girl!"

Gelsey hung up, delighted she'd shattered Diana's poise. She returned to her table and sipped her espresso. In the interval it had grown cold.

Why? Why, Dr. Z?

By the time she reached home she was frantic. It seemed as if her world were falling apart. She was a murder suspect; the police were after her; Diana was after her, too—something to do with that computer chip she'd found on Dietz. But since she'd smashed it up and incorporated it into her painting, she couldn't make a deal with Diana even if she wanted to. Meantime, Dr. Z was dead. And Tracy, her only friend, was afraid to see her anymore.

As she entered her loft, she felt desperate. She had no one to talk to now, no one to turn to for help. All she had left was her fortress and her prison, the mirror maze below.

She put water on the stove for pasta. Then, realizing she wasn't hungry, she turned it off. She poured herself a vodka, straight from the bottle she kept in her freezer. Then she stood by her window looking out as darkness crept up slowly on the industrial buildings around and the abandoned amusement park across the road.

She wished that it would rain, a soft, ripe, gentle rain that would wash her windows and skylight clean. Then she could go into the city and take down a mark. Except, of course, she could not. Employees at the bars and pubs would be on alert. The police were looking for a killer. So, even if it did rain, she could only dream.

What was it about the rain? Why did it always fill her with a longing she did not know how to satisfy? Why did rain always make her want to enter mirrorworld, the magic country of reverse?

So many questions, so many things about herself she didn't understand. Despite the numerous times she had discussed her fears with Dr. Z, she still had found no answers.

Why couldn't she break away from the mirrors? Would she ever be able to find her real self inside the glass?

Rebecca Bernstein had said something that afternoon—that she had found a notation in Gelsey's file in which Dr. Z had spoken of a breakthrough. She herself had hoped for that, but now the likelihood was remote. Could she make a breakthrough by herself? If not, then who would help her?

Later, when it was dark, and although there was still no sign of rain, she decided to go down to the maze. She had no idea what she hoped to find down there, what secret might be revealed. But she was drawn to it by a force she could not resist. It was as if she were compelled to revisit the site of some particularly gruesome crime.

Climbing down the ladder to the catwalk, she began to tremble. She knew she was truly alone in the world. She switched on the lights, then slid down the thick white rope, aware that on the floor she would no longer be alone, that there she could lose herself among her friends, the mirrors.

She stripped off her clothes, stood naked, then entered the twisting corridor. This mirrored aisle, which led directly to the Great Hall, contained no points of reference. To walk through it was akin to roaming the middle of a forest of equally spaced and identical trees. The mirrors, each seven feet by four feet, each framed by narrow pillars and angled at precisely 60 degrees, created a labyrinth of endless galleries. Gelsey knew her way through these galleries. She was not confused by the insertion at certain junctions of similarly sized and framed panels of clear glass. But if she closed her eyes and whirled around, she could cause herself to lose her bearings. Then she could become as lost as any first-time visitor.

She liked to do this. It was far more pleasureful to wander disoriented than to rush through the maze with mastery and purpose. There was an ecstasy to be found in naked bewilderment, a rapture to be savored on account of being lost and confused. To lose oneself deliberately in the maze was to enter a trance-state equal to one induced by the most voluptuous of mind-altering drugs. Space and time became distorted. She was surrounded by flowing fractured visions of her body. Light danced across the silver. Reflections shimmered as she moved. And then, if she spun, a thousand self-replicas whirled, too. She was no longer alone. She was at the hub of a great turning wheel of flickering, sparkling clones.

Once in the Great Hall, the "deceptions" were indeed "infinite." It had been her father's conceit that the confusion of the labyrinthine corridor would give way to even greater perplexity as the maze-wanderer blundered in.

Here, her father foresaw, the images would truly explode.

Here the maze-wanderer would be confronted by a burst of illusions as he viewed himself in mirrors that were crooked, bent, waved and even creased. A person of great physical presence would be challenged by distorted doubles. A beautiful face would be deconstructed. A graceful figure would be cleaved or broken. "I will take them apart," he told Gelsey once, crouching over his workbench, painstakingly bending a sheet of glass. He broke many pieces while trying to create distorting mirrors. When he finally got one right, he would rush off with it to the factory that did his silvering.

Whenever she entered the Great Hall, she expected no mercy. Here the only available images were of herself. Unless she closed her eyes, she could not escape these luminous self-portraits, finding relief only in the distorting mirrors, which, although they presented her with reflections, at least provided variations on the identical likenesses to be seen in the mirrors that reflected true. But these "mirrors of deception" also cut at her eyes. The flawed doubles they offered her were parodies. It seemed to her that by their mockery, they made comment upon her character. They told her that the face she showed the world was fake, that the self she presented was a counterfeit.

Losing herself in here, yielding to the pitiless judgment of the glass, she found herself besieged by visions from her past. They did not come to her whole, but in flashes, splinters, shards. She saw quick reflections of herself at an earlier age, little pieces of her dream-sister: a flare of flesh, a flicker of an eye, a mouth tormented in a silent scream. And there were pieces of her father, too—his flesh, eyes, mouth. But between these tiny slivers of the two of them, she saw flashes of someone or something else.

She turned and looked for whatever it was. She wanted most desperately to see it. She wondered if it was the Leering Man of her dreams. Her father had called it "the creature," sometimes "the Minotaur." It was here, hiding in the maze, visible only for instants when she moved. And so, to induce it to come out, she began to turn in the center of the Great Hall—around, around and around again, twirling, whirling, reveling at being at the hub of a great kaleidoscope, seeking a glimpse of the monster, no matter how quick or brief.

She whirled so hard, so many times, she became lost in dizziness. But as hard as she strove to see the Minotaur clearly, she caught only tiny glimpses before she collapsed in fatigue upon the floor.

Peering around, staring at each image of herself in turn, she wondered if this mirror-madness would one day cease to be ecstatic, whether one day it would make her so crazy that she would be imprisoned forever in the glass.

Oh, Doc, wherever you are—help me. Help me! Please!

The Hunt

Dr. Isaac Feldstein was not inclined to cooperate. He made that clear by staring severely at Aaron, then at Janek, while sitting very straight behind his orderly and too-large mahogany desk.

Janek stared back, blank-faced, as the doctor told them he did not believe he had a patient whose first name was Diana. In fact, the doctor said, he doubted he even knew a woman with that particular first name. As for triazolam, yes, he did prescribe it for some of his patients. He also prescribed Valium, Ativan, Dalmane and a good half dozen other sedatives of the benzodiazepine class. Under no circumstances would he reveal his patients' names or the nature of their prescriptions. If the detectives did not understand why he held to this position, they were welcome to discuss the matter with his attorney.

Feldstein, wearing an immaculate white jacket, smiled scornfully as he said all this. Then, as if to reassure himself, he gazed around at the fine appointments in his Park Avenue consulting room.

He was a short, dapper man with an oversized head, thick gray hair and a sharp, jutting chin. As he talked he angled his head back to emphasize his confidence. He was self-important, feisty, arrogant—all traits that Janek despised. Watching him, Janek wondered how he managed to keep his patients. But then he remembered that there were people who preferred a cold, imperious doctor. Better to leave everything to the despotic judgment of an all-knowing Great Physician than to acknowledge there were mysteries within the body as yet not understood.

"So, if that's all you gentlemen—"

"What's his name?" Janek asked.

Feldstein blinked. He didn't like being interrupted. "Excuse me?"

"Your attorney—what's his name?"

"Well, I don't really see—"

"Gilford Thatcher, right?"

"Well, yes. But—"

"Yeah, I thought so." Janek shook his head with disgust.

Feldstein screwed up his features. "Sorry, Lieutenant, I don't get what you're driving at."

Janek leaned forward. "I've worked a lot of cases like this. Sooner or later we find the person we're looking for. Then, sooner or later, he or she makes a deal. What I'm driving at, Dr. Feldstein, is that when we find this woman, whom you claim you don't know, and she tells us how you prescribed triazolam, knowing exactly what she was going to do with it, I'll make it my personal mission in life to see your license revoked."

He glanced at Aaron. They stood up. They didn't bother to say good-bye.

He took the Lexington Avenue subway downtown, got off at Canal Street, walked three blocks east, then climbed the four long flights to the former karate studio that housed the law offices of Rampersad & Rudnick.

This time Netti's young secretary opened the door.

"Hello, Lieutenant." Doe Landestoy beamed.

Janek peered around. Rudnick was nowhere in sight, but Netti was on the exercise platform working out with a pair of chromed barbells.

"Hi!" she yelled. "Be right with you—soon as I finish the set."

Janek watched as she completed her routine. She looked

limber and strong. He noticed she was wearing the same ensemble as on his previous visit, except that this time her sweatpants were navy and her white tanktop bore a black German military insignia.

When she was finished, she mopped her face with a towel, slung it over the back of her neck, grabbed both ends with her hands and approached. As before, her forehead, neck and upper torso were slick with sweat.

Janek looked her over. "Every time I drop in here I catch you working out."

Her eyes glowed. "I like pumping iron. Sometimes I practice a little law."

He noticed several delightful clusters of freckles on her glossy chest. *Don't start thinking about her body,* he warned himself.

"Glad to hear that. I need a good lawyer. I'm here today on my own account."

She raised her eyebrows, beckoned him to her work area, gestured him into her client's chair, sat behind her desk, mopped her face again and settled back.

"Okay," she said nicely, in the manner of a well-practiced attorney, "let's hear your story."

She listened carefully as he spoke, taking occasional notes on a yellow legal pad, nodding at strategic points to show she followed what he was saying. As he recounted his saga—exploitative ex-wife, crushing alimony, ex-wife's live-in lover, imbalance in their incomes—he found, to his surprise, that he was enjoying himself. Netti was a good listener; she inspired coherent narrative. And his depiction of Sarah, which always emerged with a bitter edge when he discussed her with Aaron, was coming out now in a far more attractive form.

"Well, it ain't criminal defense," Netti said when he finished. "But it could be fun, specially if I can do it quick." She paused. "What's your bottom line?"

"Reduce the alimony, I guess."

"Reduce it? Why not eliminate it?"

"Think you can do that?"

"I'll give it my best shot."

Suddenly he was worried: What if Netti came on too strong, antagonized Sarah, then lost the case? Might that inspire Sarah to seek even more alimony than he was paying?

"Is it smart to demand so much?"

Netti patted his hand. "Only way to go. In a case like this you've gotta break their balls."

He arrived back at Special Squad to take a call from Joe Deforest.

"Free this evening?" Deforest asked.

"What's up?"

"That attorney you're interested in, Gil Thatcher—he just phoned. He wants to take us to dinner."

"Right," Janek said, smiling to himself. "I've been expecting something like this."

He took off an hour, went over to Twelfth Avenue and walked through several new-car dealer showrooms. Everything he touched had a plastic, tinny feel to it. He was angry about the loss of his Saab and hoped Stoney would find the guy who blew it up.

He decided two things: He wouldn't buy a car, and, as soon as he was finished with the Dietz case, he would call Stoney and offer to collaborate.

La Palombe was not the kind of restaurant Janek liked. It was, first of all, very expensive, a fact made clear by its marble-lined foyer, haughty hat-check girl, hovering tuxedoed waiters, lavish floral bouquets and opulent main room where elegantly framed watercolors hung on red damask-covered walls.

The pretentious maître d' didn't appeal to Janek either; nor, apparently, did Janek do much for him. *Must be my shoes,* Janek thought, but he didn't care. He knew about the supercilious Europeans who guarded the portals of Manhattan's fancier establishments. They were the kind who, if you came in and asked politely to use the men's room, would recoil in disgust.

He didn't like Gilford Thatcher, but he hadn't expected to, so that came as no surprise. Thatcher wasn't up-front arrogant like Feldstein. Rather, he was oily and affable with the kind of perfect tan you get only if you spend a lot of time on a yacht. He was a handsome man with a leonine face and carefully cut soft black hair. He had a low-key confidential way of speaking that forced listeners to lean forward, and a smug, sometimes ironic smile.

Janek stayed silent while Thatcher and Deforest made small talk. He listened politely as Thatcher recommended various dishes and then entered into a tedious discussion with the wine steward. When, toward the middle of the meal, he noticed Thatcher studying him, he looked the attorney in the eye.

"You've been quiet, Lieutenant," Thatcher observed.

Janek shrugged. "I like to get to the point."

"Fine." Thatcher grinned. "Let's get to it. You've been asking around about one of my clients. I'd like to know why."

"I'm looking for a young woman. I think your client knows where she lives."

"Who exactly are we talking about?"

"What exactly is your client's name?"

Thatcher smiled again. "Her first name's Diana."

"The first name of the woman I'm looking for is Gelsey."

"Well, now that we've got that straight . . ." Thatcher winked at Deforest. "My client is a public-spirited individual. I'm sure she'd like to help. But if she talks to you, she could implicate herself. Obviously, that's something I can't permit."

"What do you suggest?" Deforest asked.

"That she come forward on a background-only basis."

"What does that mean?"

"No sworn testimony. Any 'crimes' referred to are off the record. She will never be called as a witness. She helps you once and that's it . . . forever."

"You're talking about full immunity," Deforest said.

Thatcher nodded. "I'll need your assurance on that."

Janek didn't like it. "Your client's running a dope 'em and rob 'em ring."

Thatcher smiled. "If you're sure about that, Lieutenant, I'd advise you to take your evidence to the D.A."

"Look, we're not interested in Diana," Deforest said.

"Glad to hear it. But my job is to protect my client. Full immunity's the only way." Thatcher gave a short nod. Then he stood. "Excuse me. I'll call her now, see how she feels about it. Meantime, you gentlemen talk it over. I'd like to settle this tonight."

As soon as he was gone, Janek looked at Deforest. "It stinks."

"Sure, it does," Deforest agreed. "But you still need to talk to the lady."

"Who's to say she'll tell me anything? Meantime, she gets immunized."

"Maybe she'll help you, Frank, maybe she won't. That's the chance you take. If after you meet her you think she bullshitted you, investigate her all you want. Just wait till the Dietz case is wrapped, then go in and develop your evidence. The only stuff you won't be able to use is stuff she tells you. Otherwise she's fair game."

"If she's smart she'll tell me everything."

"Don't let her. Go in wired. The moment she strays from the topic, cut her off." Janek thought about it, then nodded. "It's the right decision, Frank," Deforest assured him.

When Thatcher returned, he ordered coffee for three, then turned to Janek. "Assuming you guys agree to my terms, Diana will meet you tonight."

"Where?"

"One A.M. Corner of Washington and Gansevoort."

"The meat market—how convenient."

Thatcher raised an eyebrow to show he didn't know the neighborhood. "She'll drive by and pick you up."

"What's her last name?"

Thatcher smiled. "I don't think you need to know that."

Deforest glanced at Janek. Janek shrugged; he understood he had no choice.

"Okay," Deforest said, "we agree—nothing she tells Janek can be used against her. He'll record the conversation. I assume she'll do the same." Thatcher nodded. "You want this in writing?"

"Your word's fine. Anyway"—Thatcher smiled as he looked toward Janek—"I have an excellent witness here."

When Deforest got up to visit the men's room, he looked like he was going to puke. Thatcher and Janek sat facing each other. Thatcher broke the silence.

"You don't like me very much, do you?"

Janek shrugged. "What difference does it make?"

"I know what you're thinking."

"What's that?"

"Because I represent people you consider scum, that makes me scum, too."

Janek shook his head. "I understand the advocacy system."

Thatcher grinned. "You're pretty advanced. A lot of you guys can't differentiate." He paused. "So, what is it about me you don't like?"

"You got it all wrong, Counselor. I don't dislike you. I'm amused by you, that's all."

Thatcher's eyes showed puzzlement. "Amused?"

Janek nodded. "You're the kind of slick lawyer gets a kick out of making a hardball deal like tonight. But the day you want something from me you'll come on obsequious." Janek smiled. "I find that pretty funny."

As he waited on the corner of Gansevoort and Washington, he found himself growing increasingly annoyed. He knew that in a few hours the Fourteenth Street meat market would come to life, crowded with delivery trucks and wholesale butchers pushing hooked carcasses around on the permanently installed tracks. But at one A.M. the place was deserted, except for an occasional car cruising for an occasional strolling transvestite prostitute. The street lamps were dim, the meat hooks were bare, he could hear rats moving in the sewers and the old cobblestones were hard on his feet. There was a slaughterhouse aroma, too; no matter how often the purveyors hosed down the area, they could never rid it of the stench.

By one-thirty he considered going home. He knew that the delay was deliberate, that he was the object of a power play: Wear the jerk down by making him wait on the lonely street corner, then pull up, all smiles and apologies. He'd been through it many times; he guessed he'd employed it numerous times himself. But still he felt aggrieved. He thought: *Maybe I'm getting too old for this.*

At 1:35 a long white Cadillac limousine appeared out of the gloom. It slipped around the corner of Washington and Jane, then headed slowly toward him.

He'd heard about Diana's limo from Kirstin. Despite his irritation, he felt a small rush of excitement at the prospect of finally meeting the iron magnolia, as capable of taking her girls on cultural-improvement tours as she was adept at carving up their pretty cheeks.

The long car glided to a halt. As Janek moved toward it, he could see images of himself reflected in its one-way glass. When he was just a few feet away, the driver's window descended, revealing a smooth-faced Asian girl. *Must be Kim,* he thought. She was dressed in a man's white shirt, solid black tie and traditional chauffeur's cap pulled tight over helmet-cut hair. She examined him severely.

"You're the cop?"

Janek nodded. Kim gestured toward the back of the car, then raised her window, causing her sullen features to be replaced by his own.

The moment Janek opened the rear door, he was hit by a blast of cold air and the intense aroma of a dark, intensely cloying perfume. A handsome middle-aged woman with sleek platinum-dyed hair, wrapped in a gray fur coat, sat in the far corner of the seat. She was gazing at him, a feline smile on her lips.

"Please get in," she said.

Inside he was better able to make her out. She had gray eyes, extremely pale skin and fine, almost delicate facial bones. When she shifted slightly to adjust her fur, he was reminded of a pampered, silver-coated cat.

"Diana Cassiday," she said, extending her hand.

"Frank Janek," he said, extending his. After they shook, the car began to move. Janek caught a quick glimpse of Kim glaring at him in the rearview mirror.

"I hope you don't mind if we drive around. I like to cruise the city at night." Diana turned to him. "I understand you're wired?" There was a slight Texas twang to her speech, but what struck Janek was its smoothness. Her voice reminded him of velvet.

He shook his head. "No need." He showed her his tape recorder, flicked it on, then set it between them on the seat. "What about you?"

"Built in." She reached toward a console, flicked a switch, then pushed a button. A glass partition rose to cut off the driver's compartment. "Privacy," she said, as if the act required an explanation.

She snuggled farther down into her coat. The limo was so cold, Janek found himself squeezing his elbows to his sides. The solution, of course, was to turn down the air-conditioning, but the lady, it seemed, liked to wear her furs.

"Your attorney wouldn't give us your last name."

Diana smiled. "Gil can be silly sometimes. Especially as all you'd have to do is run a check on my license plate." She hummed to herself; it sounded like a purr. Then she looked at Janek curiously. "What did you say to him, anyway?"

Janek shrugged.

"Whatever it was, it surely did annoy him."

"I pretty much told him what I thought."

This time Diana's eyes were truly curious. "Why on earth did you do that?" When Janek shrugged again, Diana shook her head. The motion was kittenish. "You and I are different types, Lieutenant. I never tell *anybody* what I think."

The limo cruised east on Fourteenth. They were leaving the meat market, a move Janek found encouraging. The car, he noticed, was soundproofed, isolating them from the noises of the city. Its one-way glass made the streets look dimmer than they were. Between the hush and the muted light, he felt like he was riding in a hearse.

"I protect my girls. Whenever one of them gets into trouble, Gil's there, day or night, to get her out of it. You could say he's part of my extended family. . . ."

As Diana spoke, Janek observed her closely. There was cunning in her eyes, he thought, and also a predatory gleam. Her soft looks and graceful speech were attractive, but still he felt repelled. Was it because of what Kirstin had told him, he wondered, or a diabolical aura the woman exuded, a force field of evil and stealth? As much as he found her catlike, he was also reminded, by the way she held herself in the corner of the car, of a predaceous female spider in the center of a web, trembling with anticipation as she observed the death throes of her prey.

"When I heard about the man who was killed downtown, naturally I was upset. Something like that isn't good for business. Then, when Kirstin . . ." She made a gesture of despair. "She'd been one of us, you see." She paused again. "You must understand, Lieutenant. In my business—"

"Please, Ms. Cassiday"—he spoke clearly so that his tape recorder would pick up all his words—"don't tell me anything about your business. If you do I'll have to cut this short."

She gazed at him. "You want to ask specific questions?"

"That would make things easier."

She considered the proposal, then shook her head. "We'll do it my way. I'll tell you a story. You can take it as a parable . . . or any way you like."

"Fine, we'll try that." He thought: *With this woman, everything's a power play.*

She purred again, then began. Her phrasing was elegant, her voice subdued:

"About two and a half years ago an attractive young woman came to see me. A talented artist, she'd been referred by one of my employees. This girl told me she wanted to learn the game. That's what we call what we do." Diana paused. "Well, I looked her over, asked her some questions, decided I liked her and agreed to break her in. As it turned out, she trained nicely She had talent. I'd say she was a natural, if it's possible to use a term like that to describe somebody with a genius for our particular line of work. To make a long story short, within a few weeks she became my top producer. She seemed to know just what to do and her timing was always impeccable. It was as if she harbored a lot of anger, mostly hidden from view, but apparent when she let down her guard. Later, when I saw one of her sketches, I felt that anger again. I believe she used it to fuel herself. I asked her about that once. 'How do you happen to be so good at the game?' She thought a bit before she answered. 'I think it's because it's dangerous,' she replied." Diana turned to Janek. "Finding this interesting, Lieutenant?"

"Fascinating."

Diana purred, then continued with her story:

"After a few months I began to notice something else about this girl. For us, you see, the game is a business, a way to make a living. But for her it was clearly more. She got something special out of it. Exactly what, I'm not quite sure, but I think I'd be safe if I called it . . . pleasure. You see, Lieutenant, she genuinely liked the work, liked every single aspect of it. The power to seduce, the power to control. She even enjoyed writing on their skins.'' Diana looked knowingly at Janek. ''I assume you know what I'm talking about?''

''I do. But we won't discuss it.''

Diana grinned. ''Of course not!'' She settled back. ''This girl also had a special way of writing. She could write in mirror-reverse as quickly as any of the others could write in normal script. Amazing when you think about it.'' Diana paused. ''She's the one you're looking for.''

Janek nodded. ''Where do I find her?''

''I don't know. She left me, set up shop for herself.''

As Diana spoke, her manner changed. Whatever grace she'd displayed before gave way to a deeply felt fury. It was as if, Janek thought, a terrible blizzard had begun to blow in the middle of a summer day. He had no difficulty imagining Diana smiling as she raised a razor to punish one of her girls for recalcitrance.

''You resented that, of course,'' he said.

''She became a competitor. How would you have felt?''

''Probably the same.''

''Disloyalty's disloyalty.'' Diana bit off the word. ''Once she'd sucked me dry, she left without a fare-thee-well.''

It was such a quaint expression, Janek could only smile. But Diana didn't notice; she was reliving Gelsey's betrayal.

''At first I was glad to be rid of the bitch. I like a girl with a good professional attitude. This one was just too passionate—if you know what I mean.''

''Could you mean . . . too smart?''

She hummed. ''Perhaps that, too.''

''Look, Ms. Cassiday, it's urgent I talk to her. Why don't you just tell me where she lives?''

''You don't believe me, Lieutenant? The truth is I really don't know. She was secretive about almost everything, especially her address. She even refused to give me her telephone number. I told her that wouldn't do, that she couldn't work for me unless she was reachable day or night.

But in the end it worked out. If I asked her to call and confirm an appointment, she never let me down.'' Diana shook her head. ''A strange girl. Unique. She's obsessed with mirrors. That's where all that mirror writing comes from. She can't pass a mirror without gazing into it. But, funny thing, when she does, I don't think she looks at herself.''

''What does she look at?''

''The rest of us. I think she likes to look at us in mirrors rather than deal with us as we are.''

''And how are we?'' Janek asked.

Diana laughed. ''You're asking how I view my fellow man? This interview is turning out to be more interesting than I expected.''

''So, what's your answer?''

Diana pondered. As she did, her eyes, it seemed to him, enlarged. ''I suppose I see the world as a fairly pitiless place,'' she said carefully, ''where, in any encounter, one must move quickly for advantage knowing the other person most likely is doing the same. I admit it's not a pleasant vision, but I believe it's accurate. The will to power—or should I say overpower?—is, in my view, the most potent drive we have.'' She paused. ''Now that I've answered, do you mind if I ask a question of my own?''

''Go ahead.''

She paused. ''There're rumors about this man who was killed downtown. What was his name?''

''Dietz.''

''Yes, Dietz. There's a rumor.''

Janek went on guard. ''What rumor?''

''That he was carrying something . . . valuable. Is it true?''

Janek shrugged. He decided to annoy her. ''Where did you hear that?''

''It's all over town.''

Oh, you're slick. ''What is?''

''The rumor.''

"Which is?"

Diana twitched. "That Gelsey took something valuable off of Dietz."

"What kind of 'something'?"

"Whatever . . ."

"Is that why you think we're looking for her?"

"Is it?"

"Is that your question?"

"Not really."

Diana twitched again. He was happy to see he'd tied her in knots. Now he imagined she was calculating just how far she could push.

Janek searched her eyes. "Just what is your question, Ms. Cassiday?"

Diana paused. "What did she take?"

"Is that important to you?"

"I'm curious."

Janek stared at her, then he smiled. "Sorry," he said, "tonight I ask questions, I don't answer them."

In an instant her eyes went hard. She recoiled farther against the seat. She was not, this tightened posture made clear, accustomed to being denied.

"Perhaps if you'd tell me why it's so important . . ."

"Christ!" she exploded. "What's the big deal?"

"Is it a big deal? Is that why you're upset?"

"I'm not upset."

"You sound a lot more than curious."

"God, you're impossible! Do you have to be such a fucking—cop!"

He laughed. He'd broken her calm. "I think it's time for me to get out."

"Long past." She lifted the phone intercom from her console, ordered Kim to stop.

When Janek looked out the window he saw that they'd crossed to the East Village and were now at Tenth and Avenue C. It was not a good neighborhood, but he was happy to be making his escape. The car was too cold, Diana's perfume was too cloying and the lady had shown herself to be detestable.

He opened the door, stepped into the street, then leaned back in. Diana, deep inside her fur, glared at him from the far corner like a lynx.

"I'd be careful of my curiosity if I were you," he told her.

"Really?" Her eyes flashed. "Is that a warning?"

"Sometimes when people ask questions they give themselves away. Mr. Thatcher should have told you that."

Diana stared at him a moment, then rapped on the partition. Kim gassed the engine and the great limousine leaped forward, leaving him alone in the middle of the street.

When he arrived home he found a message on his answering machine. Aaron begged him to phone, no matter the hour, to tell him how the meeting had gone. It was a typical Aaron request. When Janek called, Aaron picked up on the first ring.

"Frank?"

"Yeah, it's me."

"How'd it go?"

"Chilly," Janek said.

"She's bad news, huh?"

"Poison."

"Figures. She tell you anything?"

"Not much. But maybe more than she thought. I've got an idea." He paused. "It's a long shot."

"Well, ain't they all, Frank," Aaron said. "And don't we always bet on them anyway?"

The next morning, with the squad assembled, Janek played back his tape of the Diana interview. Everyone was enthralled by the woman's voice.

"Very smooth," Sue commented.

"Smooth and toxic," Janek said. "So, what does she tell us?"

"She's too eager near the end," Sue said. "You toy with her and she doesn't pull back. You drive her nuts, and she still doesn't let go."

"How'd she know Dietz was carrying something? We've held that close," Ray said, stroking his mustache.

"Why do you think she's so eager?"

"Maybe . . . Kane."

"Go on," Janek said.

Ray was excited. "If I were Diana and Kane got my name out of Kirstin, then came and offered me money to lead the way to Gelsey—I'd be desperate to know why."

"What would you think?"

"I'd think that if Gelsey had something worth killing for, I ought to cut myself in on the deal."

Janek nodded. "The way Diana acted with me doesn't prove she's been in touch with Kane, but it sure points that way. Remember the other day I said Kane had jumped ahead? Now I don't think he has. It's more like we're all at the same spot."

"Looking for Gelsey," Ray said.

Janek nodded again. "Kane wants to find her so he can get hold of the Omega. Diana's looking for her possibly to help Kane, and because so long as Gelsey's on the loose it's bad for business. As for us—" he paused, "we just want to save the girl's life."

"Whoever gets to her first wins," Aaron said. "So, how do we find her?"

"Think back over the tape. What else did Diana say?"

"She called Gelsey a 'talented artist,' " Sue said.

"Right. And she referred to a sketch. So, that's one more thing we know about the girl. Now let's review it all."

He went to the blackboard at the far end of the room, picked up a piece of chalk, wrote "GELSEY," then turned to the squad.

"We know her first name. An unusual name. A name

people aren't likely to forget."

He wrote: "FACE."

"We know what she looks like. We've got two police sketches with two different wigs."

He wrote: "MIRRORS."

"We know she's interested in mirrors. She can do mirror writing. She looks at mirrors all the time."

He wrote: "ARTIST."

"Put those four things together and what've we got? 'Have you heard of an artist named Gelsey who may work with mirrors? Here's her picture—take a look.'" He paused. "We'll divide up the art community. Start with the galleries." He turned to Sue. "You and Ray take Soho. Aaron and I'll work the East Village. If that doesn't produce, we'll try Fifty-seventh and upper Madison, though I suspect she's a little young for uptown. Point is, if she's a professional artist and she's shown her work around, we should be able to turn her up." He stared at them. "Let's get on it."

Trudging through the East Village, making the rounds of its numerous little attic and storefront galleries, was not, Janek quickly discovered, much like visiting the Museum of Modern Art. Not only was the artwork itself not comparable, but a lot of what he saw looked like the subway graffiti he abhorred. But Janek didn't laugh at what he didn't understand. Rather, it aroused in him an awareness of his limitations and a sense that, however much New York had declined, it was still a magnet for young people who heeded a calling to create. So, he thought, perhaps that meant that his city still aspired to greatness, and that its underside, the awful parts he saw daily in his work, was not necessarily proof of the irreversibility of its fall.

Spending the better part of the day visiting galleries on East Ninth, Tenth and Eleventh streets, he reached home with weary eyes. He opened a beer, gulped it down, then took a long shower to relax. He was just stepping out when he heard his telephone. He wrapped a towel around his waist and went into his bedroom to answer. It was Netti Rampersad. She said she was in the neighborhood, had some papers for him to sign and asked if she could drop by.

"Sure," he said, finding it interesting that she happened to be conveniently near. "Give me ten minutes to get dressed and straighten the joint. Then, if you're hungry, I'll order in Chinese."

"Velly velly nice," she said in her Chinatown accent. Then, switching to her real voice: "Tell you what, Frank—since you're supplying the hall, the least I can do is pick up the grub."

When she arrived twenty minutes later, she was loaded down. She had used her briefcase as a base to support a large cardboard box.

"Good thing you pump iron," Janek said as he lifted the heavy box from her arms and set it on his counter. He appraised her. She looked good, wearing a clinging dark green silk blouse and a worn pair of jeans. She smiled at him, then began to unpack the food.

He watched amazed as she pulled out numerous white cartons of carry-out. She had bought moo shu pork with pancakes, General Tang's chicken, sweet and sour shrimp, lobster in black bean sauce, spare ribs, spring rolls, hot and sour soup and a large portion of noodles in sesame oil.

"I see we're into starch," he said. "By the way, are some of your friends dropping by?"

She laughed. "Anything we don't finish is yours to keep."

"I don't think I can handle eating Chinese the rest of the week."

"Geez, Frank—Chinese people eat Chinese three times a day." She gazed at him, deadpan. "All year round, too."

Amused, he set his coffee table with plates, napkins and chopsticks, while she transferred the delicacies onto serving platters. He broke out a couple of beers, then they sat down.

Netti, in the midst of chewing on a spare rib, gestured toward his workbench. "Those accordions—they your hobby?"

"They were my father's profession," he explained. "He had an accordion sales and repair shop, only one in the city, downtown on Lafayette. Fixed instruments mostly, but he'd also fix radios, toasters, whatever got broken in the neighborhood. We lived above the store."

"So, do you just fix 'em, or do you play 'em, too?"

"Oh, I can play 'em," he said. "But don't ask me. There's an old joke among accordion players: 'A gentleman is a man who can play the accordion . . . but won't.' "

He noticed that she ate like a savage, which surprised him since she was so hard-bodied and lean. She grinned when she liked the taste of something and licked her lips afterward. Soon the aromas of ginger and garlic, sesame and soy transformed the air of his apartment.

"So," he said, gesturing toward her briefcase, "what do you want me to sign?"

"Copies of your pleading." She put down her rice bowl, fished out the papers. "In layman's language, your complaint."

"I suppose I ought to read it first."

"Absolutely."

He glanced at the papers, then put them down. He didn't feel like reading the sad saga of his barren marriage. "Hell with it," he said. "Give me a pen?"

She produced a pen, showed him where to sign. Then something dripped off one of his chopsticks beside his signature.

"Uh-oh, spot of moo shu."

She blotted the stain with her napkin. "Don't sweat it. I've filed pleadings with a lot worse on them than this." She stuffed the executed documents back into her briefcase. "I'll have Doe file these first thing in the morning. Your wife'll be served by the end of the day."

"Ex-wife," Janek corrected her.

"Right. So, now we're done with business, how do you like the food?"

They devoured more of the carry-out than he would have thought possible, but there was still enough left to last him for days. While he washed the plates, she boiled water, added tea, then they settled back on his couch to sip and talk.

"I'd like to make a small confession," she said.

"Go ahead," he said. "But I don't promise to absolve you."

She smiled. "Not that kind. I haven't done anything wrong. At least not yet."

"So, what's the confession?" he asked.

She grinned, then looked down. It was the first time he'd seen her act demure. "I've had . . . impure thoughts."

"Oh, those!" He laughed but felt uneasy. He had a hunch where this tack of hers could lead.

"All right," she said, looking into his eyes, "I'll come clean. I'm feeling attracted to you, Frank. I'd like to get to know you better—if you follow my meaning." She smiled, then looked down again.

Very gracefully stated, he thought, but he wasn't sure how to respond. She was undeniably attractive, quite capable of arousing his lust, and, he was certain, a real tigress in the sack. But he had doubts: Was she serious? Wasn't she too young? How might such an encounter end?

"I guess I should take that as a proposition," he said, stalling.

"I kinda wish you would."

He nodded. "I'm flattered. A woman like you—I imagine you land most anyone you want."

"It would seem not," she said, lowering her eyes again.

"Hey," he said gently, "try and understand. If I had a kid sister, she'd probably be around your age."

She scoffed, but nicely. "Incest taboo—I'm sure you can handle it."

He peered into her eyes. Was she putting him on? Looking at her heaving freckled chest, he recalled the two times he'd come to her office and found her coated with sweat. Suddenly he was seized by a hard carnal longing. He wanted her very much.

She reached toward him, touched his cheek with the tip of a finger.

"No big deal. Sometimes I get pretty bold." She smiled. "If there's someone in your life you're loyal to—I apologize."

"No, there isn't anyone now."

"So, then . . ." she coaxed gently, "if you're anxious about getting involved, don't sweat it."

He looked at her. Her face was flushed. He liked her nonchalance.

"Okay, you're on," he said, trying to match her casual approach. "What do you say we begin by building up some trust?"

"Great idea!" She snuggled against him. "I liked you the moment I met you. Did you know, Frank? Remember how hot it was? The hottest night of the summer. But you were really cool. You were the only one there who acted like he knew what he was doing." She raised herself up to kiss him. "When you followed me into the kitchen, I said to myself: 'Hey, this guy could be fun!' " She stared into his eyes. "You don't believe me, do you?"

"I'm beginning to," he said. "I don't think of myself as being particularly attractive to younger women."

"Hey! You are! You're handsome and you keep yourself in shape. But I don't care about that. It's more the way you carry yourself. You're like a real person, not some pretty boy with body tone."

She kissed him again. He kissed her back. They stroked one another, then began to unbutton each other's shirts.

After a while she took hold of his hand. "Come on," she whispered, "let's move this into the bedroom."

• • •

His bed had belonged to his parents. Sarah had always hated it because, she'd said, it was "too old world." She had wanted everything in their house to look sleek, like furnishings from the Home section of *The New York Times.* For years Janek had kept his parents' furniture in storage, finally finding use for it when he got divorced.

When he and Netti were completely undressed and in each other's arms, she thrust her hands above her head into the grillwork of the headboard, then grinned wickedly.

"You guys all carry handcuffs, right?"

Uh-oh! He shook his head, regretting he couldn't accommodate her. "Sorry, too much like work." He gazed at her. "What about straight? Think you can handle it?"

Her eyes gleamed as she took up his challenge. "Depends how you do it, I guess."

It took them the better part of an hour to settle down. Then, though he perspired a lot and felt thoroughly exercised, he didn't feel at all fatigued.

"You're a lot of fun," she whispered in his ear.

He kissed her. "So are you."

"Let's sleep a while. What do you say?"

He agreed that that seemed like the appropriate thing to do.

They made love again an hour later, then lay entwined and talked.

"Do you mind if I ask a fairly rude question?"

"Go ahead," she said.

"Do you do this kind of thing . . . often?"

"What kind of thing?"

"You know—"

"Make love to a client?"

"Yeah, I guess that's what I meant."

"No, not often," she said. "In fact, this is the first and only time."

She got up to get a drink of water. When she returned,

she sat naked by his feet at the bottom of the bed, arms wrapped around her knees.

"You're a good guy, Janek."

"So are you, Rampersad."

She smiled. "Thank you." She gazed at him. "I like you. I think you like me. But we're not going to get involved. Just liking someone isn't enough for either of us. Still, I'm glad that didn't stop us from having fun. Meantime, I'm handling your alimony appeal. And there's also the other thing."

He studied her. "You want to talk about it, don't you?"

She looked serious. "I won't if you don't want to."

"It's all right. We've gotten to know one another. I figure now we're friends."

"Thanks. I feel that way, too. Which may have been in the back of my mind when I came on to you. Which isn't to say I wasn't greatly attracted, because you can be sure I was. In fact, still am." She lightly slapped her own face. "Geez, Netti, why're you tongue-tied?"

Janek sat up. "Let's hear it. What's on your mind?"

"This whole Mendoza thing stinks. I figure you already know that. I wonder if you know how much."

He appraised her. "Why don't you tell me?"

She nodded. "The way I see it, Jake Mendoza most likely did pay someone, probably that doofus, Metaxas, to beat the living shit out of his spouse. He probably did it because he despised her, knew she was going to divorce him and didn't feel like paying out twenty or thirty mil to cut her loose. So, okay, that may have been what happened. I don't know. I wasn't there. But I know one thing: There wasn't anywhere near enough evidence to convict him. Not legitimate evidence anyway."

"You still think that letter was forged."

"I'm sure of it." She shook her head. "I know it's an old story. You don't agree. I understand that. Truth is, it doesn't make a damn bit of difference what either of us thinks. My job is to get my client a new trial, one that can conceivably go his way. It won't be easy. In a situation like this the burden shifts to the defense."

"I understand."

"Good. Because I want to talk about something else. In looking into the case, I've discovered some interesting things—things not particularly relevant to my job. They have to do with the Clury aspect, the way it was actually connected, as opposed to the way everyone thought."

"What about Clury?"

She looked at him. "Suppose I could show you that there was another agenda, something that had nothing to do with the Mendozas. Suppose I theorized that the time connection between Edith Mendoza's homicide and Clury's quote assassination unquote was coincidental, notwithstanding the client-investigator connection that certainly did exist. Suppose I could demonstrate that someone else wanted Clury out of the way for his own reasons, someone you've never thought of in that regard. And suppose I could persuade you that because Clury was a cop, and you cops were certain Mendoza paid to have him offed even though there was no evidence at all to support that belief, certain individuals among you faked up evidence on the other totally unconnected homicide that Mendoza very possibly did pay to have committed. Suppose I could show you all that. What would you think?"

He thought: *One thing's clear, Netti isn't tongue-tied anymore.*

"You're asking a lot of suppose-I-could questions. I can't relate to a theory. If you have something, lay it out."

She smiled. "That's what I thought you'd say. But, you understand, I'm under constraints."

"You're representing Mendoza—"

"Exactly. And because of that there're things I can't say. What I was hoping—well, I thought maybe I could point you in a certain direction, and you could pick it up from there."

Suddenly a nasty thought flashed through his mind.

Could she have engineered him into bed so that they could have this conversation under the umbrella of a freshly generated intimacy?

"Is that why you came here tonight?"

"What do you mean?"

"To 'point me in a certain direction'?"

She stared at him. "I came over for one reason—to get your signature on your complaint."

"Kind of slick, though, just happening to be in my neighborhood."

Now she was mad. "I came uptown especially to see you. I called because I didn't think you'd like it if I turned up unannounced."

"But the reason you came on to—"

She got off the bed, stood before him naked, stared at him, shook her head, then started picking up her clothes. She spoke angrily:

"Is that what you think—that my brilliant quote seduction unquote was part of some scheme to manipulate you into engaging in this dialogue? Give me a break! And give yourself one, too." She stared at him. "I was as turned on as I said I was. Maybe even more." She paused. "Why don't you think back a little, like maybe to yesterday? You came down to see me about a personal matter. I didn't call on you. You came to *me*."

She was right; he was mad at himself for thinking like a paranoid.

"I'm sorry, Netti," he said. "Of course you're right."

She shook her head. Her eyes looked sad. "It's this whole weird Mendoza thing. It drives everybody nuts, doesn't it?"

"That's what they say." He gazed at her. "Please forgive me."

She finished dressing, came to him, kissed him. "Of course." She sat beside him on the bed. "It's always a mistake to mix business with pleasure. I know better. I asked your permission, but I shouldn't have even broached it. Still''—she began to stroke his cheek—''if I had a choice between bedding down with you and talking about the case, I'd bed down anytime. I mean that, Frank. So, now we've got that out of the way . . .''

They laughed. Then she told him she had to go, had to prepare for an early court appearance and feared that if she stayed she'd find it impossible to resist seducing him all over again.

He agreed that she could leave, providing she understood he didn't want her to.

At the door, after a final kiss, they stared at each other. It was as if, Janek thought, they both understood that the issue of their quarrel was still left unresolved.

''Before I go I'd like to say one final thing about you-know-what,'' she said.

''Go ahead.''

''If you ever decide to pursue it, let me know and I'll point the way. But unless you ask me, I promise you—I'll never bring it up.''

''Thank you,'' he said. ''I think that's the perfect way to leave it.''

He woke late, had to rush to make his meeting with the squad. Still, he felt wonderful, almost light-headed. On the subway, thinking of Netti, he couldn't keep from breaking into a smile. He knew there could be no future in an affair with her, but he was happy she'd seduced him. It was, he decided, probably the only way the two of them could have gotten together.

At the office he found the squad despondent. No one had turned up anything. No gallery person any one of them had spoken to could recall a girl named Gelsey who created artwork involving mirrors. Janek reminded them that they'd just begun, that the New York art scene was huge.

• • •

At four that afternoon he was peering into the window of a grungy storefront on East Fifth, staring at what appeared to be a huge gilded phallus, when his beeper went off. A punked-out young woman, hair molded into violet spikes, walked by with a springer spaniel. When she heard the beeper she stopped.

"You on fire, Mister?"

He slid into a phone booth, called Special Squad, spoke to Sue, who told him that Ray Galindez had come up with something. When he reached Ray at the David Wise Gallery, Ray explained:

"They don't recognize Gelsey here, but they represent an artist named Ruth Hibbs who works with mirror images. I think we ought to speak to her, Frank. She may know other people in the field."

"Sounds good," Janek said. "Set it up."

When he got back to Special Squad, Ray was waiting, quietly stroking his mustache. He'd arranged a meeting with Ms. Hibbs for eight P.M. Janek noticed that his people were yawning and that their eyes were pink. Understanding they were suffering from staring at ugly images, he invited them all to an early dinner at the Carolina Oyster House around the corner.

After the feast, he and Ray went to Ruth Hibbs's address. It was a small industrial building in the photo district with a freight elevator and an artist-in-residence loft on the top floor. When they rang the buzzer and nothing happened, they retreated back to the sidewalk.

"Who's there?"

Janek looked up. A black woman was leaning out the window.

"Ms. Hibbs?"

"That's me."

"We're the detectives," Ray said.

The woman studied them, then she nodded. "The buzzer system's out. I'm throwing down the keys. I'd appreciate it if you'd catch them, not let them fall into the grate."

Ray and Janek stood back, the keys were thrown, Ray ran forward and neatly scooped them out of the air.

"Nice move," Janek said. Ray, glowing, unlocked the inner lobby door.

The freight elevator, which smelled of photochemicals, moved slowly. When the doors opened on the seventh floor, Ruth Hibbs was waiting. She wore wire-rimmed glasses, a sparkling white T-shirt and tight black leather pants. When she turned to lead them into her loft, Janek appreciated the neatness with which her hair was braided into cornrows.

As soon as he stepped into the loft, he was impressed. One wall embraced a huge mirror, ten feet by ten feet. The other walls, stripped down to bare brick, were covered with paintings. The dozen or so canvases were large and, he thought, very well executed. Each was divided precisely down the middle by a thick, straight black line. On one side of the line there was a head-to-foot image of a stylized nude male or female figure striking a pose. On the other side, this same figure was precisely mirrored.

Ruth gestured them to a sitting area near the front windows. After they sat, she studied Ray's drawing of Gelsey.

"No"—she shook her head—"I've never seen this person."

"Who are the other artists who work with mirrors?" Ray asked.

"I only work with one mirror." She pointed to the large one on the wall. "I pose my models in front, then paint what I see. A double image, straight and reversed—that's my trademark. No self-respecting artist would copy another's signature style."

"Ray didn't mean copy," Janek said. "We're interested in artists who use mirrors in all sorts of ways."

Ruth nodded. "I've seen them used as surrounds. And there're a couple of people who make mirror sculptures. Jim Dargesh in L.A. bends mirrors. There's a guy in Boston, Edelman or Adelman, who creates abstract surfaces by arranging small round mirrors in series." She thought a moment. "I remember seeing a show of large-scale mirrored geometric forms sometime last year. It was at the Martinelli Gallery on Greene Street. There's also a star photographer, Leslie Kron, who shoots still lifes against backgrounds of angled mirrors. There're probably a lot more people I could think of." She stared at Janek. "Is this important?"

He felt she knew something. "It is," he said. "We'll appreciate any help."

"You say her first name's Gelsey?" Janek nodded. "Suppose I helped you find her. Would she be arrested or anything?"

"Nothing like that," Ray assured her. "We think she's in danger. We're looking for her so we can warn her—protect her if she'll let us."

Ruth continued to stare. Janek thought: *She's wondering whether she can trust us.* Finally she nodded. "I'm going to make a call."

She strode to her work space at the far end of the loft, picked up a wall phone and stabbed out a number. Janek glanced at Ray. Ray touched his mustache and smiled back. Then they both sat silent, straining to overhear the conversation.

When Ruth Hibbs came back, she squinted at Janek. "I called a friend, Jodie Graves. I think she knows the person you're looking for. The woman signs her work 'Gelsey,' but that isn't her first name."

"What's her first name?" Ray asked.

"Elizabeth. Most people call her Gelsey, but some call her Beth. She shows at Erica Hawkins on Broadway near Spring." Ruth Hibbs shook her head. "Funny—I've heard of her, but I never knew she worked with mirrors till Jodie mentioned a picture the other day. . . ."

Later that night, when he and Ray finally reached Erica Hawkins, and the woman reluctantly opened up her gallery so that they could meet, Janek received a major insight into Elizabeth Gelsey's mind.

Ms. Hawkins had shown them the portrait, titled "Leering Man," which hung in her office opposite her desk. The moment Janek saw it he was astonished. The work, he felt, cast a powerful spell, and the longer he looked at it, the more deeply he felt himself drawn in.

The image was not beautiful, nor was it intended to be. Rather, it was a dark vision, a portrait of a leering and perhaps threatening male embellished with all sorts of artifacts—coins, bits of paper money, shards of mirror glass, little springs and wheels—enmeshed in thick paint and arranged into a kind of encompassing halo around the subject's head.

At the bottom of the canvas was a very small naked female figure, lying with arms outstretched, exposed, vulnerable, as if at the mercy of the leering man whose face loomed so large above. This female's eyes, engaging the viewer, were wide open, displaying a mixture of pleasure, confusion and pain. The eyes were also very familiar; Janek recognized Gelsey's eyes as depicted in the two police artists' sketches.

But just as extraordinary, Janek thought, were the eyes of the Leering Man above—enlarged, black, meeting Janek's with an unremitting gaze. Gelsey had depicted the eyes of a person who was smirking while, at the same time, apparently suffering great distress.

After staring at the faces, becoming lost in Gelsey's vision, Janek decided it was her ability to convey different feelings simultaneously that accounted for the painting's extraordinary power. He was moved by her empathy and understanding of human failings—the anger that masks anguish, the sensual pain that lurks in a smile, the knowledge of one's own malice that erodes one's joy even as one tries to take pleasure in the bitter suffering of another.

The Meeting

Janek emerged from the Holland Tunnel, then headed west across the Jersey swamps. The rising sun chased him, burnishing the grasses of the Meadowlands shades of rust.

There were numerous ways to drive to Newark. He chose the Pulaski Skyway. It was narrow, noisy, dangerous, but he liked the way it was constructed. It reminded him of his boyhood, building bridges out of parts scavenged from other kids' discarded Erector sets. Anyway, he wanted the trip to take a while, to feel like a journey.

He hadn't slept well, his dreams haunted by Gelsey's Leering Man. At dawn he'd called Aaron, asked to borrow his Chevrolet.

"Sure," Aaron said. "But don't you want me to drive you?"

"No, thanks."

"What about backup?"

"Won't need backup on this one," Janek said.

When Gelsey woke up, later than usual, she found, strangely, that she no longer felt the fear. And yet, as far as she knew, nothing had changed: Dr. Z was dead, both the police and Diana were after her and she was still a prisoner of the mirrors.

But something was different. And if, she reasoned, the difference did not lie in the objective facts of her situation, then it must lie within, in her feelings.

Yes, that was it. Because she felt good. She felt almost . . . ebullient.

She got out of bed, yawned, stretched, then strode into the work space of the loft. Surrounded at once by all her drawings and studies, she was suddenly struck by the notion that with her latest painting in the series, the one she had turned over to Erica, she had finally finished with Leering Man and was ready to take on something new. She didn't know yet what her new subject would be, only that she would discover it when she set to work.

A new beginning, she thought. *Perhaps today is the day.*

The sun, higher now, was lifting mist off the swamps. Janek, raising his eyes from the road, watched an American Airlines jet, most likely a red-eye from the Coast, fall softly toward Newark Airport. Plumes of smoke, burn-offs from the petroleum-tank farms, marked the windless sky like hieroglyphics. Or perhaps, he thought, like letters written in mirror-reverse.

He knew where he was going. He had gone there with his father many times. His last visit had taken place thirty years before, but he hadn't forgotten the sounds, smells, revelry, crowds. Unshelled peanuts in a paper bag. Cotton candy wound around a cone. Shooting gallery with Kewpie doll prizes. Merry-go-rounds, Dodgem, roller coaster, Ferris wheel.

There were dark attractions, too—the tunnel of love, with its gloomy, watery aroma of cheap perfume and teenage sex; and the fun house (the "crazy house," his father had called it), with its cackling automatons, freaks, slanted moving floors, sudden startling blasts of wind and maze of distorting mirrors.

"Her folks were carny people," Erica Hawkins had told him. "She lives out by a deserted amusement park near Newark."

Janek remembered the place well, and also his father's friend out there, an old organ grinder named Walter Meles, with sad eyes and a drooping, yellowing mustache. His father had kept the old man's hurdy-gurdy going for years. "Walt will never be able to buy a new one," he'd said. His father had never charged Meles for repairs; in return, every summer the old man had sent him a pair of one-day passes.

And so, each August, on a very hot Sunday afternoon, Janek and his father would go to the Port Authority Bus Terminal and board a bus for Richmond Park. Once there they would ride the rides and say hello to Walt. Janek had always dreaded that part of it—not the saying hello, but the shaking of the hand. Not Walter Meles's hand, either; it was the hand of Walt's old monkey, Suzy, tethered to the hurdy-gurdy, that he would dread.

"Now say hello to Suzy," Walt would intone. The monkey would cackle, stick out its paw and Janek would have to touch it. When one time he complained, his father told him there were things in this world you have to do whether you liked to or not. "Suzy is all that old guy has," his father explained. But still, any fun Janek might anticipate on their annual foray was sabotaged by his knowledge that he would have to shake the animal's scabrous little paw.

Gelsey had always held to a superstition: that her pencils, crayons and brushes knew what they wanted to depict, and that if she could only get into sync with them, they would guide her hand and show her what to draw.

Now she stood before a large sheet of paper tacked onto a sheet of plywood nailed to her studio wall, waiting for her hand to move. The ceiling fan cut at the morning light that streamed in through the skylight, its rapid revolutions inspiring notions of circles, balls, spheres, globes.

Yes, a head. A portrait.

She swirled the black crayon through the air and then touched it lightly to the paper. And then slowly she followed it as it seemed to find a groove. And then it was as if the crayon had a will of its own, scribing with such authority that her hand seemed barely more than a support.

Still thinking of his father, Janek stopped the car before the entrance to Richmond Park. The wrought-iron gate, rusted now, was closed and hooped with padlocked chains. Richmond had been shut down ten years ago, closed by the state after its roller coaster crashed. The crash had been a major tragedy—seven children killed, forty-six seriously injured. Richmond had never reopened, yet no one had bothered to tear it down. And so it stood, rotting slowly, almost, Janek thought, magnificent in its decay, surrounded by an automobile junkyard, a warehouse especially constructed for storage of industrial wastes and a single street of decrepit blue-collar homes.

A pack of wild dogs, it was rumored, roamed its grounds. A dismembered human female body had been discovered there a couple of summers before. The killing, Janek recalled, had not taken place at the park; the body parts had just been dumped there. But that was enough to create an aura of menace and fear. Now Richmond was the sort of place one kid might dare another to enter on Halloween.

Thinking sadly of his father, Janek drove on.

Gelsey had no idea what she was drawing until, after fifteen minutes of work, she let her hand drop and stepped back from the wall to look.

And then, when she saw the form, she felt despair. She had drawn the head of a monster, the Minotaur.

I am still a prisoner of the maze.

She was about to rip the paper off the board when she heard a sound and turned. A car had driven up outside and stopped. She went to the window to look out.

When Janek found the building, he couldn't believe he had the right address. A flat-topped, windowless concrete structure with an industrial steel door, it looked more like a garage than someone's home.

He sat in Aaron's car studying the place. The number matched the one on the piece of paper in his hand. He got out, walked across the street, peered in through the eastern-perimeter fence of the amusement park. He could make out some of the wreckage of the crashed roller coaster through the weeds. Then, when he turned back, he was surprised. A wooden structure with a pitched corrugated metal roof was perched on top of the concrete building, set too far back to be seen from the street.

He walked along the side, found an exterior wooden staircase leading up to the house.

Sure, she must live up there.

He began to ascend when a young woman appeared at the top of the stairs. He couldn't make her out. The sun was behind her; she was just a silhouette. But he was certain she was his quarry.

Gelsey stared at the man below her, standing on the bottom step. She recognized him at once—the detective she'd seen on TV, the middle-aged man with the searching eyes. Her hunter. Her enemy.

''Who the hell are you?''

''Name's Janek,'' he said. ''I'd like to talk to you.''

I bet you would! ''What about?''

''You're Beth Gelsey, right?''

She didn't respond.

''Look, I know—''

''Who told you I was here?''

''Erica Hawkins.''

Erica—shit! But he must be pretty good if he found his way to her.

Gelsey didn't say anything for a couple of seconds. She knew she had to stall him until she figured out what to do. Escape was impossible. She supposed she could invite him in, offer him coffee or a Coke. But even if she put him to sleep and ran, she had no place to go.

Then an idea came to her, a way to weaken him, get the upper hand.

"What do you want?" she demanded.

He pulled out his shield, displayed it.

She placed her hands on her hips. "So, you found me. Big deal."

"Can I come up?"

"No." Her answer was sharp. "Go around to the front. I'll let you in."

Janek stood before the steel door for several minutes. *Funny how they all talk so tough.* Finally the door creaked opened. Ahead was blackness. He hesitated.

"Where are you?" he asked. "Behind the door?"

No answer. He advanced. He felt like he was entering a cave. Then, suddenly, several things happened at once—the door closed behind him, the place went pitch-black, then bright lights came on, and then everywhere he turned he saw himself.

He was surrounded by mirrors.

So, she likes to play games. This one seems harmless enough.

As he moved forward he quickly discovered that he was in a mirrored corridor with a mirrored ceiling. And then he had to smile, for the deeper he penetrated, the more distorted his reflections became. He found himself fattened, thinned, twisted, dwarfed, stretched, bent, split in two, hourglassed. In one mirror the lower half of his body was miniaturized while his head suddenly quadrupled in size. Concave, convex and irregularly bent mirrors deconstructed his bodily integrity. The effects were funny. The only trouble was that he was alone; there was no one with him to point and hoot.

Gelsey, standing on the catwalk beside the switchboard that controlled the door and lights, watched silently from above.

Gotta give him credit, she thought. *He doesn't hesitate; he moves straight in.*

Now that she had him in the maze, she would run him through her hoops. She had changed from her working garb of shirt and jeans into something a little more . . . seductive. Wandering below, he was an unwary traveler; in the endless mirrored galleries, she was queen. She stepped softly to the thick white rope, then silently lowered herself to the floor. She moved into the blue chamber, then seated herself on the stool to wait.

Janek turned a corner and found himself amid a sequence of mirrors set at angles to the perpendicular, some bending toward him and some away. At first the effect made him dizzy, but then he began to enjoy it. *Feels like I'm inside one of those 1920s German films.*

He could not move quickly—the corridor was narrow and because there were so many mirrors he wasn't always able to distinguish between open space and mirrorspace. Also, the corridor was sharply angled, full of diabolic turns. After negotiating a few of these he had the feeling he had doubled back on his route, possibly twice.

He passed beneath an arch. On it the words CHAMBER OF UNOBTAINABLE ECSTASY were written in archaic Old English script. He remembered the archway at the police headquarters in Havana, the word HOMICIDIO elegantly inscribed above.

The corridor widened, and then he was surprised again. He saw Gelsey, in a slinky black cocktail dress, smiling at him, sitting on a high stool against a brilliant neon-blue background. She seemed to be just a few feet ahead, but when he moved toward her he realized he was looking at a reflection. He turned around to look for her but she wasn't behind him either.

He turned back, moved closer to the mirror. *Maybe it's not a reflection. Maybe I'm looking at her through a pane*

He couldn't be sure. She seemed to be sitting in limbo. The bare blue chamber offered no points of reference.

Chamber of Unobtainable Ecstasy: Was she, then, the unobtainable object? *Evidently she thinks so. She's positioned herself like a lure.* She was, he recognized, most certainly that, although perhaps not the sexual lure she seemed to think. He saw a very attractive young woman with dark hair, dark eyebrows and very pale skin, whose beautiful eyes spoke to him of hurt and loss.

Thinking that sooner or later he would find his way to where she sat, he decided to move on. There were no trick mirrors in this portion; the angles were regular, the mirrors carefully and uniformly arranged. There were perfect equilateral triangles grooved into the floor, suggesting that the mirrors were set at precisely 60 degrees. But then he discovered several irregularities in this pattern, which puzzled him, as did the fact that the passage had become so wide he could not touch both sides of it at once. Every so often he would see Gelsey again. She didn't move much and her slightly mocking smile didn't change.

What was most strange was the way she (or her reflection) seemed to jump around the labyrinth, reflected in some mirrors and not in others. He couldn't figure out how the trick was done, but he was intrigued by it, and impressed.

She was, he reminded himself, a professional seductress. Such a woman would be possessed by a need to be in control. To conceal herself in the labyrinth was her way to defy him. But what a labyrinth it was! He had never seen one like it, nor imagined that such an elaborate assemblage of mirrors could even exist.

He decided that if he could see her, then she, in turn, must be able to see him. So, when he came to a panel he was certain was transparent, he stood before her and stared.

Slowly her smile seemed to widen. Then suddenly, magically, she disappeared.

• • •

Gelsey studied him. *I've got him! He looks for me but can't find me. Finally he sees me . . . then suddenly I'm gone!*

Even though he seemed to be staring at her, she knew he could not see her. Examining him now at her leisure, she decided he did not look much like a mark. Where was the fear she liked to see? The terror? The acknowledgment in his eyes that the predicament he was in had been brought about by his own stupid lust? That it was *his* weakness that had brought him to this point of danger? That he had been a jerk, a fool, a buffoon?

In fact, as she examined Janek, she saw a man who did not appear to acknowledge anything of the kind. Rather, he seemed to be searching out *her* weakness, regarding her as if she were a creature in a cage.

Janek thought: *To her I'm just a rat in the maze.* But even though she was gone, he sensed that she still was there, watching him. So he addressed her missing image:

"Okay, that's pretty good, but now I've had enough. Time to come out where I can see you."

"You've only seen the half of it." Her voice, disembodied, came to him from above.

"Where are you?"

"In mirrorworld." She intoned the word mysteriously. Her words, he realized, were being broadcast to him through speakers in the mirrored ceiling.

"I'm going back."

"You won't find your way," she taunted.

Don't think so? I can play tough, too.

"If I get lost I'll just break a few mirrors."

When she suddenly reappeared on the other side of the glass, she did not appear amused.

"What do you want?" she demanded.

He stared into her eyes, noting the same vulnerability he'd observed in the police sketches.

"Come out," he said. "I'm not going to talk to you through glass."

"It's about Dietz, isn't it?"

He nodded. "And other things."

She studied him, then seemed to make a decision. "Make two rights, then a left. I'll meet you at the exit."

Again she disappeared.

Ten minutes later they stood facing each other in her loft in the building above. They had barely exchanged a word. She had simply met him, guided him outside, then led him up the exterior stairs, making sure he saw a considerable amount of leg and butt in the process. Now, inside her house above the mirror-maze structure, she watched him as he peered around.

If the building below, with its rigorously arranged mirror maze, had surprised Janek, the wooden house above—filled with art, art supplies, tools, a workbench, mirrored panels and jagged pieces of broken mirrors—was a revelation. It spoke of eccentricity, talent and, most of all, obsession. It had been one thing to see the Leering Man in Erica Hawkins's gallery. Now he stared at twenty drafts and versions of the same subject, in various styles and formats, hanging on or leaning against the walls.

He turned to her. "I never imagined you in a place like this."

"What did you imagine?" She snickered. "A garret?"

"Lived here long, Beth?"

She looked away. "Do me a favor, don't call me that."

"What should I call you?"

"Gelsey'll do."

He nodded, peered around again. A ceiling fan whipped the air. His eyes fell on a table covered with coins, cuff links, money clips and assorted men's jewelry.

"How long have you lived here?"

"All my life."

"Really?"

"Me and my folks. This was our house." She addressed him as if he were a moron or a child.

"And the maze?"

"My father built it."

"Lots of mirrors down there."

"I like mirrors."

His eyes fell on a rack filled with huge mirrored panels. "What do you like about them?"

"The way they make things look." She studied him. "People think when they look into a mirror what they see is what they get. They're wrong. In a mirror everything's reversed." She paused. "How'd you find Erica?"

"Just followed the mirrors," he said.

She slumped into a chair. "I knew you'd turn up. I suppose I ought to feel relieved."

He took a chair across from her. "Just be damn grateful it was me."

She stared at him with disgust. It was easy to read her face: She loathed him and wanted him to know it.

Way to handle this one, he thought, *is to refuse to take any of her shit.*

Still, for all her surliness, he was struck by her beauty, and the depths he saw reflected in her eyes.

"Yeah? Why should I be *damn* grateful?" She stuck out her legs, just the way Roger Carlson had described. Then she stared at him with curiosity. He remembered Carlson's words: ". . . looking at me like I was some kind of pinned-down bug."

"There's a nasty man looking for you, Gelsey. You know why Dietz was killed?"

She shook her head, then arched her back, a sexy move on account of the way it thrust her breasts against the fabric of the dress. He thought: *She thinks seducing me is going to get her out of this.*

"You took something off of him."

"Did I?" She smiled scornfully.

"Don't play games," he snapped. "I'm not in the mood."

She tried to outstare him, snickered again, then gestured toward the table. "Lots of loot over there, Detective. Check it out. Take your pick."

He made up his mind then that if they were going to play, the game would be hardball and he would win.

"You never tried to sell any of the stuff you took?"

She shrugged.

"What about the money?"

She casually gestured toward an old wooden desk. "Bottom right-hand drawer. It's all there, every cent."

"Do you think that makes it all right? Just give it back and everyone forgives?"

She shrugged again.

"You're a pretty strange girl."

"Think so?"

"That's how you style yourself." He stared at her. "Isn't it?"

She touched one breast, then wriggled slightly in her chair. He found the gesture pathetic. Cornered, desperate, she was trying to extricate herself the only way she knew—by seduction. Still, feeble as it was, the attempt told him he had engaged her. He reached into his pocket, pulled out the Omega mock-up, tossed it into the air, caught it in his fist.

"What did you do with it?"

"If I tell you, you won't believe me."

"Try me."

"I smashed it into pieces, then worked the crumbs into a painting, the one at Erica's."

He believed her. After seeing what she had downstairs, he knew nothing she could say would surprise him.

"The guy who killed Dietz killed him for that. How does that make you feel?"

She looked at him, stunned; she didn't answer.

"What's the matter?"

"On TV you acted like you thought *I* killed Dietz."

"You got me mixed up with the reporter. Thing is, the guy who killed Dietz will kill you, too, if he finds you. He could have been the one who showed up this morning."

She pouted. "Right, I should be 'damn grateful' it was you instead."

"Tell me something, Gelsey?"

"What?"

"Why?"

"Why what?"

"Why do you drug guys and rob them? If you aren't interested in their money, what are you interested in?"

She shrugged again. "Trophies."

"Trophies of what?"

"My adventures, you know . . ."

"No, I don't. Tell me about it?"

She smiled scornfully. "Why should I? What's it to you? Are you some kind of cop-shrink or something?"

"I want to understand it. Why did you put all those guys to sleep? Explain it to me . . . if you can."

"Oh, I can *explain* it!"

"So explain," he demanded. She didn't answer. *She's ashamed.* "You wanted to humiliate them, right?"

She smiled. "Maybe something like that."

She looked uncomfortable. Another probing question and he felt she might clam up. He didn't want that, but he was getting tired of her nonsense. He decided to give her a little smack.

"You're a clever little actress," he said, contemptuously.

She snickered. "I don't see myself that way."

"How do you see yourself?"

"I'm an artist."

"Right"—he stood—"a pretty good one, too—not that I know all that much about it. So, tell me—why's the Great Artist going around drugging guys and robbing them? What'd you do—show them some leg, a little tit, get them going that way then play them for fools? You've been trying to do that to me ever since I showed up here, squeezing yourself into that slinky little dress, then playing peekaboo with me down in the maze.''

''Don't flatter yourself, Janek!''

Their eyes locked. He thought: *She's ready to fall. I can take her down anytime.*

''I've made a study of your technique,'' he said. ''One thing struck me.''

''Oh? What's that?''

''The men you go after—you always give them the option. You never ask to go up to their rooms. Always wait till *they* ask you. That's when your act gets real good. 'Gee, I really shouldn't, you being married and all. . . .' And then, of course, they ask you again. So, when you get up there and squeeze a few KO drops into their drinks, it's all their fault. Isn't it? *Their* fault. *Never* yours.''

During his attack, he observed her growing progressively more angry. Now, suddenly, she turned away. But he continued, relentless.

''Oh, you're so much *purer* than Diana's other girls.'' He spoke with studied scorn. ''You don't care about money. Uh-uh. It's the head trip that turns you on. Prey on guys' weaknesses. Put them to sleep. Then shame them with your mirror-writing messages. Know what I think, Gelsey? I think Diana and the others are the purer ones. I detest what they do, but I understand it. Money drives people to do a lot of things, legal and illegal. But to mind-fuck someone just because it gives you a buzz—I've got no respect for that at all.''

She shrieked at him: ''I don't give a shit about your respect!''

''Angry, aren't we? Maybe because I'm right. Because at bottom you don't respect yourself. Could that be it? Hmmmm?''

She gasped, outraged. Still he kept at her:

''I met Diana. A cold woman who cares only for herself, who enjoys taking advantage of people, enjoys hurting them, too. But you—you're an artist! That's the part I don't get. Have you any idea what a privilege it is to have talent?'' He walked over to her paintings, looked at them. ''Last night, when I saw your Leering Man portrait, I was actually moved. Ever since I've been asking myself: How could the person who painted that do the things she does? Why isn't the art enough for her? Why does she have to hurt people? Destroy?''

Wanting to sound more sympathetic, he altered his tone:

''Remember Kirstin Reese? She liked you, said you were a special person. That kind of person doesn't do those kinds of things. Unless . . .''

''Unless *what*?''

''The only answer I come up with is that you hurt a lot inside.'' He looked closely at her. ''I can see it in your eyes. You need help. You're crying out for it. That's what your painting says. Your bar adventures, too. They all say the same thing: 'Help me! Please help me before I break!' ''

She stared at him with something akin to the smirk she'd worn before, but he could see that it was a masking smirk. He peered back at her with all the concern he felt, and then he watched her break, slowly, before his eyes. Her smirk slipped away, her eyes enlarged, she changed position, became awkward in the chair. The vulnerability he'd observed in the police sketches now showed itself without contrivance. She looked to be on the verge of tears. The troubled little girl stood revealed.

He didn't want to hit her again so soon, but he knew no other way. He thought: *Rub her face in it. Make her see!*

''Kirstin's dead. Did you know?''

She brought her hand up to her mouth.

''Tortured first. By the same guy who killed Dietz.''

''But why?''

''To make her tell him where you live.''

''She didn't know!''

"*He* thought she did. Anyway, she knew how to find Diana. After he got that out of her he killed her. Which is just what he'll do when he finds you, especially when he discovers you smashed up his precious chip."

She'll cry now. When she does she'll turn away. That'll be all right.

But Gelsey surprised him. She didn't turn, just stared at him and began to weep without lowering her eyes. It was an extraordinary thing to witness. And he believed he understood why she was doing it—she wanted to show him her pain.

Later he would not remember how long he watched before he moved toward her and took her hand. It was a paternal gesture and she responded to it, leaning tentatively against him.

Looking down at her, feeling her body tremble, he asked himself what the hell he thought he was doing. This was not the way he dealt with criminals. But then, he realized, Gelsey was not like any criminal he had ever met.

After Gelsey let him see her cry, she didn't care what else he saw. She thought: *In some strange way he owns me now.*

And it also felt good to lean against him, feel his warmth and strength. She had never touched Dr. Z—shrinks, she'd read, weren't supposed to touch patients, although sometimes shrinks transgressed. But this tall man beside her with the searching eyes was no more a shrink than he was a mark. She wasn't sure yet what he was. A detective—what kind of man was that?

"Ever try and imagine what it feels like to be on the receiving end of a drugged drink?" he asked her. "The terror as you're going down?"

"I know all about terror," she said. She didn't want to listen to a fucking lecture. She could give him lessons in terror if she wanted to.

"We're not talking about you," he said. "We're talking

about your victims.'' He paused. ''Oh, I get it—you just feel sorry for yourself.''

She peered at him. She knew she should put up a defense. But her heart wasn't in it. He had made her cry . . . so what was the use?

''Who else is going to feel sorry for me?'' she asked.

''Jesus!'' He stood, offered her his hand. ''Come with me.''

''Where?''

''Get up! Come on!''

She stood, then allowed him to draw her across the room to the area where a dozen unframed mirror panels were stored in a wooden rack. He led her to within a foot of the first mirror.

''Look at yourself.''

She turned away.

''Go on! Look!'' He placed his hand on top of her head, then gently forced her to peer into the glass. ''Instead of playing with mirrors, why don't you use one once in a while? Take a good, hard look.''

She glanced quickly at herself and then at his image in the mirror.

''Not me! You! Why's that so difficult?''

She squeezed her eyes shut.

''Look at who you are, Gelsey. You might see something you don't like. Then you might want to do something about it. You might want to change.''

She opened her eyes. She felt his eyes on her as she gazed at herself. Then she mouthed some words.

''Speak up. I can't hear you.''

''I did try to do something about it,'' she moaned. She stared at him and wondered: *Does he like me? Does he like me even a little bit?*

Janek listened as she told him about a psychoanalyst she'd gone to in Manhattan, a wise, sympathetic, elderly man who'd tried his best to help her. For a long time, she said, she didn't tell Dr. Zimmerman about her drug-robbery activities, confessing only that she picked up men in bars and went home with them for sex. When she finally told him the truth, he was shocked, but still willing to help.

"We were going to get to the bottom of it," she said. "Then the next time I came in a woman was there. She told me Dr. Z had died of a heart attack. She offered to continue the analysis. I never went back."

She turned to Janek. "I worshiped him," she said. "I thought he could be . . ." She turned away, embarrassed.

"What?" he asked.

She smiled, then shook her head. "My good father," she said quietly. "The one I never had."

She made coffee for him. Watching her prepare it, he wondered: *Will she try to spike it?* Then he thought: *We're way beyond that now.*

They sat facing each other, sipping from mugs. Both her parents, she told him, were dead. Her father had been employed at Richmond, where he'd managed and kept up the fun house. Then he'd quarreled with management and quit to go on the road, driving a rig, hauling a fun-house-on-wheels to carnivals all over the Northeast. His mobile fun house contained a mirror maze, too, a puny one made of a few Mylar panels.

"He only cared about the maze downstairs," she said. "He spent all his free time working on it. Spent all his money on it, too."

"Funny," Janek said, "I used to come out here as a kid, but I never heard anything about it."

"It wasn't open to the public. It was just for us. For him."

A private mirror maze: Janek was astonished. "He built that whole thing just for himself?"

"You have no idea how big it is," she said. "You went through less than half of it."

Clearly it had been her father's obsession, just as the

image of the Leering Man was hers.

"My mother worked at Richmond, too," she said. "She managed the tunnel of love."

"I used to ride through there."

She nodded. "So did I. With my father. . . ."

"What was wrong with him?"

She looked away.

"Did he abuse you?"

She nodded again, then gestured toward the floor.

"In the maze?"

She stared past him. "It's an ugly story," she said.

She led him to her sleeping area, rolled up a rug beside her bed, exposed a trapdoor beneath.

"This," she said, raising the door, "is the secret way down."

He nodded casually even as it occurred to him that by offering to show him this secret way, she was inviting him to enter her world.

He followed as she descended a ladder to a series of narrow catwalks. She told him to stand still while she went to a switchboard to turn on the lights. He stood in darkness, until, suddenly, the entire maze was set ablaze. And then, for the third time that morning, he was astounded. The mirrored ceilings were transparent. The labyrinth lay bare beneath, all its intricate winding corridors revealed.

Gelsey moved back to his side and began to point things out:

"There's where you came in. You wandered through there, the Corridor. See! There's the row of trick mirrors that took you apart. And there's the row that put you off balance. Over there's the Chamber. See the blue room?" Janek nodded. "That's where I was sitting."

"I figured you were hiding in a little room somewhere. But why weren't you reflected in all the mirrors?"

"Ha! You want to know our tricks!"

He shrugged. "If it's a secret . . ."

But she was eager to explain: "First, you probably figured this out, the ceilings are made of one-way glass. When you're down there they look like mirrors. From up here they're transparent—when the lights are on below." He nodded. "Now you want to know why you only saw me in some of the mirrors and yourself alone in others." She smiled. "The maze mirrors, the ones that reflect a visitor, are all set at sixty or one hundred twenty degrees. The ones where you saw me, too—there're fewer of those—are angled to one another at forty-five degrees. So those are the only ones in which you can see a person sitting in the blue room. One of them, of course, isn't even a mirror—it's a plain sheet of glass. But down there there's no way to tell."

He thought he understood it. "Did your father figure that out?"

She shook her head. "Dad was smart, but he wasn't an inventor. He played around with other people's ideas. Some nineteenth-century guy came up with the notion of interlocking sets of differently angled mirrors. Dad discovered it when he researched maze patents. Then he built it."

"My father was a builder, too," Janek said. "He could repair anything. He repaired accordions for a living."

She peered at him closely, as if she thought she'd finally found a link.

"So," he asked, "how did you make yourself disappear?"

She giggled. "That's called the Blue Room Effect. If we move over there, I'll show you how it works."

They moved along the catwalks to a spot above the blue chamber. Gelsey pointed out that the little room was actually divided on the diagonal by a large mirror. She explained how, sitting on a stool at one side, she could control the large mirror with an electric switch, making it move back and forth. When the mirror was inside the chamber, it reflected her where she sat, projecting her image throughout the maze into any other mirror angled to it at 45 degrees. But when it was retracted, she would seem to disappear, and the chamber would appear empty.

There was more. She guided him above other sections, first to a winding, tortuous snakelike sequence of mirrors called the Fragmentation Serpent, where, she told him, the visitor, entering the serpent's mouth, faced a parabolic mirror that turned him upside down. Then onto a vast section that took up more than half the building—her father's masterpiece, the Great Hall of Infinite Deceptions.

It was here, she told Janek, that her father had abused her. The Great Hall had been their love nest.

"He would bring me down on rainy afternoons. Richmond was always closed when it rained. Then he'd make love to me. I'd see us reflected everywhere. At first I didn't know how to escape, then I learned to enter mirrorworld." She looked down, shook her head. "Once inside the glass nothing could touch me." She stared at Janek. "Trouble is, mirrorworld wasn't as safe as I thought. There was a monster wandering around in there."

What's she talking about?

"I saw it now and then. My father called it the Minotaur. You know, the mythological creature, half-man, half-bull, that supposedly lived in the center of the ancient Minoan maze. Dr. Z was going to help me figure out what the Minotaur was. Then he died." She shrugged sadly. "Want to go down and walk through the parts you missed?"

As he followed her he asked himself why he was feeling so warm toward her. She had done terrible things. She had drugged, robbed and frightened people. Clearly she was dangerous. And he knew that if she didn't get help, she would most likely do such things again. But he couldn't make himself think of her as a twisted, antisocial offender. Rather he saw her as a deeply troubled person, compelled by an irresistible impulse. He now understood the Leering Man portrait, and all the preliminary sketches and paintings he'd seen up in her loft, as a struggle against the forces that drove her to the bars.

• • •

He hesitated when he saw the gym rope. *My Tarzan days are over.* When she reached the floor, in a kind of backstage area between two segments of the maze, she seemed to sense his reluctance to shin down. She called to him that if he preferred, he could descend by a steel ladder built into the wall.

He took the ladder. When he reached the floor he found himself in an oddly shaped space surrounded by narrow angled black walls. A few moments later, one of the walls folded open. Gelsey appeared in the doorway and reached for his hand.

"Come," she said. "I'll lead you."

Beneath the mirrored ceilings, he could see nothing above except strange, confusing multiple reflections. The clarity he had obtained on the catwalks—the overview that had allowed him to comprehend the maze, follow the paths of its numerous, intricate corridors—was supplanted now by bafflement. He had no idea where they were or where they were heading. And she confused him more when, every so often, she would push at a mirror, cause it to spring open like a door, pull him into another backstage area, then reenter the maze through another door mirrored on its maze-side face.

She seemed to know every corner of the labyrinth, every secret entrance and exit. And although each mirror looked the same to him, to her each was evidently unique.

"I think I liked it better upstairs," he said.

"Relax," she goaded. "You'll have more fun."

He tried, but he didn't experience the maze as fun. He found it painful. But then, of course, he realized, bafflement was not his favorite state-of-being.

"I'm a detective," he told her. "I like to know where I am, see where I'm going."

"Life isn't like that," she responded. "Life's more like this, confused."

Perhaps she was right. But that didn't make him like the

maze better. If her father's labyrinth was a metaphor for life, he preferred to stand up on the catwalks, where the pattern could be seen and understood.

"A person could go crazy down here."

"A person did!" she said.

He supposed she thought she was that person. But why had her father taken her here to abuse her? One would think that a man, performing an act as forbidden as father-daughter incest, would commit it in a private place—an attic or a cellar. But her father had chosen to commit it in this brilliantly lit multimirrored space, a space where the taboo nature of his deed would be replicated by reflections to infinity.

Standing in the center of the Great Hall, he thought: *Now I understand what it feels like to go mad.*

"How can you stand this?"

"I had no choice," she said. "Now I'm used to it. When you're brought up living above a crazy house, it doesn't seem all that crazy. It just seems like . . . home."

He asked her how her parents had died.

"Accident."

"The roller coaster—?"

She shook her head. "Car crash. Dad was on the road and Mom was with him. I was in art school in Providence at the time. It was night. They'd been out to dinner. Dad was driving his rig without the trailer. They collided head-on with an eighteen-wheeler on the truck route between Hagerstown and Baltimore." She paused. "Sometimes I wonder if he did it on purpose, decided the time had come to pack it in."

She said that with such nonchalance, he could barely believe she was serious. But when he glanced at the mirrors and saw her expression reflected everywhere, he understood she had been masking her feelings.

He also understood that it was important to her that he stand with her now at this scene of the crime. Was she merely trying to evoke his sympathy, or was there some other reason?

"Oh, sure, you're right, a person could go crazy here," she said. "Mom used to send me down here when I was bad."

"That seems pretty cruel."

She nodded. "I'd cry and beat on the mirrors, trying to break them. Of course I couldn't. They're three quarters of an inch thick."

"Why'd she do such a thing?"

"They were carny folk—big, slick smiles on their faces, hard and bitter beneath. Think about it. The amusement-park game is a hoax. All those rides—the point of them is to make you scream. A fun house isn't fun at all, it's more like torture. A tunnel of love isn't about love or romance, it's just a dark wet place where kids can feel each other up. The whole thing's a snake-oil show. Even the stuff they sell to eat is bad for you. It's 'take their money and smile,' 'make them think they're having fun.' But have you noticed how sad such places are? That's why they close up when it rains. In the rain you can see them for what they really are—empty, flat and mean."

It felt strange to stand with her in the center of the Great Hall, looking straight at her but aware that their encounter was reproduced on every surface, repeated down endless illusory corridors. They were alone, except for their clones. How many were there? At least a million, he thought.

Gelsey understood that he was about to tell her something important. She waited for him to speak.

"You have to face the fact you've hurt a lot of people."

Yeah, well, I already know that.

"The victimizer can be as damaged as the victim. In some cases more."

Interesting. She felt at once that that was true.

"When you commit a crime you have to pay for it, and not just as an example to others, to repay society, for rehabilitation. You've heard all that too many times."

She nodded. "Is there another reason?"

"Yes. To make you feel better—because you've paid a price."

"Ah, punishment," she said.

"Yes, punishment."

"Do you believe in it?"

"Do you?" he asked.

She thought a moment before she answered. "I think I crave it," she finally said.

"You may have to do some time," he told her as they climbed the embedded ladder back up to the catwalks. "Or you might get off with community service, teaching art to inner-city kids, something like that. It'll be up to a judge. You never know who you'll draw. Carlson will testify. He was pretty bitter when I spoke to him. Maybe you can make a private settlement with him, but I think it would take more than money. You'd have to acknowledge what you did and apologize."

"I'd like to do that anyway."

She's sounding good. But is she for real?

"I don't know what harm the publicity will do you. I suppose it could possibly help—'mirror-obsessed artist-criminal.' You might get a book contract, a segment on *Hard Copy*. Ride the hype straight into the Whitney Museum."

She laughed.

"What're you looking for down there?" he asked.

They were back in her loft, sitting in the living area. She was studying him curiously, waiting for him to explain.

"You know the maze cold, right?" She nodded. "And you don't particularly like to look at yourself in mirrors, right?" She nodded again. "So, why do you go down there all the time? What're you looking for?"

She shook her head. "I don't see—"

"It's that Minotaur, isn't it?"

What the hell do you know about it? She felt defensive again.

But he went on: "Here we are, in your studio, surrounded by all these studies of your Leering Man." Janek gestured at the sketches and paintings. "Is he your father? Did your dad look like that?"

She shook her head.

"Who is he, then?"

"He who oversees, controls and knows."

"Oversees *what*? Knows *what*?"

She laughed at him. "Don't you have manners? Never ask an artist to explain her work."

He gazed back. "I don't have manners. I'm a cop. I'm still asking the questions."

She snorted and turned away.

Knowing she had every right to demand that he respect her privacy, he changed the subject to Diana. That engaged her. She didn't like Diana. She described her as "the most evil person I ever met." Then, when she recounted their last conversation, in which Diana had said that she knew Dietz was carrying something valuable and that she had a buyer for it, Janek felt he finally had some proof to support his theory that Diana had been approached by Kane.

"Maybe Thatcher told her," Gelsey objected.

Janek didn't think so. "Thatcher could have given her our sketches. We held them close, but not that close. But no one except my squad and my supervisor knows about the Omega. I'm sure Kane got Diana's address out of Kirstin, then went to her and offered her a piece of the action if she could get the chip away from you."

Gelsey told him about Tracy and the note Tracy had left instructing her to get in touch with Diana. When Janek heard that, he had an idea about how to proceed: Gelsey could call Diana, say she'd changed her mind and would sell the Omega. Then Sue Burke could take Gelsey's place at the payoff.

Gelsey objected; she didn't want anyone taking her place.

"Kane's already killed twice for the chip," Janek warned her. "He won't hesitate to kill again."

But Gelsey said she wanted to help. "Maybe it'll win me points with a judge. I need that. Please."

At first he thought she wanted to play a role in the arrest only because she thought doing so might keep her out of jail. But as she talked on, and he understood the depth of her guilt, he realized she was looking for redemption.

He thought: *How can I deny her that? If she were my own child, I'd feel proud.*

"Tell you what I think," he said, looking at her sketches again. Earlier he had noticed a huge half-completed drawing of a monster's head. Now he studied it. "I think your Leering Man is really the Minotaur."

She stared at him coldly. "Got any more flaky ideas?"

"You don't buy it?"

She marched off to the other side of the loft.

"Why don't you answer?"

"Do you think I owe you an answer?"

"No, you don't owe me anything, Gelsey. You only owe yourself."

It's funny about her, he thought, the way she moves or changes position whenever she feels cornered. He found her body language transparent and was surprised she'd been so successful in the bars. But then he remembered that the woman in the bars was someone else—her mirror twin, her dream-sister—for whose actions she, Gelsey, was not responsible.

She strode back toward him. "Suppose you're right," she said. "Then what?"

"The reason you go down into the maze all the time isn't to become mirror-girl. It's to seek."

"Seek *what*?"

"You don't see it."

"You're so fucking smart—!"

"Do you always get angry when you know the other person's right? When you talk tough like that, you give yourself away."

She sneered. "Give *what* away? Seek *what*? Speak, Janek! Say what's on your mind."

"Seek Leering Man, a.k.a. the Minotaur. That's why you go downstairs. That's why you paint. It's the same quest. You want to discover who hurt you, who even now makes you hurt. Your shrink told you the answer was down there. But you haven't found it yet. There *is* something down there, too. You know there is, but not quite where or what. That's the secret, isn't it? That's what you're looking for? Tell me I'm right, and maybe I can help. But if you deny that's what you're after, you'll never find it. *Never.*"

Later he would wonder what had made him speak to her like that, what instinct had formed the words. He often made leaps, but he didn't think he had ever taken such a chance with someone he barely knew. Normally he'd be afraid that if he were wrong he'd lose the person's confidence. Still, his little speech seemed to have found its mark. Gelsey responded as if dealt a blow.

"Dr. Z never talked to me like that. You know how shrinks are?" Janek shook his head. "They're slow. They plod. They try to get you to the point where you think it's *your* idea." She grinned at him. "You don't deal with people that way."

He shrugged. "I like to move things along."

"You're wrong, of course. There is no Minotaur. The monster is just something in my head."

"That's what Dr. Zimmerman told you?"

"It's my conclusion."

"Maybe you're right," Janek said. "But still it could be real—not a beast, not half-man, half-bull, but someone who was looking at you, someone your father invited in to watch."

"What the hell are you talking about?"

"I'm a detective. To me incest is a crime. That's how I look at it; that's how I understand it."

"So?"

"So, when you want to understand a crime, you examine everything—the people, the scene, the evidence—and ask yourself: What was the criminal trying to do? I don't mean literally. Your father was abusing you. But what was *behind* that? Why did he do it in a mirror maze, where it would not only be reflected a million times, but where a person standing on the catwalks could see it, too?"

"No one was up there." She bit her lip.

"How do you know? You were down on the floor. You couldn't see above the ceiling. But since the ceiling's made of one-way glass, someone looking down could see you."

"Wrong," she said, firm in her rebuttal. "When we went down there he'd always lock the door. No one could possibly get in or out. Anyway, I saw the Minotaur on the floor. Just a couple of flashes, but he was there."

"Hey, you can't have it both ways. One minute the Minotaur's in your head, the next he's real."

"Fuck you! Why're you doing this?"

"I'm trying to help you. Can't you tell?"

"You just met me. What do you care?"

He shrugged. "Maybe I like you. But not the way you think."

She screwed up her mouth into an exaggerated seductive smile. "No hard-on, Janek?"

He shook his head.

"So, what's your game?"

"I don't play games."

"You're just a Good Samaritan?"

"Sounds corny, I admit."

"Sounds like bullshit. What do you really want?"

A good question. He thought through his answer before he replied:

"I see a girl in trouble. I want to help her work it out."

She stared at him with her most mocking smile, and then she turned away and began to weep. He turned away, too. He didn't want to watch her cry this time. He only turned back toward her when he felt her take his hand.

"Hold me. Please."

He gently took her into his arms. "What's the matter?" He stroked her hair. "Is it so awful to meet someone who doesn't want your body, who just likes you for yourself?"

"It's not that," she whispered. "That's wonderful."

"What is it, then?"

"The rain," she whispered.

He hadn't noticed that it had started to rain. Now he became aware of water dancing on the roof. When he turned to the windows, he saw droplets washing the glass. He turned back to Gelsey. She seemed to tremble.

"It's just a light shower," he said. "It won't last."

"That's when he'd do it," she whispered. "The park would close, he'd come home early, putter around, make a sandwich, drink a beer, maybe watch a sports event on TV. All the time he'd be giving me these looks. I'd know what he was going to say even before he said it. He'd work up his nerve, then he'd smile. 'Hey, honey bunch—what do you say we go down there and, you know . . . play?' "

She was shaking now. He held her tight. He wanted more than anything to help her through this crisis.

"I'll be okay. I always feel bad when it rains. Then I go down there and spend some time. Maybe I'm looking for the monster—or something. Then I usually go into the city, hit a bar and . . . you know . . ."

He did know, of course. And now he also had a pretty fair idea of who that monster might have been.

Later, when the rain slacked off and Gelsey had pulled herself together, he asked if he could use her phone. She showed it to him in the sleeping area. Before he dialed, he wondered why Kane hadn't found her through the phone company. Even though she was unlisted, a former sheriff's deputy would know how to extract the number.

"Diana doesn't know my real name," she explained. "They all called me Gelsey. They think it's my first name, not my last."

Well, that was something; she might be troubled but she was smart. She left him alone to make his call. He could hear her in the loft, moving around.

Aaron snapped up the receiver on the first ring.

"Jesus, Frank!" he said. "I thought you were going to keep in touch."

"Sorry. I got involved."

"Is she anything like what we thought?"

"No," Janek said. "Not at all."

"Well, it's good you called. A detective named Ortiz phoned from Cuba. He was sorry you weren't here, said it's hard to put through a call. He'll try again at five. Said it's important you two talk. Urgent, too. He underlined that."

Luis . . . wonder what he wants?

Janek put down the phone and went back to the loft. Gelsey was standing at the wall, squinting at her unfinished drawing of the monster.

"Something's come up," he said. "I've got to go back to the city. I want you to come with me. You can stay with Sue Burke until we wrap this up."

She shook her head. "This is where I live, where I work."

"It's not safe. If Kane shows—"

She peered at him. "Forget it. I'm not leaving."

He could see she meant it. "What if Sue comes here and stays with you—would that be all right?"

She shrugged. "I guess she can sleep on the couch."

"She'll be on duty. She won't need a place to sleep."

Janek returned to the bedroom, told Aaron to dispatch

Sue to Newark right away. Back in the loft he told Gelsey she'd be alone for about an hour. He described Sue, warned her not to let anyone else in.

She studied him. "You really care, don't you?"

"Yeah, I care," he said. "Why's that so hard to deal with?"

"I think Dr. Z cared, too."

"I'm sure he did," Janek said.

Gelsey stood on her roof watching him leave. Just before he got into his car, he stopped and glanced back.

"Thank you," he shouted.

"For what?"

"Hospitality. Showing me the maze."

"Oh, that!" Gelsey wanted to say something, but couldn't bring herself to mouth the words. *Go ahead,* she told herself. *Ask him. Ask!*

"When am I going to see you again?" she called.

She liked his face when he smiled. "Tomorrow," he promised. "Soon enough?"

She gazed at him, then retreated back into her house.

Driving toward the city, Janek saw Manhattan magnificently displayed, its towers sharply etched against the storm clouds. Approaching the Holland Tunnel, he asked himself how he could broach to her his suspicion about her Minotaur.

That conversation, he thought, *will hurt. She won't want to listen. She'll cover her ears.*

But he knew that if he was right, it would be vital that she hear. *Help her rid herself of the Minotaur,* he thought, *and she just may have a chance.*

Betrayal

Aaron, in an orange and purple Hawaiian shirt, stared at him. Ray, at his desk, leaned forward, waiting for him to speak. What's she like, they wanted to know—the strange "mirror-girl" they had been tracking for so many days?

Janek had great faith in his people; he rarely held anything back. But now he hesitated. Gelsey had confided in him; he would not feel right if he abused her trust.

He diverted their attention by describing the maze. They listened, mesmerized. When he was finished, Ray said it sounded like something from outer space. Aaron had another thought:

"You like her, don't you, Frank?"

"Yeah, I do. It's like she's this troubled kid, she's gone wrong and now I need to save her from herself. There's so much talent there. So much intelligence. It makes me sick to think of what she's done."

He was pleased that neither of them raised their eyebrows or suggested there was a lascivious motive behind his concern.

Sue phoned in to say that she'd arrived and that she and Gelsey were getting along. Then, just at five, Luis's call came through. Janek took it in his office. Although it had been only three weeks since he'd departed Cuba, he felt he was talking to an old friend.

They exchanged pleasantries, then Luis's voice turned grave:

"Please listen, Frank. I am calling from a friend's house, someone high up in our government. What I have to say must be said in a special way. There is a chance we will be cut off. If I cannot speak as openly as I like, you will understand."

"I hear you, Luis. Go ahead."

"Before we met, you had some trouble here."

"I haven't forgotten," Janek said.

"Just this week there were important changes in that agency. People who were in charge are no longer in charge, and others, including some of my friends, now have the upper hand."

"Go on."

"These friends, people I have known for years, tell me that my role assisting you did not come about by accident. It was, they tell me now, prearranged. Do you understand what I am saying?"

Janek sat still. "I'm not sure."

"It would seem that all the things that happened—between you and personnel of that agency, between you and me, between the two of us and the lady—were planned out in advance. It was Fonseca's operation. What I am saying, Frank, is that he knew you were coming even before you arrived. Arresting you had nothing to do with papers found in your luggage."

Janek felt something throb along his rib cage. When he brought his hand to his forehead, he felt sweat.

"Still there?"

"I'm here, Luis. Go on."

"Using me that way was classic technique. Bad cop/good cop. Except I did not know I was playing a part." Luis sounded concerned. "Please believe me, Frank. If I had participated in this, I would not be telling you now."

"I know that. What about Tania? Was she playing a part, too? Was she tampered with?"

Luis paused. "Remember your last night here? We discussed whether she might have told a big lie. I cannot be sure, but now I believe that she did."

Shit!

"It is what they call 'the cinema,' Frank. The agency specializes in such dramas. I told you your interrogator was an actress. Now it turns out they were all actors. And the place they took you to was not a real installation. It was built for such things, like a stage set. Do you understand?"

I understand, all right! Why didn't I spot it? How could I have been so dumb?

"Listen, Luis . . ." He heard panic in his voice. "Who was behind it? Do you know?"

"Fonseca was what they call 'the director.' Perhaps this will be of some comfort to you: He is now in prison, accused of drug trafficking. He will soon be tried for that and for *peligrosidad.* It is possible he will be executed. The only thing I have been able to discover is that several months ago he was in New York on a covert mission working on a drug investigation in collaboration with U.S. authorities. So, my thought is that the cinema he spun around you was in exchange for assistance he received from someone up there." Luis paused. "I am only guessing, Frank. Now they are signaling me to get off. I will call again if I find out more. Believe me, I did not look forward to telling you this. Believe also that what I have told you is true."

"Thank you, Luis. You are a brave man."

"Perhaps not so brave, Frank. But you are my friend. I hope next time we will have a happier conversation."

After Janek put down the phone he sat in his chair absolutely still. He knew there was no possibility that Luis had lied; if he had knowingly participated in the cinema, he would not have called to confess it. Which meant, Janek realized, that he had been set up by someone in his own department.

It was as if, he decided, he'd been stumbling around in

a maze as devious, confusing and illusionistic as the one Gelsey's father had built. The charade was so baroque, it was worthy of Dakin. And, he remembered, Dakin's buddy Baldwin had been present the night he had met with Angel Figueras. But Janek didn't think Dakin and Baldwin were behind the Cuban cinema. He had a sickening feeling who was.

Tom Shandy, the red-haired sergeant who guarded the door to Kit's office, was not encouraging. Chief Kopta was in a meeting, then had to go home to change for dinner with the commissioner. Sure, Janek could take a seat, and perhaps Shandy could slip him in. It would make things easier if Janek would tell him what he wanted, or, if it was confidential, he could write a note to the chief and Shandy would carry it to her.

"I'll do that," Janek said. He pulled out his notebook, scrawled the word *Mendoza,* ripped out the page, folded it and handed it to Shandy. "Just give her this."

Shandy, who had pretended to avert his eyes but had seen him write the forbidden word, nodded knowingly.

"I'll see she gets it right away."

Fifteen minutes later, a half dozen detectives lumbered out of Kit's office. They had the hangdog look of big men who'd been harshly rebuked by a small, authoritative woman. One nodded to Janek, but the others walked quickly into the hall. *There'll be some hard drinking tonight,* Janek thought.

A minute later Shandy waved him through. "Try to move it along, Lieutenant. Gotta get the chief outa here."

Kit was at her desk, writing. The room smelled of the sweat of the berated detectives who'd just left.

"Be right with you, Frank. Take a seat."

He moved toward her desk, but didn't sit. Rather he stood opposite her, waiting until she glanced up at him, a curious smile on her lips.

"You don't look too happy," she observed.

"You set me up."

He spoke the words as quietly and simply as he could. He had rehearsed his phrasing in her waiting room.

"What?" She stopped writing, focused on his eyes. "What're you talking about?" She smiled more broadly, but he didn't smile back.

"In Cuba. They were waiting for me. You told them I was coming."

She stared at him, eyes steady, unblinking. Then the stale smell in the room gave way to something else. When he'd entered he'd been uncertain of his ground. No longer. Kit's reaction was too stressful, her gaze too concentrated, her attempt to appear opaque too obvious.

"Fonseca's in jail. He'll probably be executed. For drug dealing and something they call *peligrosidad.* Know what that means, Kit? Dangerousness." He paused. "You've been playing with a very bad boy."

He gazed at her. Still her eyes didn't waver. She showed him nothing and that infuriated him.

"When I came back from Cuba and we sat here together, you pretended you didn't know what happened down there."

"I didn't."

"Maybe not the details, but you sure as hell knew the drift." He glared at her. *"Didn't you?"*

She looked down for a moment, then met his eyes again. When she spoke it was nearly in a whisper. "I told him not to hurt you, Frank. He promised me he wouldn't."

"Bitch!" He whispered the insult. She trembled before it. Then he spoke loudly, hoping her staff would hear, and cluster, worried, outside her door:

"Think it doesn't *hurt* to be locked up in a closet for three days, pissing and shitting in a bucket, then some gorilla throws in a lousy crust of bread hoping it falls into your slop? Get slapped across the mouth when you ask to see the American consul? Sit in a smock cut short so it doesn't cover your balls, while a vicious anorexic, with snake's eyes and khaki nail polish, smirks at pictures of you lying naked on the floor? No, there weren't any *injuries,* Kit! Just the kind of experiences that haunt you while you're trying to get to sleep. I wasn't really *harmed*—just humiliated, made to feel like shit.'' He shook his head. ''Then they were clever. They sent over a nice young detective who treated me like a human being. I did my job. But, see, I would have done it anyway. So, tell me—*why the fuck did I have to go through all that first?*''

There was a knock on the door. Shandy stuck in his head.

''Everything okay, Chief?''

Kit waved her hand. Shandy squinted at Janek, then withdrew.

''I didn't know about any of that. I'm sorry.''

Her regret was so perfunctory, it maddened him even more.

''How'd you think they'd do it? Put me up in a luxury suite, then have me worked over by some *jineteros*?''

''Huh?''

''Tourist prostitutes.''

She shook her head. ''It was wrong. I shouldn't have gone for it. I'm *so* sorry, Frank. At the time it seemed like a good idea.'' She paused. ''Obviously it wasn't.''

Sure, you're sorry—now that I've figured it out.

''*Why?* Why'd you even think to do something like that?'' She didn't answer. Was he seeing things or were her eyes actually watering up? ''I didn't go down there to clear Mendoza. I went there for you. There wasn't anything I wouldn't have done for you. Anything! Until five this afternoon.'' He shook his head. ''I want an explanation. I'm not asking, I'm demanding.''

She nodded, stood, walked over to the window.

''You deserve that . . . of course.''

He studied her as she stared down at Police Plaza. Lights were coming on in the surrounding buildings. The sky was almost dark.

''Fonseca was here, working with DEA. The way they

explained it to me, Castro wanted to show us he wasn't in the drug business, so he was getting rid of all his people who were. One day I got a call from my counterpart at DEA. 'There's this Cuban security colonel here. He says he's got something'll interest you. Can we send him over?' " She turned to Janek. "All day long I see detectives. Three years in this job and I can tell right away if a guy's got it or not. Fonseca had it. Intelligence, confidence. You'd expect a Cuban coming in here to maybe act a little intimidated. Not Fonseca. He was matter-of-fact. He talked to me like we were equals." She paused. "Maybe I got suckered. I didn't know he was in trouble. Wait till the DEA guys find out. They'll be shitting in their pants!"

She grinned at him, an obvious attempt to warm him up. But Janek didn't warm. He thought: *I'm not giving her an inch till I hear it all.*

"Fonseca got to the point pretty quick. Mendoza's maid—somehow he knew we'd been looking for her—was in Havana working for his government. Since the case was so divisive here, maybe I'd be interested in sending someone down to talk to her. She was, he assured me, willing to be interviewed. In fact, she'd come to the Seguridad herself.

"Of course I was interested. How could I not be? Dakin's still got buddies around, guys like Baldwin, who think they own the Department. I've been wanting to clean house ever since I got sworn in, clear up Mendoza once and for all and get rid of the rest of Dakin's crowd. Maybe this Tania knew something that could help clear the case. I told Fonseca I'd send someone down."

"Right, someone."

"It had to be you, Frank." The room had grown dim; as she spoke she turned on the lamps. "You'd worked on the case, you knew a lot about it, but you weren't tainted. No one had more knowledge, more credibility. There wasn't anyone else."

"So you decided to set me up."

"It wasn't like that. Fonseca said that Tania really knew something and if I wanted to clear the case it would be a good idea to make sure my interviewer believed what she had to say. He said he could make sure you were receptive by arresting you first, scaring you a little, then pairing you with a gentle cop who'd guide you through the interview."

"Bad cop/good cop to soften me up! I can't believe I'm hearing this!"

"It's true, I swear."

"Oh, I believe that's what he said. I just can't believe you'd buy into such bullshit."

"He made sense, Frank. I didn't want any screw-ups. What I had in mind for Baldwin and the others had to be perfectly executed. I couldn't take a chance."

"No, there's gotta be more." He peered at her. "You screwed him, didn't you?" She stared back ferociously. "Sure, that's it. Fonseca sized you up: 'one tough, unmarried middle-aged female police executive. No time for a lover or a relationship. All she needs is a good fucking. I'll give it to her and she'll eat shit out of my hand.' "

"Stop it, Frank!"

"Sure, that's it." He nodded. "He fucked your brains out and afterwards you told him everything. You discussed it with him like you were . . . ha! Colleagues."

She screamed at him: "Will you stop!"

He turned; he couldn't bear to look at her. "You never stopped to think *why* he would propose such a screwy deal. What rancid pile of goods *he* was selling. No, you just took the bait, same way DEA did. A guy like Fonseca takes in everybody. Except now, it seems, he may have gone too far."

"I was *lonely,* Frank."

She moaned the word. He refused to look at her. He didn't want to feel moved.

"I'm sure you were. So are we all at times. I'm sure Fonseca was a terrific lover, too. I'm sure the whole event did wonders for your complexion, made you feel ten years younger. So, tell me, Kit—how do you feel now?''

''You're enjoying this. And you're so bitter.''

''Me?'' He laughed. ''Way back when the two of us . . .'' He shook his head. ''You were a great kid then. Fun to be with, fun to kiss. You laughed a lot and showed a lot of vulnerability. I was crazy about you. Maybe you liked me a little, too.'' He shrugged. ''You had it all—looks, guts, smarts and an ambition like nothing I'd ever seen. It burned in your eyes, Kit. You were going places, higher than I dreamed I'd ever go.'' He paused. ''Well, you got what you wanted, became the first woman to make C of D. It cost you, though. You've become a tough little lady, the kind who sells out her oldest, most loyal friend.'' He moved away from her, to the other side of the room. Then he turned toward her again. ''You got a nerve calling me bitter. I didn't betray you. You betrayed me. Or are you so far gone you can't tell the difference?''

When she answered her voice was humble. ''I said I was sorry.'' She paused. ''You know what they say—Mendoza makes you crazy.''

Sure . . . like that's a real good excuse.

''All right,'' he said, ''let's cut the crap. I got questions. I want answers.''

She nodded meekly, then sat in one of her leather easy chairs.

''Was Angel for real?''

''He's her real brother. His arrest was a fake.''

''For my benefit?''

''More for Dakin's via Baldwin.''

''That was part of Fonseca's plan?''

''Well, most of it. We worked it out together.''

This is fucking unbelievable!

''Gabelli?''

''He didn't know anything.''

''What about Rampersad? Was she in on it? Or was she just another patsy?''

''She didn't know anything,'' Kit said.

Thank God for that!

"You could have tipped me off. I'd have probably gone along if you'd asked me. In fact, I would have insisted on it, just to find out what Fonseca was up to. That's what it's all about, you know. Or didn't it occur to you it was strange he was so interested in helping us close out Mendoza? Oh, sorry, I forgot. It was all just pillow talk, wasn't it?"

She wiped her forehead with her hand.

"Jesus, Kit! Was he such a great lay it never occurred to you he had his own agenda? Have you spent so many years playing headquarters politics, you've forgotten the most basic questions a detective has to ask: *Who* had *what* to gain and *why*? That's the job around here. But you didn't do it. You didn't do anything except . . ." He shook his head.

"Are you done insulting me?"

She's hopeless. But then something hit him: Could there have been a connection between Jake Mendoza and the Cubans? Why else would they have bothered? What did they care about NYPD internal politics?

"You may be guilty of obstruction of justice," he told her. She didn't blink. "I'd consult a private attorney if I were you."

But he could tell from her stare that she had no idea of how deeply she was compromised.

"All the stuff in Cuba—it didn't hurt me as much as I said. I'm a New York City detective, for Christ's sake. We're used to taking crap." He waited until she met his eyes. "What I can't handle is betrayal. That cuts too deep."

She studied him, her old tough self again, measuring him, trying to figure out what he was going to do.

"I want a transfer," he announced. "My whole squad out of here."

"Don't be ridiculous."

"Shut up! You don't talk to me like that anymore."

She looked down at the carpet. "Okay, a transfer. Where to? Internal Affairs?"

"I want to report directly to the commissioner."

She started to protest, but he cut her off. "Shandy says you're going to have dinner with him tonight. That's when you'll arrange it."

"Tell me why?"

"I don't want to work for you anymore. Also, I'm going to solve Mendoza and I don't want to think about who might fall."

"Surely you don't think I—"

"I'm not saying what I think. I got one other case to finish up around here. I should be done with it tomorrow." He started across the room.

"Frank!" He turned. "Can't we, you know—?"

"Make it up?" He shook his head.

"Twenty years of friendship and now it's over—is that really how you want it?"

"Maybe someday I'll forgive you, Kit. But don't hold your breath."

He left without shutting the door.

The Snare

That night he dreamed of mirrors.

He was wandering through a mirror maze like Gelsey's, but far more treacherous. As he made his way, the floors rolled like the deck of a ship, and the mirrors flexed toward him, sometimes touching above his head.

The reflections were different, too. Instead of giving back images of himself, they showed the likenesses of others: Jake Mendoza, Tania Figueras, Fonseca, Violetta, Dakin, Timmy Sheehan and Kit. These simulacra were threatening. They stared into his eyes with mockery. Their expressions taunted: "You're lost, Janek. You'll never find your way out. Never!"

Early the next morning he called Ray and Aaron at home, and explained his transfer request without mentioning Kit's duplicity. He told them that since, from a career point of view, it was probably a risky venture, they should feel free to transfer out of the squad.

Ray asked if he was serious. Aaron told him that he would regard exclusion from the Mendoza investigation as an act of personal betrayal.

When he called Sue, she responded with her own special twist:

"You friggin' kiddin', Frank?" She was laughing. "You need a dyke cop like me who's, you know, politically correct."

After thanking her, he asked how Gelsey was doing.

"She's asleep. We were talking till late. She took me downstairs. Geez! I never saw anything like that!"

"Well, wake her up," Janek said. "Bring her into the city. We're going to set a trap, but not in Jersey. I don't want any jurisdictional disputes."

He stopped by Deforest's office, filled him in, requested arrest warrants for Diana Cassiday and Stephen Kane. Then he told Deforest that he and his people were leaving the division. When Deforest heard what he intended to do, he soberly wished Janek good luck.

Back at Special Squad, he briefed Aaron and Ray, instructing them to find a good location for a trap. He also told them to sign out field videotape equipment and the best body-wire unit Special Services could provide. Then he called Netti Rampersad.

"Frank . . ." She savored his name with the warmth of a casual lover. "Sorry, I don't have very good news. Sarah's attorney called to say she'll fight the alimony rollback. What I need now is that dossier you mentioned that shows how Sarah and Gilette are living high off the hog."

"I'll bring it right down."

This time when she greeted him, she was not wearing workout clothes but was dressed in an expensive, smartly cut pin-striped gray linen suit.

"Excuse the battle dress," she said. "I'm due in court."

Doe Landestoy turned away and giggled.

Janek handed her Aaron's Sarah-Gilette file. He had never read it. She put it in her desk.

"Can we go someplace and talk?"

"You can walk me over to the courthouse," Netti said.

"Where's Rudnick?" he asked on the stairs.

"In the law library. He haunts the place."

"The other night—"

"Please, Frank," she said gently, "don't tell me you've had regrets."

"Absolutely not."

"Neither have I."

"Well, now that that's settled . . ."

They emerged laughing onto Canal Street, made their way through the throng, crossed, then entered Chinatown.

"I need a favor," Janek said.

"What's up?"

"A young woman I know is in pretty bad trouble. She needs a good lawyer."

Netti opened her purse, handed him her business card. "Tell her to call me anytime."

They walked past a pagoda-shaped telephone booth. The sidewalks were slippery. Chinese men in sleeveless shirts were unloading fish off the backs of trucks.

"I wonder if you'd—?"

"—finish telling you what I started to tell you the other night?"

He gazed at her. "Are you telepathic?"

"Depends on who I'm talking to."

"You amaze me."

She smiled. "Let's hope I always do."

The air on Mott Street was aromatic: roasting barbecued ducks and ribs, scented breads.

"So, what do you want to know?" she asked.

"You mentioned the Clury angle, how it was connected, as opposed to the way everyone thinks. You said something about another agenda, someone wanting Clury blown up for his own reasons."

"You've got a good memory."

"It was a night to remember."

She smiled again. "Forget Mendoza for a while, follow up on Clury. You might discover something that'll give you a whole new slant on the thing."

"I can see why you'd want me to forget Mendoza."

"Nothing to do with my representing him. Just take a

look at the case from another point of view—the Clury point of view.''

''You're being cryptic.''

''I have to be.''

They passed a greens market. Two elderly Chinese women, with Mao-era haircuts, were picking over the vegetables.

''Mendoza's pretty rich, isn't he?''

''Like Croesus,'' she said. ''But you're changing the subject.''

''A guy like that—life sentence, no possibility of parole—can he still control his money?''

''Some convicts appoint a trustee. Jake writes most of his own checks. But he also uses his old lawyer, Andrews, as fiduciary. By the way, the only reason Andrews didn't represent him on the murder charge was because he didn't know bat-shit about criminal defense. He still doesn't.''

''So, if Jake wanted, say, to bid on a Van Gogh at auction, he could do it even though he's locked up.''

''Right. So, what're you driving at?''

''Something else I'm going to be looking into.''

Netti glanced at him. ''Who's being cryptic now?''

''Then there's the El Paso thing . . .'' he remarked casually.

''What about it?'' She was annoyed. ''You seem to have a lot on your mind.''

''Department figures it was a copycat job.''

''Naturally.'' She spoke with disdain.

''You don't really think it proves anything?''

''Let's put it this way—in a case like this I'll use every little thing I've got.''

''So, you think I ought to look into Clury?''

''I'd say that's the smart move.''

''You wouldn't be trying to mislead me, would you, Netti?''

''Anyone else, Frank, and I'd never give it a thought.

But not you. I've gotten to know you too well. And besides, you're a client.''

She glanced at her watch. ''Gotta run. Late for court.'' She kissed him quickly on the cheek, then strode off.

He stood at the edge of Chinatown, watching her take long, loping strides toward the courthouse, her mane of red hair flowing behind her. She looked awfully good, he thought.

Back at the Property building, walking down the corridor, he heard laughter issuing from Special Squad. When he entered he found Gelsey, stripped to her bra, sitting on Aaron's desk while Sue Burke taped a battery pack to her back. Ray was closely observing the procedure, while Aaron, wearing a flamboyant orchid-covered shirt, was delivering the punch line to an old police war story. Gelsey looked at ease.

''Hi!'' she said. Her voice was gay. ''I like your people.''

''We like her, too, Frank,'' Aaron said.

''But does *he* like *me*?'' Gelsey asked. ''He was so tough yesterday I couldn't tell.''

Everyone laughed.

''I found you a lawyer.'' Janek handed her Netti's card. ''Call her. She'll help you settle with Carlson. Sue and I'll take care of Stiegel.''

''Who's Stiegel?''

''The cop who took Carlson's complaint,'' Sue explained.

Suddenly Gelsey didn't look so happy. ''I really am in trouble, aren't I?''

No one said anything, but Janek could see that the others hoped she'd get out of it.

Sue patted Gelsey on the shoulder. ''You're wired. Put on your shirt so we can see how you look.''

She looked fine.

"Helping us, you'll be helping yourself," Sue reminded her.

"What about Cavanaugh?" Aaron asked. "He's not going to be happy when he hears she smashed his Omega."

"Cavanaugh's compromised," Janek said. "Kane's his boy. Kane may even try to implicate him. I think Cavanaugh'll stay quiet, no matter how pissed off."

Ray proposed a payoff site downtown, the plaza behind the Winter Garden at the World Financial Center. There were few people there at night, and although it appeared open, it could easily be bottled up.

Since both Kane and Diana had met Janek, and Kane had also met Sue, Ray felt they would need to borrow a half-dozen men from other units. One would circulate, one would pretend to be homeless, four would impersonate a night cleaning crew. Janek would control the operation and monitor Gelsey's wire from a parked unmarked police-communications panel truck.

Janek wanted to check the place out. The five of them piled into a cab. On site he looked around: The river bound one side of the plaza, new sleek buildings of reflective glass the other. The spectacular Winter Garden was far enough away that people sitting inside would be out of danger. He approved the plan, assigned Aaron and Ray the job of lining up the van and the extra men. Then he returned to Special Squad with Gelsey and Sue to throw the bait.

Sue set up the recording equipment in Janek's office, then returned to the outer room to listen. When everything was ready, Janek signaled Gelsey. She nodded, they picked up their phones, Janek dialed and settled back.

"Hel-lo. May I help you?"

He recognized Kim's crisp tone, remembered the way she'd glared at him in the limousine mirror.

"It's Gelsey."

"One moment, please."

There was a pause, then Diana came on:

"Well . . . this *is* a surprise."

"Yeah, sure," Gelsey said.

"What's on your mind, pet?"

"Still interested in that whatchamacallit?"

"The Dietz item?"

"Uh-huh . . ."

"I might be. How much do you want?"

Diana, Janek thought, was doing a bad job concealing her excitement.

"You mentioned a fifty-fifty split."

"Did I?"

"If you've changed your mind, Diana, forget it."

A brief silence. "The offer stands."

"How much can we get for it?"

"Hard to say. Maybe ten . . . fifteen K."

Gelsey looked at Janek. He shook his head.

"Not enough," Gelsey said. "If that's all it's worth, you wouldn't have been so fierce about it."

"I didn't mean to be fierce, dear. I really don't know what it's worth. I won't till I show it to the buyer."

"Surely you don't expect me to hand it over?"

"I can give you something on account, if that's what you're hinting at."

Again Janek shook his head.

"You must think I'm stupid. The only way this deal's going down is if we all three meet together."

"Impossible!"

"It's that or nothing."

Another pause. "You strike a hard bargain, dear."

"Not nearly as hard as you. Look, I've got the item. You've got the buyer. Neither of us can do anything without the other. That's why we all three have to meet. In a public place where I won't get ambushed."

Oh, she's good! Janek thought.

"I'll have to talk to the buyer, see how he feels."

"Do that. But remember, Diana—there *is* no other way. Be ready to roll at ten tonight. I'll call you with instructions. Till then . . . kiss-kiss. . . .''

Two seconds after Gelsey put down the phone, Sue burst in from the other room.

''Fabulous!'' Sue embraced her. ''Wasn't she great, Frank?''

He looked into Gelsey's eyes. ''I told you you were an actress.''

He wanted to spend the afternoon with her, build her confidence, keep her from thinking about the danger. Also, he admitted to himself, he liked her company.

He took her to lunch at a Cajun dive on Eighth Avenue in the Twenties. While they ate jambalaya and sipped beer from jelly jars, he asked about her parents.

She described her father in detail—handsome, a charmer, a silver-throated smoothy. But Janek received no clear impression of her mother. She came across, from Gelsey's description, as a shadowy presence in the house—secretive, withdrawn, ineffectual and plain.

''I don't think she had much influence on me,'' Gelsey said. ''I'm strictly my father's girl. He was a scam artist and so am I. He built the maze; I paint pictures. So, we're both visual artists, too.''

''Did he think of himself as an artist?''

''God, no! He'd laugh at the idea.''

She told Janek about other works created by other naïve artist-craftsmen: the Watts Towers in Los Angeles; an elaborate tile complex in Washington; a wall constructed out of empty beer cans in Key West, Florida.

''There're hundreds of these huge lifelong projects around the country. The men who create them, like my father, usually start out without a clear idea of what they're doing. But something drives them. They see something vaguely in a dream, then set out to construct it . . . out of masonry, metal, wood, tile, glass, whatever material they know how to use. These projects speak to people because they're obsessive. You look at them, sense the design and know they're the product of a single person's mind. You marvel at the work put in, the scale, the ambition. Few people have the will to devote a lifetime to something so grand. . . .''

Instead of borrowing Aaron's car, Janek signed out a police Ford from the Sixth Precinct. Driving out to Newark, he and Gelsey didn't talk much. He liked being with her, sitting beside her in the car. She aroused his affection in a way few young women ever had. Perhaps, he thought, she reminded him of his mother—there was something about the set of her eyes.

''What's it like to live above a maze?'' he asked as he took the turn that led to Richmond.

''Most of the time I forget it's there.''

''But there're times when you don't forget.''

She nodded. ''Then it feels strange. Like living on top of a bomb.''

He wondered if her forays into the city, spurred on by rain, had been attempts to add excitement to an otherwise quiet life. It occurred to him that for her to live above the maze was akin to an orphan living in the house in which his parents had been killed. People normally flee the scenes of injurious family crimes. But Gelsey had stayed on. He wondered why.

As they passed the entrance to the park, he asked her if there was a way they could get inside.

''This summer some kids cut a hole in the fence.'' She pointed ahead. ''About a hundred yards up the street.''

He stopped where she showed him.

''Want to go in?''

''If you like,'' she said. ''It'll bring back memories.''

They got out, she crawled through the hole, he followed, then, at her suggestion, picked up a stick in case they ran into dogs.

He was less impressed with the decay than he had been the previous morning. He guessed this was because the high afternoon sun made the ruins of Richmond appear flat, while the rising sun had endowed them with a sorrowful, romantic glow. But there was still something fascinating about an amusement park in an abandoned state. They didn't make them like Richmond anymore. The new ones were glossy and plastic. Richmond, with its patina of ruined, rusted rides, and broken, weathered sheds, would make a fine setting, he thought, for a post–nuclear holocaust film.

As they strolled through the weeds, he told Gelsey about Walter Meles and how he had hated touching Walter's monkey's paw. Gelsey didn't remember Meles—when Janek and his father had come out to Richmond, she hadn't even been born. Still, she listened with attention, and, when he finished his story, shook her head.

"Most everyone who worked here was injured somehow," she said.

The fun house was gutted. The alcoves, on either side of the door, which had contained the mechanical Laughing Man and Laughing Woman, looked forlorn without their cackling patrons of joy.

"Remember how they sounded?"

Gelsey smiled. "Scratchy. Very scratchy."

The huge painted smile that adorned the front had faded but still was visible. One of the walls, however, had fallen down. When Janek looked in he saw no mirrors, rolling floors, bats on wires, giant spiders' webs. There was no spooky lighting or scary sound effects. The fun house was but a shell.

Gelsey said, "When Dad was here this place looked great."

As they strolled, he tried subtly to guide her toward the tunnel of love. Finally, she seemed to catch on.

"Want to see where my mother worked?"

"If you'd like to show me. . . ."

He remembered the attraction well. Most customers were young hand-holding couples. One boarded a boat. He had shared his with his balding father. The boat was then pulled by a mechanical system into a pitch-black tunnel. Here the air was close, the humidity intense, the environment a jungle at night: glossy plants, mechanical alligators, chained-up live monkeys and parrots screeching out of the gloom. As one's boat passed through, along a meandering circular path, the darkness overwhelmed. But he remembered the high-pitched giggles and deep throaty laughter of lovers urging each other to greater intimacies. He also remembered wondering what it would be like to thrust his tongue inside a girl's mouth.

The tunnel, like the fun house, was seriously decayed, but they found the cement bed that had been the river, and the remains of the chains that had hauled the boats. The tunnel entrance was still defined, although most of its ceiling had collapsed. Gelsey led him into the ruins, then pointed at a shed in the center.

"That's where Mom sat. The control booth. She could see everything from there. If things got out of hand, she'd turn on the lights."

"It was so dark in here, how could she see?"

"She was used to it. The way the place was set up, if you were in the booth, the lamps in the foliage silhouetted people in the boats against the walls." Gelsey paused. "I think she lived in a state of darkness anyway."

Back in her loft, he asked if he could stand on the catwalks again. She was pleased that he was interested.

"I think last night Sue got a little freaked out," she said, opening the trapdoor. "Especially when we went down to the floor."

"It's really tough to look at nothing but yourself."

"If you're not pleased with yourself, very tough," she agreed.

Standing in the dark on the catwalks with the blazing lights on below, he was dazzled again by the rigorous symmetry of the maze. But there were places, he observed, where the ceilings were not transparent. Gelsey explained that, for structural reasons, her father hadn't been able to roof all the mirrored corridors with one-way glass. Also, there were backstage and service areas between the sections.

"Is there a map?"

She smiled, pointed to her head.

He couldn't believe there was nothing on paper.

"Didn't your dad work from a plan?"

"He made it up as he went along."

To Janek that seemed impossible; the maze was too well designed. Gelsey explained that her father had built and rebuilt portions many times, constantly correcting his work.

"I do the same thing—get an idea, sketch it on canvas, then, when it doesn't work, adjust a little here, a little there, erase this, add that, until I find my way to something I like."

"But without a plan, how do you know which mirrors are doors? To me they all look the same."

"They are the same. Otherwise you wouldn't get lost. But I've been through it so many times, I know which ones open and which ones don't." She paused. "Sometimes when I'm down here I try to lose myself by closing my eyes and whirling around. But after a few minutes I'll recognize a mirror combination or a turn in a corridor, and then I'll know exactly where I am."

She explained that the door mirrors, identical to the stationary ones, were disengaged by touching them at a point exactly five feet off the floor. Once sprung, they were easily pushed open. When pushed back, they relocked.

"When I was a kid, and opened them all up, my father thought I was a genius. But it was easy. Want to know how I did it?" Janek nodded. "I just looked for his finger smudges on the glass."

Such a strange childhood she'd had. Yet she'd emerged functional and relatively sane. Janek wondered whether he was kidding himself. Her bar seductions and takedowns proved she was disturbed, especially the fact that she hadn't engaged in them for money but solely to exercise power. It was her artwork, he thought, that kept her together. Without that, he was certain, she'd have long ago slipped over the edge.

They drove back to Manhattan. The towers glowed before the failing New Jersey sun. Once in the city, they joined up with the squad, ordered in salad and pizza, then, at eight, drove downtown in the communications van to the World Financial Center.

Janek was anxious to meet his new crew. There were four men and two women, all bright, young, alert. They had volunteered partly for the overtime, Aaron said, but mostly because they wanted to work with Special Squad.

"We're a legend. Did you know that, Frank?"

Janek smiled. "Right . . ."

They drove the van onto the sidewalk, parked it near the entrance to the Winter Garden, where, they hoped, it would look like a service vehicle. They set up one video camera facing the plaza where they expected most of the action to take place, installed the other inside a portable trash cart, which one of the volunteer cops, impersonating a janitor, would wheel around. Then they did two complete walk-throughs in which Sue played Diana, Janek played Kane and Gelsey played herself. After that Sue wired Gelsey up. Just before ten, Janek beckoned her into the van. They sat facing each other. Then Janek reached for the phone and dialed.

This time Diana snapped up her phone. Janek could hear severe stress in her voice.

"World Financial Center, behind the Winter Garden? Sure, I know it, Gelsey. In half an hour—fine. Yes, the gentleman will be with me. Yes, he'll have the money—twenty-five K just for you. That's a very good price, don't you agree? We mustn't be greedy, dear. Do as I do—take what you can get and enjoy it. That's what money's for."

After the call, Janek asked Gelsey to wait in the van while he gave final instructions to his crew. He huddled with them in the great arched glass back wall of the Winter Garden.

"They're planning to kill her," he whispered.

Everyone looked at him. Aaron asked how he could be sure.

"I could hear it in the lady's voice. Also, it makes sense. Once Kane confirms Gelsey's got the Omega, he'll shoot her in the head. He'll kill Diana, too, probably later, not here. According to Gelsey, Kim always packs a little gun."

"Wouldn't Diana expect something?"

"Yes, which is why she's probably not charging much to deliver Gelsey. She's got her own reasons for wanting to be rid of her. But Kane won't want witnesses. He'll off her and Kim soon as he can."

"Geez, Frank . . ." Sue looked worried.

"Okay, we knew it was going to be dangerous. Gelsey's understood that all along. Our job is to see she isn't hurt. The moment I sense trouble, I'm sending you all in—whether she's got stuff on tape or not. Remember, Kane's a cop. It won't take him long to smell a trap. I'm counting on Kim staying with the limo. One less gun waving around." He paused. "Let's be clear. Gelsey comes first. Making the case is number two." He met each pair of eyes, waiting until each person acknowledged his instructions. When he was sure they all understood, he dispatched them to their stations.

Walking back to the van, he broke into a sweat. There was always the feeling, on an operation like this, that something could go wrong, something he should have thought of but hadn't. One thing he felt he had going was Gelsey's ability to improvise. Her bar forays had been dangerous, but she'd always been successful. Perhaps the years of making decisions wandering through the maze had taught her to think quickly on her feet.

From the van, he sent her to her position, a semidark alcove at the rear of the American Express Building.

"Don't come out too quickly," he reminded her. "Wait till they park, then step out slowly and reveal yourself. But don't approach too close. I don't want Diana to be able to hear you from the car."

Although each squad member wore an earphone invisible to passersby, only Gelsey was miked. Thus Janek could talk to them during the operation, but only Gelsey's words would be taped.

"Everyone in motion," he instructed. "Don't wait for them to show before you get up to speed. It has to look real, like we're part of the life down here. Homeless Man—pretend you're dozing. A homeless guy wouldn't be alert this late. . . ."

Again he felt the agony of a field commander just before a battle. Was there something he'd forgotten, a touch that would certify the scene as real? Most important, was there anything that would tip Kane off?

As far as he could see, it all looked good: a normal display in front of a vast office complex at night. All the windows of the buildings were lit up, lights on for the benefit of the night cleaning crews. Inside the phones were silent, but the fax machines spewed pages and the computer screens blinked data even though there was no one at the desks. It was the great humming machine of global finance—foreign currencies, stocks, bonds, commodities—that operated twenty-four hours a day.

Diana's white limousine appeared at North End Avenue just before eleven, gliding silently to a stop by the curb. The car sat there a while, utterly still. Janek, studying it through binoculars, could see nothing but its mirrored windows reflecting back the towers of the complex.

He turned back to the alcove. Slowly Gelsey emerged. Janek was struck by her poise. Standing in a shaft of light cast by a lamp on the plaza, she looked stunning, an object of desire, dressed in black, her dark hair spilling over her shoulders.

A window of the limousine opened. A hand reached out and beckoned.

"Take a few steps," Janek whispered. "Then shake your head."

Gelsey moved forward and shook her head. After a few seconds the car door opened. He made out Diana, and an indistinct figure beside her.

"Gelsey," Diana called.

"Over here," Gelsey called back.

For a moment neither woman moved. Then Diana stepped out of the car.

Janek whispered: "As she moves toward you, retreat a little. Remember—make her come to you."

Gelsey waited until just the right moment, then took two steps back into the alcove. Diana quickened her pace.

"Stop!" she ordered.

"Backtrack two more," Janek whispered. "Make her understand she doesn't tell you what to do."

Gelsey backtracked. Diana followed.

"This is ridiculous," Diana said. "We can't do it like this. Stop!"

"Okay, take a stand," Janek whispered. "Face her, let her approach."

Diana began to speak even before she was within confidential speaking distance:

"The buyer's gotta be satisfied, Gelsey. He won't buy a pig in a poke."

"Tell him to come here and look. Tell him to bring the money."

"He doesn't want to get out of the car."

Gelsey sneered. "Is he a cripple?"

"You're out of line, pet."

"This is my party, Diana. Tell him he'd better hurry before I get bored and take a walk."

"He's paying us fifty K—twenty-five apiece. You don't

push around a man like that."

"I bet he's paying a hundred."

"Don't you trust me, pet?"

Gelsey shrugged. "Twenty-five'll be enough to get me out of this crappy town. Go get it. I want to count it. Meantime—here's a peek."

She opened her palm, showed the prototype chip, clasped her hand shut and grinned.

Diana didn't know what to do. As Janek watched, he imagined her growing realization that this time she was not in control.

"All right," Diana said finally, without an attempt to conceal her bitterness. "I'll try to get him to come out."

As Diana walked back to her car, Janek felt he had enough to implicate her in an illegal purchase of stolen goods. Perhaps not as much as he would have liked, but enough to secure an indictment.

"Fade back a couple steps," he whispered. Gelsey retreated into the gloom. When Diana reached the curb, she glanced back just before getting into her car.

There followed a short intermission. Janek tried to imagine what was being said. Diana would describe the quick glimpse she'd had of the Omega, while Kane would contemplate his best next move. Janek believed he would view his odds as good. A police trap was a possibility, but the location wasn't particularly congenial for a trap and Gelsey's hesitancy could be understood in light of her disaffected former employee relationship with Diana. Janek believed it would also occur to Kane that Gelsey knew Kirstin had been killed and would therefore want to unload the chip with minimal risk. Anyway, the object that Diana had described was certainly the Omega. There were few people about, so it would be relatively safe to leave the car, throw a few bucks at the girl, take the chip, shoot her, then split.

Just as Janek finished his reverie, the limo door opened

again. This time both Diana and Kane stepped out. Kane was carrying a paper bag.

He thought: *The gun's inside the bag.* He watched Diana and Kane approach. "Take two steps forward," he instructed Gelsey. "Stand in the light. Then hold your ground."

As Diana and Kane crossed the World Financial Center plaza, and his own people moved with apparent languor toward their final positions, Janek felt he was watching something akin to the formation of a *tableau vivant.* There was a rigor to the design these players made that reminded him of paintings by De Chirico showing lonely figures on vast Italian squares. Except in the work of De Chirico, the Mediterranean sun always burned straight down and there were *campaniles* in the background, while here the scene was played out against a black sky and looming out-of-scale office towers. Still, he felt the same strong ambience of ritual, inevitability and fate.

When each figure reached his final position, all motion stopped.

"Show it to him," Diana ordered.

Gelsey stared at Kane. "You killed Dietz."

"Never mind that, pet. Show him the goods."

"You let them think I did it. Why?" Gelsey demanded.

"What's this got to do—?"

"Everything!" Gelsey said. "Twenty-five isn't nearly enough, not for what he did to me." She turned back to Kane. "You want your little thingamajig, you're going to pay a lot more than that!"

Kane looked at Diana. "You said she was cool."

Diana shrugged. "You're pushing it, pet. Better back off before things get nasty."

"Kill me, too? Is that what you're threatening?" Gelsey turned again to Kane. "You killed Kirstin, didn't you?"

At this point Kane must have detected the artificial phrasing that creeps in when a wired witness attempts to provoke a suspect. Perhaps, glancing around the plaza, he was struck by the positions of the other people, and, in that instant, suddenly viewed the scene as false.

He's going to attack! The notion hit Janek a split second before he gave his order:

"He's going for her! Get him! Now!"

Janek flung himself out of the van, rushed across the plaza. Then everything seemed to happen at half-speed. From one side, Aaron, Ray and Sue charged in. From the other, the cop playing the homeless man and the four playing the night cleaning crew converged with drawn guns. Diana screamed. Then, trying to run back to her car in her heels, she tripped and fell onto the granite. Kane, seeing he was about to be tackled, pulled a small revolver from his paper bag and rushed at Gelsey.

He's going to take her hostage!

But Gelsey was no easy victim. She took off toward Janek and the van; Kane, pursuing, was pursued in turn by the pack. Janek, gripping his pistol in both hands, leveled it at Kane. Gelsey feinted to the side and rolled. Kane slipped. In an instant the pack was on him, while Gelsey, panting, lay in Janek's arms.

"Block the limo," Janek yelled, for it was now moving from the curb. Then he saw Diana, knees bloody from her fall, rushing after her own car, screaming at Kim to stop. A moment later the limo collided with an oncoming sanitation truck. The white car folded up. Diana, back down on the plaza floor, raged wildly at the night:

"God! What have you done!"

It was always that way, Janek thought—they never blame the breakage on themselves, instead hurl the accusation at the heavens. And because they don't take responsibility for their crimes, they never believe they are guilty of committing them.

Kim was dead. Kane was silent. Diana was inconsolable. When Kane and Diana were properly booked and locked away, Janek drove Gelsey home. When they arrived at her building a little after three A.M., she made no gesture to leave the car.

"So, is this it?" she asked, sitting still. "Case closed. We go separate ways?"

"Is that what you want?" Janek asked.

"Of course not! You've been good to me. Better than almost anyone. Even Dr. Z."

He looked at her. "So, do you think I'm the kind who gives up a friend just because a case is closed?"

She smiled. "*Am* I your friend?"

"Of course you are."

She nodded. "Thanks." She paused. "Can I call you when it rains, Janek? Will you come?"

"I'll come," he promised.

She smiled, kissed him quickly on the cheek, stepped out, then scampered up the wooden steps to her house. There she paused, waved, blew him another kiss. Then she disappeared.

As he drove back he glowed, holding the memory of her smile. But then, as he approached Manhattan, he began to feel an ache. The dark forms of the towers reminded him of Mendoza. Entering the Holland Tunnel, he steeled himself. There was still that knot to be untied.

Through a Glass, Darkly

At noon the following day he met his people at Special Squad. Though tired, they were still charged up by their success. He began by laying down new rules. They would be working on Mendoza. That meant new computer codes and passwords, filing cabinets with combination locks, a paper shredder, phone scramblers, regular electronic sweeps and new locks on the office door.

"Starting today we're the only ones in here. We clean our offices ourselves. All trash goes through the shredder. When we want to see someone, we meet him outside. When we order in food, we pay for it at the door. We don't answer questions about what we're doing, not from anyone—friend, lover or spouse. We're careful what we say, even in cars. We're not accountable to anyone except the commissioner. That includes Internal Affairs."

When they had absorbed that, he helped them work up a security schedule, making sure he, too, was assigned office-cleaning duties. Then, when that was done, he sat them down and stunned them with the news that his Cuban trip had been a setup.

"Why would the Cubans propose a deal like that?" he asked after he explained the sequence. "What could possibly be in it for them?"

Ray thought the answer was better relations. "They want us to drop the embargo."

''A good reason to work with the feds. But not with NYPD.''

''To get Tania Figueras off the hook,'' Sue suggested

''We'd stopped looking for her. Technically, Mendoza was closed.''

Aaron looked at him. ''I know you've got a theory, Frank.''

The others smiled; they knew him well.

''Mendoza has a lot of money,'' he said. ''Something like fifty million bucks. But it's no good to him because he's locked up for the rest of his life. Think about that. Put yourself in his shoes. If you were that rich and locked in a cage, wouldn't you be willing to spend whatever it took to pry yourself loose?''

Everyone nodded.

''Fonseca's a corrupt Cuban security official. He comes here, ostensibly to work with the DEA, except now it turns out he was running drugs. A guy like that, for the right amount of money, would do most anything you'd want, including pulling a con job on our Detective Division, convincing us a forgotten 'missing witness' is telling the truth when she throws doubt on the whole premise behind Mendoza's conviction.''

''You think Mendoza paid Fonseca to run the scam on Kit?'' Sue asked.

''That's the only theory that makes sense. The Cuban government wouldn't care about Mendoza rotting in prison. But Fonseca might care—if he was paid.''

Aaron nodded. ''If that's true, there has to be a financial connection. If money was paid out, it had to travel.''

''That's what we're going to look at—who paid how much to whom. Aaron, I want you to examine all large payments from Mendoza or his lawyer, Andrews, to any person or entity that isn't easily explained. Use the computer. Go back a few years. Look into anything that seems the slightest bit phony. Track it down, check it out, stick with it till you're satisfied. Sometime, somehow, money was paid out, maybe through a foreign bank account or intermediary. I'm betting sooner or later you'll find something that leads you to Cuba.''

He was pleased to see he'd fired them up. But there was more.

''There's another payment I want you to look for. This would have been made three or four years ago, about the time of the copycat killing in El Paso. Same MO as Edith Mendoza—society woman beaten to death, strung up by her heels. That's another thing Mendoza may have arranged, to make us think the real killer was still at large. He could have paid someone to do it. Which is where''—he turned to Ray and Sue—''you guys come in. Check out Mendoza's career at Green Haven Prison. Who'd he bunk with? Who'd he spend time with? Did he spread his money around? If so, to whom? You may find your Cuban connection there. You may also find someone from Texas. Look at people he buddied with who later got released. What happened to them? Where do they live? Any signs of unexplained wealth? While Aaron's looking at the money, you two look at who might have gotten it.''

''And you—what'll you be doing while we're doing all that?'' Aaron asked.

''I'll be looking at a whole other side of the thing. The Clury side,'' he said.

The bomb squad offices were situated in a former butter warehouse on Wooster Street. The old dairy vaults, with their curved brick ceilings, gave the space a cloistered, ecclesiastical look. In fact, in Janek's view, the bomb squad had much in common with a religious order. It was elite, there was an intense stillness among its members, an aura that spoke of being involved in sacred work. When Janek walked unannounced into Stoney's office, he felt as if he'd interrupted a rector at his desk.

''What can I do for you?'' the squat, blunt detective asked.

"I want to talk about Mendoza."

"Aren't you a little late?" Stoney couldn't conceal his disgust.

He really didn't put in much time at charm school.

"I was on another case. Now that's cleared. Today I start full-time on Mendoza. Are you willing to work with me or not?"

"What've you got in mind?" Stoney asked.

"Clury: Who bombed him and why?"

"You ask interesting questions, Janek. Buy a new car yet?"

"Huh?"

"I'm just curious. What kind of car does a guy buy when his old one's blown away? Or maybe he decides not to replace it. If they hit you once, they can always hit you again."

"Okay," Janek said, sitting down, "we got off on the wrong foot. I'm no longer in the Detective Division. My squad's working directly for the commissioner. We've got one case. Clury could be the key. You've already put in legwork. I want to collaborate. I'm serious."

"I notice you don't ask me to join your squad."

"If I thought you'd consider it, I would."

Stoney smiled. "Tell me about Clury. What do you know about him?"

Janek told him everything he knew, and that he'd been given two new pieces of information. The first, from a reliable confidential source, was that someone might have had a reason to kill Clury that had never been explored. The second, from a source in Cuba who had deliberately tried to mislead him, was that Clury had been investigating Jake Mendoza on Edith Mendoza's behalf.

"Well, to me that's all garbage," Stoney said. "I deal in bombs, explosives—who makes 'em, who sets 'em off."

"What did you find in Nassau County?"

"Couple of things. Clury's car was parked in his driveway all night, but none of the neighbors saw anyone tampering with it.''

''Is that important?''

''It was ignition-wired, so the bomber had to open the hood. That's taking a chance, with the car right next to the house and the guy you want to kill inside.''

''Bomber must have figured Clury was asleep.''

''He could have woken up. He's a cop. He's got a gun. He could have shot the bomber. It doesn't smell right.''

Janek thought about it; he wasn't sure yet how it smelled.

''What about the bomb signature?''

''That's not exactly like a fingerprint. But I checked it out. From the records it's only shown up twice, once on Clury's car, once on yours.''

''What does that tell you?''

''That the bomber isn't a professional. Oh, he makes a good bomb, but he doesn't do it for a living. He only does it when it concerns Mendoza.''

Interesting. ''Anything else?''

''He wasn't self-taught. Whoever taught him taught him to do it right. There're not too many places you can learn to make a bomb. Most likely he learned in the military.''

''So, that's it?''

Stoney nodded. ''Why're you so pleasant today?''

''Was I unpleasant before?''

''You didn't cooperate. I couldn't figure you, Frank. You'd lost your car but you didn't seem all that interested.''

''I guess I wasn't focusing on it.''

''But you are now. Got any ideas?''

''I'm wondering about something. . . .''

''What?''

''Not sure yet.''

Stoney smiled. ''Well, let me know when you are sure. I'll be here.'' He stuck out his stubby hand.

It chewed at Janek the rest of the day—the notion that something about the Clury story was wrong. It continued to bother him after he went back to Detective Division files and read everything he could find on Clury in the Mendoza folders. There wasn't much. Clury, although a cop, had been viewed as the secondary victim. Most of the investigators' time had been spent on Edith; hers seemed a simpler homicide to solve.

When Janek finished reading, he realized he hadn't a clear sense of who Clury was. He called for Clury's personnel file, waited two hours for the clerks to find it. A dead cop meant a dead file; a cop nine years dead wasn't even in the computer. When, finally, they brought him the material, it was after six P.M. Hungry and tired, he decided to give it a quick look, then return in the morning to tackle it fresh.

Two minutes into it he was wide awake. According to Howard Clury's military records, the deceased detective had graduated from the Naval Demolition School at Coronado, California, then served as a demolition specialist in South Vietnam, 1971–1972.

He went out, ostensibly to get coffee, but he was so excited he didn't bother to stop. Instead he walked rapidly down to the Battery, and then just as rapidly back to Police Plaza. It was after seven when he signed back into the file room. Clury's personnel folder was just where he'd left it, on the long wooden table beneath the fluorescent lamp. Approaching, he was seized by a throbbing anticipation, which reminded him of the excitement he'd felt perhaps a half dozen times in his career when he knew he was about to turn a case around. He thought: *Thank you, Netti, for steering me to this.*

There were no autopsy photos of Clury. The explosion had blown him into pieces. So, how had his body been IDed? By fragments of clothing, Janek learned—wallet, watch and ring, and, most decisively, a segment of bridgework authenticated by his dentist. No fingerprints had been taken; evidently no fingers had survived. Janek found that curious. He also found it curious that Clury's wife, Janet, from whom he'd been separated but not divorced, had come up from Florida to attend his funeral, then signed papers authorizing cremation of his remains. Janet Clury, as survivor of an officer killed on active duty, had been the beneficiary of a substantial lump-sum widow's payment plus pension.

Janek sat back. He wanted to think the implications through:

Certainly someone had been blown up inside Clury's car. But was it Clury?

If it wasn't—as the twice-used bomb signature suggested—then what was the connection between Clury's faked-up death and the Mendozas?

Timmy Sheehan's investigators had theorized that Clury had been blackmailing both Mendozas. Tania had told Janek that Clury had been working for Edith Mendoza, collecting information on Jake's infidelities to strengthen her hand in a planned divorce suit.

But suppose neither of these stories was right. Suppose Clury (who had worked for Jake Mendoza a year before) had played a part in Edith's death. Suppose he'd been paid to kill her. Suppose afterward he set up Metaxas, then arranged his own disappearance.

If that's what happened, Janek analyzed, Mendoza couldn't finger Clury. If he did he'd also implicate himself. But now that Mendoza was stirring things up in Cuba, Clury might have reason to fear that his nine-year-old charade was about to be exposed.

Clury never met me. Maybe he thought he could scare me by bombing my car.

It was a wild theory, he had to admit, but perhaps it would stand the test. For instance, suppose Clury had had some other reason to want to disappear. If, Janek decided, he could discover that, then maybe he could clear up a couple of other little dangles that had baffled anyone who had ever attempted to clear Mendoza—such as whether

Phyllis Kornfeld's claim that she had forged the Metaxas note was fact or fantasy, and, if fact, whether Kornfeld had been killed to keep her from talking or because some drug-crazed burglar got carried away.

It took him hours to get to sleep, and, even then, he didn't sleep well. He kept waking up with new combinations to be examined.

The great problem of Mendoza, he understood, was that no one who had looked into it had ever been able to figure out the sequence and the "whys."

What had been the motives of the principal players?

What, in the huge body of investigative material, was coincidental or extraneous?

Where was the entrance to the overgrown trail, which, if followed, would lead from a reasonable beginning to a plausible end?

If he could locate that path and clear it out, he might be able to trace a coherent story.

He fell asleep around two, but then was awakened at four by the harsh grinding of cartage trucks collecting refuse in front of bars and restaurants on Amsterdam Avenue. The sound reminded him of the relentless grinding of Mendoza through the years. *The mills of the gods,* he thought. Then, quite suddenly, he was seized by an idea.

He checked his bedside clock. It was four-thirty. If he got up he'd have sufficient time to shave, shower, tape on a microphone pack, then dress and taxi over to Cort City Plaza with perhaps a half-hour cushion before meeting The Dark One as he emerged for his morning constitutional.

At Cort City, waiting for the dawn, he asked himself again why Dakin had chosen to live in such a place. *Either he's as shallow and empty as the development, or he's so tormented he needs it as a refuge from his demons.*

At exactly six Dakin stepped out the front door of his building, face grim and taut, body angled forward. He took a half-dozen aggressive strides before he noticed Janek. Then, acting not at all surprised, he gestured awkwardly with his hand.

"You again." Dakin's yellow eyes sliced Janek up and down.

Janek, falling into step beside him, asked: "Clury was dirty, wasn't he?"

"Huh? What's that?" Dakin cupped his hand over his ear. "Better walk on my other side."

Janek didn't change position. "Last time you told me your hearing was better on your right. Now you're telling me to walk on your left. Cut the bullshit, Chief, and answer the question. Clury was dirty and you were on to him. You'd have taken him down, too, if he hadn't gotten himself blown up."

Dakin showed a tight, sparse smile. "Practically had my hands on his balls." He puffed his cheeks. "Another inch, I'd have had him in a nutcracker."

Bastard! But Janek knew he would have to apply some flattery. He desperately needed Dakin's knowledge.

"Was Clury dealing?"

"Naw! Too smart for that! He was tipping them off, a double agent. Most all of them are, you know—our brave undercover narcs!" Dakin's sarcasm was palpable; he was not a subtle man. "You know that. They're all slime snakes. Otherwise they wouldn't be so happy in the slime."

"How'd you get on to him, Chief?"

Dakin smirked. "I had my own agent in place. He'd penetrated the same group. But my guy was after something else." Dakin made a little squirting sound. "Oh, old Howie was raking it in, though we never found any of the loot. I figure his widow got hold of it, stashed it away. You know how it is in IA? When the suspect dies it's 'case closed.' That's policy," he added, in case Janek didn't know.

"What'd you have against Timmy Sheehan?"

Dakin snorted. "Another slime snake."

"But you could never make the case, could you, Chief?

So you thought you'd make *up* a case. Isn't that what you did?''

Dakin broke his stride. ''What're you talkin' about?''

''I'm talking about Phyllis Kornfeld.''

''Ancient history. You already beat me on that. Why bring it up again?''

''I'm bringing it up because there's a lot more to it.''

''Such as?''

''You tell me.''

Dakin strode two steps before he spoke. ''You've been in my old files, haven't you?''

''I've seen a few things,'' Janek bluffed.

''What're you trying to prove, Frank? I'm out of the Department. That's what you wanted, isn't it?''

''I want to hear the story from your own lips.''

''One of those, are you?''

''We're both one of those, Chief. We like a good confession. Today I'm here to hear yours.''

''What the hell! Woman comes to me with a good story. No point wasting it. So I put it to use.''

''She IDed Clury, didn't she? But Clury was dead. So you convinced her to finger Timmy. What I don't get is how you did it. They didn't look alike at all.''

Dakin smiled. ''Kornfeld was nuts. I could've gotten her to swear to anything. Told her there might be some reward money in it if she could make the story stick.''

''So you suborned perjury?''

''Wouldn't put it that way.'' Dakin shrugged. ''Like I said, it's ancient history. Sheehan got off. I got tossed. Kinda backfired on me, wouldn't you say?''

''I think there's some backfiring yet to come.''

''Huh? What do you mean?''

''Obstruction of justice. It's still a crime, Chief, even if it didn't work.''

The razor eyes sliced him back and forth.

''You're wired, aren't you?'' Janek nodded. Dakin stopped, then his yellow eyes flickered. ''Wasn't enough to run me out. Now you want to nail me to the cross.''

Jesus! He sees himself as a little cop Christ!

''There's more,'' Janek said.

''Is there now?'' A droplet of saliva flew out of Dakin's mouth.

''A little surprise.''

''I could use a good surprise.''

''Maybe not this one. See, Chief, Clury wasn't killed in that explosion. He's still walking around.''

''What the—?''

But Janek was walking away, toward the Baychester Avenue station.

''Alive! Can't be!''

Dakin was still shrieking when the train thundered in. Janek turned to give him a final look. Dakin's mouth was working, but no sound came out, just an expression of incredulity and rage.

Janek thought: *He may die of a heart attack before he gets to prison.*

It was nine o'clock when he got to Timmy's rent-controlled walk-up, a block from O'Malley's, on First and Ninety-fourth. The building looked pretty much like Janek's except that the graffiti was more heavily encrusted, and there was a faint odor of wet dog fur in the foyer.

Janek rang the bell. When he didn't get an answer, he went back out to the street and phoned Timmy from a booth on the corner.

''Yeah?'' Timmy didn't sound too good.

''It's Frank.''

''That you ringing downstairs?''

''I need to see you.''

''Come back later.''

''Now!'' Janek said. The battery pack he'd taped to his stomach was starting to itch.

''Tough today, aren't we, partner?''

''I got news for you.''

"What kinda news?"

"Your friend Dakin may be going to jail."

"That's *good* news. Come on up!"

Timmy's khaki pants were dirty, his shirt was stained, he hadn't shaved in a couple of days, his thick hair was out of control and his eyes glowed like a thirsty drunk's.

He cleared a chair, sweeping off a mound of clothing, then sat down on his unmade bed. Janek sat and looked around. There were stacks of newspapers on the floor, a heap of laundry in the corner. When he followed Timmy into the kitchenette, he noticed a pile of discarded orange rinds in the sink.

"How can you live like this?"

Timmy shrugged. "Free country, isn't it?"

Janek thought: *A man who lives like this doesn't like himself much.*

Mugs of coffee in hand, they resumed their seats. Then Timmy asked what he had on Dakin.

"Conspiracy to obstruct justice," Janek said. "When Kornfeld came in, her story was different from what we were told. She said another detective had paid her to forge the Metaxas note. Dakin persuaded her to finger you."

"You're kidding!"

Janek peered at him. "So, what'd you do, Timmy, that made Dakin hate you so much?"

"I was an honest cop doing an honest job. Dakin's a psycho. You know that."

Sure, but Janek also knew that when Dakin went after someone he had a reason. *And why doesn't Timmy ask who the other detective was?*

"Last time we got together—"

"A most unpleasant occasion," Timmy reminded him, raising his brows.

"—you said something I haven't been able to shake."

"What?"

"You said: 'If by some fluke you happen to stumble into

the real heart of the thing, something bad might befall you.' "

Timmy grinned. "Still think I bombed your car, Frank?"

"I'm not talking about the threat. It's that 'real heart of the thing.' What is the *real heart of the thing,* Timmy? What do you know that you haven't told anyone all these years?"

"What do *you* know, Frank?"

"Maybe more than you think."

"You were always a good bluffer."

"Not this time."

"That's what a bluffer always says."

They stared at each other. Then Janek spoke: "Maybe you bought into Metaxas a little too quick, Timmy. Maybe you knew he'd been set up, but didn't care. Maybe you wanted Mendoza so much you were willing to overlook certain problems with your evidence."

Timmy began to pace. "That afternoon, when I walked into his hotel room—it seems like . . . just yesterday. I can still remember the way the furniture was arranged, how the light broke in through the gauzy curtains. The smell from the bathroom, too—steam and blood. Soon as I walked in there, saw Gus lying in the pink bathwater, I thought of you, Frank. A phrase of yours started going through my brain."

"What phrase?"

"I remember just how you used to say it: 'Too slick, I'm not buying in, partner.' It was those words that hit me when I walked into that bathroom. Gus in the tub, wrists cut neat, knife in the soap dish, suicide note on the dresser. It was just . . . too goddamn perfect. As was the money order, and the real sincere look in Peña's eyes when he confirmed Gus's story. Too slick, too good to be true. But then I thought: 'Hey, someone's left me a nice package here. If the writing on that note checks out, I could wrap this thing up, put Mendoza away for offing Clury, come out a cop hero from this thing.' " Timmy paused. "You know how it is, Frank. You always want to catch a great case. That's how you build a legend. That's what makes the young guys look up to you, whisper about you when you pass them in the hall. 'Hey! There goes Sheehan. He's the one broke Mendoza. Great case, great detective. You can learn a lot from him.' You were already a legend, Frank. This was my chance to be one. So I bought the scene, just the way it was laid out, even though I knew it was phony. And once you do a thing like that . . . there's no turning back."

Timmy let his arms hang loose. The gesture seemed to be an expression of regret, but Janek wasn't satisfied.

"All right," he said, "you made a deal with yourself. The scene felt wrong, but you bought it anyway. Still, you must have asked yourself: Who laid it out so neat?"

Timmy shook his head. "I didn't care."

"Of course you did. You *had* to."

"It looked good, so maybe it was good. And if it was fake, I didn't give a shit. I liked what I saw so I bought it. Like buying something pretty in a store."

"Pretty?"

"Attractive. You know what I mean."

"When you see something that appealing you never ask yourself why?"

"That's you, Frank. Not me. I buy what I like. I don't torment myself."

Could be true, Janek thought. *Timmy never doubted his hunches.* But as for torment, Janek couldn't agree. Timmy was clearly tormented. The crazy look in his eyes, his crummy grooming, stained clothes, poor housekeeping—all spoke of a person in distress. *Maybe his problem is he's tormented and doesn't know it.* But still, he thought, there had to be more. "The real heart of the thing." What had Timmy meant?

"Your instincts were good," Janek said. Timmy tipped an imaginary hat. "I mean it. You were right about Mendoza. He *did* have Edith killed. And you were right about Metaxas—he *was* too good to be true."

"So, who was the hit man?"

"Now you're curious. Couple minutes ago, when I told you Kornfeld IDed someone else, you didn't even ask me who."

"You've aroused my curiosity."

"Gotta be one of the players, right?"

"Guess so." Timmy paused. "Who? The maid?"

"Not the maid." Janek stood, looked at his watch. "I gotta go. Nice to see you."

"The fuck!"

Janek turned to him from the door. "What's the matter, partner?"

"Who're you kidding, Frank? If you know who the hit man was, tell me, for God's sake!"

"Maybe I will . . . when you tell me why Dakin hated you. Bye, Timmy." Janek slipped out the door.

A minute later, leaving the building, he imagined Timmy standing at his window, watching him walk away. He was about to turn to see if Timmy was really there, but then decided not to. *Better if he doesn't think I care. That'll torment him even more.*

They had tasty morsels for him at Special Squad:

Sue and Ray went first. There'd been two Cubans at Green Haven, since released, who'd fraternized with Jake Mendoza: a car thief named Cabrera, living in Albany, where he reported regularly to his parole officer; and a drug dealer named Villavicencio, believed to be a member of a major importing ring, who'd managed to transfer his parole obligation to Miami so that he could take care of his aging mother.

"Things can get fairly lax in South Florida," Ray added.

As for a Texas connection, Sue and Ray believed they'd struck gold. A suspected mafia strong-arm named Tony Collizzi had been Jake Mendoza's cellmate. Collizzi, residing in Houston, had been released, after serving fifteen years for homicide, just one month before the copycat killing in El Paso.

"I may have a match on that," Aaron said. "Just before Collizzi's release, there was a fifty thousand-dollar disbursement, and shortly after the copycat job, another fifty thousand was paid out. The transfers were made by Mendoza's lawyer, Royce Andrews, to an account Mendoza maintains in the Cayman Islands Bank. Impossible to trace money going in and out of there, but if we could find Collizzi's name on flight manifests around those dates, Texas cops might want to haul him in."

"What about payments to Cubans?"

"Three months ago there was a two-hundred-fifty-thousand-dollar transfer to a numbered account in Panama. The day after you got back from Cuba, there was, get this, a million dollars transferred to the same account."

"Fonseca's account?"

"Probably, but we'll have a hell of a time proving it," Aaron said. "There were also a couple of smaller transfers of twenty-five thousand dollars to the Caymans."

"Could've been a finder's fee paid to Villavicencio."

"What'd you want us to do now?" Ray asked.

"You and Aaron check the flight manifests to the Caymans, direct and indirect routes. Look for people who went in and out the same day. When you get matches, run them down." Janek paused. "You know what I like about this? If we can connect Mendoza to El Paso, he'll have to go to Texas for trial. Murder-for-hire is a capital crime down there. They use lethal injection."

They all exchanged looks.

"What about me?" Sue asked.

"You're going on a special mission."

"Nice place, I hope?"

"Sarasota. You're going to check out an honored member of our tribe, the widow of a killed-in-action cop."

• • •

The following morning he received a call from Netti:

"Mixed news. First the good stuff. Your ex was badly shook when she heard about our dossier. She's willing to give up alimony. We're negotiating a one-year phase-out."

Janek smiled. "Great!"

"Bad news is that Carlson doesn't want to make a private settlement with Gelsey."

Shit! "What'd you offer him?"

"Restitution, damages, a written apology. He didn't want any of it. He wants to see her in jail."

"Have you told her yet?"

"She's taking it fairly well. I don't know, Frank. It's a weird situation. Carlson says she tried to kill him. He's talking about upgrading the charge to attempted murder."

"Maybe if he saw her, face-to-face, he'd melt a little bit."

"Can't take a chance. If she shows up for a meeting, he could call a cop. He might even call you."

"Want me to talk to him?"

"If you take her side, you could make a lot of trouble for yourself."

"What're you going to do?"

"Keep upping my offer. But the way I read him, he won't be interested. Basically, he wants her head."

Ray found Collizzi's name on flights in and out of the Caymans, both before and after the El Paso copycat job:

"Can't believe it, Frank. He used his own name, flew direct via Miami."

"He got a hundred thousand," Janek said. "There ought to be some sign of it. Fly out to Houston, check out his life-style, then go down to El Paso and talk to the cops handling the case."

"The pieces are starting to fit, aren't they?"

Janek nodded. Later he marveled at how quickly the case was coming together—as if Mendoza were a puzzle left incomplete nine years before, each hole still receptive to the dust-covered pieces still lying beside it on the floor.

Sue called from Sarasota. She liked the city, liked the people, liked her motel, which was on the beach. She'd even found a lesbian bar. "Actually, it's a gay bar," she explained. "They tolerate women."

"Glad to hear you're having fun," Janek said. "What about Janet Clury?"

"She lives in a nice one-story house, three-hundred-thousand-dollar job on a finger. That's what they call a man-made spit of land." Sue paused. "Frankly, I find it a little phallic."

"Is she living with someone?"

"Not now, though she's been known to have a boyfriend or two. She's comfortably set up. Besides the house she's got a BMW and a good job as a hospital administrator. She's nice-looking, expensive blond dye-job, not too flashy, cut at a good salon. Every afternoon after work she goes to a local mall, works out at a health club, shops at a health-food store, then goes home. So far no visitors. Last two nights she's stayed in watching TV. I've seen the screen flickering from the street."

"Watch her a couple more days," Janek said. "If nothing happens, we'll try and stir things up."

Timmy called. He was drunk. He woke Janek up.

"It's your old partner," he announced. "Who set me up? I gotta know."

"Forget it, Timmy. I'm going back to sleep."

"You don't fuckin' care, do you, Frank?"

"Sure, I care."

"Not about me."

"Go to AA. Get off the sauce. Then maybe we can have a decent conversation."

"That's all you gotta say?"

"You know the deal: You tell me why Dakin wanted to

nail your ass, I'll tell you who set up Metaxas.''

Janek hung up. The phone rang again. He unplugged it for the night. It took him hours to get back to sleep. He kept having visions of Timmy staggering toward him down a corridor of mirrors.

He rented a car, drove out to Newark. Gelsey greeted him from the top of the exterior stairs.

''Looks like it's going to rain,'' she said.

''I heard it on the news. That's why I came out.''

When they were inside and he realized he'd interrupted her painting, he urged her to go back to work. She picked up her brushes, turned to her canvas, while he brought her up to date on Dietz. Diana was still in jail, he told her. Thatcher hadn't been able to get her bail.

''What we want to do is soften her up, then let her plead to something less than extortion and attempted murder in return for testimony against Kane. So far she's holding out, but I know she'll break. A woman like that can't take jail.''

''I almost feel sorry for her,'' Gelsey said. ''She really did love Kim.''

''Whenever you start feeling that way,'' Janek said, ''just remember what she did to Kirstin.''

Gelsey dabbed at her canvas. Then she stopped and shook her head. ''Netti can't seem to work things out with Carlson.''

''I heard,'' he said. ''Give it time.''

She turned to him. ''I'm going to have to go to jail, too, aren't I?''

''I don't know. But soon you're going to have to turn yourself in. You have a good lawyer. You helped us solve a major case. Nine judges out of ten'll suspend your sentence. I'm pretty sure you'll get off.''

''I might not.''

''There's always a 'might not,' Gelsey. You can't think about that.''

''Jail would kill me.''

"It won't. You're a strong person." But he didn't like thinking about her serving hard time.

Later, after it started to rain, she asked if she could sit beside him on the couch. Then, when she rested her head against his shoulder, he gently drew her closer with his arm.

She turned to him: "You have an idea about the Minotaur."

"Did I say that?" The rain was falling steadily, streaking the windows, washing the skylight.

"I just have a feeling."

"I'm not a shrink," he said.

"I know. You're a detective."

"If it was in your head, the way Dr. Zimmerman—"

"He was wrong. It wasn't just in my head." She paused. "I think you know that, too."

The rain began to fall hard, exploding like thousands of little firecrackers against the metal roof. Gelsey started to shake. He held her tighter. Was the sound getting to her, or was it memories of loneliness? He imagined how she must have felt when it rained, alone in her strange house, the water beating on the tin, the maze with its mysteries and terrors beckoning from below.

"Why don't we go down and take a look?" he said finally. "Maybe we'll find something. It's worth a shot."

"I'm scared."

"Of the maze?"

"Not the maze," she said. "The Minotaur. I'm afraid of what he might turn out to be."

When they were on the catwalks and the lights were on, he walked with her above the places where the ceilings were opaque.

"What's down there?" he asked as they stood above a blocked-off portion.

"Storage area."

"What about there?" he asked, pointing to another.

She looked down. "That's just some dead space between three mirrors."

"Are you sure?"

She thought a moment. "Yes, that's where the corridor turns back on itself."

After asking her to identify three more such areas, and finding her more tentative, he asked her what was wrong.

"It's easier when I'm down on the floor," she said. "I know the maze better there. I'm not used to analyzing it from above."

He suggested she go down while he remained on the catwalks. Then he could walk above the places where the ceilings were opaque and call down his questions.

She agreed, shinned down the rope, then together they worked their way methodically through the maze, verbally mapping its invisible areas. She opened mirrors that were also doors, confirming the existence of each storage and backstage section. It was only when they reached the Great Hall that she became confused.

"No," she said when he asked her about a small area with an opaque ceiling off the Great Hall. "No, there's nothing there."

"I'm standing right above it, Gelsey," Janek said. "There's a covered space, maybe five feet by five."

"Impossible." Her voice was agitated. "I knew this part very well."

They continued. When there were no other hard-ceilinged areas she could not identify, he guided her back to the one off the Great Hall. Again she insisted there could be nothing there.

"Maybe just more dead space," he offered.

"Maybe . . ." She didn't sound convinced.

His original notion was that the person Gelsey had seen, whom her father had dubbed "the Minotaur," had been standing on the catwalks. Then this person's image, caught somehow by one of the mirrors, had shown up reflected in the Great Hall. But now he wondered if there might not be a hidden room below, a place where a voyeur might have been concealed. Gelsey had explained every covered space except for one.

He guided her around the space, urging her to search for a mirror that would open like a door. When she called to him that she could find nothing, it occurred to him that if he had been her father, and had wanted to create a secret chamber, he would not have placed the opening mechanism in its usual position five feet off the floor. *He'd have put it where she wouldn't expect it,* Janek thought, *perhaps in an opposite position, very low.*

He asked her to meet him at the bottom of the ladder. Then he climbed down to the floor.

When she greeted him she seemed disturbed.

"What's the matter?"

"I'm getting tired, that's all," she said.

"Want to do this some other time?"

"No. Let's see it through."

As she led him rapidly through the maze, he was again awed by its complexity. There was no possible way to know where he was in relation to the configurations of mirrors he had seen just minutes before from the catwalks. The reflections defeated any attempt to define real as opposed to illusionary space. Occasionally she led him through doors, shortcutting her way to the Great Hall. When, finally, she stopped before a series of sharply angled mirrors, he could only guess that they had arrived.

Gelsey was sweating.

"You all right?"

"I get like this when it rains."

"Is it still raining?" She shrugged. He looked around. "Are we near . . . where the bad stuff happened?"

She nodded, pointed across the Hall, then lowered her eyes.

"Were you always facing the same direction?"

"I don't remember. Anyway, it wouldn't make any difference. No matter which way you face down here, you see everything . . . reflected to infinity.''

He detected weariness in her voice, almost, he thought, despair. He felt it would be wrong to push her further.

''Let's go back up.''

She shook her head. ''You're on to something.'' He didn't answer. ''I feel you are.''

He studied her. She looked stronger.

''Okay,'' he said, ''I want you to press on these mirrors. Apply the usual pressure but not in the usual place. See if you can spring one open.''

''You really think there's something behind?''

''Let's find out,'' he said.

She shook her hands to loosen her fingers, like a safe-cracker preparing to break into a vault. Then she began to explore the surface of the first mirror panel. When nothing happened, she moved to the second. Janek observed that she was sweating again, that the stress was building up. Suddenly she stopped. She was crouched on the floor. She glanced up at him, eyes catching fire from the silvered glass.

''I feel something.''

''A spring?''

''I think so.''

''All right,'' he said. ''Remember, I'm here beside you. Whenever you're ready . . . open it up.''

She stared at him, then turned back to the mirror. But he felt she wasn't looking at herself, rather at something beyond its surface. Then she placed her fingers on the glass and pressed. The panel swung open. A small room was revealed.

At first they both recoiled. The room was dusty and the air that escaped was stale. Then, as Janek craned forward, he saw the props: a small stool, with a cloak folded neatly on top, and, on the floor beside the stool, a rubber mask. He reached for it, picked it up, unfolded it, stared at the image. It was a trashy fun-house monster mask with horns, the kind sold in novelty shops around Times Square.

"Is this the Minotaur?" he asked, holding it up. Some of the face had rotted away. There was a hole in one of the cheeks and, because the rubber had lost resiliency, the horns hung soft.

"Yes!" There were tears in her eyes.

He handed it to her. She didn't want to take it.

"Don't be afraid of it," he told her. "It's just an old piece of rubber."

Even as he spoke he knew that the mask was a lot more than that—that it was all the terrors of her childhood, the source of her art and of her pain.

When they returned upstairs, Gelsey placed the mask on her coffee table, then stared at it. The rain, Janek saw, had tapered off.

"Dr. Z had a collection of masks," she said. "They were firm and beautiful, not like this. I'd look at them during sessions. They spoke of marvelous places—ancient African kingdoms, South Sea islands . . ."

"I think you should just throw it away," he said.

She shook her head. "I'll cut it up and use the pieces in my paintings. Glue them to the canvas, then paint them over."

He liked that: destroy a personal demon by incorporating it into a work of art. It struck him as a healthy version of the use she'd made of the trophies she'd taken off marks, perhaps a civilized variation on the tribal practice of ingesting an enemy one had slain.

"Who wore it?" she asked suddenly.

He'd been dreading the question.

"Who do you think?"

"One of his buddies, I guess." She looked at Janek. "No?"

"I have another idea." He shrugged. "Of course I have no proof."

She looked around the room, at her many versions of Leering Man.

"My mother, wasn't it?" Janek didn't reply. "Yeah, it figures." He was surprised at how easily she seemed to accept the notion. "She let him do those things to me. Maybe even suggested them because she didn't want him to do them to her. Maybe she even got off on it." Gelsey grinned; Janek recognized the smile of a person trying to disguise the deepest perplexity. "Ever hear of anything like that?"

He nodded. "It's a lot more common than you think."

She shook her head. "I wonder if Dr. Z knew. He told me he thought the secret was hidden in the maze. Well, now I found it. And, funny enough, I feel better for it. I'm almost . . . pleased." She paused, tried to smile again. "I guess I must have suspected it. Because, you see, I'm not all that surprised."

He studied her. She was a strong person, but not as strong as this.

"You're entitled to cry," he said.

"I've been doing a lot of that lately. Too much."

"Things are changing for you."

"True."

"Go ahead," he said. "Let yourself really feel it. It'll be healthy for you if you do."

"The pain? Oh, I *feel* it!" She spoke bitterly. She glanced at him. "Dammit, Janek—will you come over here and sit beside me, please?"

He moved to a place beside her on the couch.

"I pity her," she said. The tears were flowing now. "I really do pity her. For being part of something so tacky, so fucking sordid. I wonder if she wore a monster's mask because she felt like a monster." She turned to him. "Does that make any sense?"

"Yes, it does."

As he held her, it occurred to him that the pity she was feeling now for her mother was similar to the pity he had felt when he had first seen Leering Man and realized that a powerful artist was engaged in something as sleazy as picking up and drugging men.

"I'm not a big quoter," he said. "But there's a line from the Bible: 'For now we see through a glass, darkly . . . but then shall I know even as also I am known.' I think that's what you did today. Looked through the mirrors to a place where you could see yourself." He embraced her. "I think it's always better to know, don't you?"

"Yes, always." She hugged him. "And you helped me. If it weren't for you, I don't think I'd have ever found the Minotaur." She turned to him. "Thank you for that. It probably seems strange, but I'm grateful."

"Soon you'll start feeling free."

"I'm already beginning to," she said.

Mirror Maze

With each passing day the puzzle became clearer.

Ray phoned from Houston. Janek, listening, imagined him slowly stroking his mustache:

"Me and two El Paso cops—Cody and Martinez, both great guys—have gotten a good fix on Tony Collizzi. Seems Tony's been living very well since he got out of Green Haven. Signs of unexplained wealth all over the place. Fancy high-rise condo. Snazzy bronze-metallic Cadillac. Numerous sharp-cut Italian suits, kind that cost you a grand and a half. 'Course none of this fits with his so-called job as parking-lot manager. So, on a hunch that Collizzi's arrogant and sloppy, we start checking out his old credit-card slips. We got enough now to place him in El Paso the night of the copycat: gas purchases, restaurant and bar bills, motel, the whole bit. Also, there were some latents on the rope and some hair and skin samples collected at the scene. Soon as we get positive lab reports, Cody and Martinez will haul him in."

"Good work, Ray," Janek said. "How do your new cop friends feel about Mendoza?"

"They want him bad." Ray chuckled softly. "Way they figure, if they get enough on Collizzi, he'll turn Mendoza over. Then they'll have a classic murder-for-hire case. Texas juries love 'em. Most of the time the guy does the hiring gets the needle."

Netti invited him to lunch in Chinatown. They were to meet in a second-floor restaurant on Pell Street. It was a cool, windy, sparkling day, the light so dazzling they both wore sunglasses. Approaching from opposite directions, they nearly collided at the restaurant door. Netti stood back, removed her glasses, squinted.

"Well, look who's here," she said, pretending they'd met by accident.

Janek squinted back. "How're you?"

"Maybe we should stop meeting like this."

"Yeah . . . I guess we should," he said.

At the table she fixed him with a happy smile, then recommended they share a bass. Soon a cook wearing a headband embellished with Chinese characters appeared in the dining room with a short-handled net. He approached a large aquarium a few feet from their table, scooped out a live fish, then carried it, dripping, back to the kitchen. Fifteen minutes later the waiter brought it out on a platter, cooked whole and covered with a spicy black bean sauce.

Netti tasted it. "Um, good! Have a bite."

She grasped a portion with her chopsticks, offered it to Janek. He leaned forward, took the morsel neatly between his lips, sat back to devour it. The texture was like silk.

"Best fish I've had since Cuba."

She had papers for him to sign; she pulled them out of her briefcase.

"What're these?" Janek asked. He was more interested in his half of the bass.

"Your agreement with Sarah. Alimony ends next month."

Janek laid down his chopsticks. "I thought there was going to be a phase-out."

Netti smiled. "They agreed to immediate cessation."

"How'd you manage that?"

"By threatening to put Sarah under oath, then examine her about her life-style. When her attorney heard about

Honolulu, he backed down real fast.''

Janek stared at her. ''You're a great lawyer, Netti. But why make me think I'd have to pay her for another year?''

She shrugged. ''Didn't want to excite you too much. Wanted to bring you along slowly. Wanted to surprise you, then see the expression on your face.'' She paused. ''Generally speaking, I like it when a client thinks I'm better than he thought.''

Oh, that convoluted mind!

After lunch, in the midst of thanking her for her tip on Clury, he casually mentioned that he'd discovered some things that were not going to rebound to her client's advantage.

She waved her hand. She didn't want to discuss it. She mumbled something about how, if he ever told anyone what she'd done, she could get disbarred. It was then, for the first time, that he understood that she had pointed him toward Clury fully aware of the consequences to Mendoza. That, he thought, took courage, being perhaps the most grievous sin a criminal lawyer can commit. But he respected her greatly for having committed it. She had sized her client up, and, understanding he was a killer, had violated the special ethics of her profession. By doing that she had not only put herself at risk, she had placed her destiny in his hands.

''I won't mention it again,'' he promised.

With dexterous manipulation of chopsticks she extracted the fish's cheek, then offered him the piece.

''Take it,'' she urged. ''It's the tastiest bit.'' Her eyes expressed her gratitude.

When he signaled the waiter for the check, he discovered it was already paid.

He turned to Netti. ''Why?''

''This is a celebration lunch. When a case is won, your attorney picks up the tab.'' She smiled. ''You'll get my bill in the morning.''

''It'll be a pleasure to pay it,'' he said.

On the street, sunglasses back on, about to part, Janek asked how things were going with Carlson.

"Not good. He won't budge." Netti shook her head. "I'm going to call Gelsey this afternoon. I hate to give her the bad news, but it's time to turn herself in."

Sue called from Florida. After three days of watching Janet Clury, she'd seen no change in the woman's pattern.

"Work. Mall. Gym. Store. Home. Then she watches crap on TV. Meantime, it's hot down here and I'm getting bored. Just give me the word, Frank—I'm ready to move in on her and squeeze."

"I'm going to send down Aaron to do that," Janek said.

Silence. "Any particular reason?" She couldn't hide her disappointment.

"I think it'll be more threatening coming from a man. But you'll still have plenty of fun."

"How's that?"

"When Aaron leaves you'll be waiting outside, ready to follow Janet when she makes her move."

"And if she doesn't?"

"She will. Or I've got this whole thing wrong."

"Okay," Sue said, breathing steadier. "I can get off on that. Maybe you're right, maybe Aaron will scare her more. Still, I hope one day you'll let me show you what I can do."

He wrote up his report on Dakin, added the tape he'd made of their final conversation, addressed a covering letter to the Manhattan D.A. recommending prosecution for obstruction of justice, then sealed the package and locked it in his filing cabinet. He wouldn't send it until he captured Clury. But he wanted it ready to go.

The following morning, cloudy and raw, Aaron picked him up at his apartment. They ran into heavy traffic on the FDR, but still had time to make the flight. In the car, Janek explained what he wanted Aaron to say to Janet Clury and exactly how he wanted him to say it:

''Start out casual: 'Has your husband been in touch with you lately?' That should make her jump. 'What the hell're you talking about? Howie's been dead nine years!' When she says that, look her straight in the eye, then give her a half-snicker. Start in on her pension. That'll be the first thing to go. Then we'll seize all her property to pay back nine years of pension fraud. When she asks, 'What's fraudulent?' explain she obviously knew Howie hadn't been blown up. Tell her there'll be criminal charges. She'll be extradited to New York for trial. Could be a lot of jail time because New York jurors don't like folks who defraud their impoverished city. Whether she plays it cool or frantic, doesn't matter, so long as you leave her with the feeling she's in terrible trouble. Remember, you're sending a message: It's not that we *think* Howie's alive, we *know* he is. Try not to spend more than fifteen minutes with her. When you leave, you want her panicked. When you get to the door, hesitate, then say something like: 'If you hear from Howie, tell him Janek might be willing to deal.' Don't stick around, don't explain. Leave, drive straight to the airport, fly back here tonight.''

''What about Sue?'' Aaron asked. ''Shouldn't I stay with her and help?''

''Sue will handle her end fine.''

At La Guardia, Aaron patted the fender of his Chevrolet, then handed Janek the keys.

''Take good care of her, Frank.''

''Right,'' Janek promised. ''I'll even fill up the tank.''

He drove the car out to Newark to pick up Gelsey and bring her back to the city to be booked. He had promised her that it would be quick, that Netti had everything arranged. She'd be photographed, fingerprinted, arraigned and immediately bailed out. He'd have her back home right after lunch.

On their way in, he could see she was nervous. To distract her he asked questions about painting. What did she like best about it? Creating the images? Moving around the paint? Working with her hands? Or was it the result, taking pride in what she'd achieved, reliving the feelings she'd released?

"It's all of that," she said, "and something more. I call it soothing the hurt. See, I think that's what artists do. We're injured people. We paint, sculpt, whatever—to try and heal our wounds. At least a little bit."

A few moments later, the Manhattan skyline came into view. The towers loomed, silver forms against a dark, cloudy sky. The clouds looked almost purple, Janek thought—purple like a bruise.

He stood beside her during the booking procedure. Rain poured down outside. Stiegel, as expected, didn't show, so Janek listed himself as the arresting officer. There were papers to be signed for the bondsman. Netti worked hard to move things along. But there was still a sleaziness about the process that he wished Gelsey could have been spared. Beaten-up furniture, scuffed floors, disinterested guards and cops, people yelling, quarreling, whimpering, faces creased with helplessness and fear. The air was stale, tainted with the mingled aromas of whiskey breath, body odor, exhaled cigarette smoke. Once, when the thunder clapped, Gelsey grabbed for his hand. He held hers tight, finally felt her relax. Then, when they took her away, she looked back at him, panicked, with the eyes of a frightened doe.

As he stood in the rear of the courtroom waiting for her to come out, he was again struck by the tawdriness of the system—the alienated dialogue between judges and lawyers; dehumanizing deal-making; battered, abused public facilities he'd always taken for granted. Where, he wondered, amid all this filth and taint, was the vaunted Majesty of the Law?

As Netti had predicted, the entire procedure took two

hours, but Gelsey was shaking when she emerged. She had told Janek that although she had often been frightened in men's hotel rooms and apartments, she had managed to keep her cool because she knew she was in control. At Central Booking she'd had no control over anything. She'd been but one in an endless stream of beasts prodded and corraled through the stockyards of Justice.

"It's not that I'm so fancy," she said when they were outside the courthouse. The rain had stopped but the steps still were slick. "I've eaten plenty of shit in my life, but in there I felt helpless." She paused. "Jail's like that, isn't it?"

"No one wants you to go to jail, Gelsey," Netti said. They were walking on either side of her, descending the broad granite steps to the street.

"Yeah, sure. No one except Carlson. Look, I know I did bad stuff." She was fighting back her tears. "I deserve to be punished. I know that, too."

She looked at Janek, again grasped hold of his hand. "I just don't know if I can take it."

Janek took her to lunch at a fish joint on South Street, a rowdy place filled with workmen talking loudly over plates of mussels and clams. The moment they sat down, Gelsey began to castigate herself, saying how it was good for her to have gone through booking and arraignment, how the experience had helped her to see what she really was: a doper-girl, a felon, a thief.

Janek didn't quarrel with her, just listened. He thought: *She needs to run herself down, needs to let it out.* But the whole time his heart was crushed with grief.

When their food came, Gelsey brightened. "Know what I'm going to do when this is over?"

"What?"

"Destroy the maze. Sell the building. Look for a loft here in the city."

"Sounds good. But why not sell the building with the maze intact?"

She shook her head. "Nobody'll want it. Nobody'll understand it. And for me, now it's finished. You helped me solve the mystery of it, Janek. I look at it now and all I see is a lot of stupid glass."

"So, it's no longer art. That's what you're saying. One day it's a great naïve work, the next it's a pile of shit."

She shook her head. When she spoke it was with the same bitter contempt she'd just applied to herself. "Oh, sure, it's art. It just doesn't *feel* like art anymore. To me now it feels like terror and pain. So, why not tear it down?"

He didn't challenge her. He understood why she would want to destroy it, considering the evil ways her father had used it against her. But he hoped she'd change her mind. The maze was magnificent, and once broken up it could never be rebuilt. More important, he felt she would do nothing for herself by trying to punish the scene of her suffering. Yes, the maze had terrorized her and held her in its thrall, but now, having understood her pain and having rendered harmless its source, she could leave it to dazzle and entertain others. He resolved to broach this to her when she was in a less bitter state.

There was a bill from Netti in the office mail. It was typed on formal invoice stationery:

TO FRANK JANEK,
FOR PROFESSIONAL SERVICES:
One Chinese Carry-out Dinner
(Payable on Demand)

He laughed, carefully placed it back in its envelope, then stored it in his personal file.

• • •

That evening he sat alone at Special Squad, reading, waiting by the phone. At 7:20 it rang. It was Sue. She was whispering, excited:

"I'm at the mall, Frank, the one Janet goes to every afternoon. I'm standing at a phone bank. She's at another one, fifty feet away. I figure she's on line with Clury. She's yakking a lot and looks upset. About five minutes after Aaron left, she stormed out of her house, peered around, then got in her car and took off. Wait a sec . . . she's listening . . . now she's nodding. He must be trying to calm her down."

"When she leaves, stay with her," Janek said. "But don't forget which phone she used. Note the time, come back in the morning, copy down the number, then go to the locals and have them subpoena records from the phone company. If she's using a credit card—"

"She isn't. I saw her feed coins to the slot."

"Then Clury's probably not too far away. Remember, he's a cop. He may figure she was trailed. He may try and come in behind you, so watch your back."

"I never thought of that."

"Be careful. If Janet doesn't head home, she may be leading you into a trap."

"What do I do?"

"Drop the tail, go back to your motel, get a good night's sleep."

"Right." She paused. "Whaddya think he'll do, Frank—now that he knows we're on to him?"

"One of three things. He'll either run, go nuts and try to bomb us, or get in touch to see what kind of deal he can make."

On his way out to La Guardia to pick up Aaron, he thought about the real possibility that Gelsey would have to go to prison. He knew now that he and Netti had been deluding themselves. As soon as Gelsey's story came out, more victims would come forward, more complaints would be filed, the felonies would mount up, the pressure for a sentence would grow. Despite her assistance in trapping Kane, a fair judge would have to take into account the violence of her crimes and the ways she'd terrorized her victims.

It was after midnight when Aaron's plane touched down. He emerged tired but still high on his interview with Janet. He described it as they walked through the terminal, then across the parking lot to his Chevrolet:

"She's the cool-blonde type, but she wasn't all that cool when I got done with her. All that stuff about heavy-duty jail time—I swear, Frank, she was ready to pee in her pants."

"She denied everything."

Aaron nodded. "She bugged out her blues." He bugged out his to demonstrate. "What'd she do afterward?"

"Drove fast to a public phone in a mall."

"Clury must have told her never to call him from the house. I wonder if she still cares for him. Or if they made some kind of deal."

"The pension was the kiss-off. All she had to do was act sad at his funeral, cry a little on the commissioner's arm, then sign the cremation papers."

Aaron smiled. "Come to think of it, I didn't see an urn in her parlor."

"Now she knows the string's played out. The old crime's come back to haunt."

"Think Clury'll show?"

Janek shrugged. "Sue asked me the same thing. We'll have to wait and see."

But his mind wasn't on Clury anymore. He could think only of Gelsey: her misery as she endured four or five years in a woman's prison and her state when she emerged.

The next morning Ray called from Houston.

"Evidence tests positive. Cody and Martinez just picked Collizzi up. They're tanking him. They'll start sweating him this afternoon. Charge is capital murder. What do you want me to do?''

''You've done all you can,'' Janek said. ''Now it's up to the El Paso police. Come home.''

Sue called at eleven A.M. The night before, Janet Clury had gone straight home from the mall. In the morning, when she left for work, she looked calm, as if nothing had happened.

''Her call tracked back to an address in Crystal River, Florida, about a hundred fifty miles up the coast. The phone's listed to a Mr. Dan Dell. I just called there to see what would happen. A lady answered. Nice voice. She said: 'Good morning, Dan's Bait and Charter.' ''

A Florida bait and charter! Every cop's retirement dream!

''Anyway, I was wondering—do you want me to go up there and check it out?''

Ten to one he's already left.

''Sure, take a look,'' Janek said. ''But apply the KISS principle: Keep It Simple, Stupid. Nothing fancy.''

''What do you consider fancy?''

'' 'Mind if I take a little picture of you, sir?' Or pretending you know something about fishing.''

Sue laughed. ''How about I swagger in real butch and tell him me and my girlfriend are looking for a very private charter?''

Could work. Clury's been out nine years. Probably doesn't know we have out-of-the-closet gay detectives now.

''Sure, try that,'' Janek said, ''but don't forget to call in. Aaron'll be here. Ray's flying in from Texas. It's all coming together. A couple more days, we ought to have it wrapped.''

He borrowed Aaron's car again, drove out to Newark. On his way he asked himself: *Why am I doing this? What am I looking for?*

She was painting when he arrived. They talked casually. He liked sitting on her couch, talking, watching her work, while her ceiling fan slowly stoked the air. He felt comfortable with her, as if he'd known her forever, as if there weren't anything he couldn't say.

She took a break to make some tea. After sipping in silence, she turned to him with an inquiring smile.

"What are we all about?" she asked softly.

"I've been wondering myself. What do you think?"

"The Mirror-obsessed Outlaw Artist and the Cop with the Searching Eyes. Obviously we like each other. But why? We don't have much in common."

"Does that bother you?"

She smiled. "You're very special to me. You know that."

"As you are to me."

"Still, it's strange, isn't it?"

"Strange and wonderful, I think."

"It *is* wonderful," she agreed. "Somehow we found each other. We didn't know we existed, but we were searching for each other anyway. Two lost souls, right?" She smiled to mock the cliché. "I feel so lucky. It's as if you've freed me. Now I can change, become the person I was meant to be." She paused. "The only thing I worry about is what I can give you in return."

"Don't ever worry about that," he said. "You've given me a great deal . . . more than you can possibly know."

Driving back in the dark, he noticed a car following, one headlight slightly dimmer than the other. He realized he'd seen this same signature several times since he'd left Richmond Park.

Am I being followed? Is it Clury? Could he possibly move so fast?

After he emerged from the Holland Tunnel, he slowed, made sure the other car was still behind, then sped uptown, turned the corner, turned again onto empty Washington

Street, then quickly parked, cut his lights, pulled out his revolver and slid down in his seat.

A few seconds later the other car, a battered maroon Oldsmobile, drove by. As soon as it passed, he started up again and followed.

The other driver drove slowly. *He's looking for me.* Then Janek noticed him weaving. *Maybe he's drunk. Maybe it isn't Clury after all.*

Approaching a stoplight, Janek decided to make his move. When the other car halted, he pulled up right beside it and turned to look. Timmy Sheehan stared into his face.

Janek rolled down the window on his passenger side.

"Hi, partner! Lost?"

"Hey, partner! What're you doing out so late?"

"Pull over after the light. We'll talk about it," Janek said.

Timmy pulled over. Janek parked behind. The street was silent. There were no pedestrians. It was an area of old brick warehouses, deserted at night.

When he got out he heard the faint thud of rock music issuing from one of the unlicensed late-night basement clubs in TriBeCa. Walking to Timmy's car, he felt like a traffic cop approaching a speeder he'd signaled to the curb.

He opened Timmy's car door. The interior smelled of gin. There were crumpled potato-chip bags and empty beer cans on the floor. *He would have a ratty old car like this.* Janek sat down in the passenger seat, shut the door.

"Why're you following me, partner?"

"Who set me up, Frank?"

Janek met his eyes. "Time's come to spill, Timmy. Why does Dakin think you're slime?"

Timmy stared at him, grinned secretively, feigned a yawn, then suddenly tried to hit him. The blow was awkward. Janek grasped hold of his fist, pushed him back behind the wheel.

"Want to punch out your old partner? What's the matter with you?"

"Fuck you, Frank!"

Timmy swung at him again, this time with more serious intent. Janek pulled back, but not far enough. Timmy's fist clipped his shoulder.

"Okay, that's enough. . . ."

But Timmy didn't stop. He began to flail, his blows wild and ineffective. Janek caught them open-handed, but then his shoulder began to hurt and he grew annoyed.

He wants me to smack him. That's really what he wants.

Finally, Janek hit him back. The moment his fist flattened Timmy's lips, Timmy stopped swinging to wipe away the blood. Panting the aroma of cheap gin, he peered down at the stain on his handkerchief. Then he looked at Janek, hurt, surprised.

"You're bleeding now. That's what you wanted, isn't it? What'd you do, Timmy?" Janek spoke gently. "Better tell me. You'll feel better."

Timmy wiped his mouth again. "Maybe I took a few bucks. Who the hell cares?"

"How much? How many times?"

"One time. Maybe ten, fifteen K."

"Cut the 'maybe' crap. You know exactly how much you took."

"Around fifty," Timmy said. "More or less."

"Who from?"

"Drug dealer."

"When'd you do this?"

"Seven, eight years ago."

"The same dealer Dakin lined up. The one who swore you tried to hire him to kill Kornfeld. What was his name?"

"Keniston."

"Right. So Keniston had it in for you. All Dakin had to do was skew his hatred a few degrees. And you spent all the money on booze, too, didn't you? You don't have a pot to piss in now except your pension."

Timmy nodded.

Janek stared at him. "God, you're pathetic!"

Timmy shrugged. ''Everyone can't be the Great Fucking Detective like you, Frank. Some of us are just slime, you know.''

''That how you see yourself?''

''Maybe. What're you going to do now, partner? Turn me in?''

Timmy's eyes were glowing. A thin line of blood, running down his chin and the side of his neck, had stained the collar of his shirt.

He wants me to turn him in. He'll revel in it.

''I wouldn't bother,'' Janek said. ''You're punishing yourself more than any prison could. Do yourself a favor, Timmy—go to AA, get your head straight before you get too hungry for your gun. Because that's where you're headed, my friend. Maybe you'll eat it in a service-station washroom or early one holiday morning when even the dogs are asleep. But you'll eat it. Sooner or later you will. You know it, too.''

Janek opened the car door, was halfway out before Timmy answered.

''Would you care if I ate it, Frank?'' He showed his secretive grin again. ''Would you mourn me?''

''Sure, I'd mourn you, Timmy. You were my partner. I haven't forgotten that.''

He fled the car, and, when he was back in his own, took off fast. Following the river uptown, he thought about police work and some of the strange people who did it: Kit, Dakin, Clury, Timmy. He thought about cops, how they lived and the awful ways their lives often turned.

Our music is so maudlin, he thought, *like an old-fashioned amusement park on a crappy off night in autumn. The hurdy-gurdy grinding, the fun-house robots cackling. Cheap, tawdry, rinky-dink. God help us all.*

Sue called in early from Crystal River. Mr. Dan Dell had not been at his bait shop when she stopped by. Mr. Dell, it seemed, had left town for parts unknown. But there was a picture of him on the shop wall, posing, like Hemingway, with a huge blue marlin hanging from a block and tackle.

"Does he look like Clury?" Janek asked.

"Maybe," Sue said. "Hard to tell."

"Describe him."

"Stocky, smaller than the fish, thick neck, thick brush mustache."

"What about his cheeks? Scarred?"

"I couldn't tell. The sun was full in his face."

"Eyes?"

"He was squinting."

Most likely Dell is Clury, but her description doesn't nail it.

"I think I got his prints," Sue said casually.

Janek smiled. *Good girl!* "How'd you manage that?"

"I spotted a pack of Marlboros beside the register. I asked the nice lady, who turned out to be the new Mrs. Dell—small, blond, a younger version of Janet—if it would be all right if I helped myself. 'Sure,' she says, real nice, 'they're Dan's. Might as well take the pack. They'll just dry up.' So I took it, dropped it dainty-like into my purse. Now I got it properly bagged and IDed. Want me to bring it home, Frank?"

"No, I want you to throw it in the sewer. Take it to the nearest locals, have them lift the prints, fax them to me, then stand by."

"Yes, sir, Lieutenant Janek, sir!"

The prints on the cigarette pack matched Clury's perfectly. After that it was classic follow-up. He made all the textbook moves:

He kept Sue in Florida to check on Dell. When the local DEA agent told her that, although there was no hard evidence, Dell was suspected of using his charter boat to pick up drugs dropped by runners into the Gulf, Janek suggested that the DEA begin proceedings to seize his property.

He sent Aaron back to work with Sue and the Crystal

River cops. They set up a twenty-four-hour watch on Clury's boat, house and bait shop, got a court order to tap his phone and followed young Mrs. Clury whenever she went out.

He sent Ray over to the NYPD pension department to explain that Clury wasn't dead. The department immediately cut off Janet's checks, put liens on her accounts and property and filed charges against her for criminal fraud.

Janek personally went over to the bomb squad butter vault to inform Stoney that Clury was still alive. He made sure Stoney understood that it was his excellent work tracking the bomb signature that had made Janek think to call up Clury's file.

Stoney appreciated the compliment, but worried about the outcome. "Put a bomber in a corner," he said, "he's likely to throw a bomb."

"Killing isn't going to help him," Janek said. "He's got two choices: deal or run."

Stoney didn't agree. "Bombers are psychos. Once a bomber, always a bomber. And when one comes after you, he's not going to come with a gun."

It was Sunday afternoon when Clury called. Janek was at home, watching a Yankees game on TV. The caller didn't identify himself, but Janek knew who it was. Clury's voice was deep and harsh:

"There's a phone booth on your corner, Amsterdam and Eighty-seventh. I'll be calling there in four minutes. Don't miss me." *Click.*

Janek pulled on a sweatshirt, slapped a cassette into his micro tape recorder, rang impatiently for his elevator, then took the stairs. Out on the street, he jogged to the corner. A teenager, possibly a drug messenger, was snarling into the phone.

Janek tapped him on the shoulder. "Pardon me, I'm expecting a call."

The boy turned, mouth curled with contempt. "Yeah? Hot shit!"

Janek flashed his shield. "Get lost, kid."

The boy dropped the receiver, took off down the avenue. Just as Janek replaced it, the phone rang.

"It's me," Clury said. "Put that tape recorder away. Otherwise I don't talk."

He's near. He can see me.

Janek obeyed.

"You're a clever cop, Janek. Gotta admire the way you put the scare into Janet. Your guy was right behind her, right?"

"Something like that," Janek agreed.

"Well, it ain't worth shit, Detective, because you got nothing but a middle-aged cop who decided to drop out of the game. A cop who got worn down doing undercover work. So instead of quitting officially the way you're supposed to, he walked away."

"Some people might call that desertion."

"Would they? Big deal!"

"Anyway, I got a little more than that," Janek said.

"Pension fraud? I never took a cent. That's between Janet and the Department. Nothing to do with me."

"There's homicide."

"Whose are we talking about?"

"I count four: Edith Mendoza, the guy in your car, Gus Metaxas and Phyllis Kornfeld."

Clury laughed. "Edith? No one's ever going to figure that one out. Guy in my car? Who's he? Way I heard it, they found some body parts which got cremated nine years ago. Metaxas? He killed himself. No one can prove otherwise. Kornfeld? You gotta be kidding. She was killed by a robber. You'll never tie her to me."

You don't know I've got Dakin in my pocket. "You blew up my car," Janek said.

"I didn't. I was fishing off the Keys that night. I can prove it, too."

Yeah, you probably can.

"So, you got it all figured, don't you, Clury? Why'd you bother to call?"

"I want to work things out. Sure, I can disappear. But I don't want to see Janet hurt. My new wife either."

What a nice man!

"We'll have to meet and discuss it."

"No problem. Just you and me. No one else. I'll pick the time and place."

Go for it!

"Sorry, can't do that. You'll have to surrender at my office. Think it over. If you're interested, call me back. I'll be at home. No more phone booths. Think about this, too. The Department wants Mendoza closed. If you help me close it, maybe something can be worked out. But you'll have to surrender first." He waited a beat, then hung up.

He's watching, he reminded himself as he walked back to his building. *Move with confidence so he sees you know you've got him by the balls.*

After two days of silence he wondered if he'd made a mistake. He thought: *Maybe I went too far. Surrender is more than he can tolerate.*

But he still didn't see how Clury could disappear again, since, this time, he'd be a wanted man. Also, he was nine years older. He had a nice life as Dan Dell in Crystal River. Could he walk away so easily from everything—wife, business, bank accounts? What were his choices? At first Janek thought he had him boxed. Now, after two days, he wasn't sure.

Maybe, he thought, *Stoney's right. Maybe Clury will throw a bomb.* But Janek didn't see the point of that. He viewed Clury as an ice-cold killer, not a nut case. Everything he'd done, the way he'd set up Metaxas and murdered Kornfeld, was amoral, logical and totally self-serving. So, why now try to kill the cops who were after him? He had to know that if he did that he'd only provoke the formation of a posse.

On the other hand, Janek reasoned, how could Clury walk away from his sweet life in Florida and his new, young, pretty wife? His only reasonable choice was to surrender, with the hope that he could make some kind of deal.

Clearly he wouldn't plead to a homicide count or anything that would earn him heavy time, but he might be willing to go in for a couple of years just to clean the slate. Yes, Clury's best bet was to help close the Mendoza case, which he might believe he could do without implicating himself. His biggest problem would be to explain who was in his Cadillac when it blew. If he was smart, and Janek believed he was, he would come up with a plausible explanation and some proof to back it up.

What he would not know, of course, was that Phyllis Kornfeld had identified him years before to Dakin. Nor would he know that under the Dead Man Statutes, such "hearsay" could be presented in court, and that Dakin, desperate to save *his* ass, would eagerly testify.

But there was another side to the thing. Suppose Mendoza had paid Clury to kill his wife? How much money could Clury have gotten? Fifty thousand? A hundred? Not nearly enough to run away on, not nearly enough to take himself to a new life. So, maybe what Clury had said was partly true: Perhaps he was, as he claimed, a burned-out cop who decided one day to walk.

Still, Janek knew, he hadn't walked without money. So, where had he gotten it, if not from Mendoza and Janet's widow's pension? Dakin had said that Clury was dirty, that he hadn't been dealing but had been a double agent. What if Clury had stolen from the group he'd penetrated? Not the kind of chicken feed Timmy had taken off Keniston, but real money, the kind big-time drug dealers keep lying around—a million, maybe even two? Then his dropout walkout made some sense. And whatever he got to kill

Edith Mendoza would have been a little extra cream on top of all that milk.

Yeah, Janek decided, it must have been something like that. What he couldn't decide, however, was which of the two men was most evil: Howard Clury with his bombs and hands-on homicides, or Jake Mendoza with his money and hired killers.

When Clury finally did call early on Thursday, a few minutes after midnight, Janek was about to fall asleep. He groped for the phone beside his bed.

"Yeah?"

"It's me." Clury's voice sounded less harsh than before. "I'm ready to meet."

Janek thought he heard a note of resignation, as if Clury had been chewing on his options and concluded that none of them was good.

"Glad to hear it," Janek said. "How's tomorrow morning? My office is in the old Property building in the Village."

"No, you don't get it. I'm calling from Newark."

Janek rolled over, then sat up, awake. Suddenly his heart began to pound.

"What're you doing there?"

"I'm talking on my cellular from the hall of mirrors. You know the one. Your girlfriend's with me. You've got an hour to get your butt over here. The door'll be unlocked. If you don't show by one-fifteen, I'll blow her and the whole place up." A pause. "Oh, yeah, just to show you I'm not bullshitting, here she is to say hello."

"Frank!"

Clury cut her off: "That's enough. Get back on the floor."

Jesus! Janek strained to hear the skirmish: Gelsey's protest, then the sound of a slap followed by a cry. It was the first time she'd ever called him Frank. He knew he was ready to kill for her.

"Frisky little thing, ain't she?" Clury chuckled. "Maybe too hot and young for an old-timer like you."

"If you—"

"Yeah, yeah, if I harm a fair hair on her fair head you'll personally cut off my balls. Something like that, right? Now listen good. You wanted a meeting. You're about to get one. So cut the crap and get over here. And don't even think about bringing someone with you. See, I've turned your girlfriend into a walking bomb and it won't take much to make me set her off."

Trying to stay calm, knowing that only if he did would he be able to deal with this terrifying threat, Janek dressed quickly, then triple-armed himself, securing two seven-shot Beretta pistols, one to each ankle, then strapping on his shoulder-holstered Glock. He stuck his tape recorder into his pocket and hurried down to the street.

There was no time to borrow Aaron's car, so he stood on Broadway trying desperately to flag down a cab. Several passed. Maybe he looked too crazy waving his arms in the wind, with bits of refuse clinging to his shoes.

Finally a taxi stopped. Janek stuck his head in the front window, flashed his shield.

"Want to make two hundred bucks?"

"*Da,* yah." The cabby grinned. He was one of the new Russian drivers struggling to learn the city and the language. Janek got into the front.

The cab was a heap, it squeaked and shook, its shocks were shot and the passenger seat had busted springs. None of that mattered. What mattered was getting to Newark before Clury's patience ran out.

"*Da,* Jersey. First I go Newark Airport, yah?"

The driver, Valyenkov, wanted to practice his English, so Janek nodded, pretending to listen to his chatter even as he tried to work out some kind of plan.

Clury, it was clear, had followed him to Gelsey's, most likely even before his Sunday call. He may even have followed him the same night Timmy did, and, distracted by Timmy's inept tail job, Janek hadn't noticed. At this point, he knew, the how didn't matter. What counted was the why. What was Clury after? What was he planning? Capturing Gelsey, turning her into a bomb, then exploiting her jeopardy to compel a middle-of-the-night meeting in the maze—what could he possibly hope to gain?

"Newark tough town." Valyenkov grinned. "Many car crooks, yah?"

"Yeah, lots of crooks."

Ahead he could see the glow of the airport and the flares that demarcated the burn-off towers at the petroleum storage farms. He could smell their pungent fumes and the marsh gas coming off the Meadowlands and the stink of soot and chemical waste.

I should never have sent in Aaron to frighten Janet. I should have known that would set Clury off. I should have had Sue watch her, no matter how long, until Janet gave Clury away. I was stupid. I couldn't wait, even though the case had been going on nine fucking years. Had to push it. Didn't have the patience. Now I got a mad-dog bomber to deal with and a girl I love who'll get blown to bits if I screw things up.

"Good food. No?" Valyenkov pointed to a diner. Trucks were parked in front.

"Yeah, good food."

He looked around. They were driving by the burn-off towers. The looming steel skeleton frames and huge gas storage cylinders dwarfed everything.

So, what does Clury want? What if he doesn't want anything? What if he just wants to kill me? Maybe Stoney was right: Put a bomber in a corner, he'll throw a bomb. Clury hates me. He's had three days to figure out that no matter what he does I'm going to take him down. So, if he's going down, why not take me with him? And, since he thinks Gelsey's my girlfriend, why not inflict extra punishment by killing her first before my eyes.

"I've been fucking stupid!"

Valyenkov turned. "I am stupid? Why you say?"

"Me, not you," Janek explained.

"Oh, okay, I understand. . . ."

So, why the mirror maze? Why does he want to meet there? Maybe he likes it because of what a bomb'll do to all that heavy glass.

His problem was that, since he had no idea of what to expect, he would be forced to improvise. Angry as he was at himself for leading Clury to Gelsey, he knew he would not be able to save her life if he went in burdened with guilt.

It was 1:10 A.M. when he got out in front of her building, paid off Valyenkov and sent him on his way. The wind was fierce, carrying smells of autumn leaves and rust. He stepped back to look up at Gelsey's loft. For a moment he thought about entering through her trapdoor. If he could get onto the catwalks, he'd be able to see exactly where Clury stood.

He rejected the idea. Too risky. Clury might hear him, might even have forced Gelsey to take him in that way. Anyway, even if he saw them from above, he would never be able to find them easily on the floor. The maze was too confusing. As soon as he entered it he'd be lost. Gelsey was the only one who understood it. If he could just manage to separate her from Clury, she might be able to find a place to hide.

He decided to obey Clury's orders, enter the maze through the front. *And if he's up on the catwalks, he can watch me stumble through.*

He pulled open the front door. The gleaming tunnel embraced him. He shut the door, cutting off the wind.

It was not difficult to make his way through the Corridor of Distortion. Its mirrors, each one different with a unique capacity to deform, were meant less to baffle than amuse.

But Janek did not stop to smile at the images of fat Janek, thin Janek, Janek-as-pair-of-legs, Janek-as-hourglass. Rather, he hastened to the Chamber of Unobtainable Ecstasy, hoping he would see Clury and Gelsey in the blue room—since he knew the secret of its effect.

The chamber was empty. He saw only images of himself. And, as on his previous visits, it was impossible to differentiate between real space, through which he could advance, and mirrorspace, which blocked his progress. The only way through, he knew, was to move slowly, hands outstretched to feel for the glass.

He wound as quickly as he could through the Fragmentation Serpent; it seemed to him unlikely that Clury was waiting there. The sinuous corridor, with its parabolic mirror-as-mouth, was lined with silvered cubistic surfaces that broke up his body into conflicting planes.

Then, as he left through the serpent's narrow tail, he caught his first glimpse of Clury and Gelsey in the Great Hall of Infinite Deceptions. It was impossible to know exactly where they stood since the mirrors projected false images everywhere. The closer he moved toward them, the more reflections of them he saw: lustrous clones, repeated and repeated, surrounding him on all sides, mixed with an equal number of replicas of himself.

"Lots of mirrors, right, Janek?"

Everywhere he turned he saw Clury, bull-necked, smiling as he spoke. Gelsey, standing beside him, looked serene. Only her eyes betrayed her fright. She was wearing a T-shirt and shorts, her hands were bound in front of her with rope and there was some sort of pack, presumably containing the bomb, mounted like a child's school satchel on her back. The worst part of it was the way Clury controlled her. He held a leash attached to a chain-link choke collar around her neck.

"Yeah, lots of mirrors. Bother you, Clury?" He tried to sound tough, indifferent, as if he felt at home in the maze and was used to dealing with punks who held his girl hostage.

"Just so you know, if little darlin' here breaks loose, I can set her off by remote."

Clury opened his hand to reveal a slim black object that looked like a television control module. The mirrors reflected it a thousand times.

"Why're we meeting here?"

" 'Cause here I can see if anyone else comes in, no matter which direction. That's how I know I'm having a one-on-one. See, Janek, I'm not interested in surrender."

"What are you interested in?"

"A deal."

"A deal made under duress is no good. You know that."

"I got something to say."

"So say it."

"First, put your gun on the floor. Carefully." He held out his remote unit to show that his thumb was poised on the button.

I know what he wants. He doesn't want to talk or deal. He's going to kill us both, then set things up to look like Gelsey and I killed each other. He's good at that. It's what he did with Metaxas. He spent the last three days figuring out just how to do it.

Janek shrugged, unbuttoned his jacket, removed the Glock from its holster, stooped, set it carefully on the floor.

"While you're bent over pretty like that, put down your ankle weapon, too."

Janek removed the Beretta from his right ankle holster, laid it beside the Glock, then stood up.

"Now back off."

Janek edged backward until his shoulder grazed the wall of mirrors. He watched as Clury, leading Gelsey by the leash, approached his guns, stooped and picked them up. The mirrors reflected the action: a thousand Clurys and Gelseys moving together, each image showing them from a slightly different angle, a thousand Clurys and Gelseys moving down endless mirrored corridors, approaching from every direction at once.

It was then that the concept hit him: Amid all these moving images of humans dancing across myriad "mirrors of deception," there was no way to tell which were reflections and which were actual people. Intuiting that this insight was the key to victory, Janek began to move. Suddenly the Great Hall became alive with images. It was as if a great crowd of people had filled it up. The only strange thing about this crowd was that its members had only three faces—a thousand Janeks, a thousand Clurys, a thousand Gelseys mingling and milling around.

"What're you doing?" Clury yelled, his words echoing off the glass.

"You've got my guns. What's the problem?" Janek bellowed, circling, then doubling back.

"Why are you moving?" Clury's pockmarked cheeks skipped across the silvered surfaces.

"I don't want to get shot." Now Janek could not distinguish between the genuine Clury and the counterfeits.

"You *will* be shot if you don't stand still." A thousand Clurys aimed Janek's Glock.

"What're you going to shoot at, Clury?" Janek said, walking faster. "Me or one of my clones running around in here?"

Clury leveled the Glock in the opposite direction. Or at least Janek hoped so—there was the possibility that Clury had him in his sights.

"Go ahead, shoot me if you can," Janek taunted. He liked his tone. It built up his confidence. He wanted to distract Clury, make him forget about using Gelsey as a shield. By focusing on Clury and ignoring her, he hoped to cause Clury to ignore her too.

"Stand still or I'll blow up your girl."

Janek laughed. "She's not my girl. And you won't blow her up."

As he moved clockwise around the room, his mirror-twins moved in all directions. He felt as if he were revolving at the center of a rapid counterwhirling merry-go-round.

"Don't push me!" Clury looked confused as his eyes scanned the images skimming across the gleaming walls.

"Too much glass in here. Blow her up and you'll kill us all." Janek paused. "Maybe that's what you want." Janek, dancing, knew that if he stopped, Clury would shoot him down. "No, I don't think so," he added. "You're not the suicide type. You're a killer, Clury. But a bomb's a coward's weapon."

"Bullshit!" Clury twirled like an enraged bull.

I've got him now!

"Yeah, a coward's game. Wait till no one's looking, then set it up. Back off, crouch down, watch it blow. Can't do that in here. You'll be sliced to ribbons."

Clury fired the Glock. Janek winced. The explosion, rebounding off the glass, echoed harshly in his ear. On the other side of the Great Hall a mirror panel shattered, then fell in pieces to the floor.

Janek crouched, pulled out his left ankle Beretta, fired back across the Great Hall as he rose. Then he was off again. Across the room a clone of Clury splintered and crashed.

Clury let go of Gelsey's leash. The moment he did, she ran to one of the walls. Now the three of them were separated, their images crisscrossing on every mirror.

"Don't stand still!" Janek yelled to her. "Move! Move!"

A thousand Gelseys nodded at once. A thousand dreamsisters began cavorting through mirrorworld.

Clury fired at Janek again.

I can't waste ammo returning shot for shot. He's got two of my pistols, maybe another of his own.

Janek was also aware that this game of hide-and-seek could not go on too long. Concealment among the mirror figures was possible only as long as everyone moved. Once one of them slowed or stopped, he or she would become a target. The endgame would be determined by fatigue.

"Get out of here!" Janek yelled to Gelsey. "Take off that damn pack and run!"

Clury laughed. "She can't take it off. And if she runs out of here I'll blow her up."

Gelsey's eyes, a thousand pairs, gleamed with fright. It was the same frightened look Janek had seen when she was booked—the panic that seized her when she was not in control.

No choice now. I've got to kill him.

Janek fired across the room. As Clury ducked, a panel bearing his image broke into shards. Janek saw Gelsey run to one of the walls, then, head down, push her tied hands against a mirror. When the panel sprang open, she crawled into the blackness. The panel shut after her. Janek heard it click.

"Fuck! Where'd she go?" Clury, panicked, fired four times in four different directions, wheeling 90 degrees between each shot. Sheets of glass splintered and crashed to the floor in different parts of the Hall. Janek watched as four Janek clones broke and fell.

He, of course, knew exactly where Gelsey had gone: into the chamber of the Minotaur.

If I stop he'll stop, just to get off a good clean shot.

Janek rushed along the walls, watching his likenesses whirl around. Suddenly he stood still. Then, assuming combat stance, he held out his pistol in both hands. Clury stopped, too, took careful aim. They fired together. Mirrors shattered at either end. They fired again. More panels crashed. Janek became aware of something skidding across the floor but knew he mustn't turn to look.

Clury fired again. Janek fired back. At the end of the third volley, Clury cried out and fell.

Get to him before he sets off the bomb!

Janek ran forward, pistol outstretched, while Clury, bleeding, groped for his module.

Janek fired at his leg. Clury yelled in pain, but still had

enough strength to grasp the module from the floor.

Kill him!

Janek, stepped closer, fired. This time he hit Clury in the stomach. Clury rolled over, clutching his unit. Janek squeezed his trigger but his pistol was empty. Clury grinned. Janek leaped upon him. He had wrestled him over, was lying beneath him, his own back against the floor, when he felt the blast.

All he would remember afterward was the tremendous sound followed by a hard shower of silver shards. He remembered pain in his hands and the feel of Clury's blood, warm, viscous, spurting upon him. He remembered the foul smell of Clury's body and the multiple images of himself that filled his eyes, broken images all around the wrecked room, reflecting his fear, pain, despair. He remembered thinking: *I can lie here now and watch myself die.*

Later, when he understood that only his hands had been cut, that he was lying beneath a badly bleeding dead man covered with slivers of shattered glass, that the blood all over him was not his own, he wriggled free, sat up, peered around dazed at the wreckage and saw nothing but broken mirrors. The mirrored ceiling had fallen in, exposing the catwalks, which, he was surprised to see, were still intact. Most of the stage lights were still on, illuminating the debris, and many of the wooden frames that had held the mirrors stood undamaged.

Gelsey!

She had been harnessed to the bomb. Had she gotten loose? He turned to look for the chamber of the Minotaur. Surveying the wreckage, he understood that the bomb had exploded someplace else. Then he remembered, in the midst of the shoot-out, seeing the backpack skidding across the floor. So, she had gotten loose and emerged from the Minotaur's den to heave it away.

Pulling himself to his feet, ignoring the wounds on his

hands, he made his way through the rubble to seek her out amid the broken glass. He found her finally within what was left of the little room. She was dead yet her body was unmarred. One of Clury's bullets had torn into her chest.

He sat beside her, hugged her to him, and then he wept—for her, the loss of her, the loss of her art to the world. He wept for a long time, until he heard the sirens. Then he let her go, walked out of the ruins of the maze and thought: *The mirrors are all broken now.*

It was cold and clear the day Gelsey was buried in a small, sparse cemetery near Richmond Park where many carnival workers were entombed. Walking to the site, his hands still wrapped in bandages, Janek noticed a headstone marking the grave of his father's friend, Walter Meles.

Erica Hawkins attended, along with her gallery staff, several art collectors, a girl named Tracy, Netti Rampersad and the members of Special Squad. During the brief service a flock of crows broke from a tree, then streaked across the New Jersey sky.

After the burial, Janek and Netti spoke.

"Mendoza's being extradited to Texas on capital-murder charges," Netti said. "I've withdrawn from the case. I've decided to give up criminal-defense work, too."

Janek protested. "You're so good at it, Netti. Just because—"

She shushed him. "It's not because of that. Truth is, I hated representing slime. I thought it was a game. Now I see it wasn't. I'm going to specialize in a different kind of law now: women's issues—domestic relations, spouse battery, workplace harassment—all stuff that turns me on. It's going to be great. I can get righteous as hell and break balls right and left."

"Yeah, I think you'll be very good," Janek agreed.

"I've decided to dump my Chinese accent, too," she said. "It doesn't amuse me anymore."

• • •

It took him a week to finish his report on Mendoza. As he wrote it he thought often of mirrors: mirrors of illusion, mirrors of deception, mirrors which, purporting to reflect the truth, had concealed it for nine long years.

At the end of his report he wrote:

All of us who, at one time or another, looked into Mendoza saw only what we wanted to see. For some of us that was a corrupt Department, for others a straightforward if bizarre homicide case, for still others a puzzle of such complexity that it defied understanding, and, as we constantly reminded each other, made us crazy, too. The truth is that Mendoza was a kind of mirror into which anyone who peered saw only himself and his beliefs. For nine years it reflected our diversity and humbled us because we could not comprehend it. It is time now for us to retire the file. The mirror is broken. Mendoza is finally closed.

One night a week later, when he came home and was unlocking his inner lobby door, he heard his name.

He turned. Kit was standing behind him, wearing a raincoat over her NYPD sweats. She appeared even smaller than usual. Her normally sharp eyes looked tired and her small Greek features were clenched into an expression of loneliness and fear.

"I've been waiting out in my car, Frank. Still work late, don't you?"

He wanted to look away, but he didn't. "Something I can help you with?"

"I read your report. Congratulations. You tied it all up. There isn't a dangle left." She paused, bit her lip. "Tomorrow I'm going to resign. That's what the commissioner wants. I'm going to do it before he asks."

"Then?"

"Oh, there're lots of opportunities. I've had offers through the years. Heading up corporate security departments, that kind of thing. Chances to make some real money.''

''I wish you luck, Kit. I really do.''

''That's not what I want from you,'' she said.

''I know. But I can't give you what you want.''

''Yeah, I figured.'' She looked crushed. ''You're right, of course. I'd feel the same. There're some things in this world you just can't forgive.'' She wiped her eyes, brightened, tried to smile. Then she backed off, waved. ''Take care, Frank.''

She studied him a moment, then turned and left.

Late in October he spent a weekend with Aaron at a fishing camp Aaron owned on a creek in Ulster County. They barely spoke, just fished. When they needed to communicate they'd gesture or grunt.

Janek managed to catch a decent-sized trout. It tasted good. But not good enough, he thought.

Just before Thanksgiving he went into Timmy Sheehan's favorite bar, O'Malley's. Timmy wasn't there; he'd moved to Arizona and hadn't called to say good-bye.

Janek started drinking a little after six. By eleven o'clock he was roaring drunk. Just before midnight a big man, about thirty, with Irish features, who'd been sitting four stools down from him at the bar, told him to shut the fuck up.

Janek studied the man in the bar mirror, then he nodded, got off his stool, pretended he was going to leave, turned and shoved the big Irishman to the floor. The fight lasted all of two minutes. Afterward he and the Irishman embraced, slobbered over each other, bought each other beers. When Janek left hc had a sore chin, two black eyes and a huge amount of self-disgust. When he got home he vomited into the kitchen sink. Then he called Sue.

''If I'm going to eat it, tonight's the night,'' he said.

She came right over, bawled him out, helped him undress

and got him into bed. At the door she told him she respected him as much as ever.

"It's just nice to find out you're human," Sue said.

It was an exceptionally cold winter. Deforest was named to replace Kit. After that, at Janek's request, Special Squad was transferred back to the Detective Division.

The squad worked several cases, nothing interesting, nothing that taxed Janek's mind. One day Luis Ortiz called from Miami. He and his family had commandeered a small plane, fled Cuba, were seeking asylum in the States.

Janek flew south to meet them. He ended up staying a week. There was a huge welcoming party thrown by Luis's Florida-based relatives. Janek attended but drank only club soda, no rum, not even beer.

Luis, he thought, looked as alert as ever. He told Janek he wanted to find work as a cop. Janek neither encouraged nor discouraged him. When Luis asked him why he was silent, Janek shrugged.

"It's something I can't explain," he said.

In March, Sue won the Department martial-arts competition in her weight class, 108 to 115 pounds. Special Squad attended and cheered her on. Afterward Janek took everyone out to a celebration dinner at Peloponnesus.

That spring there would be rainy afternoons when the rain was soft, the sky iron-gray, and the droplets clung, large and crystalline, to every leaf and blade of grass. On those days Janek would sit in his office watching the water slide lazily down the panes. Then his thoughts would turn to Gelsey, seeking out her demons, wandering alone amid her father's mirrors—and then his eyes would fill with droplets, too.

We gave each other so much. If only we could have given more.

• • •

One night, he had a dream in which he walked alone, barefoot, through the deserted city—a city of rubble, a city of broken glass.

When he woke up he asked himself: *Is that wreckage all that's left?*

Late in April, Janek sought an interview with Joe Deforest to discuss his future in the Department. When he entered he peered around Kit's old office, then sat in the chair in front of the new chief's desk.

He told Deforest he'd been thinking about resigning, giving up the work, but he didn't see himself as a bait-shop-and-charter type. When Deforest asked him how he did see himself, Janek said he wanted to go back into the ranks.

Deforest studied him curiously. "What do you mean?"

"I mean put on a uniform and walk a beat."

"You can't do that! You're a detective-lieutenant, for Christ's sake!"

"I want to give up the shield and the lieutenancy. I want to be an ordinary cop."

"I never heard of such a thing! You must be out of your fuckin' mind!"

"That's what I want."

"How old are you, Frank? Forty-four? Too old to walk a beat."

"There're cops ten years older doing it."

"Yeah, the walking dead. Give yourself a break. Take a sabbatical. Apply to a university, get a master's or a law degree. We don't waste resources here. You could position yourself for a high command."

Janek shook his head. "I've served this division well. It's time to give me something back."

"Yeah, well, I'll look into it," Deforest said. He quickly ushered Janek out.

• • •

On the first of July, Janek, dressed in a blue uniform bearing a silver shield, formed up with the ranks in the basement of the Ninth Precinct house. He was assigned a twenty-four-year-old partner, handed the keys to a car, then sent out on his first street patrol in twenty years

Author's Afterword

There are many acknowledgments to be made.

As must surely be apparent to anyone who has seen Orson Welles's great baroque thriller *The Lady from Shanghai,* its final mirror-maze sequence was the inspiration for the ending of this book. I first saw the *noir* classic as a teenager in 1958 at the Museum of Modern Art in New York. I never forgot the mirror-maze sequence, and, when I obtained the videotape, I think I viewed the scene more than a hundred times.

On the subject of mirror mazes, there are probably no more than a half dozen significant ones in the world. (I don't count the tacky carnival variety in which the mirrors are made of Mylar.) The best ones are at the Glacier Garden in Lucerne; on the Petrin in Prague; in the Musée Grevin in Paris; and an extraordinary new one, designed by the contemporary maze designer Adrian Fisher, at Wokey Hole Caves in Somerset, England.

Adrian Fisher has been helpful to me. His Minotaur Designs has spun off a company for the purpose of designing mirror mazes. I have a feeling we will be seeing several soon in the United States.

I am also indebted to Mr. Fisher's *Labyrinth: Solving the Riddle of the Maze* as well as Janet Bord's *Mazes and Labyrinths of the World* and Jeff Saward for his *Caerdroia* magazine, the journal of his nonprofit Caerdroia Project, devoted to exchange of ideas on the subject of labyrinths and mazes. As for the theory of mirror mazes, I know of only one article, written by Jearl Walker, which appeared in *Scientific American* in 1986. Without it, the nineteenth-century patents of Gustav von Prittwitz Palm and the mentioned books, I doubt I would have been able to work out the binding metaphor of this novel.

I am indebted, too, to the following scholarly works: *The Mirror & Man* (University of Virginia, 1985) by Benjamin Goldberg, an excellent, gracefully written overview of the history of mirrors (Mr. Goldberg was of personal assistance to me, too); *Herself Beheld: The Literature of the Looking Glass* (Cornell University Press, 1988) by Jenijoy La Belle, a superb work of feminist literary criticism, from which I drew numerous ideas; *The Double: A Psychoanalytic Study* (University of North Carolina Press, 1971) by Otto Rank, the definitive work on the psychological phenomenon of doubling and mirroring; and *Father-Daughter Incest* (Harvard University Press, 1981) by Judith Lewis Herman, a compassionate, heartrending book about a dark subject. Finally, I am indebted to my fellow crime writer, Dr. Jan Šmíd; to my exemplary editor, Peter Gethers; and to my old friend Edward Hunter, magician extraordinaire, who encouraged and nurtured my mirror obsession and taught me the Blue Room Effect.

A special note about the late Michael Ayrton, brilliant sculptor, writer, author of the novel *The Maze Maker,* a man whose life was literally transformed by the concept of the labyrinth and the Minos-Pasiphaë-Minotaur-Daedalus-Icarus myth.

To explore the maze that Ayrton designed at the Erpf estate in Arkville, New York, is to feel the presence of a great artist working out a great obsession. Although Ayrton's maze and maze-related sculptures and writings did not deal with mirror mazes, his sculpture of Daedalus and Icarus resides in a mirrored chamber at the center of the maze. I am indebted to Sue Erpf Van de Bovenkamp for allowing me to explore this extraordinary work of art.

Ayrton's work has been an inspiration. In *The Maze Maker,* impersonating the voice of Daedalus, he wrote the lines that are quoted at the beginning of this novel. He also wrote:

"Each man's life is a labyrinth at the center of which lies his death."

I believe no one has ever said it better.

—W.B.

About the Author

William Bayer's last Janek novel was *Wallflower.* He is also the author of the noir thriller *Blind Side, The New York Times* bestsellers *Switch* and *Pattern Crimes,* and the Best Novel Edgar Award–winner *Peregrine.* He has recently served as president of the International Association of Crime Writers, N.A. He and his wife, food writer Paula Wolfert, divide their time between homes in San Francisco and Martha's Vineyard.